PRAISE FOR
# Promises Reveal

"Few writers can match the skill of Sarah McCarty when it comes to providing her audience with an intelligent, exhilarating Western romance starring two likable protagonists. The fast-paced story line hooks the audience."
—*Midwest Book Review*

"Entertaining . . . Kept this reader turning the pages. I've got a soft spot for Western historicals, with their hard times and smooth-talking cowboys. Ms. McCarty delivers on both of those fronts."
—*Romance Reader at Heart*

"I absolutely adored the chemistry and witty banter between these two spicy characters, and the sex, as always, was titillating, sizzling, and realistic . . . I don't know how she does it, but I want more and more and more. You will too once you read this fantastic tale."
—*Night Owl Romance*

"A must-read . . . Enticing and erotic . . . I am already craving more!"
—*Romance Junkies*

"Highly entertaining . . . Plenty steamy . . . and a great compliment to the series."
—*A Romance Review*

"A delightful tale with lots of intense passion . . . Outstanding! Not to be missed by fans of historical Westerns who enjoy a strong dose of erotic fiction."
—*The Romance Readers Connection*

# Running Wild

"[Sarah McCarty's] captivating characters, scorching love scenes, and dramatic plot twists kept me on the edge. I could not put it down."
—*Night Owl Romance*

"McCarty . . . skillfully brings out her characters' deepest emotions. Three strong heroines and three mouthwatering heroes . . . will tug at your heartstrings, and the well-written sex scenes will not disappoint."
—*Romantic Times*

*continued . . .*

THE SHADOW WRANGLERS

# JARED

*≫⋅≪*

## Sarah McCarty

BERKLEY SENSATION, NEW YORK

**THE BERKLEY PUBLISHING GROUP**
**Published by the Penguin Group**
**Penguin Group (USA) Inc.**
**375 Hudson Street, New York, New York 10014, USA**
Penguin Group (Canada), 90 Eglinton Avenue East, Suite 700, Toronto, Ontario M4P 2Y3, Canada
(a division of Pearson Penguin Canada Inc.)
Penguin Books Ltd., 80 Strand, London WC2R 0RL, England
Penguin Group Ireland, 25 St. Stephen's Green, Dublin 2, Ireland (a division of Penguin Books Ltd.)
Penguin Group (Australia), 250 Camberwell Road, Camberwell, Victoria 3124, Australia
(a division of Pearson Australia Group Pty. Ltd.)
Penguin Books India Pvt. Ltd., 11 Community Centre, Panchsheel Park, New Delhi—110 017, India
Penguin Group (NZ), 67 Apollo Drive, Rosedale, North Shore 0632, New Zealand
(a division of Pearson New Zealand Ltd.)
Penguin Books (South Africa) (Pty.) Ltd., 24 Sturdee Avenue, Rosebank, Johannesburg 2196,
South Africa

Penguin Books Ltd., Registered Offices: 80 Strand, London WC2R 0RL, England

This book is an original publication of The Berkley Publishing Group.

This is a work of fiction. Names, characters, places, and incidents either are the product of the author's imagination or are used fictitiously, and any resemblance to actual persons, living or dead, business establishments, events, or locales is entirely coincidental. The publisher does not have any control over and does not assume any responsibility for author or third-party websites or their content.

PRINTING HISTORY
Berkley Sensation trade paperback edition / April 2010

Library of Congress Cataloging-in-Publication Data

McCarty, Sarah.
    Jared / Sarah McCarty.—Berkley Sensation trade pbk. ed.
        p.   cm.
    ISBN 978-0-425-23240-8
1. Vampires—Fiction.   I. Title.
    PS3613.C3568J37   2010
    813'.6—dc22                                    2009051633

PRINTED IN THE UNITED STATES OF AMERICA

10   9   8   7   6   5   4   3   2   1

*To my mother:*
*My friend, my inspiration,*
*and the person who always insisted*
*any dream was in reach*
*if I wanted it badly enough*
*to work toward it. Thanks, Mom.*

## ❧ 1 ❧

THE scent of fear came to him on the wind. A woman's fear. Sharp and acrid, it fouled the night around him. Jared slid his rifle off his shoulder, adrenaline coursing through his system, feeding the restless anger that seemed to be always with him these days. The cold metal slid into his palm. He closed his fingers around the stock in a gesture so familiar, it was more reflex than planned. Immortality had done nothing to dull his survival instincts and 249 years of vampirism had done noting to touch his code of honor. And in his world, men did not stand aside while a woman was being harassed.

The scent came again, this time mixed with the stench of vampire lust. He backtracked the wind, slipping into the shadows, shielding his energy as he scanned for the intruders. This was Renegade land. The people within this section were his responsibility. And if some son of a bitch thought he was going to terrorize a woman under his protection, he had another think coming.

A trace of the woman's energy whispered across his senses. Intensely feminine. Intriguing, but alarmingly weak. She was shielding herself but without any degree of skill, which meant she was either newly converted or untrained. More than likely the former. In the last six months, all known vampire women had either been gathered up by the Renegades for protection or fallen victim to the Sanctuary for experimentation.

The Sanctuary's belief that only a certain type of vampire should survive into the future had launched the immortals into a civil war. If the situation wasn't brought under control soon, it was going to imperil the mortal world, and that could be catastrophic for everyone. Especially since his sister-in-law's pregnancy had opened a whole new world of possibilities to the Sanctuary leaders: that of improving their numbers through the specific breeding of immortals, which up until Allie's pregnancy had been believed impossible.

He shook his head at the idiocy of it all. The laws of nature were there for a reason. They created harmony and tampering with them was not going to work out the way the Sanctuary wanted. Especially if they started messing with the mortals, and word was that was happening now. Vampires were part of the food chain, and when a food source was killed off through disease and manipulation, no one was going to survive. Not that a Sanctuary fanatic could be convinced of that. They were a bit set in their belief that their supremacy justified whatever they did. Unfortunately for them, the Renegades weren't so convinced of the Sanctuary's superiority. Renegades believed in choice.

A faint cry came from the other side of the meadow. Slipping into the shadows of the trees, Jared probed the area with his mind. One hundred yards ahead and slightly to the right, three vampires—two male and one female—were standing close together. The men radiated no energy at all, but the woman was emitting frantic signals bordering on panic.

Jared closed the distance carefully, slipping into the shadow of a tree, donning the illusion of the next, blending his energy with the plant energy, hiding behind a mirror image of the tree. As the scene came into view, it was evident why the woman was radiating panic. The two male vamps were playing a game of cat and mouse with her, feinting in to lure her out from the scant protection of the group of trees she had at her back, building her fear, probably getting off on it as she bared her fangs.

Jared's free hand clenched and unclenched in a habit left over from his outlaw days. Though he fought with talons, mental energy, and specialized weapons now, the small ritual of limbering up his fingers still centered his focus. Some things just stuck with a man even into immortality. He slipped deeper into the shadows surrounding the clearing where the two male vamps had the little female cornered. She had her back against a tree and was talking fast, but he didn't think threats and blackmail were going to hold those two off for long. They were hungry and horny. Never a good combination in a vampire.

A worse combination in members of the Sanctuary. That group tended to think they were entitled to indulge their baser instincts. And those guys were definitely Sanctuary. He didn't even need to see the telltale insignia on their shirts, glowing white in his night vision, to know that. The fact that they thought their urges entitled them to corner a woman on Renegade land, this close to a D'Nally werewolf stronghold, said all that needed to be said. They were not only arrogant, they were stupid. And their kind of stupid deserved to die.

One of the men grabbed for the woman's arm. Blood sprayed as she slashed with her talons. The man's curse almost overshadowed the woman's threat.

"Touch me again, and I'll hurt you."

Though he seriously doubted the woman had the muscle to back the threat, the fact that she was throwing threats rather than screams impressed the hell out of Jared. Sanctuary scum were known for their single-minded pursuit of their goals rather than their compassion. He'd had only a glimpse of her before the men had moved in. His two biggest impressions were a wealth of tawny hair and slenderness. Too slender, which made their ganging up on the woman more despicable and made them more in need of learning a lesson.

He cast his senses out into the scene, probing deeper into the male energy, finding the flickers at the edges of the one the woman had swiped that indicated weakness. Jared smiled as he glided closer. That's what he wanted. Just a little opening. A touch of opportunity. The moon slipped free of a cloud, bathing the scene in soft white light. He let his mind wander along the beams, a hiss of energy, invisible to all. They shouldn't have felt him, none of them should have felt him, but the woman looked up and her big eyes turned unerringly in his direction before looking away.

*Stay away.*

The whisper in his mind was soft and sweet, lightly accented, stunningly feminine, like nothing he'd ever sensed before, tuned specifically to his brain pattern. He followed the intriguingly unique path back to its source, sending calm with it.

*Stay still.*

She didn't respond to his order, just slashed at her attackers, going for their throats with a desperation that vibrated outward along with her order.

*Run!*

Again the intrusion into his mind. She was covering for him. Jared smiled at the generous, misguided effort and set his gun aside. It'd be a cold day in hell before a Johnson walked away from a fight, especially against two little pissants like this. It would be an even colder day in hell before he left a woman helpless and alone to fight as best she could with his mind on saving his own ass.

He broke out of the shadows in a burst of energy, spinning the other vampires around with a mental thrust. Weak. No challenge at all. He slit their throats with ruthless efficiency, holding them enthralled while he went for their hearts.

*Oh, don't make them watch their own deaths.*

The feminine entreaty broke through his barricades again, laden with the compassion he'd long since abandoned. He glanced over his shoulder. The woman was staring at him, her face creased with horror and disgust. With a mental command he turned her away.

She fought, but she wasn't as strong as she would like. With her back to him she whispered, "I'll still know."

He didn't want to be hindered by a five-foot-nothing conscience. Dammit to hell, he wouldn't be, but the horror and acceptance in the woman's thought wouldn't go away, and in the next split second, he blocked the vamps' knowledge and delivered the killing blows. The bodies hit the ground with discordant thumps. The woman jumped. He took her gloved hand and pulled her away from the tree. "They were going to rape you."

The statement came out harsher than he intended, fueled by the illogic of her position. The men didn't deserve her mercy.

"I know, but there's no need for cruelty." Her voice had the same softness as her thoughts. It was completely out of place amidst the residual violence and the cold reality moonlight cast on the bloody scene. Annoyance built along with frustration as the woman stumbled when he pulled too hard. He didn't need this complication, didn't need to be reminded he had a conscience. For the last hundred years he'd been quite content to focus on right and wrong, and leave the sorting out of the repercussions to others.

"Sorry." The fact he felt compelled to apologize ticked him off further.

"It's all right." She hopped over a raised bush, her booted feet sinking into the snow. He frowned. She should have glided over the snow's surface. He'd never met a vampire who couldn't levitate as easily as he breathed. He checked her energy again and got the same reading as before. Weak.

He shifted his grip to her upper arm, supporting her as she struggled with her balance. It'd been a long time since he'd touched anything besides other male vamps or weres. And then mostly in battle. The delicacy of the woman's build slid through his consciousness, reminding him of other times, other lives.

He gentled his grip, all of his upbringing slamming to the fore. Women were delicate, gentle, and were to be protected from the harshness of life whenever possible. Though that mind-set had moved out of popularity since his day, this woman brought it back with a vengeance. Another thing he didn't appreciate. Especially since, if he mentioned it, she'd probably bite his head off.

Keeping his body between her and the corpses, Jared steered the woman back the few feet to where he'd left his gun. When she would have glanced over her shoulder, he pushed her ahead, giving her nothing to look at.

"They're dead?" she asked as he grabbed his gun.

"As doornails."

There was a little hesitation and then, "Thank you."

He straightened, keeping her within his grip because he got the sense she'd flee if he didn't. "You're awful particular about the way you're rescued."

"There was no need to be cruel."

He looked at her then, raising his brow. "They weren't exactly inviting you to a tea party."

"You didn't like them being cruel to me."

She spoke with an accent he couldn't quite place. "You got that right."

"Because I was smaller and had no defense."

"And you're a woman."

She brushed that point aside. "They were no match for you."

He shook his head, easily seeing where she was heading. "I hardly think it's the same."

"It is the same." With a twitch of her lips, which he supposed was a smile to placate him, she tugged her arm free. "Thank you for sparing them that last moment."

The shape of her arm left an imprint of energy in his grasp. He curled his fingers around it. "You're welcome."

The moon tucked behind a cloud. His vision switched over. Even in the starkness of black and white, she was a stunning woman, with high cheekbones, a high forehead, a narrow nose, and full lips. Very full, very kissable lips. But she was thin. Too thin, and that thinness accentuated the Slavic cast to her features, which went with the slight accent to her voice. "You're not from around here."

"Not originally."

He raised a brow. "You're awfully tight-lipped for a woman who's just been rescued."

She looked toward the men. She rubbed her palm over her jean-clad thigh. "I must be in shock."

He got a feeling it would take a lot more than what had happened to shock the pretty little vamp. However, the sight of the dead men upset her. Her unease radiated off her in waves. "If you wouldn't keep looking at them, your stomach wouldn't revolt so hard."

"I'm not looking at them. I'm looking past them." She waved with her hand. "My pack is over there."

"Uh-huh." He spotted the brown leather backpack just on the other side of the tree. "Stay put, and I'll get it."

He had made it halfway to the pack when she took off. She was trying to mask her energy but not her footfalls. He grabbed up the pack and threw it over his shoulder, frowning. The most basic of vampire skills was skimming over the earth. There shouldn't be any footfalls. He headed after her, closing the distance easily. The harsh rasp of her breath punctuated every frantic step. His frown grew deeper. His little vampire was unnaturally weak. And, he let his senses flare out, company was coming. Catching up with her was not difficult, grabbing her up and tucking her under his arm no hardship, though her shriek did about split his eardrums.

"Quiet," he warned as he put on a burst of speed.

"Put me—"

He slapped his hand over her mouth.

*We've got company.*

She went absolutely still in his grip.

*Put me down.*

*You're too weak.*

*But—*
*Be quiet.*

The patrol was fanning out, trying to surround them. He tested the minds of those coming at them. Two were strong, one medium, but the fourth was weak from going too long without feeding. Jared turned in that direction, sending a suggestion deep into the vampire's mind, sending him away in pursuit of a noise that didn't exist. Having the woman with him, he couldn't indulge his need to take them on. Silently—just one more shadow in the landscape—he broke through the hole he'd created in the trap. He slowed his pace to an easy lope once they were clear, focusing against his will on the woman he carried. Her energy was like nothing he'd ever felt before. Linking with his in slow pulses before releasing. Testing, lingering, tempting even.

"Are we safe?"

"We lost them."

"Then could you put me down?"

"Why?"

"Because I'm going to be sick."

Vampires didn't get sick. He took a sharp right into the cover of sheltering bushes and set her down. They were far enough ahead of the others that they could spare the time. She swayed. He steadied her with a hand on her upper arm. His fingers met around the curve. He was a big man, but not so big that he was used to having that happen.

"When was the last time you ate?"

She leaned over, bracing her arm against a tree. "Vampires don't eat."

"Force of habit." He changed his phrasing. "When was the last time you fed?"

She waved away his concern, her hand going to her stomach. "It's just the stress."

"Of what?"

He couldn't take offense at the look she shot him. It was a pretty stupid question. "Guess nearly being taken captive and raped by the Sanctuary vamps would put a crimp in your tail."

She nodded and retched, a horribly violent sound. Her hand slipped on the tree. He stepped forward, wrapped his arm around her waist, and held her head. Even as she tried to push him away, she was retching again. Nothing came up. He damn near lost his own meal though as the spasms continued. He opened his palm over her stomach. She was too small to endure this.

"Easy," he murmured in her ear. "Just take slow breaths."

"I can handle throwing up."

"I don't think I can."

She shot him another look. "Nobody's asking you to."

Surely she didn't expect him to just walk away and leave her to her suffering? "I saved your life; you're my responsibility now."

Her torso jerked, but she didn't retch. "Convenient."

He smiled. "It works for me."

She stood there for a couple more minutes, shoulders bent, chest heaving. When no more spasms occurred, she straightened. He dropped his hand from her head, but not too far. Just down beside her cheek. He brushed a few strands of hair away. She bared her fangs at him. He had the irrational urge to kiss her. Instead, he took a step back.

"Better?"

"Yes, thank you."

"Then let's get moving."

She held out her hand. He cocked an eyebrow at her.

"My pack?"

He patted the strap. "I've got it right here."

"I can carry my own pack."

He listened to the forest. The spots of silence indicated the others searching, working in ever-broadening circles. "And I can carry you if you don't get moving. Those two had friends."

"I'm not going with you."

"A woman alone isn't safe out here."

"I'm not safe with you, either."

He stopped and turned. "You're about as safe as you're ever going to get."

Her hands settled on her hips. "Why? Because the big, bad male vamp beat up the other two vamps?"

He took two steps back and grabbed her hand, impatience at her rejection of his protection roughening his voice. "Because I'm the big, bad vamp who can beat up all the other vamps who want you as their own personal tidbit."

He gave a yank, and she stumbled toward him. He kept her momentum going through sheer muscle. She trotted behind him, putting as much resistance as she could into every step.

"If you don't cooperate, I'm going to pick you up and carry you again."

Her talons sank into his wrist. "I don't want to go with you."

"I don't care."

He wasn't leaving her for the Sanctuary vultures. He glanced behind them and, with a surge of energy, created a tiny whirlwind to erase their tracks from the snow. If those who followed found the spot, and were good trackers, they'd sense the lingering energy, but they'd have to be good.

"Levitate."

"You levitate."

She was determined to be difficult. He tugged her into him. She landed against this chest with an "oof" and a flash of talons. "Hellcat."

He spun her around, wrapped his arm around her torso, pinning her arms to her side, picked her up, and headed west. After five minutes of riding in that position, she caved.

"All right," she gasped. "You win."

He didn't stop. He didn't trust her for a minute. The woman had spent the entire time stewing, her energy whirling with concentration, which meant she'd probably been planning, too. He'd lived long enough to know a pretty exterior didn't mean an empty head. His brother's wife was a prime example. The woman was as sweet as candy to look at, but underneath there was a will of iron and a razor-sharp brain.

"I'll tell you what." The other males had split up, one heading in their direction. He stopped. "You can ride piggyback."

"I don't think so."

"Then you stay the way you are." In a couple of miles he'd lose their tail, and then he'd put her down.

"I don't like you," she informed him in icy tones.

"You don't have to like me, little vamp. All you need to do is live."

"And if I don't want to?"

He almost missed a step. "I'm sure you've figured out by now that, as vampires, we don't have much of a choice."

She always had a choice. Raisa prided herself on creating choices where none existed, but right now, the only one she could come up with to deal with the big vamp was to kick him between the legs. Frustration never created her best ideas. She tried a different tact.

"Please put me down?"

He glanced down at her and slowed. He had beautiful eyes. More green than hazel and glowing with the force of the personality behind them. There was a flicker of his energy. A softening? She tried again.

"Please?"

He stopped. The slow glide down his body was more seduction than release. Awareness shuddered along her senses.

She looked up as her boots sank into the snow. The man was not just big, he was massive. He had to be over six feet tall with wide shoulders that just screamed "give me a reason." The leather coat he wore did nothing to reduce the image of power and mass. He wore the Stetson on his head without any affectation. The same with the rifle in his hands and the scuffed cowboy boots on his feet. Not a newcomer to the West, then. With startling speed, a shaft of energy shot out from him and surrounded her, catching at that flutter of awareness. She instinctively caught it, muted it, and sent it back. Not a newcomer to vampirism, either, if he was so adept at mind reading. Rats. It would have made things easier if he were new.

"I always have a choice," she told him.

He probably would have looked more convinced if she hadn't stumbled right then.

With an easy tug that spoke of a man familiar with his strength, he saved her from her own clumsiness.

"Uh-huh. Well, not today."

Yes, today. Every day, for that matter. Until she found the man she'd been sent to find, her only choice was to keep looking. And to avoid being captured, either by the Sanctuary or the Renegades once she'd "accidentally" wandered off the course set for her. Just twenty-four hours out of the compound and she'd failed on that one.

She tugged her hand. The man didn't let her go, didn't even seem to notice she was trying to get free. She'd told Miri she wasn't going to be much good at this, that she needed to put her faith in someone else. Miri hadn't even hesitated, just gave her the "look," told her the information she'd needed, and then blithely pinned all her desperate hopes on her. Raisa sighed. It sucked being a woman's last resort.

"I don't have time for your ego trip."

That pulled the stranger up short. His eyes glittered at her from beneath the brim of his. She had to tilt her head way back to meet his gaze. Too many conversations like this and she'd develop a crick on top of the other aches and pains that were her daily companions. The edges of his wide mouth twitched. "You got somewhere else you need to be?"

"Yes."

"Where?"

He just had to be the type to pin a woman down. She pushed her hair off her face, grimacing when her fingers immediately caught in a snarl. The Sanctuary had been on her at the break of twilight, long before she'd had a chance to braid it. "It's not polite to pry."

His gaze followed her hands, lingering on the spot where her fingers tangled. "Just consider me the rude sort."

This time the touch of his energy made her blink. Now that she wasn't fighting for her life, merely running for it, she could appreciate it. It was deep and dense, very powerful, with a tendency to wildness that intrigued her. She tested the imprint she had in her mind of the man she had to find. It didn't match. Thank God.

The relief behind that "thank God" made her blink again. She'd never had a "thank God" moment before, and that was quite an admission for a woman who was 270 years old. She eyed the man again. Her initial impression was still big, but now that she'd slowed herself down she could appreciate the way those powerful shoulders sat atop an equally powerful chest. Now, through the opening of his coat, she could appreciate the flatness of his abdomen beneath the forest green of his shirt, not to mention the way his denims showcased, in loving detail, his lean hips and well-muscled thighs. And what it did for everything in between . . .

She licked her lips. One of the best inventions in the last two hundred fifty years was blue jeans. There was nothing, absolutely nothing, more flattering to a man's physique than well-worn denim. A chuckle drew her gaze up. The man was staring back at her, watching her admire him. The blush started in her toes and kept climbing no matter how hard she tried to suppress it. By the time he pushed his hat back, revealing a handsome, square face with startling hazel eyes, her cheeks were on fire.

"I take it you don't find my rudeness objectionable?"

The heat in his gaze slid into his energy. With a pulse of power, it surrounded hers. Instead of finding the intrusion objectionable, she found herself leaning toward it, embracing it. Raisa pulled herself up short. She did not have time for this.

"Your rudeness is objectionable."

"But my body isn't?"

There was no help for it. She was going to have to bluff her way through the embarrassment. "You have to know you're a handsome man."

"Never hurts to have it reinforced."

"I don't suppose it does."

"But?"

"I have things to do that don't include you."

"Well, now, that is going to be a problem."

"Why?"

He looked over her shoulder. She felt his energy fan out and scan. She piggybacked hers to his, keeping under his radar. With her debilitating weakness, it was about the only way she could afford the luxury of scanning. She felt the Sanctuary patrol at the same time he did. They were back at the bodies of the first two, but they wouldn't be for long. Soon they'd be coming after them. However, the patrol was far enough behind that if she could get away from the stranger, she'd be able to disappear. The man's grip tightened around her hand. "Because I've decided to keep you."

He'd decided to— Oh, for heaven's sake! She planted her feet. "Look, Mister . . . ?"

"Jared." With a mere twitch of his arm, he popped her forward.

"Look, Jared." She struggled to find her most persuasive tone of voice as she awkwardly trotted beside him. She wasn't used to running while being levitated, and she couldn't get the rhythm right. She pried at his fingers with her free hand. She managed to work her pinkie free. It gave her hope. "You can't just decide to keep a person."

"No. I can't." The glance he cast her was beyond amused. "But the vampire law does say I can keep an unattached female in need of aid."

Vampire law was totally archaic and chauvinistic, and didn't appeal to her in the least, but that line of argument wasn't going to get her any further than tugging on her hand had. "My need for aid has passed." She shooed him along with a wave of her fingers. "You can go about your business without having to worry about me."

"Well, Miss . . . ?"

The arch of his brow was not only a prompt, it was as sexy as all get out. Why did she have to meet this man here? Now?

"Slovenski. Raisa Slovenski."

That brow twitched again. Her name and her accent always marked her as a foreigner to this land. "Well, Raisa, the way I look at it we'll have plenty of time to discuss the beginnings and endings of my obligations as soon as I get you to a safe place."

"But—"

"No buts. About all you have to decide is whether you want to run"—he held out his hand—"or be carried."

She wrapped her arm around her ribs where she still felt the bruise of his last carry. Some choice. Take the pain from his carry or the pain from the exhaustion. In the end her dignity made the decision for her. She placed her palm in his, a tiny trill of pleasure at the contact spiking through her energy as she did. "I'll run."

But she was definitely discussing the endings of his obligations later.

# ❈ 2 ❈

IT was almost sunrise before Jared found a safe cave on the back
edge of D'Nally territory. For himself, he wouldn't worry so
much about where he spent the day, but he had Raisa with him, and
that meant extra precautions. There were too few women of their
kind, and what the Sanctuary did to them was too horrible to risk
her in any way. Not many women, even immortal ones, survived
the genetic manipulations nor the repeated rapes the Sanctuary put
them through in their pursuit of their master race. And even if a
woman survived physically, her mind was pretty much shot.

Jared had encountered women in his mortal days who had been
worked over by men, and while he'd managed to distance himself
from his emotions long enough to get them home, he couldn't seem
to achieve the same with the women the Sanctuary tortured. Couldn't
block their energy, couldn't get past the "if onlys" that might have
come together in such a way that he could have saved them. Which
is why he did as few of those rescue missions as possible.

He glanced over at the woman. She was sitting on the ground,
her back against a boulder near the wall, head down, fishing through
her pack. As far as anyone knew, all the women had been gathered

up by one side or another in the last year. Stragglers occurred, but they were few and far between, most of them protected by strong families or their men. She pulled a brush out of the pack. She was a very pretty straggler to be all alone.

"What happened to your people?"

Raisa paused with the brush halfway through her long hair. The strands glowed like sunlight against the black of her turtleneck. His fingers twitched as the highlights rippled with the brush strokes, like sunlight dancing on water. He bet her hair would be silky to the touch, soft against his skin.

"I don't have any."

"You're alone?" He couldn't conceive of it.

She shrugged and resumed brushing. "For now."

Something primitive surged inside him and every muscle pulled taut at the implication that she might be looking for a protector. He leaned against the cave wall. "Well, for now, you can consider yourself with me."

She stopped brushing, took a breath, and held it a second before releasing it. Her lips shaped silent words in a measured pace. She was counting, he realized. To ten, from the way her lips parted on the last word, revealing the pearly white of her teeth and the barest hint of fang.

"I'm glad you brought that up."

He'd say she was about as far from glad as a woman could get.

"I'll be leaving come nightfall."

Not likely. "To where?"

She licked her lips, a nervous habit he bet she'd quit if she knew how much it gave away.

"My destination."

It was the weakest hedge he'd ever heard. "You don't lie much, do you?"

A blink that was as revealing as the licking of her lips prefaced her "What makes you say that?"

He adjusted his position against the wall, amusement taking the stress off his weariness. She had a very expressive face. "The fact that you telegraph every lie before you say it."

"Well, fiddle."

Fiddle? "So, just where do you plan on heading tomorrow?" She didn't answer immediately, probably because she couldn't come up with an answer over the chaotic panic of her energy. He sighed. "If you're working on another lie, you might as well give it up."

Her face wasn't the only expressive thing about her. Her big brown eyes met his, delivering a punch he felt in his gut. The woman didn't have a clue where she was going or what she was going to do.

She paused, the brush held just above her shoulder in an unconsciously feminine pose that thrust the delicate curve of her breast against the front of her turtleneck. Normally he leaned toward full-figured women, but there was something about Raisa that honed his attention to a razor edge, whet his appetite, made him want to cup those small breasts in his hands while at the same time sending all sorts of protective, possessive urges into a mad gallop.

She cut him a glare from under the thickness of her lashes. Even that glare, laden with self-directed anger, sent a whisper of pleasure along his energy.

"I take it from that glare we're done arguing the subject?"

She resumed brushing her hair. "I am."

"Good, then I'm going to get things ready for sleep."

She didn't say a word as he headed toward the back of the cave, but her energy trailed him in a seductive lure, tempting him to turn around, to answer the challenge she presented. To claim her. If he thought she had any idea of what she was projecting, he would head back to where she was sitting and teach her everything she needed to know about him. Jared sighed. He didn't think Raisa was even aware of how often her mind touched his, let alone how her energy liked to slide between the soft edges of his in an unconsciously soothing gesture. Dammit to hell.

With a wave of his hand he removed the illusion of a wall. The safe place was exactly as he had left it. Small, secure, and well out of the way of the sun, it was the perfect place for a man to hide until things were safe. Unfortunately, it was really meant for one person, and even as small as Raisa was, it was going to be a tight fit getting them both in there. He smiled inwardly, imagining just how tight a fit it was going to be. She was bound to kick up a fuss.

He glanced back around the corner. Raisa was still brushing her hair, the long strands pulled over her shoulder in a honey-colored spill, looking as sweet as the candy he remembered. A snarl snagged the bristles. She frowned and yanked at the knot. His fingers curled around the urge to remove the brush from her hand and take over the job. Hair like hers would require a lot of maintenance. Thick and curly, it probably snarled a lot. She yanked at the brush again. The woman didn't have the patience a husband would have for the job.

He reentered the main cavern. He didn't need to look at the sky beyond the entrance to know that dawn was coming. He could feel it in his bones. He gathered up his gun. Raisa didn't look up until he got to her side even though she had to know he was there. "It's time to rest."

The brush slowed. Her eyebrow arched. "With the Sanctuary on our heels?"

"Unless you can walk in sunlight, I don't see a choice."

She looked first at him and then toward the back of the cave. Her lips pursed. "I can stand guard."

"There's no need."

If someone disturbed the alarms he'd set around the cave perimeter, he'd waken.

She put her brush in the bag and flipped her hair back over her shoulder as she stood. She was dressed entirely in black, which gave her the illusion of blending into the darkness of the wall behind her.

"You're that fond of surprises interrupting your sleep?"

He took her inventory from head to toe, starting with the thick

mass of her hair, down over her slender shoulders and her compact
little body, to her slim thighs and small feet encased in black boots.
She was the kind of woman who made a man think in terms of protecting and claiming. He brought his gaze back to hers. "Sometimes."

The roll of her eyes made him smile. "Get over yourself."

She grabbed her backpack and looked around. "So, where are
we hiding out?"

He motioned to the back. "Around the corner."

With an easy sidestep, she scooted around him and headed toward the cavern. The cave wasn't that big. It didn't take her long to
get there, just five steps, but for him they were well worth focusing
on. The woman had a way of walking that was saucy and inviting,
yet completely in control. She was definitely a woman comfortable
in her own skin. His interest deepened.

As soon as he drew up alongside, she cocked her head toward
the interior. "That's it?"

"Yup."

"We aren't both going to fit in there."

He didn't miss the emphasis that she put on the word we. "It'll
be tight."

"Uh-huh. I'd say more like obscene."

Again that foreign urge to smile twitched the corner of his lips.
"Necessity doesn't allow for modesty."

"Neither does lechery."

"Lechery?" He chuckled and leaned his rifle inside the opening
before reaching for the strap of her pack. "It's been a long time since
I heard a word like that."

She clamped her hand down on her bag. "It's been a long time
since I've had an opportunity to use it."

"Now that . . ." Her muscles were no match for his. The bag
came off her shoulder. He tossed it to the head of the small cavern.
"I find very hard to believe."

"Believe it." She pushed her hair out of her face. "I think we need to go back to plan A. You rest in your cozy little cavern, and I'll stay out here and keep watch for trouble."

With her hair off her face, he could easily see the blue smudges under her eyes and the lines of strain beside her mouth, along with an unnatural pallor to her skin. He was not leaving her anywhere.

"You're not well."

"I'm fine."

"When was the last time you fed?"

"Yesterday."

He tipped her chin up. "I won't tolerate you lying to me."

She didn't give an inch, just matched him stare for stare. "Your tolerance is not my concern."

The primitive something stirred again. He squeezed her chin between his fingers, having difficulty keeping the growl out of his tone. "It is now."

"Why?"

"Until someone takes the responsibility from me, you're mine."

Her fingers wrapped around his wrist. Her big brown eyes still didn't flinch from his. He felt the prick of her talons. A tiny feminine threat that put a spark under that primitive emotion swirling and hovering. "Then you're just going to have to adjust your truth meter or suck it up."

The sting of her talons blended with the hot arousal that surged through him at her challenge. "You fed yesterday?"

"I already answered that question."

He stared into her eyes and probed into her mind. He found an image of a middle-aged man in hunting camouflage, and then her mind snapped closed.

He ran his finger over her full lower lip. "So you did. How often do you need to feed?"

If she needed to feed often, it was going to complicate things. He had a mission to complete and a limited amount of time to do it.

"It depends."

"On what?"

She yanked her chin out of his hand before ducking back into the cavern. Bending over to grab her backpack, she presented him with another view of her body, one he deeply appreciated. She turned back around. She noticed the direction of his gaze. The twist of her lips was wry. "On none of your business."

He stepped into the chamber, crowding her back as he sealed it off with a manipulation of energy and light. "And I already told you, everything about you is now my business."

She glanced under his arm and licked her lips. Evidently, she was just beginning to believe he meant it. He motioned to the floor.

"Lie down."

She took half a step back into the wall. "I don't think so."

He broke her death grip on the pack, settling it beside them. "Relax. I don't have the patience to wrestle with you, right now. I need my rest."

The glance she sent him was pure skepticism. "I can see you're in danger of collapse."

While he might not be, she was. "Appearances can be deceiving."

She didn't look relieved. He tested the edges of her mind. It was closed. Her glare let him know she knew what he was doing as she said, "You're going to have to convince me of your exhaustion the old-fashioned way."

He deliberately focused on her breasts, which rose and fell with each rapid breath. "Is that an invitation? Because I had my mind set on sleep, but if you want a turn beneath the blankets, I can probably work up the interest."

There'd be no working up to it. In reality, he was astonishingly ready. And he didn't like it. He thought he'd eradicated his emotions over the last hundred years, settling for blank calm over the upheaval of conversion. And he didn't like the fact that this little vamp could disturb it with nothing more than her presence. He didn't intend to feel again. Ever.

Her hands fisted at her side. "You're being obnoxious."

She said it with strict precision, each syllable colored with that intriguing accent that said English wasn't her native language. And dammit, if it didn't make him feel guilty for his previous off-color response. He sighed, trying to ignore the prick from his conscience.

"What I am is tired, so whatever it takes you to get to sleep, I'm willing to throw myself on it." He sat down on the hard floor. He confiscated her backpack, mushed the contents around until they resembled some sort of pillow, and then lay down on his back. She stood above him, mouth working, eyes flashing small flicks of vampire flame. Her energy lashed his with the same agitation. He kept his grin to himself.

"Good night."

"That's my pack."

He watched her from under his lashes. "Unless you've got a reason it can't do double duty as a pillow, it's staying put."

"It's mine."

He shrugged. "You're not using it."

Her hands opened and then clasped into fists. "That doesn't give you the right to take it."

He tipped his hat down over his eyes to hide his smile. No, it didn't, but as he didn't think she'd be leaving without it, using it as a pillow was another way to insure she stayed put. "The oldest law in the world gives me the right."

"And that would be?"

"Might makes right."

She spluttered and fussed. He could hear her angry breaths and the shuffling of her feet. "If you kick me, I'm going to kiss you."

The shuffling stopped. "You're insane."

"Nah, just tired."

He reached up and caught her hand. The fineness of her bones sharpened his desire. She was the complete opposite of him. All softness and talk. He tugged. She tumbled against him with a squeal of outrage.

"Good thing none of those Sanctuary hounds are anywhere near here, or we'd be lab bait for sure, what with you making all that noise."

In reality, he'd soundproofed the chamber with one of Slade's discreet little devices. For an ex-outlaw and saddle bum, his brother had turned out to be quite the scientist.

"It might be preferable."

He didn't dignify that with a response. She wiggled and wormed for what seemed like forever, teasing his libido with the feel of her breasts and hips rubbing against his chest and hip. His cock hardened. His senses focused. He held his breath. She kept wiggling. He swore under his breath at the hot, sweet torture.

"What are you doing?"

"Trying to get comfortable." Another contortion and she picked something up and threw it. It bounced off the wall and hit his boot. A stone.

Clearly he wasn't going to get any sleep until she was settled. He angled his arm under her head. His hand fell naturally to the small of her back, her cheek to the hollow of his shoulder. Her breath hit his chest in moist puffs he could feel through his thin cotton shirt. Arousal started a thick chug though his system. Shit, it was going to be a long eight hours.

She pushed at his side. "This isn't exactly an improvement."

He couldn't agree with her more. With her sexy little body snuggled up to his, the chances of him getting a decent rest were somewhere between zero and zilch. "Tough."

She wiggled this way and that for a minute or two more and then she rose to her elbow. "I need my blanket."

She reached past his face. Her unique scent covered him, along with her body, as she fished in the backpack. She knocked his hat askew with her elbow as she tugged.

"Can't you just adjust your body temperature?" he asked, pushing his hat back.

"I'm not good at that."

From where he sat, she wasn't good at a lot of things that were commonplace for a vampire.

"Then a blanket isn't going to cover it." The cave was dark and dank, the floor cold. If she couldn't adjust her body temperature, she'd be an icicle by morning. He rolled onto his side. From there it just took a matter of anchoring her thigh to his and then rolling back, giving her a little "umph" with his right arm to pop her the rest of the way on top of him. She landed a bit higher than he planned. Her breasts pressed into his cheek. He slid her down, setting his jaw against the urge to open his mouth against that softness and test it with his fangs. Raisa gasped. Before she could explode in outrage, he put his hands on her hips and drew her down. With one hand, he clamped her cheek to his chest, letting her kick and struggle as he reached over his head. It took several yanks, but he eventually got the blanket out. It was wool and soft from frequent use. He tossed it over her, releasing her cheek to tuck it in around her. "There. Now you can sleep."

She grunted, her anger palpable. "This is not a step up."

"You're warm."

"It's outrageous."

He settled his hat down over his eyes, leaving enough angle that he could sneak peaks at her. He found watching the expressions chase across her face enthralling. "Why?"

"I don't even know your full name."

He gave her side a nudge, moving the sharp point of her hip bone off his cock. Two squirms that had him gritting his teeth and the soft curves of her body melded into the hard planes of his. "It's Johnson. Jared Johnson."

"Well, Jared Johnson, I can't see where you'll get a bit of sleep with me crushing you."

Crushing? Another smile tugged at his lips. As if there was enough of her to crush a fly. He stroked her hair off her face. "I'm tired enough to sleep through a bronc busting. I think I can manage."

She was tired, too. He could feel the weariness dragging at her.

He adjusted the blanket up over her shoulders. A shiver went through her. He upped his body heat to warm her faster. He couldn't maintain it that way forever, but he could long enough to heat her up.

"So maybe you could just close your eyes and let us both get some shut-eye?"

She stared at him for a long, suspicious minute, but then she either accepted he wasn't going to let her lie on the floor or the warmth surrounding her took the decision out of her hands. Her head relaxed against his chest. "You are a very strange man."

He cupped her head in his hand, just in case she got the urge to struggle. "Weariness will do that to a man."

With an astuteness that startled him she said, "I think it's more than weariness."

He didn't want her analyzing him, or feeling sorry for him, or any of the other emotions women liked to bring into the moment. "Trust me, I'm just tired."

"I don't believe that." He noticed, for all her beliefs, she wasn't pulling away. The warmth was definitely getting to her, draining the tension from her bones. A stab of guilt poked his conscience. She must have been cold the whole time he'd been carrying her.

"Believe me, I'm bone weary."

Weary of fighting what he'd become, weary of longing for who he'd once been. Weary of being alone.

"Well, I'm-just-tired-Jared, brace yourself." She smothered a yawn behind her hand. "Because in the morning—"

"You mean night?"

"I found it was easier just to think of night as morning after I turned."

"That would work."

She nodded. "I thought so." Another yawn. "And in the morning, we'll be going our separate ways."

Not in her current condition, and not without someone to protect her. He held her as the minutes passed, counting her breaths, measuring the loss of tension in her muscles by the number of limbs

that relaxed against him. First her shoulders and thighs, then her
calves and lastly her hands. He poked the backpack under his head,
moving the lumps into a better position. It was a collection of odd
shapes. "Just what do you have in here?"

"My things."

"Anything breakable?"

A pause, as if she had to think about it. "No."

"Good." He gave the bag a shake, resetting the contents, and
lay back down. "That's better."

She was almost asleep. He should leave her be, but he liked the
intimacy of the moment with her lying trustingly on top of him,
allowing him to care for her. It'd been a long time since he'd felt
this closeness. A long time since he'd had a woman depend on him.
He found he wanted to prolong it. "Raisa?"

"What?"

"Does your name have a meaning?"

"In your language, it means light."

He continued to stroke her hair, letting her name and its meaning settle in his mind. Raisa. Light. It was, he decided, a pretty name
for a pretty little vampire condemned to live in the dark.

# ❋ 3 ❋

**THEY** were being hunted.

Jared opened his eyes and stared at the roof of the cave, his senses flaring as the knowledge came to him in a thrust of energy. The fact that it was barely dusk meant the hunters were werewolves. That was a plus. Vampires made for a much trickier confrontation.

Raisa slept on top of him, a softly curved, sweetly trusting, completely oblivious weight. He gently eased her to the side. She moaned as soon as her shoulder hit the cold floor but didn't wake. Just shivered and pulled the blanket over her.

Sitting up, he frowned down at her. She should be awake, her senses screaming the same warning as his. But she wasn't, which just highlighted all the more why she needed protection. He lifted her head gently and eased the backpack under her cheek before getting to his feet. With a subtle manipulation of energy that went no further than the illusion, he removed the concealing barrier. Raisa murmured. Jared glanced at her. She was frowning in her sleep, looking completely insubstantial beneath the blanket. The urge to return to her was overwhelming. The need to wipe the frown from her face almost a compulsion, which made absolutely no sense. He barely knew the woman.

His gaze lingering on her, he flexed his fingers, loosening the muscles before reaching for his rifle and stepping out into the cave.

It only took a second to restore the barrier, this time with a time limit on the duration. Just in case he didn't make it back. He wasn't really worried, but there was always an off chance something could go wrong, and Raisa seemed to be the type who'd bitch up a storm if she were entombed for eternity. He smiled as the illusion fell back into place, irrationally amused at the thought of her angry, those brown eyes snapping with that inner fire he felt in her and all that passion she suppressed raging free. He bet she'd be the type who brought intellect to an argument. The type to keep a man on his toes.

He glided to the front of the cave, staying out of the fading light, taking stock of the situation as he did. The falling night was crisp with the promise of snow, ripe with the energy of those who tracked him. They were making no attempt to hide their presence, which just served to make him suspicious. Either they were extremely cocky or they thought he was stupid enough to be so easily tricked. Either way could work for him.

He waited ten minutes, until the light had faded to the point that it would be just a discomfort on his skin, before he slipped out of the cave. When he was two miles away, he released the barest hint of his energy, keeping his path due west toward the heart of the mountains, away from civilization. If they were smart, and he was sure at least one of them was above average in the brains department, the unwavering determination of his path would get them thinking along the lines of why he was heading so purposefully in that direction and perceive his presence as a potential threat to the secret compound the Sanctuary had there. Which would keep them from exploring the area where he'd tucked Raisa.

An echo of their energy bounced back to him. They were taking the bait. Whatever was in that compound must be mighty important to have them charging after him just because he was heading in that direction.

Jared would have loved to actually check out the compound. That was his primary reason for being out here, but with the complication of Raisa, he didn't dare risk it. He had a duty, first and foremost, to get her to safety. He hit the button on his cell phone that sent out the single signal—too short to be traceable—that said he was aborting his mission, but that it was safe for someone else to try. If the three key Sanctuary leaders were truly going to gather here in the next few days, the Renegades needed to know it. Catching the bastards in one place would go a long way toward ending the civil war that had started six months ago.

There was just nothing like a bunch of immortals throwing a hissy fit to upset the natural way of things. And things were getting pretty upset. If they kept it up, the mortals would figure out they weren't alone in the world, that their Halloween tales were actually reality, and then there'd be hell to pay. And mortals far outnumbered immortals. With werewolf birth rates down to near zero and conversions failing right and left, the immortals were fast approaching qualification for the endangered species list. Which was a hell of an ironic note when a body thought about it.

Jared slid along the shadows of the tree line, slowing his pace, letting the hunters catch up, feeling their simmer of elation when they recognized they were closing the distance. They were too confident, probably relying on the fact that there were four of them and only one of him to be the deciding factor in the battle. His fingers flexed. That overconfidence would be the death of them.

The ping of regret that hit him at the thought had no place in his life. It was a kill-or-be-killed world, more so now than before, with too much on the line to waste time with a conscience. Especially now that his sister-in-law's pregnancy was known. The rarity of the pregnancy had fueled the latest rounds of Sanctuary kidnappings and experimentations. Before they'd been toying sporadically with the possibility of creating life, something that rarely occurred with mated pairs of weres and never with vampires—but an actual pregnancy among the vampires had raised their fanaticism to a fever pitch, inspiring claims that it was a sign from the creator that their time was here.

Allie's pregnancy was raising hope and panic among the Renegade vampires and weres as well. Hope, because there was nothing bleaker than a future without children and family to build on, and panic because the pregnancy had occurred when she was only half converted. If that information got out, no woman, whether immortal or mortal, would be safe from Sanctuary males. Their conviction that their genes were the foundation for a master race would ensure that every fertile female would be impregnated, or would end up a broken shell with screwed-up DNA and a fragmented mind. Jared had seen a few of those women. It had left him, along with the rest of the Renegades, vowing to prevent it from happening to anyone else. They might be a dying species, but that didn't give them a right to prey on and destroy others to achieve their ends.

He checked his back trail. The enemy was following, the original four plus two others who'd been masked before. Either tiredness or assumption had them not hiding their presence as they should. He shook his head. Assuming the maximum scanning distance was a constant for all vampires was stupid. Each vampire had different skills and abilities, making assumption a dangerous prospect. He made a note to go over that again with his own men.

It seemed to be both human and vampire nature to become complacent, and complacency was the number one frailty that Jared counted on to win most battles, mainly because he was a patient man. He could wait centuries to get his revenge. Had been, in one case. His grip tightened on the stock of his rifle. The vague image he had of the woman who had turned Caleb, now fractured and fragmented into a nearly indistinguishable blend of energy and features, surged in his mind. He made it a point never to hurt a woman, but when he found that cold bitch, he was going to throw away his scruples. She'd taken everything from him and his brothers, putting them on this road, into this war.

If the unknown vamp had walked away from Caleb that night two hundred fifty years ago, Jared would have married up with Diane, had a little boy with the Johnson hazel eyes and square chin, maybe even a couple of daughters with Diane's bright personality and blonde hair, grown old spoiling his wife and his grandchildren, died at the end of a natural life span, and by now be just so much dust in the ground.

He eased his grip on the rifle when the crack of wood reached his ears. The only thing he'd ever wanted was a normal life. Losing their parents at an early age had made the bond between the brothers strong, but it had also made surviving hard. They grew up tough and independent of everything except each other, but whenever they'd ridden through a town and Jared had seen the men with their wives and children, he'd felt the ache inside—that hunger for the normal family life he'd lost. Sometimes all that had kept him going had been the determination to regain it.

He'd been on the verge of doing just that when Caleb had converted him. He knew, by rights, he should blame Caleb, but he couldn't. He understood his brother too well, had felt the overpowering drive of vampire emotion that obscured reason until a body learned to control it. No, he didn't blame Caleb, but he did blame the bitch who'd converted Caleb when he was at his weakest.

That wasn't the kind of thing a body did to a person. It was as foul as what the Sanctuary did to women, and when he found the bitch, he'd show her what it meant to betray a Johnson.

Mid-leap over a large boulder, Jared felt it. A surge of energy joining the other six. It cut through his shields with the efficiency of a well-honed knife. Every synapse in his brain snapped to attention, fine-tuning through the shock of the contact with that sweet feminine vibration. Raisa.

Dammit! How had she gotten past the barrier? He landed awkwardly on the other side of the boulder and pulled up, erasing his footprints from the snow as he mentally cast for more information. There was no change in the energy of the men hunting him. Which meant they didn't know that the woman followed. He frowned, the strength of the signal almost deafening him. How could they be unaware?

Along with awareness came a jangle of emotional discord so unfamiliar that it took him a moment to place that it came from him. Panic. And rage. Panic at the fact six vampires were between him and Raisa, rage at the risk she'd created for herself by not following the mental order he'd placed in her subconscious to stay put.

Gathering his emotions back under control, Jared cast out a false trail of energy, sending it forward in the direction he had been going, trickling it out with a repeating pattern that would feed back to the energy probing so it would always stay ahead, fading into the distance, keeping the illusion of distance between the pursued and pursuer.

He settled his hat more firmly on his head. The enemy would probably figure it out eventually, but by then he'd be long gone, and Raisa with him. And if he managed to finagle enough time in which to paddle her ass while he was at it, he'd be indulging himself with the pleasure. The stupid fool.

Jared circled around and headed back, doubling his speed, taking particular care to mask his presence, fighting the need to abandon protecting himself in order to protect Raisa. He was too far away to project an energy shield over her, but everything primitive in him, everything ruled by the vampire, ordered him to try. To guard her at all costs. The urge was damn hard to ignore.

He was so focused on Raisa that he almost ran over one of the Sanctuary vampires. Jared came to a halt just five feet away. It was a rookie mistake and if his natural shielding hadn't been a reflex rather than a conscious endeavor, he'd be dead. Instead, he was undetected, two arm lengths away from his enemy. His fangs exploded into his mouth. His talons extended. The man was studying the snow, tracking the energy trail Jared had laid down, his frown indicating his level of concentration.

It would be so easy to kill him. A swipe of Jared's talons across his neck and his head would separate from his body, and there'd be one less fanatic cluttering the world. The bloodlust surged. The Sanctuary vamp looked up, sensing the threat.

Jared controlled the energy, controlled the wildness flaring inside. Killing the SOB would only alert the others, and until he got Raisa to safety, he couldn't risk a confrontation. Just another thing to add to the list of things she owed him.

He glided behind a tree, waiting out the man's suspicion. After a few seconds, the man continued on. Jared made another note to his mental list. Train the men in trusting their instincts. In his experience they were never wrong, and if this man had trusted his, Jared wouldn't have been able to slip behind their line. Considering the prize the slip was costing the Sanctuary, relying on what only could be seen or obviously felt was a damn expensive habit in which to indulge. Raisa's energy increased its call, reaching out to his, slipping along invisible channels to hook deep, raising his vampire and a primitive response. His cock hardened along with his anger. Jared stayed where he was, letting another Sanctuary vampire glide past, holding his position through sheer force of will as the storm inside raged for action. As soon as the last of the patrol was a safe distance past, he came out of hiding, streaking back toward that feminine call, every beat of his heart, every pass of his breath, blending into a savage thirst for dominance.

**SUDDENLY,** he was just there. A big black force blocking her path. Raisa swallowed her scream and ducked as Jared reached for her arm. He had her before she was halfway into the move, his lean fingers wrapping around her upper arm, the sheer strength behind the grip making her attempted escape laughable. Raisa very carefully settled her weight into her boots and adjusted her pack on her shoulder. Only when she had the wild flare of her senses under control did she look up into his face.

Jared's anger hit her like a blow, hard enough that she flinched away before she got a grip. She was no longer a servant who had to fear a man's anger. She glanced at his face. It was a long way up, and when her gaze got there, all she could do was blink. Not a speck of the anger she could feel surging off him showed in his face. Every lean angle, every hard plane was set in an impassive wall of neutrality. Apparently, he was a master at hiding his emotions, but the man was angry, savagely so.

Raisa pinned a welcoming smile on her face and pretended she didn't feel the violent energy seething around hers, probing the edges, looking for weakness. "Hi."

Jared yanked her into the shadow of the trees. "You, little hellcat, have a nasty habit of not staying where I leave you."

"I got claustrophobic in that little cave."

And she had been hoping to get out of his reach before he came back.

"Uh-huh. Claustrophobic or not, that barrier should have held for at least another six hours."

Well, at least she knew he hadn't intended to bury her alive, which had been her first horrified thought when she'd woken up alone in the cave, locked in stone. "Well, it didn't."

His grip on her arm eased. She stepped back, resisting the urge to rub the strange tingles lingering there. His gaze dropped to her arm, those potent blue-green eyes of his narrowing. "Did I hurt you?"

She was tempted to say yes, just to see what he'd do. "No."

"How'd you get past the barricade?"

"I unlocked it. It wasn't hard."

His brows snapped down and the flames flickering at the edge of his gaze flared.

"What?" she asked. "Don't you like hearing you're not all pow-erful?"

"I don't mind hearing that at all."

"Then, what's your problem?"

"That wasn't a flimsy protection."

She took a step back, putting some distance between herself and all that seething energy. Jared had an uncanny curiosity to go with his uncanny face, uncanny power, and unnatural strength. Even for a vampire. And she'd intrigued him. That was not good. She did not need him fixating on her. The Sanctuary's obsession was bad enough, but having Jared tail her would be the ultimate complica-tion in a life already complicated beyond belief.

She stretched her smile a bit and widened her eyes just a frac-tion, going for vapid. "You're right. It was a wonderful barrier, well constructed and complex."

The only problem was he'd left his prints all over the important parts. He really needed to work on clean up.

Jared's right eyebrow went up. "You wouldn't by any chance be humoring me would you?"

"Absolutely not." She was lulling him into a false sense of secu-rity. "That goes against every one of my principles."

"Then why exactly are you praising a barrier that obviously didn't work?"

She looked around for a way to escape. There were woods on two sides, a meadow behind Jared, and a cliff behind her.

"Because you're bigger than me, faster than me," she answered honestly. "And I'm hoping that if I put you in a good mood, we'll be able to shake hands and part friends."

"Really?" There was something in his voice, and it wasn't mak-ing her rest any easier. "You think a little sucking up will get you all that?"

She shrugged. "It doesn't hurt to try."

That "something" spread to a note she recognized as he drawled, "No, it doesn't."

Humor. The irritating man had a sense of humor, and her honesty was apparently stroking it.

"But in this case, you're doomed to disappointment." His drawl stretched a bit to accommodate his amusement. "No amount of honesty or sweetly feminine placating is going to convince me to let you strike out alone."

God, he was still stuck on that. She slapped her hands on her hips. That was really too much. "Who on earth appointed you my guardian?"

He didn't even take a breath between her question and his answer. "The Renegade Council."

"You're Renegade?" She took a step back. A quick glance over her shoulder showed a clear shot to the cliff.

"Yes."

"Well, I'm not, which means your council has no say over me."

"Unfortunately, one of the drawbacks to being female is you're either Sanctuary or Renegade with no point in between."

"I don't agree with your philosophy."

Another discreet glance and another step. Not all vampires could fly. As big as he was, it went against logic that Jared could. That skill seemed to be relegated to the smaller-boned, lighter vamps. She couldn't fly, either, but she might be able to trick him over the edge.

"Your agreement isn't necessary," he told her, his energy pulling into tight focus.

"So you say." It was now or never. The winter-burned bush on the edge looked like it could hold her weight. She gathered her strength and shifted her grip up to her backpack.

Jared waved a hand toward the cliff. "You'll never make it. I'll have you in two steps."

A little primitive shiver of awareness went through her at his use of the word "have." There was something so elemental in the way he said it, a hint of possessiveness that wasn't hitting her sense of independence with the note of discord it should. Good grief, had the Sanctuary messed her up more than she was aware? Had the mental manipulations taken a deeper hold than she'd thought?

"What's wrong?" He took a step toward her, reaching out, a frown on his face. With a blink she realized she'd projected her distress straight into the waiting arms of his energy.

She pulled the wayward emotions back. "I don't like your attitude."

His chin angled down, the shadow from his hat hiding the color of his eyes, only leaving the flickers of energy at the edges of his irises dancing like flames in the darkness. "That panic went a whole lot deeper than annoyance."

"Maybe you should try looking at the situation through my eyes. A self-proclaimed bad-ass vampire kidnaps me—"

"Rescues you," he corrected, the flames in his eyes becoming more noticeable.

As if she cared if he got annoyed at this point. Men with as much arrogance as Jared carried around deserved to have it tweaked now and then. "As I was saying, I get kidnapped, locked in a tiny airless cell—"

"It wasn't airless."

She waved away his interruption. "The reality is, I have trouble with small spaces."

"I didn't notice any trouble last night."

She breathed out a sigh and wrapped her fingers back around the strap. "You really can't help arguing, can you?"

"Not when you lie to paint a more favorable picture of yourself."

It wasn't a lie. Normally she panicked when closed in, but last night she hadn't. She didn't know the why of that any more than she knew how she was going to save Miri, but she'd figure it out. She always figured something out. She sighed and hitched up her slipping backpack. "Where have you been all your life? Manipulating reality is what people do when they're telling a story."

"You can stick with the truth while telling this one."

Wind gusted over the ridge, blowing her hair around her face and a shiver down her spine. Damn, she hated the cold. "What's the point?"

He took one step, closing the distance it'd taken her three to create. "The joy in telling a story is in the magic of spinning the tale, not in the number of exaggerations you can create."

She watched warily as he reached over her shoulder. "So you say." Her backpack flipped open. "And who's to say I was exaggerating?" she asked, twisting her neck to see what he was doing. The blanket slid from the pack. He dropped it around her shoulders, encompassing pack and all as he drew it around her.

"I do."

"That's because you're six-foot-plus and more brawn than—" She reconsidered finishing that statement.

"More brawn than what?"

"Than a five-foot-tall woman of undisclosed weight."

The twitch of his lips was definitely amusement. "Now there's another difference in how I'd tell the story." He pressed the edges of the blanket into her hands. "I'd use the word insufficient to describe your weight."

She grabbed the edges tightly, steadying herself in the aftermath of the riot of her senses at his nearness. "No one asked for your version."

The edges of his lips quirked up, this time reaching a smile. And again she blinked. That hint of softness took his expression from hard-edged nasty to downright sensual with just that tiny shift of muscle.

"Just your lucky night that I'm offering it for free."

Right. Her lucky night. So far she'd had to pick her way out of an illusion trap, dodge a patrolling band of Sanctuary vampires, and now she had to sweet-talk her way out of the clutches of a too-handsome-for-his-own-good Renegade do-gooder. Yup, luck was what she had. Bad luck. "I'm a very lucky woman."

Jared's head tilted to the side as he took a step back. "Now why do I feel my suspicions acting up when you start agreeing with me?"

"Probably because you weren't toilet trained properly as a baby."

The little smile spread to a grin. Again she blinked. A grinning Jared was positively lethal. "What makes you so sure of that?"

She hugged the blanket to her as the rattle of treetops heralded the next wind. "Your uptight and controlling nature."

His eyes narrowed as the wind gusted around them. Though she tried to hide it, she knew he hadn't missed her shiver.

"Well, since my uptight and controlling nature and I are going to be your bosom buddies for the next couple weeks, you'd better get used to it."

"A couple weeks? I can't stay with you for a couple weeks! I have a life to live."

His hand came under her chin, lifting her face to a fast-fading strip of moonlight. "No one's stopping your living, just who you're living with." He tilted her head to the right, his muscles easily overwhelming her stubbornness.

"You have no right—"

"We've already gone over my rights."

She jerked her chin. "While trampling mine."

"Tough times call for tough adjustments." His thumb pressed her lip and withdrew. He watched the spot for a heartbeat, then pinned her gaze with his. "You're anemic."

"So?"

He frowned. "You knew?"

"Yes."

"Why didn't you tell me?"

"Because it's not unusual."

His frown deepened. "Why?"

She rolled her eyes and jerked her chin off the shelf of his fingers. "If I knew that, I could fix it, couldn't I?"

He caught her chin again. "You need to feed."

"No, I don't." She'd just gotten over the vomiting and pain of the last feeding. She wasn't going through it again until she absolutely had to.

"You're weak."

"Only compared to you."

"You'll slow me down."

She had an easy solution to that. "Leave me behind."

His grip on her chin tightened to near pain. "As Sanctuary bait? I don't think so."

"How do you know I'm not one of them?"

That made him pause. He appeared to debate the issue for two seconds and then shrugged. "I don't, but whether you are or not is immaterial. You're going with me." He dropped his hand to her shoulder, frustrating her plan to bolt. "However, it does bring up the question of what you're doing out here in the middle of nowhere, alone."

"Well, I didn't start in the middle of nowhere. I had help getting here."

"By the men I saw you with."

"Yes. They had some sort of take-me-to-their-leader fetish." She cast him a look. "Not unlike yourself."

He smiled and then, when she shivered, he pulled her against him. Her cheek settled naturally against his chest. God, he was big. And warm. As she stood in his arms, fighting to keep from snuggling in, he seemed to get warmer. In another minute she realized he was. He was regulating his body heat. Elevating it for her. He put her hands under his shirt. His abdomen sucked in on a quick gasp.

"I'm sorry."

"Nothing to be sorry for. I'd just forgotten how cold a woman's hands can get."

When she tried to withdraw them, he shook his head. "Stay put until you warm up."

It was the sweetest thing anyone had ever done for her in over two hundred years. She tried to think of the moment as a purely clinical one, tried to think of his stomach as an impersonal fire-place, but the longer she stood there in the cold night air, the more aware of him she became. The ridges of muscle beneath her hands, the raw masculinity he exuded with every breath, his heat, the draw of his power. Jared of the Renegades, she decided, was a very dangerous man. She withdrew her hands from his skin.

"All warm?"

He wasn't even breathing heavy. Apparently, she didn't have the same effect on his senses that he had on hers. "Yes, thank you."

He grabbed his gun. "Then let's go."

"Go where?"

He pointed northwest with the rifle. "Up that slope."

Slope? It was a mountain! "What's up there?"

"Food."

She looked at the slope and then back at him. "There's no need to climb the mountain on my account."

He caught her arm and turned her in the direction he wanted her to go. "There's every need."

"It's not going to make a difference."

"That I'll have to see for myself."

She dug in her heels. "I don't see why we have to go up so you can make a point."

The corner of his mouth twitched. "Because that's the way I'm going."

It was the opposite way she was supposed to be heading. "I can't go with you."

He didn't look back, just kept on walking. "I wasn't aware that I was giving you a choice."

She braced her foot on a log, grabbing his wrist with her free hand for added strength. "You have to."

He popped her over without even so much as a tug on her arm. "Why? Do you have a man to get back to?"

The push of his power was suddenly stronger, coming at her from multiple angles, testing for the truth.

"Yes."

The growl surrounded her, spinning her around. She couldn't see anything. She stepped closer to Jared, searching the forest. Then she looked up. Jared's eyes were red, brilliant with heat and energy. And anger. Oh hell. She took a cautious step back, watching him carefully. She might have just jumped from the frying pan into the fire.

## ❧ 4 ❧

**D**INNER was served.

Raisa took a breath. As dinners go, it wasn't bad. Young, healthy, physically fit, the woman would have sustained a normal vampire for a good month. But Raisa couldn't bring herself to even take the step that would bring her close enough to do a test nibble on the young hiker.

She motioned to the man—obviously the woman's boyfriend—Jared also held in thrall, "Why can't I have him?"

That her choice of wording wasn't the best was evident from the deep rumble that emanated from Jared's chest. Jared had been doing a lot of growling since she'd announced she had a man waiting for her. Raisa wasn't even sure he was aware of making the noise, but every time she said something that stroked his growing sense of possessiveness, he growled. She pushed her hair out of her face. "I'll take that as a 'no.'"

"The woman's blood is good."

And that was just the problem. The woman's blood was good. So was the woman. Raisa had scanned her mind the minute Jared had brought her to them. She never fed from good people. It struck

her as morally wrong. Like taking advantage of the innocent. "Can't
we look for someone else?"

"You need blood now."

"Actually, I'm fine for a few more weeks."

"No, you're not."

As he wasn't going to hear anything else on the matter, she wasn't
going to argue with him. She waved to the couple, trying another
tactic. "If we feed from them, this will completely ruin their honeymoon."

"They have a lifetime to make up for it."

"But a woman only has one honeymoon." She looked at the
young couple. Both had brown hair, fine skin, and that healthy glow
that came from an active lifestyle. They had no money but a lot of
love. Both were going to school, working two jobs to make ends
meet, and in the midst of the stress of their lives, they had married,
a smile on their lips, hope in their heart. This weekend in the mountains was all they could afford, and they didn't care. To them the
time together was a precious gift they cherished. God, to be in love
like that. She tilted her head and smiled at the magic of it. "She sold
her iPod to buy him those gloves."

"Only because he gave her his."

It was just so sweet. When she was human, she would have given
her eye teeth for a man to think that much of her. Heck, as a vampire she still would, but vampire men were possessive and unemotional, more interested in dominating than treating a woman with
tenderness. Tears misted her eyes.

Jared shook his head and looked down that long blade of his
nose at her. "You get too close to your meals."

She brushed the back of her hand across her eyes. "They're human, like we were once."

"But we're not anymore." His hand in the middle of her back
pushed her forward. "So all this emotionalism is for nothing."

Maybe to him. She hopped to the side and faced him, holding

her hand up to keep him from coming after her. "I won't do it. This weekend is all they could scrounge, and I'm not ruining it for them by taking their blood and leaving them weak."

"Dammit!"

Raisa folded her arms across her chest. His curses had no effect on her. Her stubbornness apparently had none on him. He grabbed the young man by the back of the neck, hauling him toward him, the exasperation he felt with her evident in the quick movement. Obviously he thought if he drained the male, she'd see things his way.

"And you're not drinking from him, either," she pointed out quickly as Jared angled his head for the bite, his fangs gleaming in the moonlight. His eyebrow went up, but he did stop.

"I'm not?"

She licked her lips and played her hunch. "No, you're not. You don't need the blood. The only reason you're doing this is because you're trying to force my hand, but even if you suck him so dry he's useless in bed for a week, I'm not drinking from her, so your plan is completely illogical." She waited a second for him to absorb that before adding, "And you are not an illogical man."

He slowly straightened, his eyes glittering with sparks of frustration. "I'm not?"

She held her ground as his energy whipped around her, seething with the frustration she could see in his face. "No."

"And you're seriously so concerned about these two having the perfect honeymoon that you're willing to put yourself at risk?"

She waved the last aside with a quick flick of her wrist. "I told you, drinking from either of those two isn't going to change anything. If you weren't so stubborn, you'd accept that."

"I would?"

"Yes." She leapt over the warning in his voice, rushing for the win. He was weakening. She just knew it. "As for their honeymoon, weren't you married in your before life? Or at least engaged?" A snowflake fell and then another as she searched his face for some softening. "Don't you remember the anticipation of the wedding, the endless excitement of knowing at last you were going to be together?"

Another growl rumbled. "You've got your centuries mixed up. These two have been screwing like rabbits for years."

The snowflakes, shining almost silver with her night vision, gathered and fell in loose spirals of brilliant clustered beauty. "But there will only be one first time after they've promised themselves to each other," she said softly, Jared's face fading out of focus, remembering back to her own before life. "Only one first night of the rest of their lives . . ."

She blinked as the wind gusted around them, whipping the snowflakes into stinging projectiles. Where had that come from? As quickly as the storm started, it stopped.

"You're a Goddamn romantic."

He made it sound so bad. "So?"

"Life is not romantic."

"Mine is."

He stepped back from the young man. She didn't release her breath until his hand fell to his side. "That's why you're a fucking vampire."

"I'll thank you to watch your language."

To her surprise, his eyelid twitched. With what? Shame? "Sorry," he amended. "That's why you're a *darn* vampire."

She chose to ignore the sarcasm and concentrated on the concession couched within. In her day, a man watched his language around a woman and from the clues in Jared's speech, he came from a similar time. "Apology accepted."

The muscle in his jaw ticked. She took the two steps necessary to get to his side. The man had made major concessions for her, she could make one for him. She placed her hand on his sleeve, the skin of his forearm blessedly hot. "Thank you for not ruining their honeymoon."

He glanced down at her hand on his arm, and then at the enthralled couple. He shook his head again and sighed, "I must be losing my mind."

"You're just a good man."

"I'm neither a man nor good, I'm a f—" He cut her another glare. "A darn vampire."

She patted his sleeve. "I know." Picking up her backpack, she asked, "Shall we go?"

She made it halfway across the clearing, far enough away that the roar of the stream over the rocks was a melodic backdrop to the softly falling snow by the time Jared caught up. Two tugs and he had her pack off her shoulder and onto his. She grabbed for the blanket, which slid off her shoulders, catching a glimpse of the couple out of the corner of her eye as she did, and stopped dead. Despite the cold, despite the perfectly good tent just a few feet from them, they were tearing at each other's clothes, their desire for each other so rich, she blushed. As she drew the blanket over her shoulder, Jared came back to her side, reeking with impatience. The couple had been embracing when they'd come upon them, but it hadn't been anything like this. There had been more hesitation, insecurity. "What did you do?" Jared shrugged and hitched the blanket up, scowling at her as if her need for it was her fault, which in his eyes, it probably was.

"You wanted them to have a memorable honeymoon; I insured it."

"By giving them a false level of desire?" That wasn't any more right than taking the blood of innocents. Unless a vampire was incredibly strong mentally, mind influence only lasted so long and when the falsely induced lust faded, the couple would spend their life wondering where it had gone.

He grabbed her hand and turned her away. "No. I just improved his technique."

Raisa planted her feet. Jared stopped, exasperation the predominant emotion under his scowl as he faced her. "Now what?"

"What do you mean, you improved his technique?"

For the first time Jared didn't met her gaze. "There's too much back-assward information out there for a kid these days."

"As compared to my day when there was none?"

He arched his brow, all his arrogance back. "Speak for yourself."

"I am." She touched his arm. "So you educated him?"

"Just righted a few wrong notions."

"And her?"

"Just removed a few ludicrous inhibitions."

She was going to ask what, and then decided she didn't want to know. She had more than her share of inhibitions, and if she blushed at the wrong time during Jared's explanation, he would have something to torment her with for days. "That was just so incredibly sweet."

"Just a means to an end." With a jerk of his chin he asked, "Can we move on now?"

Whether Jared wanted her to believe it or not, he was a nice man. If he hadn't been, he wouldn't have listened to her argument, and certainly wouldn't have helped the young couple the way he had. There were so few nice men left in the world. A good one should always be rewarded. She looked up the incline, her heart sinking at the steepness. She hated "up," but as his reward for his accommodating her wishes, she wouldn't utter a word of complaint the whole way up the darn mountain. "Of course."

**THE** woman did not know how to shut up. Jared gritted his teeth as another "Why does the way he wants to go have to be up?" filtered past his shields.

It was part of the endless litany he'd been forced to endure since the first hint of an incline. No matter how he tried to block Raisa out, her energy seemed to find a way, probing at his until her thoughts intruded on his. He'd tell her to knock it off if it weren't for the fact that she seemed totally oblivious that she was projecting.

And that she'd been amusing herself for the last mile coming up with all the adjectives she could think of to describe his butt. He'd never known women admired men's butts, but Raisa had elevated her appreciation of his to an art from. And that appreciation was about the only thing keeping him from snapping at her for the non-stop complaining of the last hour.

He sighed as the footsteps behind him stopped. He turned. Raisa was poised at the other side of a log, eyeing it as if were a snake coiled to strike. Snowflakes glittered in her tawny hair like a fairy crown as he heard, *I'm gelding him. One more log like this in the path, and—snip, snip—his frolicking days are over.*

Despite the gravity of the threat his lips twitched. "Is there a problem?"

*Just another monster log to lift my aching legs over, you sadistic monster.*

In contrast to the viciousness of her thoughts, her smile was tooth-achingly sweet. "Not at all."

Aching? He touched his mind to hers, slipping through the path of her forward projection. Her legs weren't merely aching, they were knotted and trembling from exhaustion. And she hadn't said a word. Not a damn word. She'd hid her emotions, her pain, her utter weariness and instead filled his head with the unimportant chatter about his butt and her hatred of the direction up.

"Son of a bitch!"

He was at her side before the curse finished, catching the wash of exhausted tears in her eyes before she blinked them away and her chin came up. And that sweet, totally beguiling, totally misleading, smile curved her lips.

"Give it up." He could shake her for being so foolish. Grabbing her arm, he forced her to sit on the log. "Why in hell didn't you tell me you were hurting?"

"Because I didn't want a lecture."

"Well, brace yourself. You're in for a he—a heck of one."

He lifted her right leg, anger, mostly at himself, putting too much force behind the maneuver. She tipped back. He caught her arm and tugged her forward. She didn't stop when she got upright, just kept on coming until her forearm rested on his shoulder as he massaged and worked the slender muscles around her right knee. Hell, there wasn't anything to her—no substance, no strength, just a crazy sense of humor and a smile that could melt polar icecaps. He found a knot and dug his thumbs in. Her moan shivered past his ear. "Oh, that feels good."

About a million other ways to make her feel good crowded his head, none of them appropriate, and certainly nothing a man did with a woman who expected him to watch his language around her. Her hand slid over his shoulder and her forehead fell to his collarbone, giving him more of her weight. He shifted his feet to accept it more easily. She was more than exhausted. She was played out. He switched his attention to her other leg, finding the same trembling, same knots, same feminine delicacy. And beyond bitching about having to climb, she'd given no indication of the distress she was in. Either she was the most stubborn, self-sacrificing woman in the world or this was normal for her. He went back over all she'd told him, the last lingering in his mind.

*Actually, I'm fine for a few more weeks.*

A vampire was strongest after feeding, the results holding for a week or two and then fading over the next few. "Have you been trying to tell me that this is you at your strongest?"

She didn't lift her head. "Finally, the man catches a clue."

The muscle in his hand spasmed, and she sucked in a whistling breath. That didn't make sense. He massaged the cramp. "Are you newly turned?"

Her "What makes you say that?" was a vibrating moan.

He controlled the surge of lust the shuddering betrayal inspired, keeping his drawl even, with effort. "My sister-in-law had trouble at first."

"Your brother is married?" He turned his head, and her hair blew across his face. He inhaled the lingering scent of honeysuckle. "You sound shocked."

She pushed her hair back. This close he could see the black and taupe flecks adding dimension to her brown eyes. He'd always been partial to brown eyes.

"I've never met a settling-down vampire."

"Maybe you just haven't met the right vamps." He caught a few strands of hair stuck to her lips and eased them off. Her skin was very smooth but chilled. "And that doesn't answer my question."

She sighed and sat up straight. He missed the warmth of her body, the responsibility of taking her weight. "Yes. It has always been this way."

"And how long has that been?"

"One hundred nine thousand, five hundred four days."

He chuckled at the bright way she announced it. "Not that you've been counting."

"My life took a downward turn after that." She shrugged. "How about you?"

"Slightly less time as a vampire. And being turned definitely changed my life."

Those long elegant fingers settled on his arm. "For the good I hope."

He stopped as he realized it actually hadn't been bad. He still had his brothers, still got to work with the horses he loved, and while he'd had to say good-bye to the century and the woman he'd loved, he would have had to do that anyway. Something Allie had been pointing out to him relentlessly for the last six months. She had a real problem with the hostility between he and Caleb, and just couldn't accept that they were comfortable with it. Since the day she'd met his brother, she'd been picking at the fabric of their relationship. She'd be thrilled to know her persistence was paying off. "It stayed pretty even, if you must know the truth. Just a couple kinks in the wire."

He straightened.

She looked up at him. "What kind of kinks?"

"My brother and I had issues."

She frowned. "That is not good. Have you settled them?"

"We're working on it."

"You have been a vampire for almost as long as I have, and you are just working on it?"

He shrugged, feeling an unwarranted flick of discomfort under her frown. "It was never a priority before."

"How could it not be?"

He held out his hand. She took it. He pulled her up. "You sound like Allie."

That cute frown deepened along with her accent. "Who is this Allie?"

"My sister-in-law."

The frown cleared. "Then I don't mind the comparison."

That piqued his curiosity. "Why not?"

"Because you admire her."

"What makes you think that?"

"The way your expression softens when you speak of her. Is she a fun person?"

He pulled her to her feet. "She's a pretty little thing with more courage than one woman should have and a sense of humor that keeps everyone around her laughing."

"You like her."

"It's hard not to." He bent to pick up his rifle. "She makes my brother happy."

Bark sprayed off the tree above Raisa's head. A explosion of sound trailed the spray of bark. A force on her arm yanked her down. She fell on her back, landing on a rock, the fall knocking the wind from her. She no sooner got it back than Jared threw himself over her, squashing her flat, his shoulder pressing into her jaw. Above her head, she saw more bark splintered off the tree and heard another explosion. A snowflake landed in her eye. She blinked. Realization dawned. "Good God! Someone is shooting at us!"

She pushed at Jared's shoulders. He pushed back. "Stay down, you little fool."

The next bullet hit lower down the trunk. The next wouldn't miss. Her pushing became frantic. "The fool in this situation would be the one setting himself up as target practice."

"Roll."

His arms came under her, and then up was down and down up as they rolled into the shadow of the trees. He took the brunt of everything on his elbows and knees, sheltering her with his big body as the echo of the gunshot reverberated around then. Before she could catch her breath, Jared half lifted, half tossed her behind a tree. He handed her the rifle. As her fingers closed around the stock, he said one word: "Stay."

And then, with animal-like grace, he spun around, fading into the shadows.

She could feel his energy fanning out, encompassing the forest around them, feel his hesitation as he found what he was looking for, felt the tension fine-tune the flow, and then he was heading off, perpendicular to where the shots had come from, easily traceable to her. But then, everyone was easily traceable to her. She had a talent for following energy that others couldn't see or feel. She sent a thought out on his trail.

*Be careful.*

His response was short and to the point. *Be quiet.* And then as if in apology to the harshness of his order, there came a stroke of calm.

Raisa sighed. He was a very nice man, and if things were different, she might have just lingered in his company for the uniqueness of the experience, but Miri was relying on her. Miri, with her incredible strength and absolute belief that her mate could save her from the Sanctuary's torture if only Raisa could find him and let him know she lived.

For a moment, Raisa felt the weight of responsibility weighing her down. She didn't know anything about being a hero, didn't know anything about this war she was caught up in. She'd spent the last two hundred of her almost three hundred vampire years experimenting with the changing times and cultures. Relishing the freedom to learn all that had been denied her as a virtual slave. In between avoiding the lecherous pursuits of the rogue male vampires who saw her as an opportunity to be exploited, that is.

She'd learned very early on that she was different, lacking the skills that put female vampires on an equal footing of sorts with the males. Blood did strengthen her, but just marginally, and every time she drank it she got so sick for so long that she put off doing it until there was no other choice. The best she could make out, she was actually allergic to blood. Animal or human, it made no difference. The more she drank the sicker she got, but if she didn't drink it at all, she'd die faster. And she hadn't reached the point where suicide looked good.

She grabbed the rifle. With a last glance in the direction Jared had gone, she mouthed a good-bye and headed down the mountain, taking care to mask her presence. Her muscles were still tired but since "down" was working on a new set of muscles, she made good time. Part of her scanned for other energy, part of her stayed locked to Jared. She just needed to be sure he was alive. She stumbled when his energy cut off. An abrupt cessation of hope.

"No." She leaned against the tree, sucking air into her lungs only to have it catch on a sob. *He couldn't be dead. He couldn't.*

"I'm not, but in about five minutes you're going to wish I was."

Jared! She spun around. He stood between two towering pine trees, looking as dark and as imposing as the forest as he glared at her. Yanking the rifle up, she slammed the stock into her shoulder, hoping he'd believe she would actually shoot him. She couldn't let him take her away from her mission. The Sanctuary had to believe she was doing what they had ordered her to do. Otherwise, they would kill her, and if she died, so did Miri's hope of rescue. "Stay back."

"I don't think so." With his hat pulled low over his brow, his eyes still glowing red from the heat of battle, Jared looked every inch the dangerous outlaw he was. "Put the gun down, Raisa."

"No." She didn't ever want to hurt him, but especially when he looked like this, the twilight emphasizing the breadth of his shoulders. The rising moon cast a faint light that glinted off the faded patches on the thighs of his jeans and drew her eye to the strong muscles beneath that flexed with the step he took toward her. She tightened her finger on the trigger. "Don't make me shoot you, Jared."

"You won't shoot me."

"I won't like it, but I will."

Another step. "What makes you think a little bullet's going to hurt me anyway?"

"Because you brought it to hunt Sanctuary vampires. I guess it must have some efficacy against vampires."

"Not only pretty, but clever." Another step. His energy reached out and surrounded her—calm and soothing, beckoning. The bastard. "You can't trick me."

His head cocked to the side. "I wasn't aware that I was trying to. If you pull that trigger, watch the recoil."

"Thank you."

She couldn't let him come any closer. She searched up and down his big body, looking for a target. His head was out. She could never shoot anyone in the face. That left his torso or his legs. She lowered the muzzle. Over his broad chest, down the center line of his abdomen, hesitating when she got to the waistband of his jeans. Worn almost white, they followed the lines of his narrow hips and strong thighs with loving detail. Jared was a man—vampire—in peak condition, and it showed in the easy way he moved and in the way the well-honed muscles of his thighs pressed against the pale blue denim of his jeans. She lowered the gun some more, angling over the creases of his jeans until she reached the toes of his scuffed boots. Maybe if she shot his toe, it would slow him down.

"Give it up, Rai. You don't have it in you to shoot anyone."

She brought the gun back up just as slowly, counting time in heartbeats, her courage in breaths. She couldn't afford to be swayed by a handsome face and handsomer manner. She had to get away, finish what she had started. Locking on Jared's energy so she'd know if he moved, she closed her eyes and remembered one of the few happy moments of her childhood, before the famine had taken her father and her mother's laughter. Before hunger had become her companion and loss a constant. Remembered back to when she'd finally mastered swimming after months of trying. She'd been such a slow learner, but every day when she'd gone out, her mother had given her a hug and encouragement, and on the day she'd finally— finally—paddled four strokes to shore, her mother had held her face between her hands and whispered, pride in every word, "I told you, Raisa, you can do anything if you want it badly enough."

With her mother's words echoing in her head she opened her eyes and stared at a point over Jared's shoulder. Courage welled with the memory. "You're wrong. I can do anything."

Before he could answer, she pulled the trigger.

## ❧ 5 ❧

JARED launched himself at Raisa before the bullet hit. For a critical spit second, incredulity that she'd pulled the trigger clouded his realization that she'd aimed over his shoulder. Behind him there was a thud, in front of him Rai, her face white as a sheet, horror in her eyes as he flew at her. She dropped the gun and threw up her arms up to protect her face. He took her down easy, twisting to absorb the shock of impact, rolling to get her out of the way in case whatever she had shot at was still moving.

He leapt to his feet, spinning around as he did, talons at full length, fangs fully extended. He cast out his energy, feeling for a threat, finding none, even though he could clearly see there before him, in the snow, lay a man—a were—blood spilling from a wound high on his shoulder and pooling on the frozen ground in a dark, spreading splotch. Snowflakes drifted into the pool of blood, disintegrating in the heat. His senses should be screaming. They weren't. That was not good.

Jared grabbed the rifle, levered another round into the chamber and put it on Rai's lap. Her fingers closed reflexively around it.

Meeting her wide gaze, he ordered, "If anything else moves, pull the trigger."

She blinked. "But what if—"

He cut her off. "No what-ifs. Pull the trigger, and I'll sort out anything that needs sorting later."

Another blink and then those incredible lips firmed. A quick nod and she got her elbows under her. Satisfied Raisa would do as he'd told her, Jared turned back to his attacker. The attacker that shouldn't have gotten within a hundred feet of him without his presence being telegraphed by his energy.

"Did I kill him?" Rai called.

She didn't sound too excited by the prospect. He remembered the horror in her eyes and the way she'd begged for the vampires who'd attacked her. Unlike him, killing what needed killing wasn't something she probably did on a daily basis. "No." He nudged the paralyzed were with his toe. "Just winged him."

"Winged him? How could I just wing him from that close?" She sounded both horrified and disgruntled in one breath.

"Talent, sunbeam. Pure talent."

"What does that mean?" She had a penchant for worrying about the wrong things at the wrong time.

"Nothing for you to get your tail in a twist about, so be quiet a second and let me concentrate."

"And what, exactly, do you need to concentrate on?"

The edge to her voice and the nervous twitch of her energy warned him she was going to go all soft on him again. "Nothing you need worry about."

The sound she made was a ladylike version of his own snort of disbelief.

He gave the were another nudge. "Sucks, doesn't it?" he asked the chemically frozen were. "Having your own technology used against you?"

The were couldn't answer, immobilized as he was by the paralyzing agent loaded into the bullet, but the antipathy rolling off him in waves spoke volumes. "Slade thought that Sanctuary cocktail should be spiked a bit to include weres in its effects." He bent and started checking the assorted pockets of the man's camouflage jacket. "I can't say that I disagree."

"Who is he?" Rai asked.

"Just an overly friendly were, sugarplum."

He let her stew over the nickname while he removed the pistol from the were's shoulder holster.

"What are you going to do with him?"

"Kill him eventually."

She gasped but hushed for a second. A trickle of energy teased his mind, knocking gently. When he wouldn't answer the knock, she slid in, utilizing that neat way she had of circumventing his defense. *You can't kill a defenseless man.*

She was wrong. He could easily kill him. The bastard had definitely planned on killing him, then probably raping her. With her weakness, she wouldn't have stood a chance against the brute. *Stay out of it, pumpkin.*

*Are you going to keep calling me silly names every time I talk to you when you don't want me to?*

He found a small electronic device in the were's left pants pocket. *That's the plan.*

*It won't deter me.*

He didn't imagine it would. *That's why I've decided to amuse myself by seeing just how many I can come up with, sweet cheeks.*

He felt the move as her hand went to her cheek.

With a glint of amusement he tacked on. *Those weren't the cheeks I was referring to, by the way.*

Another gasp and then another bit of silence before she was back. *You're outrageous.*

*Nah.* He slipped the device into his pocket. *Just a connoisseur of beautiful asses. Much like yourself.*

Dead silence. He never knew he could sense a blush, but Raisa's was coming loud and clear over the connection between them—a wave of heat and awkward feminine discomfort as she gnawed on the possibility that he'd heard her mental litany up the mountain. He smiled. She was a cute little thing. And finally, blessedly silent.

He removed the throwing knives from the were's ankles. "So, asshole, mind telling me what you're doing up here, and why you jumped us?"

Not surprisingly the were didn't answer. A probe of his mind revealed nothing other than the disturbing fact that he'd been hunting Raisa. Jared turned the were over and searched his back pockets. The crinkle of paper in the right one drew his fingers there. The were's mental tension increased. "What's this?"

Jared pulled it free, opened it, and froze. It was a picture of Raisa. Not the Raisa he knew with the sharp wit and terminal optimism, but a woman with sunken, pain-filled eyes that radiated anger, but Raisa all the same.

"What is it?" she asked.

He didn't answer, just refolded the paper and put it in his pocket and asked her, "Aren't you supposed to be keeping an eye out for his companions?"

"What makes you think there're more?"

He motioned to the downed man. "Wolves travel in packs."

The were's start confirmed what he suspected. There were more. "He's a were?"

"Yes."

"That's better than a vampire, right?"

That was the McClarens' and D'Nallys' opinion. "So I'm told."

And he had met some weres who put all but a few vampires to shame for fighting skill and cunning. Derek McClaren for one, and Ian and Creed of the D'Nallys for a couple others. Jared stood. He had about twenty minutes of paralyzing effect from the bullet before he'd have to start watching his back. He came to Raisa's side. Her big brown eyes studied him warily. The picture in his pocket crinkled with incriminating insistence.

"Why couldn't I sense him?"

He pulled the small electronic device from his pocket. "I suspect this might have something to do with it."

She took it from him, holding it in her open palm for a moment before closing her fingers over it. Her eyes took on that unfocused look that said she was concentrating inwardly.

"It has a strange vibration to its energy."

"You can feel something?"

"Yes, now that I'm holding it."

He took the device from her hand. He held it for a good two minutes, concentrating, but to no avail. He didn't feel a thing. Absolutely nothing, which was unusual. Everything gave off some residual energy of its function—the people who touched it, its power source. But this device lay in his palm like dead air.

"Are you sure you're not imagining things?" he asked her, giving the object a squeeze.

She cut him a disgusted glare. "Positive."

"No need to get feisty. Just asking a question."

She stared at his closed fist. "I've always been sensitive to energy."

That was possible. Every vampire, when they turned, developed some special skill, usually an enhancement of something they already had. He'd never met another vampire gifted with the ability of see-and-throw energy, but that didn't mean they didn't exist. And apparently Raisa was one of them. That unique energy that flowed around the edges of his, slipping into the folds with familiar ease, soothing the raw edges. Too familiarly and too easily. If she could do with her energy what he could do with his, he needed some distance between them until he figured out how involved she was with the Sanctuary. She could be a Sanctuary collaborator. That would certainly explain her resistance to killing Sanctuary warriors. Or she could be just another victim with a soft heart, his vampire whispered, uncomfortable with anything that put her outside its acceptance.

Jared pulled his energy away from Raisa's. It wasn't as easy as it should be. A ping of hurt came from her to him. He had no reason for the guilt that flicked through him. She reached for the device again. He shook his head and put it in his shirt pocket. "I'll keep this for Slade to check out."

He grabbed up her pack. Her energy flowed around him, seeking a reading of his emotions. He blocked it.

None of the hurt he could sense inside her at his move showed in her voice as she asked, "What about him?"

"I'll take care of him in a minute."

Her lip slid between her teeth, pressing into the plump fullness, honing his attention. She had a gorgeous mouth—full lips behind which he could see even white teeth. Her mouth held an appeal for him he couldn't afford to indulge.

"You can't kill him."

He shot her a look. "Why not? He was going to kill me."

Her jaw flexed. The flesh around her teeth glowed as white as the gleam of the enamel on the teeth pressing into it. "It's not right."

"Are you worried for my soul or yours?"

"I don't understand?"

He walked over to where her blanket had fallen, scooped it up, and tossed it to her. "Just what I asked. What's your worry about how that piece of shit dies? He wanted to kill me, rape you, so what does it matter how he meets his end?"

She rolled the blanket up in a ball. The snow, falling heavier now as the storm gathered, sheltered her in a swirling flurry. "Because we're not them. We don't kill because it suits our purposes or makes life easier."

"Speak for yourself."

"I am."

"And your point would be?"

She settled her weight into her shoes, shoulders squared. "I can't let you kill him in cold blood, no matter what he intended to do."

"You can't?"

"No."

"How do you intend to stop me?"

"I'm going to start by appealing to your moral barometer, and then I'll resort to physical methods."

He shook his head, marveling at the woman's ego. She barely reached the center of his chest and was about as big around as a matchstick. On top of that there were dark smudges under her eyes, her skin was pasty white, and every time the wind gusted she shivered. And she was going to get physical with him?

"You go right ahead, then, and give it your best shot." He took the rifle from her. The fact that she didn't even try to hold on to it showed how poorly prepared she was for a battle. He glanced over at the were before looking pointedly back at her. "You might want to turn your back so your scruples won't be offended."

"Why? If I let you do this, turning my back won't alleviate my culpability."

"But it might spare your sensibilities."

"Thanks, but no thanks."

He steeled himself against the energy radiating off her. It wasn't easy. The soft strands of feminine entreaty slid neatly between his darker rage, wrapping around the edges, tugging them away from the black burn of anger and into the gray area of his conscience.

"Give it up, Raisa."

"You keep telling me that."

"Because it's your only option."

She shook her head, her hand completely dwarfed by the folds of the blanket clenched in her tight fist. It was a small hand, white and dainty. Not particularly beautiful, not particularly elegant, just a normal hand belonging to a normal woman, so there was absolutely no reason for his gaze to be locked on it or for an uncomfortable feeling to take up residence in his gut.

"I have others." She walked toward him, her steps carefully measured, her gaze locked on the were. When she got within two steps of the man, Jared put himself in her path. She didn't slow, didn't look up, just stepped around him and kept going. He was torn between grabbing her arm and waiting to see what she would do. Curiosity won out.

She stopped halfway between him and the were and turned around, still holding the blanket in front of her like a shield, that chin set at an angle that defined stubborn. "Let's just go."

"What? Suddenly you're in a hurry to go with me?"

"Considering the alternative, absolutely."

Her eyes were suspiciously moist. The uncomfortable feeling in his stomach intensified. Guilt. She was actually making him feel guilty for doing what needed to be done. Son of a bitch. In four quick strides he was beside her and at the were's side, his talons extended. He only needed one swipe to sever the were's head from his body. In an equally fast move, Raisa was attached to his arm like a leech, her stomach curling dangerously close to the razor-sharp edges of his talons. He swore and retracted them immediately, grabbing her by the back of her coat and holding her up. Shock was the predominate emotion on her face as he warned, "Don't you ever do something so foolish again."

The snarl in his order lingered in his chest. She'd come damn close to getting her abdomen laid open. He tossed her a safe distance to the side. She landed on her feet, a sleek little cat who darted between him and his quarry once again. "No, Jared."

His teeth snapped together at her persistence. He kept his voice as even as possible as he laid out the facts. "It's not your decision."

She spread her arms wide, as if a three-and-a-half-foot span of slender muscle was a barrier to anything he wanted to do. "You can't do this."

He took a breath, the raw flick of her emotions churning his own. He didn't like her so close to the paralyzed were. Frozen or not, the other man represented danger, and Jared's instincts demanded he be between Raisa and any threat, no matter how slight. "If I don't, in about twenty minutes he's going to be on our asses hunting us."

Her arms lowered. "We'll outdistance him."

"Uh-huh." Was she crazy? He watched the were. At the first twitch of muscle, he was dead. "You're too weak."

"Then you can leave me behind."

Crazy didn't begin to cover it. His head snapped up. "Not a chance in hell."

"That's my choice."

He shook his head, adding a mental thrust to his flat declaration. That had been decided the minute he'd laid eyes on her. "No, it's not."

Raisa opened her mouth to argue, and then froze. She spun to the right, and then just as quickly to the left, her chin lifting, her focus intensifying in a subtle surge of energy.

"Oh heck."

"What?"

"They're coming."

"Who?" Or maybe he should have asked what?

"More weres."

"How many?"

She closed her eyes and concentrated. She opened them, anxiety shadowing her big brown eyes as they met his. "Five."

Shit. "'Oh heck' means we're about to be knee-deep in enemies?"

"Yes."

"Oh heck" meant a woman broke a nail, put a run in her stocking. It did not mean they were about to be overrun by Sanctuary.

"I really need to teach you to swear."

She grabbed his hand. "We have to leave."

They couldn't go anywhere until he determined which way to run. He scanned and detected nothing. "Are you sure your nerves aren't acting up?"

"I'm not the nervous type."

No, she wasn't. She yanked his arm in a frantic bid to get him in motion. When he didn't move, she gave another tug and grunted, "I really can feel them."

"I can't."

"I can't help it if your senses aren't as developed as mine."

His first instinct was to dismiss the claim, no one had better senses than him, but then he paused. Raisa had never been anything but brutally honest. Even when it was to her detriment. Disarmingly so. And there was no way she could hide the distress coming off her in waves or the nervous flicks of energy surging right and left. Either she was a damn good actress or she really could sense what he couldn't.

Shit. They were a good two days' run from a known Renegade stronghold, which only left them one option. The D'Nallys' secret back door entrance. Using that was as likely to get him killed as standing here waiting for trouble to show up. Shit, again. He turned the gun on the were and fired.

Raisa moaned as if she'd taken the bullet. Softhearted little fool. He grabbed her hand and took off running, dragging her behind him, calling over his shoulder as he did. "And you can stop whining for that piece of scum." It irritated the hell out of him that she wasted sympathy on that were. "I only wounded him in order to keep him off our butts for another few hours."

Provided the double dose of paralyzing agent didn't stop his heart, but she didn't need to know that.

"One less wolf to worry about," she wheezed.

Damn, she was already out of breath. "Yes."

He scanned the woods around them. The thick fall of snow obscured the shadows. He still couldn't feel any energy, but the hairs on the back of his neck lifted in warning. "Where are they?"

She didn't hesitate. "Three behind and one each on the left and right."

Too many to risk a flat-out fight. At least with Raisa with him. She was too vulnerable to attack, and he didn't trust his ability to fight through the distraction if they threatened her.

Jared took a sharp left, heading downhill, knowing the weres would be expecting them to head up toward the nearest known Renegade stronghold on the other side of the mountain. The *Oh, thank God, not up* from Rai made him smile. In the midst of everything bad, she could make him smile. "You are one strange woman."

There was hesitation in her "Thank you," a shimmer in her energy that made him wonder if he'd hurt her feelings. He told himself he didn't care. Told himself that it was good she was distancing herself until he knew what was up with a Sanctuary were having her picture in his pocket. But the longer he did without the soft touch of her energy, the more irritated he became. She tripped. He only realized it when there was a hard jerk on his arm. He looked back and down. She was on her side in the snow, dangling from his hand, her shoulder up against a log, a dazed expression on her face. Grabbing her under her arms, he lifted her up out of the snow, cursing under his breath as she shivered and rubbed her hands together. "Are you all right?" he asked in a barely discernible whisper.

She nodded, teeth chattering. "F-fine."

He brushed the snow from her hair and her clothes. She'd lost her blanket somewhere along the way. At this rate she wouldn't survive the night. She'd either succumb to the cold or the weres. "We've got to keep moving. There's safe passage ahead."

She nodded as if she wasn't on her last legs. "Lead on."

He rubbed her hands between his. "I'll warm you up when we get there."

She nodded at the promise. "I'll h-hold you t-to that."

Damn, he didn't like this. She was freezing; cold drained the small bit of strength she had left. He didn't know if she could make it even if he carried her. She touched his arm with her hand. That soft energy wrapped around him again. "I'll make it."

She'd snuck inside his mind again. He put his hand over hers. Her fingers were like blocks of ice. "I know you will."

If it killed him, he'd make sure of it.

He studied the terrain over her shoulder. As far as he could see through the blowing haze of snow, their back trail was clear. He didn't insult Raisa again by asking if she was sure they were being followed. His gut was in full agreement.

He looked down at her. Damn, her head barely came to the center of his chest. "Just remember, the faster you run, the faster you get warm."

She gave him a faint smile and a game nod of her head. There was nothing left to say. He wrapped his fingers around her upper arm and set off running, risking the energy expenditure to levitate them both. The cave trail was only five miles away. If they got there undetected, they should be fine. As long as the D'Nallys didn't cut their throats for entering their territory without an invite, that was. He didn't tell Rai that. She had enough on her mind just trying to keep up. Two miles into the run, Rai grabbed his shirt and tugged.

"Something's wrong," she gasped.

He kept running, lifting her up when her feet tangled with his and threatened to bring them both down. "What?"

"They turned."

He stopped. "I don't understand."

She wrapped her hand across her stomach holding her side, a frown on her face as her breath wheezed in and out of her lungs on a hoarse rasp. He had to wait for her to get enough wind in her to answer. "They turned as soon as we did."

"You mean when they tracked us?" Shit, if they had a tracker who could do that, he and Raisa were in serious trouble.

The shake of her head was immediate. The damp strands of her hair clung to her flushed cheeks. Her eyes were fever bright above, picking up the deep shadows of her snow-drenched hair. "No. They turned . . . when we did . . . as we did."

Son of a bitch.

Her hand went to his shirt pocket, patting at the bulge there when she ran out of breath.

Understanding flared immediately. "A tracking device?" he asked.

She shrugged, wheezed a bit, and then said in a long exhale. "I don't know. I'm not familiar with this kind of thing, but there's a steady ebb and flow to its energy."

Like maybe it was pinging signals off other devices. He picked up the small device and turned it over. There wasn't a switch or lever on it anywhere. It was just a small innocuous-looking sealed black box. Which was too bad because Slade was going to pester him to hell and back for details about it. Raisa peered over his arm, breathing a bit easier with the rest. "Does it have an off switch?"

He had that ridiculous sense of disappointing her when he told her, "No."

She bit her lip and thought for a minute. That faraway inward focus came into her gaze. Then she blinked and focused on him, that tempting mouth that always seemed on the verge of inviting a kiss tipped up at the corners. She snatched the controller out of his hands, turning it over in hers. "Do you think they're so confident that we don't know this is a transmitter that they'll follow this signal wherever it goes?"

Understanding of what she was getting at was immediate. He cupped her chilled cheeks in his hands and kissed her hard and quick, her startled gasp bathing his lips in the promise of her taste. "Did I say clever before?" He took the device out of her hand as she stood there blinking at him. Hell, a man would think she wasn't used to being kissed. Jared smiled and flicked the end of her nose. "You, sunbeam, are a wonder."

While she stared, not blinking, not moving, except for the pink of her tongue coming out to touch where his lips had been, he summoned a deer from the forest. A doe answered his call. She had eyes as soft as Raisa's and a manner just as sweet. He held her in thrall as he motioned to Rai, "Give me your bra."

She clutched her chest like he'd just demanded her jewels.

He held up the device and said, "I need something to tie this to her." He motioned again with his fingers. "Give me your bra."

"Turn your back."

He raised his eyebrow at her. "Can't you just slip it off under your shirt?"

"I'm not that coordinated."

He turned his back. "Now that's disappointing to hear."

Cloth slid along skin in a seductive whish that sent his imagination galloping. Her "Live with it" as her bra slapped over his shoulder made him grin again. The garment was laden with the scent of her body. A flowery perfume underlay a richer scent, one that made his vampire sit up and take notice. He snatched the garment off his shoulder. It was simple cotton. Nothing fancy. Nothing like he'd buy for her if she were his. She was definitely a silk-and-frills woman if he'd ever seen one. He clipped the device onto one of the straps, ignoring the sense of connection he got from handling the soft garment. He approached the doe. Rai was right beside him, her shorter legs taking two steps to his one. "Are you under the impression that I need help?"

"I just wanted to make sure you didn't put it on too tightly."

He slanted a glance down at her, taking in the way she was biting her lower lip. "If it falls off, it's not going to do us much good."

He wrapped the band around the deer's neck. Despite the doe being enthralled, Rai stroked her neck soothingly. "But it doesn't need to stay on that long. I mean, if it doesn't fall off, they'll catch her, and they'll be angry."

And they'd take that anger out on the deer and that bothered her. "I'll only fasten one hook, weaken the material, and plant a suggestion for her to rub it off."

Raisa nodded, the high pitch to her energy dropping off as relief flowed through her. He shook his head as he fastened the garment to the doe. She had to be the softest woman he'd ever met. Completely unsuited to the life of a vampire, yet she'd been one longer than he. It boggled the mind. He slapped the deer on the haunch and sent it up and east.

Raisa rubbed her hands up and down her arms. "I hope she'll be okay."

He picked up his rifle. "You'd do better to hope they fall for that trick."

"I know." She was still staring after the deer. "It just seems so wrong to use something so sweet and helpless."

"Life isn't always fair."

"True." She took a deep breath that rasped with weariness. As the doe bounded out of sight, she held out her hand. "We'd better get moving."

"Yes." He took her hand in his. Her fingers barely spanned his palm. A woman like her shouldn't be out here in the wilderness running for her life. She should be tucked away somewhere safe, away from any threat, kept happy and comfortable doing things that wouldn't tax her strength. She should have someone watching over her, easing her way. A father, a brother, a husband.

Allie would call that view chauvinistic and outdated, but he couldn't help it. It came naturally to him to protect women, to show them courtesy. He'd been raised in a time when women were to be pampered and cherished. No matter how the centuries changed, he couldn't seem to shake that aspect of his upbringing. Up until Raisa, he hadn't realized how much he had missed a woman's acceptance of his care.

"You ready?" he asked. Another deep breath and she nodded. He pulled Raisa into his side and headed down the mountain, taking more of her weight than she wanted to give him, stilling her mental protest that she was too heavy with a brush of calm. His reward was that addictive, soothing wrap of her energy around his. He levitated them over a fallen tree. She shivered against him as the wind whipped a stinging barrage of snowflakes into their faces. Everything protective and what his sister-in-law would call archaically male surged to the fore.

Her shirt was wet. Her skin cold. If he didn't get Raisa to shelter soon, she'd end up a frozen caricature of herself. He splayed his fingers over her waist, appreciating her softness even as she determinedly put one foot in front of the other. The woman was a mass of contradictions. She took on Sanctuary weres without batting an eye, yet finishing the job when she missed her kill gave her an attack of conscience. She jumped when he thought she'd stand, whined when he thought she'd be quiet, and displayed an incredible determination when other women would have given out. She was unpredictable, sweet, sassy, and as intriguing as all get-out. And he was taking her straight into a den of woman-hungry males. He shook his head. It was definitely not turning out to be his day.

## ❈ 6 ❈

THE D'Nallys didn't kill them, but they were entirely too fond of Raisa for Jared's peace of mind. At least the males. Jared felt another growl rumble in his chest as yet another well-muscled, well-favored D'Nally stepped into their path and murmured a greeting to *his* little vampire. His fangs ached with a need to sink into the man as he reached for Raisa's hand in the traditional pack greeting of an unmated male toward an available female. The only thing that kept Jared from severing the limb was the way Raisa leaned back against him to avoid the contact. He tucked her under his shoulder and snarled at their armed escort. "Are we going to some place in particular, or are you just taking us for a stroll around the compound?"

Creed, the leader of their escort, tucked his rifle into his arm. His brow arched and the corner of his mouth twitched, but beyond "Someplace particular," Creed didn't say anything more.

The man was all hard angles bristled by a day's growth of beard, but the minute Raisa shivered, his brown eyes narrowed and he stopped. As if in synch, the rest of the four guards halted. The visual inspection they subjected Raisa to was as intense as any his brother Slade would give. Raisa shuffled her feet. The touch of her energy was tentative. He caught it in his, wrapping his around it in a soothing stroke as she stared right back at the were. Nothing in her expression gave away the uncertainty he could feel streaking through her. She shivered again, and the big were turned his head, his yellow-flecked brown eyes narrowed on Raisa. "She is not well?"

The question was not unexpected. Healthy vampires didn't feel the cold. "Not particularly."

The were's brows snapped down. He touched Raisa's shoulder. "What's wrong with her?"

The snarl rumbled from Jared's soul. The were removed his hand. "She's cold."

A small smile played around Creed's mouth as he met Jared's gaze. "You will have to do better than that growl if you wish to keep the males from this one."

Rai's hand wrapped around the back of his thigh. Lust and territorial rage spread through him, spiked by her instinctive request for his protection.

"She's under my protection."

Creed's smile was indulgent. "The extent of your claim will be observed, but as she doesn't wear your mark, courting is allowed."

"As flattering as being courted sounds," Rai piped up, "I'm not in the market."

Creed's smile, when he bestowed it upon Rai, was extremely gentle, an emotion Jared hadn't believed Ian's badass first in command was capable of. "But for now we will get you to a place that is warm, eh, little one? You would not want to meet suitors with blue lips and frozen toes."

It irritated the hell out of Jared that, rather than shoot down the offer, Raisa smiled that sweet smile and thanked the arrogant bastard. Right before she shivered. Creed's frown returned. He motioned the men forward. The pace was noticeably faster than before. And when another hopeful stepped in front of them, he was elbowed aside none too gently by the guards. This time the sound that rumbled in Jared's chest was a growl of satisfaction. Rai protested and moved to see if the man who'd landed on his ass in a snowbank was all right. Jared checked the instinctive move. The were, seeing Jared wasn't going to let her rush to his side, got up with an easy flex of muscle that revealed his bid for sympathy for what it was. A shot at Raisa's notice.

"You're too soft," Jared informed Raisa as the young man touched his forehead in a wry salute as Jared hustled her by. "If you don't toughen up, this lot is going to run right over you."

Raisa glanced over his shoulder. "They didn't have to shove him."

As far as he was concerned, the escort hadn't shoved the impudent pup hard enough. He was still smiling and still hopeful. "Unless you want him in your bed tonight, I suggest you stop encouraging him."

Raisa gasped. Creed chuckled. Her hand tightened on Jared's. "I was just—"

"Making eyes at him," Jared finished for her.

She stopped so suddenly, that, if he hadn't had his arm around her waist, the were behind them would have goosed her with his knee. As it was, he had to carry her two steps before she fell back into rhythm.

Her "I was not making eyes at him" was as stiff as her body.

"It's a different culture, sunbeam. What you think of as innocent consideration could find you flat on your back with a husband you weren't expecting."

He felt Rai's start of fear. As well as Creed's disgust.

"Among our kind, your concern might be mistaken for interest. But D'Nallys recognize outsiders have different ways," Creed explained, that odd gentleness that Jared didn't trust in his voice. "You do not have to fear rape, little vamp."

Raisa didn't relax, her eyes darted from man to man under her lashes, as if expecting one of them to jump her at any moment. Low growls from the escort, each aimed at Jared, punctuated every step they took. The D'Nallys didn't like the implication. Jared ignored the threats, too, satisfied that Raisa was reining in that potent femininity of hers for the moment. He didn't give a shit if the D'Nallys resented it.

Creed stopped in front of a large log home sporting big windows and opened an ornately carved front door. Warm air from the interior flowed over them. "The D'Nally offers you the comfort of his home."

Jared nodded with the appropriate formality. "Thank you." With pressure at the base of her spine, he pushed Rai through the opening, the urge to get her warm barely stronger than the need to get her away from the other males. Creed halted him before he could follow.

Jared glanced down at the hand on his arm and then at the were. There was no gentleness in the man's face now, just the ruthless clinging to purpose that the clan was known for. "Don't scare her again."

"Don't tell me how to handle my woman."

Creed smiled darkly, revealing his sharp canines and the aggression so inherent in his kind. "She's not yours."

Jared stepped into the other man's space and bared his fangs right back in an equally feral smile, meeting Creed's power with his own. He removed the were's hand from his arm, restraining himself from breaking it with sheer force of will. "She won't be yours."

Creed shifted his grip to the rifle. "While she is here, she is also under D'Nally protection, subject to pack law, and her wishes will not be disregarded for yours."

"I never thought they would."

"You will also not be allowed to abuse her."

"Warning her of your customs is not abuse."

"You frightened her needlessly. You know pack law always gives a woman a choice."

"Up to a point." Jared knew once a woman lay down with a man, even if only he felt the bond, all choice was gone. The woman became his sole responsibility.

Creed inclined his head. "But until that point, she will be protected in her right to choose."

"Protected from what?"

"Vamp males are known for their indiscriminate mating." Creed's lip curled in disgust. "She is a woman who thinks in terms of forever. That will be respected."

It was a warning. The snarl ripped from Jared's throat without thought. No one told him what to do with his woman.

Creed stepped back, a mocking smile on his lips. "Snarl all you want, but she is a woman whose compatibility to were mating has been scented by all. If she becomes someone's mate, she will not be leaving."

Great. Just what he needed. Weres on a mating mission. "She's not a paragon. She's as contrary as they come."

As one, the weres around him smiled, purely male smiles of anticipation, making Jared wonder if their escort had been picked at random or from the pack's most eligible males. Creed was no exception.

"Then she should fit right into the pack."

Shit.


**HE'D** kill every damn were in the pack before he let them get their paws on her, Jared decided as Raisa came out of the bathroom wrapped in a too-big heavy terry robe, steam billowing around her, framing her in a fragrant cloud.

"Warmed up?" he asked, keeping his voice as neutral as possible, which wasn't all that neutral. The woman stirred all the rough edges of his personality.

She nodded and clutched the neck of the robe closed. "Yes, thank you."

Her hair was still damp, falling around her too-thin face in a sub-dued mass of waves. As soon as it dried, it would be that wild tangle of honey curls that tempted a man to wrap his fingers in the tawny mass. Her lips were soft but not relaxed, reflecting the tension he could see shadowing her gaze.

"What's wrong?"

She crossed the room, her bare feet making wisps of sound as she came to where he stood in front of the wood-burning stove. "Are we going to be here long?"

"For a bit, why?"

She shrugged. "I was just wondering."

Weariness and nervousness came off her in an undulating wave. "You wouldn't, by any chance, be feeling a little hunted?"

She shot him a startled glance and then a rueful smile. "Hard to believe, but even the Sanctuary made me feel less pursued."

Jared could understand that. "The D'Nallys are a rather intense clan."

"Don't they have any women of their own?"

"Yes, but it's not that simple."

He tugged one of the wing-back chairs over closer to the stove. She flashed him that smile and a touch of soft energy. "Thank you."

She kept the robe closed around her legs as she sat, denying him a glimpse of anything other than the tips of her pink, slightly-pruned-from-the-bath toes. After years of watching and appreciating the most blatant displays of female flesh, he'd forgotten how erotic a women's modesty could be. The anticipation of maybe catching a glimpse of what was always hidden, the temptation of the possibility of getting the woman to flash a bit of ankle, maybe to catch a hint of the top curve of a breast, a bare arm, a dimpled knee . . .

Longing hit him like a sledgehammer. Longing for a time when things were simpler, when he understood the rules and was com-fortable with them. The robe's neckline gaped as Raisa scooted back on the seat. Jared caught his breath as the shadowed valley between her pert breasts became visible, a dainty hollow that was just deep enough for his kiss. On either side, the small mounds swelled in a creamy firm expanse. His mouth watered. If he kissed her there, she'd taste of soap and clean, willing woman. His fingers twitched as he stared. She had very white skin. It glowed warm in the soft light of the room. Like the finest cream.

Raisa's gaze followed his. She gasped and clutched the lapels closed. Color moved up her throat. The move caused the bottom part of the robe to gape. Jared got a glimpse of slim thighs and fragile knees with little dimples, and then he heard another gasp. Her hand came down and whipped that gap closed. He stared uncomprehendingly for a second, his blood pounding in his veins, his fangs extending, his energy reaching for her. All because he'd caught a glimpse of her knees. Son of a bitch.

Jared shook his head and grabbed a throw off the couch. Raisa sat there, clutching her robe closed at her knees and chest, eyeing him with the wary, hunted look she'd worn while walking through the D'Nally compound. He didn't think she took a breath during the three steps it took him to get back to her side.

As he handed her the throw, he realized her feet didn't touch the floor when she sat back. How in hell could so small a woman raise so much havoc inside him?

"You're looking at me funny."

"Just admiring the view."

"There's not much to be admired."

She tucked the throw around her hips. The forest green brought out the brown of her eyes, the richness of her skin, the thickness of her lashes as they fanned her cheeks in a slow blink. He pushed a wild corkscrew curl off her forehead. It wrapped around his fingers.

"There's all kinds of pretty, sunbeam."

"Well." She hooked a finger around the strand of hair and pulled it from his hand, "What kind of pretty makes it not so simple for the weres? Why are they focusing on me?"

"Because you smell good."

Her hand opened over her chest. "I smell?"

"To a were, some women smell like heaven on earth."

She glanced at the window and the door, and then back to the windows. "Why?"

"No one will hurt you, Raisa. The weres are real strict about that, and for all they're a hot-blooded bunch, they hold their traditions dear."

"That's not an explanation of why."

"Weres are not happy unless they're mated. If ever there was a species that craves happily ever after, it's a were."

"So why do they not just marry?"

Her accent was back. She must be very nervous. "Because, when they mate, compatibility is determined by more than just a mental need. There's a chemical compatibility that has to exist. If a were doesn't find that perfect match, they live alone."

"A lot of people live alone."

"Weres' social position, emotional well-being, everything depends on their mating, so when a viable female comes into their midst, they tend to sit up and take notice."

She tucked her legs up under her. "Viable."

"Unattached."

"How do they know I'm unattached?"

"You don't wear another's scent."

He waited for her to process that, what it meant. When she did, her face went fiery red. "There are some things I will never get used to about this life."

Jared smiled, remembering his own frustration when he realized the weres knew he hadn't marked her. "I know what you mean."

Her lips slipped between her teeth. "That's why you're staying here with me, isn't it?"

"One reason." The other reasons he was staying with her were too revealing.

A knock sounded at the door. Jared straightened, his senses telling him who was on the other side of the door and territorial aggression surged forward. "Stay put."

Raisa nodded, her eyes as big as saucers. Jared crossed to the door, threw it open, and stared at the man standing there. "What in hell do you want?"


**THE** man on the other side of the doorjamb shared Jared's height and arrogance. He also had the most shocking eyes—a glowing amber that created a deep contrast when framed by his long dark hair. He radiated power and aggression. Raisa remembered what Jared had said about her scent. She tucked the throw closer about her, not wanting any stray whiffs to get away. The stranger frowned at Jared. "I thought you were advised not to scare her anymore."

Jared's shoulder flexed under his shirt as he brought the door forward to close it. "I'm not the one scaring her."

The man stopped the door with the flat of his palm. "You don't get to have everything your way, Jared."

"I don't see why not. She's my woman. I brought her here."

"But she's not yours by pack law or vampire law, which means she gets to choose."

"It's late, Ian. She's exhausted and not in the mood for this."

Ian slid past Jared. "Which is why I'm here. To see if she needs anything."

Raisa swallowed as the door closed and the amber-eyed man strode across the room, Jared close behind. She was trapped in a room with two of the most dominant creatures on God's green earth, and both thought she smelled good. She started to stand. The man held up his hand, forestalling her effort. "No, stay comfortable."

It wasn't a matter of comfort—it was a matter of advantage— and with her sitting and him standing, he had all of it. He got to her side before she could get to her feet, trapping her within the chair. She mastered her start of fear. Calm stroked along her fear. Jared. She clung to his energy as the big were squatted before her and lifted her chin. "I'm Ian D'Nally. Leader of the D'Nally weres."

Pulling out her manners wasn't as easy as it should be.

"Raisa Slovinski. You have a beautiful home. Thank you for sharing it."

He searched her face, his thumb rubbing her cheek. Behind him she heard a rumble. Jared. She sent her energy along his. They couldn't afford to alienate the weres. She'd gleaned from the edges of Jared's mind that this was the only safe place for days, so she bit her tongue when Ian tilted her head to the right and then the left.

"Why are you so weak?"

"I don't know."

"Is it a recent thing?"

"No."

"Have you been living alone?"

"Yes."

"For how long?"

This was beginning to sound like an interrogation. "Almost three hundred years."

"I find that hard to believe."

"I don't care what you believe."

Ian smiled, and a distinct possessiveness entered his touch. "You should. How did you come to be on my mountain?"

"I was dragged here."

"By whom?"

This was definitely an interrogation. Raisa met Ian's gaze squarely. "What gives you the right to question me about anything?"

The man smiled, revealing white, even teeth and larger-than-normal canines. "Little girl, I can do whatever I want. I'm the D'Nally."

She jerked her chin off the shelf of his hand. "Which means nothing to me."

"If you mate with one of my pack, it will mean everything to you."

"I'm not mating with any of you."

Instead of bristling, he nodded. "That is, of course, your choice, but don't think a blanket 'no' is going to discourage my men. Your arrival has caused more than a few fights already."

"Over what?"

"Over the opportunity to court you."

She didn't think she'd said more than one "Thank you" in the way of encouragement. "I can't help it if your men are unstable."

"No, you can't, but you should understand that they regard you as a prize worth fighting for."

She did not want to be a prize. "You said I'm weak," she hastened to point out.

Ian glanced over at Jared before rising to his feet. "Then it will be up to your mate to be strong for you."

"She doesn't need a were."

Ian shrugged. "She needs a man. As weak as she is, she is a sitting duck for the Sanctuary."

She opened her mouth to protest. Jared squeezed her shoulder, cutting off what she was going to say.

"She has me."

"But you are not her mate."

"Don't you ever think of anything else?" Raisa asked, exasperated.

Ian shook his head. "Not much. Forever's a long time to be alone."

Yes, it was. For a moment, Raisa shared the loneliness she saw in the big were's eyes, and then Ian blinked and she was alone in her emotions as his expression regained that hard impassivity and those amazing eyes dimmed to amber in that extraordinarily masculine face.

"The women must go nuts over you."

The words just popped out. Ian laughed, and Jared growled. Raisa wanted a hole to open up in the floor. Ian touched her cheek. "Would you be wanting to throw your hat into the ring?"

"No, she wouldn't," Jared snarled.

Who the hell was he to tell her what to do? Raisa cocked her head to the side and smiled at Ian. He was a handsome man with a kindness that appealed to her. "If things were different, maybe."

That fast, the easygoing leader was gone and Ian's intensity narrowed to a laser precision, pinning her to the chair. "Different how?"

She got the impression it wouldn't matter if she told him she wanted the moon delivered to her feet, he would give it to her. Jared's hand came down over her shoulder, warm and hard. Possessive. In front of her, Ian's gaze narrowed on the gesture. Dangerous lights began to spark in the depths.

"She's an outsider, Ian," Jared said in a careful drawl.

Ian blinked and then smiled a smile that did nothing to soothe Raisa's nerves because she could feel that incredible will of his seething behind the polite facade. The were would make a deadly enemy.

The backs of Ian's fingers grazed her cheek. "But a better friend."

It was her turn to blink. He'd read her mind? Weres could do that?

"Yes." Ian glanced up at Jared, his long hair falling over his right shoulder. "She doesn't have control of her thoughts or energy. That is dangerous."

"I know."

"She needs to be taught."

"I don't think it's a matter of teaching but of strength."

Ian considered her for a moment. "You could be right. She's very weak."

Raisa leaned back into the cushions, wanting away from Jared's aggression, Ian's interest, just wanting . . . away. Deep in her abdomen, she felt the first curl of hunger, followed quickly by a twist of pain. The exertion of the last two days was taking a toll on her reserves. She gritted her teeth against the agony to come, keeping her voice even and her thought patterns balanced as desperation clawed inside. "*She* is sitting right here."

"And very prettily, too," Ian agreed with an irritating arrogance before returning his attention to Jared. "She cannot be allowed out without a protector. She would raise havoc with the men. So much uncontained femininity would be too much temptation."

*Uncontained femininity?*

"I'll handle it," Jared answered.

She almost got a crick in her neck trying to see Jared's face. He was impossibly tall, standing while she was sitting. "What do you mean handle it?"

"It would have to be according to pack law for it to be respected," Ian continued as if she hadn't spoken.

There was barely a pause. Jared's jaw muscles flexed and tightened, and a purely male smile tilted the corners of his generous mouth. "Of course."

Raisa did not like the sound of that "Of course." She liked even less the satisfaction in his smile. Before she could ask what either meant, Ian was kneeling in front of her again. "In the meantime, Miss Slovinski—"

"Raisa," she corrected. Jared rumbled his dissatisfaction. It vibrated down the chair back and into her spine. She ignored him. She'd never grown to accept being addressed formally as natural. She wasn't better than anyone else and wasn't comfortable pretending that she was.

Ian inclined his head, a small smile playing around his mouth. "Ah, more hope for the hopeless." His glance at Jared was nothing less than a prod. "If you are not careful, my friend, you may find me your first challenger."

"I look forward to it."

Aggression rolled off Jared in hard waves that crashed into the equally hard waves of aggression coming off Ian. Good God, she was surrounded by rampant testosterone.

"In the meantime, Raisa . . ." Ian pressed his thumbnail into the inside of his right wrist, sending the potent, life-giving scent upward. "I offer you my blood."

The hunger surged, as it always did at the sight of fresh blood.

Starving, withered cells cramped in an agony of hope that this time they'd be fed, that it wouldn't be just another pointless taunt. Jared swore. His energy raged around her, pushing at her mind. She blocked it out, her world narrowing to that single spot of red, anticipation building as the first drop plumped into a round promise of salvation, growing until it was too big to balance on the were's dark flesh. It slid down the inside of his wrist in a potent lure. She leaned in, or maybe Ian brought his arm closer . . .

"Dammit, Ian, that's not part of the game," someone snarled through the haze.

"All's fair in this game, my friend."

"Then you won't mind if I rip off your head."

"For the pleasure of her bite, I'll risk it." The rich blood came closer and along with it a masculine scent that was not unpleasant. "Feed, little one. Take what I offer freely."

The argument, the order, flowed in the background of her need. All she could see was that offering, all she could feel was hope. She'd never fed from a were before. Maybe it would be different. Even possible. Hunger bloomed to a relentless twining demand that cramped her stomach in an agony of pain. She gasped and doubled over, closing her eyes against the whimper. Ian and Jared swore in synch. Arms came around her, supporting her, an incredible energy wrapped her in comfort—Jared. That drop of blood smeared against her lips. Rich, vital, and wrong. Oh God, wrong.

She turned her head. Another pain hit, sucking the breath from her lungs in a long moan. Hands stroked her head. A mind pushed at hers, and then another, slipping through the splintering pain, taking over.

*Feed.*

The order came in tandem. She might have been able to resist one of them, but the two together were too much, manipulating her muscles and instincts, forcing her to do what they wanted. She bit down, feeding as they demanded, all the while screaming a protest, knowing what they didn't as the were's rich blood slid down her throat. Knowing the price she was going to pay for daring to hope.

They forced her to take four swallows before her body rebelled, all that hope imploding in an agony of searing burn. The blood ate at her mouth, her throat, her stomach like a pool of acid. Wrong. So wrong. The silent scream welled from her soul, spreading outward, that one word riding the crest: *wrong*.

More swearing that came at her from a deep, distant well, licking at the flames burning her from the inside out, and then she was free. Free of their control, their mental presence, but not of the consequences.

She threw herself to the side of the chair as nausea clenched her stomach. A hand on her head kept her from pitching to the floor. Violent and terrible, the nausea ripped through her in tearing spasms that knew no end, just kept clawing at her stomach long after the last of the blood had been expelled.

A hand slipped across her stomach and she was lifted. She howled with the sheer agony.

"Jesus Christ, Raisa."

More agony and then she was on her hands and knees, Jared's big body behind hers, his hand on her forehead keeping her head from slamming into the floor. His energy probed the morass of reaction, stroking a spot here, a spot there, searching, seeking, finding. The pain stopped with a suddenness that left her gasping. She collapsed, her arms and legs trembling, her body shaking. She was lifted and turned. She had a glimpse of Ian's grim expression before Jared's came into view. It was white, rigid with emotion, whiter lines etched beside his eyes and mouth. Flames raged in his eyes. He'd stopped the awful pain. No one had ever done that for her before. She tried to lift her hand, but couldn't get it more than an inch off the floor. It flopped back. "Thank you."

It was a bare thread of sound, hoarse from her vomiting, and in no way reflected the depth of her gratitude. It had no impact on Jared's expression, just seemed to bounce off the wall of his control.

She sighed, an unreasonable sadness invading the momentary peace. She liked it better when he smiled. He was incredibly appealing when he smiled.

As if hearing her thoughts, Jared's lips tilted in a grim parody of what she envisioned.

*Sleep.* The ruthless command surged into her mind, driving out all other thoughts, taking over. As the last echo reached the deepest corner of her consciousness, the world faded to a deep, soothing black.

## ⇥ 7 ⇤

"I guess that answers any question of compatibility," Ian said from where he knelt beside Raisa's still form.

Jared carefully lifted her against his chest, not wanting to disturb the calm he'd forced on her body the same way he'd forced the agony in the first place—by thinking he knew better than she did as to what she needed. Because he'd convinced himself she'd been refusing to feed out of a weird sense of scruples. "Yes."

He couldn't get any more out, wrestling as he was to draw the agony out of her body into his. He'd never felt the like before, it was a howling wild beast that gouged holes in his innards. Sweat beaded on his brow and dripped down his face in red trails of guilt. He couldn't forget the one word her mind had projected at the first taste of Ian's blood. *Wrong.*

"Is it bad?" Ian asked.

Jared nodded. "I don't know how in hell she's survived it."

She was so small and delicate. An old-fashioned woman from his time, who, if she hadn't been turned, would have spent her life under a man's protection. She was the type of woman a man sheltered, cosseted, spoiled. Protected. Except he was her protector and he'd failed her.

Ian picked up Rai's hand. He balanced her palm in his and touched his thumb to the fan of delicate bones beneath her skin a second before saying, "I don't think she is surviving."

"I don't want to hear it."

Ian placed her palm on her abdomen. "She's dying, Jared. Just doing it the hard way."

Through slow starvation. Everything in Jared rebelled at the thought. "No."

"I'm not any more in favor of it than you are, but there's no changing the reality."

"She won't die." He wouldn't let her die. "I'll get her help."

"Think Slade might have an idea what's going on with her?"

Jared clenched his jaw against the next wave of pain, grateful it wasn't as bad as the first. "He's got ideas about everything else. This won't be any different."

Jared wouldn't allow it to be.

"How the hell do you think she's survived this long?"

Jared relaxed the muscles in his jaw, took a slow, deep breath, and wiped at the bloody sweat dripping in his eye. "Through sheer force of will."

"She's got that."

"Yeah. The pain's passing now. I'm going to put her to bed."

With a provoking arch of a brow Ian asked, "Need any help?"

Jared resisted the urge to kick the too-handsome were in the teeth. "No."

It should have been awkward getting to his feet with a woman in his arms, but it wasn't, mainly because her weight was nothing. She was too thin, too sweet, too close to death.

*Wrong.* Again the word played in his head. If something was wrong, then something, someone, somewhere must be right. The conviction grew as Jared carried Raisa into the bedroom and brought her to the big sleigh bed. Ian's bed. Again, everything in him rebelled. And again, the sense of possessiveness welled, primitive and all encompassing. She didn't belong there. She didn't belong with Ian. He didn't know much about her, but he knew that.

Hot on the heels of that though came the thought of his sister-in-law. Allie was only compatible with her mate.

*It's not going to make a difference.*

Over and over, Rai had made that statement, a certain hopelessness coloring the phrase, which could only mean one thing. She knew she was dying. But how? Did she already have a mate and had lost him? Again, that violent negative reaction inside him that he had to suppress. He untied her robe and rolled her out of it with calm efficiency, before tucking her under the sheets. She'd be horrified if she knew he was doing this, and he was old-fashioned enough to appreciate that modesty in her, to understand where it came from. They'd grown up in the same time, shared the same sense of right and wrong. Tucking her hair behind her ear, his fingers lingered there in silent promise before pulling the sheet over her shoulder. She could trust him to take care of that part of her.

She shivered, and he dragged the extra blanket from the foot of the bed and pulled it over her, too. He touched the soft wool. It was strange for a were to have so many blankets. Their bodies naturally adapted to temperature. Not as well as a vamp, but well enough. Only humans required so many blankets. Or immortals with a bad metabolism. Did Ian, along with the ability to read minds, have precognitive abilities? A human lover? Jared shook his head. Of the two, the latter was more likely.

If he did have a human lover, it was a risky prospect at any time, but especially in these troubled times. The Sanctuary would target any female of interest to any were or vamp. Only mated women could get pregnant, therefore, the Sanctuary had their radar focused on those women and their mates. And the unknown hormone interaction that so rarely resulted in offspring.

Jared stroked Raisa's hair. All the rich yellows and ambers trapped in the curls glowed in a fluctuating pattern against the white sheets. She looked like an angel. Pure, white, and fragile. An angel very much in need of protection. And according to were custom, he'd offered her his—offered his muscle, his skill as a fighter, his guidance in exchange for the right to keep her safe. In some ways were society was pretty primitive, with might making right. Whenever a man took on the role of protector, he volunteered to put himself between the woman and all comers, maintaining the right of protection only through his defeat of all challengers. If a woman's protector lost a challenge, the winner of the fight would become her new protector. A protector didn't have the same rights as a mate, but being a protector gave a man the ability to keep others away from the woman in his care. A real advantage in were society. The next caress ended at the corner of that seductive mouth. Jared smiled. And right now the advantage was his.

IAN was on him as soon as he entered the room, two glasses in his hands. "Is she better?"

"She's not in pain, if you want to call that better."

Ian handed him one of the glasses. He nodded his thanks as the scent of good whiskey stung his nose.

"At this point I'm calling it a hell of an improvement."

So was Jared. He ran his hand through his hair. "Me, too."

"Where'd you find her?"

"About halfway up the mountain. A couple of Sanctuary vamps had her cornered."

Ian's lip lifted in a snarl, his heritage very evident in that moment. "I'll have the heads of the sentries who allowed them access."

Jared dropped into a chair and took a sip of his drink. The alcohol burned all the way to his stomach. "I'm not sure you can blame the sentries."

"Why?"

"Because they've got a new device. Something that masks their energy."

"Shit. Combine that with the scent-masking spray and they've got a real advantage."

"Yeah."

"I'd like to know who they've hired to be able to come up with these very clever gadgets."

"So would Slade."

"I bet it'll burn his ass that he's trailing on this one."

"Yeah."

"Did you get to keep the device?"

"I had to dump it. Rai sensed a tracking device in it."

"Raisa sensed it?"

"She might not have control of her energy, but she has an affinity for all energy."

"Better than you?"

"Apparently so."

Ian whistled. "You didn't sense it?"

"Not one bit." Jared took another sip and savored the burn. It blended nicely with his frustration. "No matter how hard I concentrated."

Ian tossed back the rest of his glass. "That's not good."

"No. It isn't, but there might be a chance the device is still on the mountain. We attached it to a doe and sent it northwest." He mentally fed Ian the energy imprint of the deer for tracking.

Ian finished up his drink. "I'll send some men up the mountain to look for it."

"Good. And until Slade finds a way to defeat it, I'd suggest relying on more traditional methods of rat control and using more men to patrol."

"Agreed." Ian rolled to his feet and went over to the decanter. He poured another glass and then held the decanter up in a silent question. Jared shook his head. He could process one glass, expel it through his pores as he would any poison; two would have him puking, and his vicarious experience of Rai's recent bout was too close for him to go there, even for the best sipping whiskey he'd tasted in a hundred years. "No, thank you."

Ian resumed his seat. "One upside of having more men out on patrol is that there will be less here to challenge you for the right of protector over Raisa."

"I'm not afraid of a challenge." He'd actually welcome the opportunity to take the edge off his temper.

"I'm sure you're not, but I don't think you understand just how appealing her scent is to a were. I don't think many of the challenges will be token ones."

Token challenges referred to the pseudo-challenges made by male weres to boost a woman's self-esteem.

"Shit."

"Uh-huh." Ian lifted his glass in a toast. "And speaking of shit, how compromised is your mission now?"

Jared wasn't surprised Ian knew the reason he was on the mountain. Among the Renegades, the chain of command was Caleb, Jared, and then Ian. The cohesion they'd achieved was the only edge they had against the Sanctuary's much larger numbers. Not to mention the Sanctuary's larger bank account, which allowed them to manufacture all sorts of interesting devices to complicate the Renegades' lives. Devices like the energy masker.

"On hold unless I can come up with something to do with Rai."

"If the information's correct, this will be the first time the Sanctuary leaders will be together."

"I know." It could be a once-in-a-lifetime opportunity to end the civil war for good. "I signaled Caleb to send someone else."

"I hate to point out the obvious, but you could leave her here and still go."

"I could, but if I did, I'd no doubt come back and find Rai married against her will."

"And that would worry you?"

"She's under my protection."

That irritating smile curved Ian's lips. "That's the only reason?"

"It's the only reason you need to focus on."

Ian shook his head. "You keep telling yourself that, and while you do, my men will keep Raisa busy."

Jared just bet they would. "You really wouldn't object to a marriage between a vampire woman and a were?"

"Honestly? I wouldn't be adverse to one of my men finding happiness with her. There have been so few matings this last century, any possibility brings a wild hope. And, as she's not from here, there would be no power struggles."

"You think a were would give up family and pack position to marry Rai?"

"I can think of twenty of my men who would be grateful for the opportunity."

Great. Just what he wanted to hear. "I won't let her be railroaded."

Ian shrugged his shoulders unconcernedly. "Then you'd best care for her."

Which would mean either leaving her here or staying with her. "Hell of a choice."

Ian rolled to his feet. His glass settled on the tabletop with a decisive click. "But at least you have the pleasure of making it."

Jared stood, too. "Very true. Where are you staying?"

Ian headed for the door. "With a friend."

A lady friend, Jared had no doubt. "I appreciate you giving up your home for our visit."

"The D'Nallys only extend the best hospitality to potential mates."

"She's not here to seek a mate."

Ian put his hand on the knob. "But she could be."

"No, she couldn't."

Opening the door, letting a rush of cold air and blustery snowflakes fly in, Ian looked over his shoulder and smiled that damn cocky smile of his. "As I said, that decision is not yours to make."

LIKE hell it wasn't. Jared slammed his glass down on the table so hard it rattled. He steadied the piece of furniture while anger rolled through him. Rai was his responsibility, and no damn were was going to twist the rules to trick her into a forever she didn't want. He went to the windows and drew the curtains. As he got to the last one in the living room, he looked out. The D'Nally compound was compact, neat, with small log structures set out in squares with streets between. Most of the homes were dark now. Most weres, with the exception of the full moon, tended to be daylight dwellers. Night runs were fun, but not a way of life.

Jared looked around, appreciating high walls that stood like stark sentinels against the night sky, shielding the inhabitants of the village. The first D'Nally had picked well when he'd chosen this hidden valley. Plenty of land and wildlife, with fresh water and high walls on all sides, it was hard to detect and there was little danger of an attack. Especially now that Slade had manufactured a few devices to continue to protect the weres' privacy.

However, continued technological developments could soon endanger the weres. Weres hunted by scent and energy. The Sanctuary now had found ways to circumvent both. If the Sanctuary ever found out the secret entrance to this place and they could cloak their energy while attacking, the element of surprise could give the Sanctuary the edge they needed to overwhelm the fierce clan. That couldn't be allowed to happen. There weren't many packs like the D'Nallys. Old-fashioned, with a sense of honor that went as deep as their history went back, they made deadly enemies and loyal friends. They saw right and wrong in black and white, something Jared appreciated along with the fact that when push came to shove, a D'Nally would always do the right thing.

A light went on in a house down the street. A pale gray light seeped between the clouds and the edge of the high peaks. Dawn was coming. He lowered the light-blocking shades and pulled the curtains closed over them. He dropped the reinforced bars on the front and back doors before heading to the spare bedroom. A rustle of sheets and a moan drew him up short as he passed the master bedroom door where Rai slept. He touched the smooth wood, sending his energy through it, seeking the edge of Raisa's.

Pain.

Sharp and swift, the reality lashed at him. She was in pain. He opened the door, his vampire rising. Raisa tossed on the bed, a frown on her face, her hands clenched around her stomach. She turned onto her back, almost tumbling off the mattress, another moan slipping past her lips. Her feet drew slowly up toward her hips, making a tent of the covers. A thick swathe of hair obscured the right side of her face from his view. She didn't open her eyes. Either she was so exhausted that even pain couldn't wake her or she was so used to the pain it no longer registered as abnormal enough to wake her.

Which made it his turn to frown as he approached the bed. When he'd put her to bed, he'd positioned her in the middle. Now she clung to the edge as if the middle were a place to be feared. Or, he reconsidered, as if she feared the precious seconds it would take to get from there to the edge in case she needed a fast exit. He tucked her hair behind her ear, his fingertips lingering on the outer curve, tracing the near point at the top. Her flesh was cool to the touch. She twisted on the bed and hitched over to her side. Her cheek settled into the curve of his palm, as if made for that spot.

Jared slipped his other hand beneath the covers, beneath hers, to the soft flesh of her abdomen. She was warmer there, softer, the lack of musculature reinforcing her vulnerability. Ian was right. She needed a husband.

He rubbed his thumb across the smooth expanse of her abdomen. Her skin was very different from his. As was her energy. More gentle than aggressive. Smoother, rather than rough and jagged. He opened his palm over her stomach, sending his mind into hers, slipping through the cracks in her defenses, letting her emotions pour through him, searching for the source of her pain.

*Hungry.* She was so hungry her very cells cried out for nourishment. Along with the current cry he had impressions of others from episodes past. Thousands of previous cries for nourishment that went ignored. He didn't know how she lived with the constant scream without going insane. But at least he knew why she had such compassion for others. Living with that agony for 270 years was enough to make anyone sympathize with almost anything.

He smoothed his thumb over her eyebrow. "Rai?"

She shook her head against his call and pushed his hand away, rolling all the way to her side, her legs dragging the opposite end of the covers to the middle of the bed in a rumpled pile of blue as she pulled her knees into her chest. As Jared watched, an unfamiliar feeling of helplessness keeping him company in the dark, a shiver shook her from head to toe. She was cold and hurting. He didn't know what he could do with the latter, but he knew he could do something about the former. He kicked his boots off and unbuttoned his shirt. Tugging off his socks, he lifted the covers and slid beneath, slipping his arm under her head, spooning against her back. She mumbled a protest. He raised his body heat, tucking his thighs under hers, giving her at least one thing she craved. Warmth.

*Sleep.*

She moaned and snuggled into the pillow. Jared opened his palm over her stomach, letting her pain flow into him, following the path back to the source, finding the bits of debilitating energy rapping out calls of distress and muting them. He sighed with relief right along with her as the rigidity began to leave her muscles.

"That's it, sunbeam. Relax."

He felt the hunger twist through her, calling for relief. Everything in him rose to answer. The beat of his heart sounded louder in his ears, the rush of his blood felt hotter in his veins. Every one of her breaths against his wrist whipped across his flesh like a lure.

*Wrong.*

The word whispered through his mind in a memory. A warning. A clue.

Ian had been wrong for her. The men she'd fed from before had been wrong. It didn't mean every man was wrong. Just the ones she'd tried until now. Her cheek rubbed on the artery on the inside of his wrist as his heat permeated the chill surrounding her. His pulse centered at that point, eager, willing, throbbing in invitation. His heart rate increased, pushing more blood through his arteries and veins. More than enough to feed her. His body was ready, more than ready to supply what she needed.

Jared rested his head on the pillow behind hers, tucking his legs under hers, cocooning her in his strength. He took a breath. Ian was right. Rai did smell incredibly sweet, like the first day of summer. Like wildflowers in bloom. Like temptation. Like hope.

A sharp edge of pain sliced outward from her to him. She groaned and pushed at his hand, his leg. Her cheek turned away from his arm. A bead of blood appeared at her temple. It was natural and right that he kiss it away. Her taste spread through his mouth. If she smelled of a summer's day, she tasted like Kentucky sipping whiskey. Hot and potent with a kick that took a man's legs out from under him. He wanted more.

*Wrong.*

The warning whispered across his conscience. Raisa had been through hell already once tonight, when he'd forced her to take Ian's blood. She'd never survive that torture twice in one night. Another bead of blood welled at her temple. Vampire sweat. Vampire stress. Vampire agony, and she'd been enduring it alone for more than two centuries.

His heart twisted. She should never have been alone. Not for one year, one month, one day. He held her to him as he stole that evidence away, his lips lingering on the fragile skin with the tracery of veins beneath. But she wasn't alone now. His arms were around her, his strength protected her. Another bead of sweat welled. More of her taste spread across his tongue. Arousal joined the need pounding in his blood. There was no need for her to suffer while he was here. The longer he held her, the deeper the conviction grew. The longer she shuddered and ached, the more his vampire roared. She needed, and he needed to provide. It was his right.

*Right.*

Yes, the thought resonated in his mind. Her lips quivered against his arm, inches from an artery. It was very right. He pressed up. The edge of her fang stung his skin, not deep enough to draw blood, just enough to alert the vampire in both of them. He adjusted his arm so her lips were positioned directly above the artery.

"Jared?"

His name sighed between her lips, against his pulse, kicking it up to a hard pound.

Raisa was waking, pain passing from her subconscious to her conscious mind. In the half life between sleep and wake, her instincts took over. He felt her tongue lap delicately, her fangs graze inquisitively before they tested, clenched, prepared to penetrate.

*Wrong.* This was wrong. He caught her shoulder and pressed back. Her anguished "No" as she rolled to her back away from his blood scraped his conscience raw. "Easy, sunbeam, just give me a minute."

"So hungry."

"I know."

A tug and she was rolling toward him. Her shoulder got caught on his chest. He lifted her, giving her room to face him. A swathe of her hair fell between them, blocking her mouth from his skin. He pushed her hair away from her face. The wild curls just sprang back, getting between his flesh and her mouth, hot licking barriers of silk that were too soft, too delicate for his hypersensitized flesh that wanted the sharp, hard bite of her fangs. He gathered them up in a loose ponytail in his fist, anchoring her mouth against his chest.

Her energy surged and ebbed, the edges darkening with panic as she became more conscious. "I can't."

"Yes, you can." He arched her neck back. Her fangs, as dainty as the rest of her, flashed a brilliant white. "It's right."

She shook her head. "It's never right."

The curve of her lower lip beckoned. "But this is."

Her big brown eyes widened as he raised his head, kissing the plump flesh before running his tongue over her teeth, lingering on those feminine fangs, feeling the shock waves go through her as he did. "Taste how right it is."

He sealed his mouth to hers, his energy to hers, riding rough-shod over her fear, searching for the base instinct that thrived in everyone, vampire, were, or human. The instinct that overrode fear of pain and failure. The instinct for survival. Hers was very strong and got stronger with every brush of his tongue, every thrust of his belief.

*Right, sunbeam.* He reiterated.

"Oh God!" The despairing whisper escaped the seal of their lips. "Don't do this to me."

"I'm not doing anything," he whispered back. "This is us together."

"You're making up fairy tales."

"Fairy tales are good. They always end in happily ever after."

"Not for me."

*This time, for you.*

He didn't know how he knew that, but he was sure.

He raked his pinkie nail across his chest. Blood rose immediately. Raisa whimpered as the rich, life-giving scent blended with the scent of their desire. He urged her mouth to his chest, anchoring her with his fist in her hair, his belief. Her tongue touched his skin just below the cut, a hesitant step toward trust. Fire burned outward from the spot. Her need screamed. His vampire roared.

With a thrust of power, he implanted the order in her mind. *Take from me.*

With a helpless moan, she did. Those fangs sank erotically deep, drawing from him everything he ached to give, letting him provide for her needs the way a man should provide for his woman, replacing pain with pleasure, starvation with sustenance.

His head dropped back as he merged his mind with hers, listening for that echo of agony, ready to pull her away if he heard it, but swallow after swallow, second after second, there was only the elated scream of her cells as they finally, finally, got the nourishment they needed.

Jared opened his palm on her skull, supporting Raisa as she fed, his pulse finding and matching the rate of hers, slowing hers when it got too fast, steadying her through the heady experience, accepting the stroke of her energy across his nerves, her hands over his back as she took from him what she needed.

*Yes, baby. Feed.*

He felt everything she thought, everything she experienced. Joy and elation as his force poured into her. Amazement as, for the first time since she had turned vampire, she felt the flush of power that came with the turning. And then he heard it, that quiet little voice in her head he'd been dreading, the one that confirmed his worst fear. In a gentle statement colored with the roll of her accent, it whispered, *Right.*

As much as Jared wanted to argue, he couldn't. Whatever this was between them was right.

## ≫ 8 ≪

IF she wasn't careful, Rai was going to find herself in trouble. Jared wiped the snow from the back of his neck and turned to find Rai standing a few feet away, packing another snowball in her hands. In the early evening dark, her cheeks were rosy with health, her eyes bright with mischief. Her energy reached to meet his, vibrant with the renewed health his blood had given her, warm with her increasing regard.

Around her stood four male weres, one of which was Creed. Each of them wore a smug smile. Creed held a sled. Jared mentally gave him a "Fuck off." He didn't like their presence around Raisa any more than he liked the way she made him feel. Uncomfortably possessive, on edge, happy.

"She's falling in love with you."

Jared turned to Ian, ignoring the flick of Rai's energy that indicated disappointment in his refusal to play. "I know."

The were's eyebrows arched at the dryness of his tone. "Most men would find that a good thing."

Jared shrugged. "She's just caught up in feeling good for the first time."

And he wasn't stupid enough to believe that meant any more than it did, but he wanted to.

"You don't find it significant that she can take only your blood?"

He was trying not to. There was a whole lot about Raisa he was trying not to attribute too much significance to. The woman was experiencing the way her life should be for the first time. Just because he was the one who had given her the blood that allowed her to do that didn't give him special rights over her. His conscience-less, possessive vampire hissed a mental, *Yes, it does*.

He told it what he'd told himself every minute since he'd given her blood. A woman had a right to feel good without a man pressuring her.

"I thought you wanted to talk."

Ian's gaze left Raisa and focused on him. "I do."

"About what?"

"The meeting."

"It's still going on?"

"Yes."

Try as he might he couldn't keep his attention from Rai. The need to touch her visually was as strong as it was to touch her mentally, physically. "Same place?"

"So it's rumored."

He'd been so busy with Raisa he hadn't checked in with Caleb, an anomaly that would have his brother worried.

"When?" He watched Creed climb into the sled, watched as Rai snuggled in front of him, imagined the were's pleasure as that cute butt settled between his thighs. Rai laughed as she lost her balance. The were caught her, his strength easily righting her, his arms not unwrapping from around her as he signaled the others to push them off. Raisa's scream of excitement gouged Jared's good humor as the sled took off down the hill.

"Are you listening?" Ian asked.

Jared forced himself to pay attention. "Yes."

"Caleb is worried about you."

"I'll call him later."

"Good. And in case you're interested, the meeting's rumored to be one day from now."

"Shit." That centered his attention. He'd have to run flat out for a full night to get there. To make that happen he'd have to be at full strength, which he wasn't after feeding Rai last night. "It'll be tough just getting there, let alone undetected."

"Caleb wants to know if there's any chance you can back up Jace."

Caleb would. The man didn't know the meaning of the word impossible, and he knew as well as Jared the edge Jace was walking right now. None of the brothers knew why, but something was eating Jace, making him take more risks than usual. And that was saying a lot for their wild brother.

The sled hit a rock buried in the snow and went airborne. Rai's scream held more fear than excitement. Ian grabbed his arm as he tensed. "Creed won't let her be hurt."

"He'd better not." The tenuous hold he had on his temper wouldn't withstand Rai being injured. The couple tumbled across the snow, and while it was obvious Creed had picked up a few bruises, Rai popped up, wiping the snow from her eyes, her laughter coming clearly to him in the night air.

"If you can back up Jace, you're going to have to leave immediately to make the meeting," Ian continued.

Jared couldn't take his eyes from Raisa, couldn't keep his mind from reaching out to hers. He didn't think it was accidental that he met a wall of resistance. Raisa was miffed that he'd ignored her invite to play. "Yes."

"If you take Raisa with you, she'll be at risk."

"I know." He probed her mind again. This time he got a mental huff before the door slammed shut. Irritation twitched.

"She's welcome to hang out here while you take care of business."

"Thank you."

Despite his resolve, his mind reached for hers again, restlessly seeking the connection, needing, he admitted ruefully, that feminine touch of hers that soothed the raw edges of his emotions, the jagged edges of his energy.

"I'm sure my people will devote themselves to making her stay a pleasure."

The amusement in Ian's voice was hard to miss. Jared sighed. There wasn't a chance in hell the were had missed his distraction.

"I just bet they will."

Ian glanced over at the small group. "She's a very beautiful woman. A bit old-fashioned in her ways, but that only enhances her appeal. A woman who can hold her own without increasing a were's natural dominance is pretty much irresistible."

Jared knew exactly what Ian meant. That unique combination of strength and spirit that promised peace and acceptance drew him as well. He watched as the men helped Raisa to her feet. She accepted their help as her due, accepting their fussing over her without any insult to her pride. And why wouldn't she? In the time she'd been raised, it was exactly what she'd been trained to do. To be the object of a man's attention, to offer him strength and support without seeing it as a detraction to her own. To the ultra-dominant weres she was the ultimate treat. "She does have a way about her."

Creed brushed the snow off Raisa's coat, his hand coming damn close to the cute curve of her butt. The growl erupted of its own volition, mentally and physically closing the distance between them. Raisa's head snapped up, her mind immediately reaching for his, looking for the threat.

*What?*

Creed glanced over. The smile that curved his lips was nothing short of a challenge as he brushed again, the arrogance in the gesture increased by the fact there wasn't any snow left. And this time his palm did graze the upper slope of her rear.

Jared held his gaze, sending a command to Rai. *Come here.*

Raisa frowned, said something to Creed, and then obeyed, levitating across the snow with ease. The alacrity with which she responded to his command soothed a little of his frustration. Creed's frustration at her obedience to another man's order, Jared's specifically, eased his anger.

"If you marked her," Ian said conversationally, "you wouldn't have to worry about the men courting her in your absence."

Jared didn't need the reminder. He was having a hard enough time resisting his vampire's demand he do that very thing, without Ian adding fuel to the fire with logic. "Mind your own business."

"You're on D'Nally land. Everything here is my business."

Rai was just a few feet away, a hint of anxiety in her gaze. "Not this."

Her energy reached him first, soft and sweet, quickly finding the turbulence of his anger and smoothing over it, infusing her particular brand of calm. Two steps farther and she was in front of him, her tawny hair spilling over her shoulders with all the colors of sunshine. On her head sat a black knit hat. One that hadn't been there when she'd left the house this morning. This close, he couldn't mistake the scent clinging to it. Definitely male. His growl rumbled past his control. Creed's.

Raisa's tongue flicked over her lips. "What's wrong?"

The gleam of moisture left by the pass of her tongue held his gaze. "I have to leave."

It came out blunter than he had intended, but he did have to leave, not only to back Jace but to get away from his baser instincts that seemed to dominate whenever he was around her. The instincts that would take choice away from her.

She blinked and then said, "I'll pack my things."

"You'll be staying here."

Stubborn didn't begin to described her frown or the thrust of emotion that backed her "No."

"You can't come with me."

"You can't leave me behind."

The panic in her built. She was afraid to be without him. Afraid for him. He plucked the hat from her head. The curls sprang to life, bouncing around her head before settling around her face. "I'll come back."

That didn't soothe her. Her hands fisted at her side. A second passed. And then another. Suddenly she said, "You're going on a mission."

He hadn't even felt her probe. He crumpled the hat his hand. "Yes."

"I can help."

No way in hell was he letting her within grabbing distance of any Sanctuary member. "The only thing you could do is slow me down."

"I'm stronger now."

From his blood. Damn, it was arousing as hell knowing that he could provide for her at that level. "Not that strong."

"You don't know that."

He grazed the back of his hand across moist remnants of snow on her cheekbone. "I'm not putting you in danger."

"You'll be in danger."

As if there was any comparison. "I'm trained for it. You're not."

"What am I supposed to do while you're gone?"

"The D'Nallys would be honored to extend you shelter," Ian offered.

Rai looked from Jared to Ian and then back at Jared again. Her energy withdrew, and her face closed up. A coldness settled between them as she nodded at Ian. "How convenient of you to provide a place for him to dump me." She held out her hand to Jared. "Could I have my hat please?"

"No. And I'm not dumping you."

"Dress it up any way you want, it amounts to the same thing." She snapped her fingers. "The hat please? I must give it back."

Her English was slipping. A sure sign she was ticked.

Ian took the hat, neatly preventing the building argument. "I'll make sure this gets back to its owner."

"Thank you." With one last glare at Jared, Raisa turned on her heel and marched away, that tight little ass swishing with a feminine challenge to which everything in him demanded he respond.

"That woman just begs a man to claim her."

Ian's admiration was not what Jared needed to hear. Raisa wasn't begging any man, just him, and it was getting damn hard to resist. "Well, it won't be me."

Ian cocked his brow. "You're leaving her here unclaimed?"

"Yes."

"You're a damn fool."

"No doubt."

But he wasn't an ass, and taking advantage of Raisa's gratitude for giving her back her strength would make him into one. She reached the group of men. They accepted her easily into their midst. That didn't bother him nearly as much as the fact that she settled so comfortably there, accepted their attention, smiled at their words. He changed his mind about one thing. She could do whatever the hell she wanted when he wasn't here, but while he was, she wasn't entertaining a bunch of horny weres.

"Where are you going?" Ian called.

"To set a few ground rules."


**WANT** to go again?"

Raisa forced a smile as Creed grabbed her hand and headed up the hill. "Okay, but this time I'm driving."

"Not a chance."

"I can't do worse than you. You drove us off the ledge."

"It was a rock in the snow, and you didn't get hurt. I protected you."

Yes, he had. From the time she'd arrived, he'd set himself up as a man she could trust, protecting her from the other weres, Jared, and her own stupid expectations. She wished she could feel for him what he needed.

"Still doesn't change the fact that you wrecked the sled."

"Just a tumble, sweet thing." He tugged her even with him. "Trust me this time, and I promise we'll make it to the bottom unscathed."

Raisa glanced up the hill. She didn't have the heart to tell Creed she was tiring, that the energy from Jared's blood was seeping off. Mainly because she didn't want to believe it. The climb appeared so much steeper than it had earlier in the evening, the bright moonlight reflecting off the snow-covered rocks in spools of white, emphasizing the deeper black of the shadows. She marked a spot a third of the way up the hill. She could make that. And when she did, she'd pick a new one. One foot at a time.

Creed glanced down at her. "Everything okay?"

She nodded and took the first step. Today had been the best day of her life physically, and even though it was turning out to be the most taxing emotionally, she didn't want it to end. One-third up the hill, just short of her mark, she had to stop. She recognized the tension, the horrible tension, that gathered in her stomach. She held herself perfectly still, hoping against hope that she was wrong, that maybe she'd just pulled a muscle, that this wasn't happening again. She couldn't go back to the way it had been before. She couldn't.

"Raisa?"

She pulled her hand from Creed's. The first pain hit her hard, harder than ever before, striking brilliantly from out of her complacency, doubling her over. Sweat beaded her brow, ran down her temple, and fell to the snow, marring the pure white surface with washed-out red splotches.

"Shit." Creed's arms came around her, strong and warm. "Jared, get over here!"

As Creed's hand covered hers, she heard Jared's shout. She felt the probe of Creed's mind at the edges of hers, surprisingly strong and very knowledgeable in the way it found the crevices in her control. His palm spread across her stomach, supporting her as he whispered in her ear, "You hunger."

She grabbed his wrist, unable to pull away or draw it in as another cramp doubled up on the first.

It'd never started this hard before. She had to go weeks to reach this level of pain. And now, just twelve hours after taking Jared's blood she was in this condition? Oh heck, she was in so much trouble.

The next pain left her hanging in Creed's arms, too wrapped in the consuming agony to support herself. His other arm pressed against her mouth. "Feed."

She shook her head. "Can't."

"Yes, you can. Just a little nip."

"It wouldn't be a little," she gasped.

"I'm a big man." His lips brushed her ear, sparking enticing shivers. "I can give you all you need."

The temptation was there. As well as the fear. What if he made her sick? Worse, what if taking his blood didn't make her sick but it did what Jared's had? What if it shortened her ability to last between feedings even more?

The next pain gathered. Her fangs extended. She opened her mouth. What did any of that matter? Anything was better than this.

With a shocking abruptness, she was yanked out of Creed's arms. She landed softly in a snowbank, staring up at the night sky. "Get your fucking hands off her."

Jared. She pushed herself up on her arms. Not an easy task with the snow collapsing beneath her. He was facing off with Creed, the broad set of his shoulders reflecting the dark seething quality of his energy. Jared was an extremely intimidating sight when angry. But across from him, Creed wasn't looking like any sort of slouch. He matched Jared for height and breadth, and as far as sheer aggression went, he was also on par. If things came to a fight, it would be bloody and vicious and long, because both men were lethal predators, and both, judging from the way their energies clashed against each other, were prepared to fight to the death. She couldn't let that happen. Raisa dug her fingers into her stomach, as if through physical force she could hold the pain back long enough to function.

"Who the hell are you to tell me what to do?" Creed snarled.

"Her protector," Jared snarled right back.

Creed snorted. "Is that what you're calling it?"

Jared's snarl vibrated down her spine. "Yes."

"Were she were, your brand of protection would not be allowed."

Like a kick in the gut, Creed's meaning took. The weres thought she was Jared's whore. Suddenly the men's interest took on a whole different light.

"Raisa's not a were," Jared growled.

"She can choose to be."

"And then what?"

Creed smiled, his canines gleaming. "Then you can expect her man to come call."

"You?"

"Yes."

"You're not compatible."

"So you say."

"Is that true, Raisa?" Jared asked over his shoulder. "Are you compatible with Creed?"

She wasn't a fool. There was more at stake than a simple answer to the question. And as fuzzy as her thinking was, she wasn't going there right now. "What's true is I'm not sitting in this snowbank anymore."

Snow crunched as Ian came up beside her. "Nor should you have to."

She held out her hand. He took it, pulling her out. He didn't stop when she got to her feet, but gave an additional tug, sweeping her into his arms as she stumbled. "The two of you can fight over whose right until you bleed stupid, and if there's anything left, you can present it to the Council."

Raisa slipped her hands over Ian's shoulders, feeling uncomfortable doing so. He was not the sort of man who inspired warm touches.

"Relax. I don't bite pretty little vamps when they're down."

"And when they're well?"

He smiled a wicked smile that made even her tired heart flutter. "Then it's up to them."

She stopped with her hands halfway to his neck. "Oh."

"You, however, are safe. We established last night that we're not compatible."

Yes. They had. He shifted her in his arms. She clutched at his neck. It was awfully quiet behind them. "Are they killing each other?"

"No."

She leaned her head against his chest as another pain gathered. "I didn't mean to cause a fight."

"You didn't cause a damn thing."

"Ah." The small cry escaped her determination to be stoic.

"How bad is it?"

"Not that bad."

The look he cut her as they reached the porch was skeptical. "Anyone tell you, you're a poor liar?"

"I've mentioned it a time or to," Jared said in a low drawl, leaning around them to open the door. His eyes were more green than blue, and around him, his energy flailed with barely contained rage. As his gaze met hers, that energy changed direction, lashing out at her with blinding speed. She flinched back against Ian's chest.

"Back the hell off." Ian growled.

Jared pushed the door open. "And leave her with you so you can play knight in shining armor? I don't think so."

Ian shouldered past him. "You're being an ass."

"And you're overstepping your bounds."

"I'm leader here. I have no bounds."

"You're holding my woman."

"I'm holding an unclaimed woman who needs to feed."

Ian placed her on the couch. She curled there in a fetal ball as they argued around her.

Ian knelt beside her. "I'd offer you my blood if I could."

She grabbed his hand, squeezing in an effort to contain the uncontainable. Her "Thank you" came out a whimper.

"Get the hell away from her."

Ian's hand paused on her cheek. He didn't move away. "Do you want to deal with him now, little vamp?"

"Unless you want me to rip your throat out right now," Jared snarled, "you'll get the hell away from her."

Unless she wanted bloodshed, Raisa didn't see where she had much choice, as much as that scared her. "I guess."

Ian studied her face for a heartbeat more. His head canted a bit to the side. "Jared is ticked right now at all the males around you, but he won't hurt you."

"Speak for your Goddamn self."

Ian shook his head. "He is also an idiot. No one would blame you for sending him packing."

Raisa could feel Jared's frustration and his need. It beat at her in relentless waves. She could also feel his guilt that she hurt.

"I don't want to send him packing." She reached over Ian's shoulder and held out her hand, palm up in an invitation. Jared took it, his grip surprisingly gentle as he took Ian's place, his thigh muscles straining the fabric of his pants as he squatted down. His hand slipped under hers, cradling the convulsing of her stomach muscles. "I thought we were finished with all this."

"Me, too."

Another pain hit. Her stomach contracted. Energy pulsed through his hand. It didn't help. She turned her face into the cushions and screamed breathlessly, releasing the pain, frustration, and sheer inevitability of her existence.

"Come here, sunbeam." Jared's arms encircled her, tugging her off the cushions and against his chest. Shards of pain splintered off the knot in her stomach, sparking new flames of agony to burning in her chest, her arms, her legs. Her fangs ached. Her talons sank into his shoulders. He winced. The scent of blood tainted the air. A hand came into her line of vision, closing over Jared's shoulder. Ian pulled Jared back, ignoring his snarl.

"You can't afford the blood loss right now, Jared."

"Tough." He ripped his shirt open. He lifted her head.

"I can." Creed volunteered, meeting her gaze over Jared's shoulder. Little red flicks of flames danced in his eyes.

"You're not compatible," Jared snapped.

"As her mind opened to mine, so will her body."

Jared stiffened. "Get him the hell out of here, Ian."

"Short of killing him, I don't think that's possible."

"Then kill him."

Creed snorted. "It's not so easy to kill me, vamp."

Raisa moaned as both males' energy came at her. Both strong, yet so different. She wouldn't have a prayer of keeping them out of her head, and she didn't know how she would deal with that chaos on top of what she had already endured, but then a third interceded, slipping between her and them, forming an impenetrable wall that didn't touch her, yet blocked Jared and Creed. She glanced at Ian as the men swore at being blocked.

"You can deal with them later."

Yes, she could. "Thank you."

He motioned with his hand. "For now, you must feed."

She shook her head. Ian's shield rippled with displeasure.

"Weres do not allow their women to suffer."

"Neither do vamps," Jared snapped.

She squeezed Jared's hand and took a careful breath. The scent of Jared's skin was so close—spicy, male underlaid with the intriguing scent of musk. She could hear the beat of his heart. With every thump, his blood whooshed through his veins. All the blood she needed. She curled her lips down over her fangs. She shook her head. They didn't understand. "No."

"Yes," the three men snapped in unison.

"Why?" She gasped as the clench of agony eased to bearable. "So I can feel good for an even shorter time, next time?"

"I'm not going to allow you to suffer, Rai," Jared snarled.

Creed was equally emphatic. "You will feed."

She shook her head. "It's not up to either of you."

Creed cut a glare at Jared. "A mate would take better care of her."

"Since she doesn't have a mate, she'll just have to deal with me."

Creed's tone was implacable with resolve. "A were would not wait on permission."

Neither was he, Jared decided. Another shudder racked Rai. The muscles in her abdomen wrenched with the inner agony she was trying to shield. Beside him, Jared could feel Creed and Ian's impatience, their instinctive need to protect a female. It matched his own. And Creed, at least, wasn't going to last much longer in a passive role. He'd always been a ruthlessly straightforward man. And now he saw Raisa as his potential mate. He wouldn't be able to let her suffer without intervention.

*As her mind accepted me, so will her body.*

Jared's vampire howled at the thought of the were offering his blood to Raisa. Of her bending that pretty little head, of that sunshine hair spilling across the were's dark skin, of those plump lips parting, those little fangs piercing before she partook of the offering.

She was his. Only his blood should pass her lips. Only his arms should come around her. He focused his energy and thrust through Ian's shield, shattering it, guiding the shards back into the two weres' minds, forcing them back as he ruthlessly plunged into Raisa's. Pain greeted him with greedy hunger. Despair trailed in its wake. She thought this was all there was for her. That the few minutes she'd had of pleasure were part of her punishment for her past. Another blinding burst of pain blocked from him the memory of the reason she thought she deserved to be punished.

Jared brought her mouth to his chest as he punched through his skin with his talon, letting his blood smear across her lips.

Her moan vibrated against his chest. He didn't care about the resistance in her, the need she had to protect herself for the future she saw looming. All he cared about, all his vampire demanded, was that she not suffer any more right now. He would force her to accept anything in order to make that happen. Nothing mattered more than that. With another brutal thrust through the fogging layers, he found that primitive part lurking within her vampire and brought it to life with one word: *Feed.*

Her fangs scraped, stopping his heart with the sheer pleasure of anticipation as he waited that split second before they sank deep, and his heartbeat took off, the ecstatic whisper of *Yes* racing with his blood from him to her and then back as her energy intertwined with his, ebbing and flowing with her hunger, going deeper each time, not drawing back quite as far after each blending. He wrapped his arms around her, hunching his body over hers, shielding her from the view of the others.

"That's it, sunbeam. Let me make you feel better."

*Let me take care of you.*

The last went no further than his own mind.

Her strength built as his dwindled.

"She's taken enough, Jared."

Whereas Ian's comment seemed to come from a distance, Rai's protest exploded into his mind with crystal clarity.

*No!*

He stroked his mind over the wild protest. *All you want, sunbeam.*

She could have anything she wanted of him.

"Jared, that's enough."

He lifted his head and snarled at Ian. The reach of Creed's hand was just a blur of movement, but he caught it, lashing out with his talons, snarling with satisfaction when he connected and the scent

of were blood filled the air. Raisa needed him. They would not in-
terfere.

"Stay away."

"I can't." Creed's mind slipped through the crack in his anxiety
about Rai, flowing with a smooth skill uncommon in a were. More
energy blended with Creed's. Ian?

*She's taken enough, Jared.*

Rai's mind merged so completely with his that she couldn't help
but overhear. And again came that desperate cry. *No!*

This time, however, the stroke of calm that found her was not
his. Creed, enhanced by Ian, covered his efforts and hushed them.
Something they'd never be able to do if Jared was at full strength.

*You're killing him, Raisa. Taking too much.*

*No. He has enough.*

*Yes. I have enough*, Jared thought. He'd always have enough for
her.

*No, he doesn't. He hasn't replenished from last time.*

*He'd say—*

*He would never deny you.* Hard, implacable, Creed took advantage of Jared's weakness to command Rai's attention. *He'll let you
suck him dry.*

Yes, he would. Anything she needed he would provide. No matter what the cost. Raisa needed to be strong to survive. Jared pulled
her closer, slashing at Ian as he grabbed his shoulder, his talons
meeting flesh. Ian didn't let go.

"Do you want to kill him, Raisa?"

Another *No*, wilder than the last.

"Then let go," Creed whispered aloud and into their heads. *You
need to let him go.*

Raisa's vampire fought with all-consuming need for his blood while
Raisa fought with every bit of her humanity. The scream that tore
through her as she withdrew her fangs echoed the howl from his
vampire. She wasn't strong enough yet.

Jared pressed her head into his chest. Her hand came between them, pressing back. She'd drained him to the point that he couldn't even win that small battle.

Her eyes met his. Her face faded in and out of focus. Her eyes rounded with horror. "Oh no."

He touched his finger to her cheek, blooming with the pink of health. "Next time we need privacy to do it right."

His head fell back. She scrambled from his arms. They felt empty without her.

"How could you let this happen?" Her energy snapped and crackled at the weres.

"Neither of you exactly gave us much of a choice."

"Bull."

Jared heard a gasp and then smelled the rich feminine promise of her blood. He caught the wrist she lifted to his mouth, brought it to his lips. He allowed himself one sip of her intoxicating richness before he sealed the wound with the stroke of his thumb. "No, baby."

"Don't you 'baby' me." She shoved her wrist in his face. "Feed."

He owed Creed and Ian for the shield they threw up between his mind and hers. Weres could be very effective telepaths at close range, though Creed and Ian were amazing for weres. He made a note to inform Caleb of that idiosyncrasy.

Another gasp preceded her removal from his side. His vampire snarled. His human side sighed with relief. He didn't know how long he could resist Raisa. She affected him like no other.

"Thank you."

"Thank me later. Right now, feed." Ian's scent came strong to his nostrils, the allure of his were blood potent. Jared resisted. Taking blood between were and vamp opened a mental door for the weres to their minds. The brothers had agreed their allegiance with the weres was too shaky to give them that leverage.

"You know the rules."

"Fuck the rules. They won't do you a bit of good if you're dead."

Ian had a point.

"Besides, if I'd wanted your secrets I'd have them by now. The D'Nallys aren't ordinary weres."

Ian's face blurred in and out of focus. Raisa's hand touched Jared's shoulder. The purity of her energy fortified his. "Feed, Jared."

He shook his head, "Stay out of it, Raisa."

This was too critical a decision to be made in haste. The shake of her head, which he couldn't see, trembled down her arm, communicating to him through her touch.

Softly, regret in her voice, she whispered, "I can't."

Using her ability to slide into his mind, adding her power to Creed's and Ian's, she betrayed him with the simplest of commands.

"Feed, Jared."

## ✤ 9 ✤

HE wasn't going to make the meeting.

Jared accepted the reality as he sealed the wound at Ian's wrist, and with a single push expelled the two weres from his mind. He was Raisa's mate, and she was his first priority. Inside, his vampire prowled, loose and in charge, angry and possessive, out of his control, wanting only one thing—to deal with the woman who'd betrayed him.

He got to his feet, holding Raisa immobile in a mental grip. He cut both weres a glare. "Get the fuck out."

Neither of them moved. Ian spoke. "She did what she had to, Jared."

"She did what she wanted, and to hell with the consequences." Something he was beginning to believe was a habit among female vampires.

"You took advantage."

"From my side, keeping you alive and strengthening our advantage is a win-win situation."

"Not from mine."

"You're just pissed you didn't get your way," Creed growled, moving closer to Raisa.

"Yeah, that's it." He caught Creed's eye. "Don't bother. She's never going to be yours."

"She's not yours, either."

"In a few minutes she will be."

Creed sneered, "Against her will?"

"She made her choice." When she'd taken his choice from him, she'd made her choice.

Ian came up beside Creed. "Yes, she did."

Creed spun around, confronting Ian. "That clearly violates pack law."

"She's not yours, Creed."

"She could be."

Ian's eyes met Jared's, and he sighed. "No, she couldn't."

Creed bared his fangs at Jared. "You hurt her and I'm coming after you."

"Why wait?"

Ian frowned. "Don't push this, vampire, or I'll finish it."

"You think you can?"

"I think there's a lot you don't understand, and until you do, you might want to accept my support and stop escalating this issue."

"And if I don't feel like it?"

"Then you will die."

The statement pushed into his mind with incredible strength. Jared blinked. Ian was a were of many surprises. Common sense warred with primitive demand. "If you want peace, get him out of here."

"Leave, Creed."

"No."

Ian turned slowly, head down, shoulders square. "You challenge me?"

Creed didn't immediately back down, didn't move. "The woman comes first."

Ian waved that concern away with his hand. "He won't hurt her."

Creed didn't move and didn't unlock his glare from Jared's. "You can't be sure."

Ian's lips twitched. "Yes, I can. Look at him without jealousy, and you'll see what I see. "

For another heartbeat, Creed stayed as he was, shook his head, then nodded once to Ian and stepped back, a sardonic smile tugging his lips as he glanced at Jared. "You do realize, sooner or later, you're going to have to unfreeze her?"

"What's your point?"

"She's not going to be happy."

"Get the hell out."

Ian grabbed Creed's arm and turned him toward the door. Creed stopped before passing through. "Just remember, vamp, if you mess up, I'll be there to pick up the pieces."

Jared flashed his fangs. "Like hell you will."

Ian shoved Creed through before adding his own warning over his shoulder. "Don't mess up."


**THE** door closed quietly behind the weres. Jared dropped the bar across the door. He did not want to be disturbed, and both Creed and Ian were the disturbing type. Sure the door was secure, he walked over to where Rai stood frozen, her energy and her spirit contained in a trap of his making. Helpless, vulnerable to whatever revenge he wanted to exact.

He touched a curl near her shoulder. It wrapped around his finger in a silken embrace, linking them together. The tawny shades caught the light from the table lamp, shifting from dark to pale as he drew his hand away. The ringlet stretched, holding on until the last second, maintaining the contact longer than he though it could. Defying him. He rubbed the strands between his fingers. She had pretty hair.

Jared looked down her body. All of her was pretty—a neat little package shaped perfectly to his taste. The black turtleneck shirt and pants she wore just emphasized the femininity that radiated off her. He brought the end of the curl to the corner of her mouth. She didn't blink, didn't move, but moisture gathered in her big brown eyes. The strand of hair slipped. He caught it with his thumb, prolonging the contact, the violence within him swirling with frustration.

He released her from his control. She blinked those thick lashes over her eyes. The color rose in her cheeks. Healthy color. Still holding the strand of hair, he touched her cheek. "You don't take a man's choices away, sunbeam, even to save his life."

Her moment of disorientation detonated in an explosion of anger. "Get away from me."

She took a swing at him. She would have connected, too, if she hadn't pulled back at the last minute. That display of softness settled over the last of his anger. Jesus, she needed a keeper. He caught her wrist and pulled her into his chest. "How in hell have you survived the last few centuries?"

"None of your business."

"Now that's where you're wrong. Everything you do is my business. Ian gave you to me."

She yanked her arm, her hair bouncing around her face. "I'm not Ian's to give."

"Then how about we just leave it that I've decided for both of us."

"You don't have that right."

He caught her other wrist before she could wallop him on the side of his head. She immediately started kicking at his shins. He let her land four kicks. On the fifth, he said, "Ouch."

Immediately, she stopped. He shook his head. "You, baby, have too soft a heart."

That got a rise out of her. "I do not."

To prove it, she kicked at him again, this time with everything she had behind it. He dodged the kick, the effort jarring loose his smile. She also had quite a temper.

It was simple to use her momentum to turn her. Crossing his arms over her chest pinned her against him. She struggled and kicked. He let her expend her frustration, resting his chin on her shoulder. Breathing deeply of her scent, his vampire prowled impatiently, waiting for her to settle. Waiting for her to accept.

Finally she slumped against him, jerking when she felt his arousal. Her jaw set, and then she leaned back, letting him know without words she wasn't intimidated by him. His smile broadened. She was all hellfire and compassion. And as much as that combination should conflict, it worked for her.

"I saved your life," she muttered.

"So you did."

"Twice."

"Guess that means that I own you now."

"That's not how it works."

"It is if I say it is."

She elbowed him in the gut with enough force to drive a punch of air from his lungs. Spinning out of his arms, she slammed her hands down on her hips. "This isn't the nineteenth century! You can't just own someone."

"I'm not owning someone. I'm owning you."

"Never."

He cocked his head to the side. "That sounds personal."

"Of course it's personal. We're talking about me."

"Well, look at it this way—you get to own me."

She looked him up and down, and managed to put a fair amount of disgust into her tone. "Assuming I want to."

He grinned. "Yeah. Assuming that." It was easy to catch her hand and tug her back into his arms. "Do you?"

"No."

"Would you prefer Creed?"

He saw her lips shape around a "yes," and then she shook her head, that inner honesty pulling the punch out of her anger. "I don't want to be owned by anyone. I had enough of that before."

"Before when?"

"Before I became a vampire."

"Explain."

She sighed. "I was a servant, which for a woman is as close as you come to being a slave and not wear the title." She pressed her palms against his chest. "I have no wish to revisit the experience."

He lowered his head. "Tough."

Destiny, fate, or just plain bad luck had hooked them together. Now she needed him, and he needed her. Her softness, her compassion, and that old-fashioned propriety that drew him like the sweetest of honey. "Neither of us have a choice."

"We can walk away."

"Try it." He kissed her right cheek and then her left. She wouldn't have any more success than he had, and he'd only gotten as far as a thought.

"Let me go, and I will."

"Later." He found the corner of her mouth. His vampire hissed in satisfaction as a hint of her taste teased his tongue. Spicy hot and addictive. He slipped his tongue into that tiny notch, taking advantage of her ensuing gasp to slide farther within the tempting haven of her mouth.

"Sweet baby."

Her hands stopped pushing. Her fingers curled inward. Her talons teased in tiny pinpricks as she came up on her toes, her lips parting, her breath mingling with his.

"Yes. Come here."

He hooked his arm behind her back, encouraging her to arch farther, widening his stance as her toes nudged his.

"Jared."

"Right here."

Her hands slid up his shoulders. "This is so wrong."

"We'll figure it out later."

"Later will be too late."

He slanted his mouth over hers, licking along the smooth seam until she shivered.

"Open."

"Think, Jared. You don't even know who I am."

"My vampire does."

"Your vampire is just horny."

The word seemed incongruous coming from those lips. "You make even swear words sexy."

"I did not swear."

"Yes, you did." He extended the talon on his index finger and placed it at the base of her neck, poking through the material of her turtleneck, tickling her skin. She shivered, and her mouth took on a softer cast. "All sexy and enticing. I find I like it when you talk dirty to me."

With a quick downward movement, he sliced the turtleneck open and slid his hands under the stretchy fabric.

"Ah, sunbeam, you're silky soft all over."

Her fingers dug into his neck as she tugged herself up. "You're not soft." Her breasts rubbed against his chest in short, jerky movements.

"No, not soft at all." He cupped her buttock in his hand. Lushly feminine, the curve filled his palm. He was so damn hard he was about to break in two.

She grunted and bounced against him. "You're too tall."

She was trying to get into his arms. "Then we'll adjust."

He lifted her up. Her legs immediately came around his waist, strong and slim, locking them together.

"Oh yeah."

Kisses sprinkled along his jaw, his neck. And then back up again. "Do you make love as well as you give orders?"

"Better." He caught her head in his palm, directing those kisses to his mouth.

Her fingers riffled through his hair, sliding up before wrapping in the strands and tugging down. Her "Prove it" dragged a chuckle past his desire.

"Any time."

She rubbed those pretty breasts against him, the slippery material of her bra easing the friction. "I was thinking now was a good time."

"I'm not dense, sweetheart. I got that."

"You couldn't prove it by me."

He hooked his talon behind the elastic of her bra strap and gave it a flick. The severed strap slid down her arm. "In a hurry, are we?"

"Yes."

He slit the other strap before walking her back against the wall, smiling as she jerked when her spine made contact with the cool surface. He reached for the hem of her shirt and tugged it up until it caught under her arms. "Let go of me."

She shook her head. "You feel too good."

"I'll feel even better against you without the barrier of clothes."

Her head cocked to the side as she considered the option. Her fingers slid back over his neck, her nails scratching erotically over the ledge of his collarbone. Her eyes, melting with passion to the color of warm chocolate, met his. With a witchy smile, she lifted her hands over her head, crossing her wrists and leaning back, perking those breasts up toward his mouth, figuratively and literally offering herself to his pleasure.

Desire crashed over him with the force of a tidal wave, almost wiping out his control. His fangs exploded into his mouth, aching with the need to accept her offer. He traced the tendon running down the side of her neck. "Dangerous, sunbeam. Very dangerous."

Her lids lowered over her eyes, adding a sultry challenge to her expression. "Afraid you can't handle me?"

He braced her weight on one hand. With the other he lifted her shirt up and over. The neck obliterated her expression for a heartbeat. When he tugged it free, she was still tossing that challenge at him from behind the shield of her lashes. Her lips curved in the slightest of smiles.

"Oh, I can handle you." He wrapped the excess shirt around her arms, effectively trapping them above her head. Her breasts, small and tip-tilted, quivered as she took a hoarse breath. He tucked the material between her arms, locking them in place. His mouth watered, imagining how sweet those swollen tips were going to taste on his tongue. How perfect her cries were going to sound to his ears as he sucked and nibbled them to tight points. "But I'm not rushing."

Her smile just got more confident. She ran her tongue over her small sexy fangs and arched her back, pushing her pelvis down on his. "We'll see."

So they would. He lowered his head. She met him halfway, catching his lower lip between her teeth, licking the inner lining in teasing little flicks that drove him crazy for full contact. Wrapping her hair in his hand, he tilted her head, bringing her mouth into alignment with his, her growl of frustration adding one more intriguing element to the passion arcing between them.

He caught her chin in his hand, and she pulled him closer. "Slow down, baby."

She shook her head, fighting his hold. "You have to hurry."

Buttons flew everywhere, hitting the floor in little pings of excitement, as she tore his shirt open. "Why?"

"You have to hurry before it's over."

He had to think on that a second. "Sunbeam, are you worried about coming too soon?"

"Not me, you."

Now she wasn't making sense. "If that's the problem, why are you rushing?"

"I don't want to lose the feeling."

He needed another second. "If you lose it, I'll help you find it again."

She shook her head, leaning forward to lick at his chest. "Oh no. I know how that works." Her mouth skated to the right, finding his nipple with unerring accuracy, lapping it lightly when he wanted her to bite. "You fall asleep, and I'm left watching you snore."

No way in hell could he ever fall asleep on her. "I think you're safe."

"You don't fall asleep?"

He put an end to her teasing by simply lifting her up while tilting her head back. "I don't snore."

"Like that's some comfort."

He caught her lower lip between his teeth, pulling at it gently, measuring her response by the increase in her respiration, the increase in her heartbeat. "Rai, it's been a long time for me, so even if I'm quick off the mark the first time around, I guarantee you I'll be ready to go again before you get to missing the feeling."

She had one hand nearly free of the tatters of her shirt. "I've heard that before."

Anger cut through his patience. "If you don't want me taking you like a barbarian, you'd best not raise the beast by talking of other men."

"Raise the beast?"

She twisted so her nipple brushed his lips.

"My vampire side doesn't like being reminded he's not the first."

She rubbed her breast against his mouth in a blatant invitation. "If he performs really well, maybe he'll get to be the last."

His laugh buffeted her nipple. The small peak drew diamond hard. He touched his tongue to the flat tip, drawing her taste back into his mouth, savoring it before answering. "That, my little vamp, is a given."

He caught her under the arms, lifted her up, and tossed her over his shoulder. Her squeal made him chuckle. Her fists thumping him on the butt had him slapping hers. Another squeal, and then he gave her a toss onto the mattress.

She landed awkwardly, her hands stretched over her head, her torso arched, her feet hanging toward the floor. He ripped his shirt off and let it drop to the floor. Her eyes opened wide as she took in his chest. Her tongue came out to play over those pouty lips. His cock jerked within the confines of his jeans. He ripped them open and shoved them down, barely remembering to kick off his boots as she parted her legs suggestively. All the while those hands remained anchored above her head in a visible sign of submission to his need. "Hurry."

He came down over her, stepping between her legs, lowering his hips to hers, his stomach, his chest. Everywhere her skin touched hot embers burst into flames.

Lowering his head, he kissed her cheek, her ear, and whispered, "All of a sudden, I'm not in that much of a hurry."

"Darn it!"

"No swearing, sunbeam."

"That wasn't a swear."

"It's about as close as you get, and if I have to watch my language, you have to watch yours."

"I'm not teasing you."

He caught her wrists just as she was about to slip them free, pinning them to the bed. "But you are rushing me."

"I just want to feel good, too."

The truth hung between them. "Too? Sunbeam, hasn't this ever felt good to you?"

"For a bit, but then it's over."

Had her lovers been idiots? "Well, tonight it's not going to be over."

Not when he had such a hot, willing woman panting beneath him, one who aroused his sense of humor as much as his passion.

Two slashes freed her from the constriction of her pants. He ripped them down and off, along with her underwear. His cock fell onto her stomach in an erotic little spank. She gasped and arched up. "We're a long way from that, baby."

That got her attention. She shook the hair out of her eyes and asked, "We are?"

"Oh yeah. I've got a lot of tasting, touching, and sipping to do before then." She eyed him warily. He grazed his lips along her neck, just above her jugular. She tensed. "That doesn't interest you?"

She tucked her chin in, blocking his progress. "Of course it interests me. I'm just trying not to get my hopes up."

"Is that why you're blocking my efforts to get closer?"

She nodded. "That always is what puts an end to it."

From "that," he gathered, she meant taking her blood. It was easy to understand why previous lovers had lost their heads. Raisa was the sweetest woman and bound to go to a man's head.

"You're with me now."

"What does that mean?"

With a push of his finger and a smile, he lifted her chin, tucking his mouth into the hollow beneath. "Go ahead, baby, get your hopes up."

He removed the shirt from around her arms. Her fingers flexed. He could imagine how they'd feel on his skin. Firm. Caring. Teasing. He smoothed his fingertips over her upper arms, trailing them over the inside of her elbow, over the roundness of her forearm, to the sensitive inside of her wrist, encircling it, and bringing her arms down over his shoulders before turning his attention to her. Her skin was so clear—cream with the slightest hint of peach undertone. Her lips, full and pouting, had that same peach tinting their full curves, and above the Slavic cast to her cheekbones, those incredible eyes. Eyes that looked at him with hesitation, passion, and hope. A hell of a lot of hope.

"No need to look so anxious, Rai. This is going to be fun. For you especially."

"Why especially me?"

"Because I've spent every minute since I met you contemplating which spots on your body would be the most sensitive." He took her earlobe between his lips and sucked carefully. Her shudder and gasp were exactly what he was looking for. "Which would make you shake. Which would make you sigh." He bit down. "And which ones make you cry out loud . . ."

"That's a good one," she gasped and arched up.

"Yup. I'd say it's got you warming up nicely."

Her legs came up around his hips, and the warm, soft nest of curls cuddled against his groin. "What else have you been thinking about?"

He skimmed his lips down her neck. "Your breasts. I've had many a fantasy about those pert little breasts."

"What about them?"

He smiled. Talking turned her on. "I wonder how they'll feel against my tongue. Whether you prefer a light touch, or hard."

He closed his lips over the left nipple and sipped lightly.

Still holding his face with her hands, more following than guiding, she gasped. "Hard. Definitely hard."

He shook his head, not releasing her breast, letting her experience the new sensation before saying, "I think it's too soon to tell."

Her fingers curled into his hair. Urgency rose along with lust as she pulled on his hair, begging for the harder touch she thought she needed.

"Such an impatient lover," he whispered against the peachy-pink of her areola, kissing around the puckered surface, smiling as it drew up tighter, as her nipple prodded his cheek in a potent little demand. He took it into the heat of his mouth, supping, then sucking, and finally settling in to suckle in earnest, drawing from her an intangible nourishment that spiked his passion, his emotions, and his need. A sexual need to be sure, but also a need for something else. For her. To bind her to him, mark her, possess her. To own her laughter, her spirit, and that sassy little tongue that could either make him laugh or moan, depending on how she used it. Rai groaned and arched. He took more of her breast into his mouth, applying a bit more suction. Her thighs convulsed around his hips, pulling him closer.

*That's it, baby. Welcome me.*

*Hurry.*

*No way.*

There was no way in hell he was rushing this first time.

Her heels drummed on his back. *This is not my first time.*

*It's our first time.* Her frustration came at him in a curl of energy, tinged with anxiety. She really was worried he'd leave her behind.

*Relax. You're going to be with me all the way. All you have to do is stop worrying and concentrate.*

*On what?*

*This.*

He lashed her nipple with his tongue. The spark of sensation shot through her in a bright sparkle. Her attention focused inward with a single-mindedness that might have scared him if he hadn't understood her. She wanted it to be right between them with the same fervor that he wanted it for her.

"Oh . . . Do that again."

He did. Following the sensation into her center, feeling the explosion of pleasure that radiated outward as it found its mark, the echoes reverberating against his own desire, throwing him off center. He'd never been with a woman who could slip in and out of his mind. Never anticipated the havoc all that hot feminine need pouring over his desire would wreak on his self-control.

She gasped. A flick of pain came from him to her. He was holding her too tightly. Easing his grip, he gentled the moment of panic, moving up so he could kiss her slowly and leisurely, rubbing his lips over hers, ignoring the parted invitation of her lips for thorough investigation of the edges, lingering in the corners when she flinched, touching the sensitive flesh with his tongue when she arched her neck, enabling more of the caress. Giving her tenderness when she thought she needed demand. Smoothing his tongue over the narrow dents left in her lower lip by her teeth. Replacing pain with pleasure until, with a broken gasp, she lifted, forcing a connection he was only too willing to maintain. She tasted sweeter than wine, more potent than whiskey, addictively perfect. He needed more, so much more. The line of her jaw beckoned, then the hollow beneath her ear, the dip between neck and collarbone, the high curve of her breast. Her right nipple was still puckered, but the left, not so much.

He cupped the small mound in his hand, plumping it to his attention. "Poor neglected baby. She needs some attention, too."

Raisa's enthusiastic *"Yes"* caught his vampire's attention and brought it roaring forward. Her palms cupped his cheeks, smooth where his were callused, so small and yet capable of holding him in ways no amount of strength could maintain. He went with her direction, fighting his vampire's selfish demand that he take the step back from the edge of the bed that would bring his aching cock into alignment and just rut on her until he exploded.

Resisting was harder than it should be with the erotic images pouring from her mind to his, images of his mouth on her breasts, between her legs. And behind each image the secret desire she didn't want known. Ah, hell, that one might just be the nail in his coffin.

He dropped his forehead against her breast and slowly squeezed off the connection of their minds, enduring the protests of her vampire along with his. He couldn't give her what she needed if she kept bombarding him with her joy at each caress. Not when his own pleasure was about to detonate. "I've got this, sunbeam."

The start that went through her bounced his chin on her chest. She was very on edge, in more ways than one. Her hands jerked open. "I'm sorry."

"No need to be sorry." He cupped her right breast, surprised to see his hand was shaking. Shit, if he wasn't careful, he'd be coming at her like a green kid. A brush of his thumb over her sensitive nipple had her arching into his touch. He opened his mouth, letting her be the one to press her nipple in.

"This is good," he murmured before closing his lips around the hungry little bud. Very good, better than anything he'd imagined or dreamed.

Her breasts were small but highly sensitive. Every lap, brush, and tap had her breath catching in her throat, her hips working against him, her energy straining to entwine with his.

*More.*

The desperate little thought slipped past his shields. He glanced at Raisa's face. The same desperation was etched there. He released her nipple with a little popping kiss. "I'll give you all you can take. Just relax and let me."

Her lower lip slid between her teeth. "Promise?"

"Absolutely. Now close your eyes and let me build on this little feeling."

Her "It's not little" brought forth his smile again along with a tidal wave of lust. For a second he went under, his fingers pinching her nipple in hard pulses that fed into the lash of his tongue on her other breast. Her gasps did nothing to deter him; rather they inspired a hot, glittering incentive to inspire more of those groans that rolled over him in the hottest of compliments.

"Yes." *Yes, yes.*

She wanted more. He wanted to give it to her, but his control was shaky this first time. He kissed his way down her torso, over the concave hollow of her stomach, skimming the well of her navel, finding the downy soft hair beneath, catching a few strands in his teeth, smiling when she yelped before moving down farther, letting her scent roll over him in potent encouragement before he parted the full outer lips and touched his tongue to the spice within.

"Oh my God!"

That was his reaction, too, as her flavor spread through his mouth. An addictive, honeyed spice. More.

Her hand came down and wiggled between his mouth and her pussy. The growl welled from his core. Nothing would keep her from him. Her hand jerked back. "Jared?"

"Mine."

"I'm not sure."

"I am." He snuck another taste, which led to another and another. His tongue glided across the moist flesh, gathering the rich cream in a heady feast. Her heels gouged into his buttocks. Her breath came in hard pants that echoed the hard thud of his heart. He parted her folds and found her little clit. It was engorged and as eager as the rest of her. Eager for his touch. He homed in on it, letting her cries and her tension feed his desire. He tested her with a finger. Her snug little sheath clamped down on him immediately. A few flutters of his tongue and her sheath rippled. She was close. So was he. It was going to be a close call getting her to the finish line ahead of him.

He laved her gently, holding her put when she would have jerked away under the initial slash of sensation. And then she was pulling him to her, her fingers sinking through his hair, her talons into his scalp.

"Oh God, oh God, oh God."

He was right there with her. Cradling her in his arms as she shattered, kissing her once, twice before climbing up over her, nudging her tight sheath with his cock, then easing it in past the hard contractions. Fighting for control, restraint, and determined to make this the experience he'd promised. A second orgasm crashed over her, catching him by surprise. Barreling through his barriers, her energy wrapped around his, pulling him in physically and mentally, until he couldn't tell where he ended and she began.

*Come with me.*

The warm entreaty dragged him into the storm. Raisa's pleasure magnified his, blending, mixing, escalating until there was nothing but the two of them.

The need hit him as hard as the pleasure. He leaned down, the rhythm of her pulse pounding in his ears, calling to him. He scraped his teeth over her artery. Her head fell back.

"Yes." *Yes.* They needed this to complete the cycle. Needed the joining. He bit down. Her scream echoed around them as he came hard and deep, filling her with his seed as she filled him with her essence. *His.* The thought rode through him as he marked her. Irrevocably, forevermore his.

## ❈ 10 ❈

JARED'S lips brushed her temple. "How did you get turned?"

"Ah, the big question."

"Yet so easy to answer."

Raisa snuggled her head into his shoulder. She experimentally pinched his side. There wasn't an ounce of fat on him. Just long, lean cuts of muscle slabbed attractively over heavy bone. She glanced up into his face. He was looking down at her, his mouth soft, his expression indulgent. If his expression was anything to go by, he was going to be a very generous lover.

The corners of his mouth eased into a smile. "Very generous."

She tried to put resentment into her tone, but she didn't think she was too successful. "You peeked into my mind."

His finger wove through a curl at her temple. "That seems inevitable between us."

She slid her thigh up his, the hair on his leg tickling the inside of hers. A shiver went through her, and she kissed the rise of his pectoral muscle, just to the left of his nipple. His energy pulsed. Hers answered. She bit down. Just a little. He shuddered, and his shaft rose thick and strong against her stomach, the broad head throbbing with the urgency between them, setting the pace for her desire.

She liked that. "You're a very sexy man."

His smile was very sensual. "And you, sunbeam, are ignoring my question."

She inched her hand across his chest to weave through the mat of hair in the center, understanding, as the strands wrapped around her fingers, why he liked to play with her hair so much. There was something intrinsically satisfying about being bound to him in even this insubstantial way.

"There doesn't seem a need to mess up this moment with ickiness from the past."

"So it was . . . icky?"

A note in his voice made her look up. "The conversion wasn't, but the time before was."

His arm tightened around her. She rubbed her cheek on his skin, accepting the protective cloak of his energy around her. "Honestly, Jared, being a vampire was the best thing that ever happened to me."

"You're shitting me."

"No," she shook her head. "Before I was turned, I was a bartering tool. My family was poor. My job as a daughter was to raise their status. They loaned me to a relative in America."

She shuddered. "That, as they say these days, was not pretty."

"I'm sorry."

"There's nothing to be sorry for. It was ages ago."

This time his sympathy was couched in a kiss, brushed across her hair. She patted his chest and continued. "But once I was turned, I was free." She tugged at the dark hair under her fingers, watching his naturally dark skin lift ever so lightly to the pressure. "I never had that until I was a vampire. Even though I'm the sickliest vampire in history, being the walking dead let me be free for the first time in my life."

Jared's hand came over hers, stilling her playing. "And what did you do with your freedom?"

She glanced up. "The very first thing?"

"Yeah. The very first thing."

"I learned to read. And then I read and read and read. I think I spent my first century living in libraries. Good books, bad books, children's books, fiction, nonfiction. Oh, it was a feast for my mind."

And a balm for her soul to read about a world bigger than the immediate need for survival that she was used to. To see that other people thought like she did, had fully formed philosophies that reflected the half-gelled ones she'd struggled to live by. That other women had been where she had and made something of their experiences. It had been liberating, enlightening, not to mention fascinating. She tucked her thigh higher over his and tilted her head back. "Do you like to read?"

His smile was gentle, letting her know he'd been in her mind again. She sighed. Maybe it really was inevitable between them. "Yes."

"Do you have a favorite book?"

"My reading is more for information."

She propped herself over him, shaking her hair out of her face. Lamplight played over his harsh features, softening the edges, bringing out the green in his eyes, highlighting the intelligence there. "Oh, who do you think you're kidding." She cocked her head to the side. The man was way too curious and intelligent to not like to read. "I bet you're a Tom Clancy type of man."

His laugh was beautiful to see. And strangely, it seemed to fit his face better than sternness. She touched the corner of that grin. He immediately turned his head and caught her fingertip in his mouth. The hot lick of his tongue burned down to her core. She folded her arms on the firm ledge of his chest, placing her hands on top of each other. As she rested her chin on the back of her fingers, she had a moment of sudden insight. "You used to laugh a lot before you turned vampire, didn't you?"

His hand hesitated before coming down on her back. His expression went from soft to hard in the space of a breath. "I don't remember that far back."

"If you don't want to talk about it, you can just say so."

He walked his fingers up her back, under her hair to the nape of her neck. "I don't want to talk about it."

She had an image of a man's face, vaguely familiar, and then a pulse of anger so hard it made her jump.

Jared's thumb settled on the pressure point under her ear. "Suffice it to say, my conversion was not a liberating experience. Unlike yours. And don't think I didn't notice you didn't answer my question. How were you turned?"

She didn't mind telling him. It didn't matter anymore. "The place my parents sent me was a saloon. After all those months of travel I arrived to find out my new beginning wasn't what I had thought it would be. My mother's cousin, Nicholai, who needed help, was actually looking for a prostitute to pick up business. I wasn't agreeable to the plan. We discussed the issue. My nerves were a bit frayed from weeks of seasickness. I wasn't as diplomatic in the presentation of my position as I could have been. I got the bad end of the argument. Nicholai brought in friends to help persuade me."

His friends had been bigger than Nicholai and just as mean. She'd been terrified, and strangely determined. The more they beat her, the more she'd clung to the word "no" until she'd been past feeling anything and their arms had tired. Jared snarled, and the muscles beneath her cheek tightened. He was in her mind again. She quickly closed her mind on the memories and did her best to sooth the rage that poured from him in a waterfall of emotion.

"A man came upon me in the alley where they'd tossed me."

"They threw you into an alley?"

"I wasn't much to look at before they started beating on me. I'd been sick for the entire voyage. I don't suppose my looks improved with bruises." She shrugged. "I think they thought I was as good as dead."

More rage rolled off him. More need for violence. "The bastards."

"They were that." It took everything she had to contain the lashing fury of his emotions. "Anyway, he asked me if I wanted to live. I said no. He laughed and said he thought I might have a change of heart." She shrugged. "He was right. I did. He stayed with me only long enough to tell me the rules and then moved on."

Jared's grip on her was miser tight, as if the threat still existed. As if he could protect her from the pain of the memory. "What about your inability to take blood?"

"That," she admitted ruefully, "was one of the reasons he moved on. I think he felt guilty for that."

"He damn well should have."

"Why are you so mad?"

"He had no right to convert you against your will."

"Do you seriously think I could have comprehended what he was offering me?"

"It was your choice."

She shrugged. "Well, like everything else at that time in my life, it was made for me, and since it worked out, I'm fine with it."

"You shouldn't be."

"It happened, I can't change it, and it's provided me with opportunities I never would have known otherwise." To put it mildly. "And it definitely beat dying on top of a garbage heap. Do you know how much garbage reeks in summer heat?"

Her attempt at levity fell flat. Jared's thumb came under her chin and tilted her face to his. "I'm sorry those men hurt you."

He was still stuck on the fact that she had been beaten. The fury that rolled off him was as strong as if it had just happened. And it struck her as so incredibly sweet that he would be angry on her behalf. Especially as the men were long since dead and she was obviously over it. She stretched up and kissed his chin. "Thank you, but it's long passed."

He hiked her up so his mouth could meet hers. "I still don't have to like it."

She wrapped her arms around his neck as he rolled her beneath him. "Well, I suppose you could kiss me and make it all better."

His head tilted to the side, and his lids lowered over his eyes while his mouth took on a distinctly sensual tilt. "I suppose I could."

**SOMETIMES** opportunity just dropped into a woman's lap. Raisa eased out from under Jared's arms. Being locked up in a pack leader's house while her guard/lover slept the sleep of the exhausted definitely qualified as one of them.

She drifted soundlessly across the floor, grabbed Jared's shirt off the chair, and slipped her arms into the sleeves. A thrill at her newfound strength coursed through her. Jared stirred. She suppressed the emotion. The man was too connected to her, his emotions constantly tapping hers, and if she wasn't careful to stay focused, she'd ruin everything. She couldn't afford that. She rolled the too-long sleeves up. She'd found Ian's office earlier today. If she was very lucky, the information she needed to feed the Sanctuary would be there.

Jared stirred again. She glanced toward the bed. If he caught her, he wouldn't be happy. He had a sense of honor that went bone deep, and he wouldn't ever understand why she needed to do this. Especially as she couldn't tell him. Couldn't tell anyone except the mystery man who was Miri's mate. Miri had been wild with desperation when she'd made Raisa promise to tell no one. She owed Miri her life and her sanity. She'd keep her promise to her. She slipped from the room and headed down the hall.

Raisa paused at the window before Ian's office door. She cast out with her energy but didn't feel anything. Easing the curtain aside, she lifted the blind and peeked out. Muted daylight burned her eyes. Nothing stirred beyond the porch. No sign of Creed or Ian or any other were. That was good. The hint of twilight in the sky was not good, however. She only had a few minutes before Jared woke.

It was a simple manipulation of energy to pop the electronic lock. With one last look around she slipped into the office. She scanned again for any residual energy from cameras. There was none.

The door clicked shut behind her. There was no sign of a computer, no sign of a laptop. There were, however, five file cabinets. Shoot! Ian would be the old-fashioned type. She closed her eyes, sensing for any remnants of the were leader's touch, any clue as to where she should start searching. The file cabinet in the right corner held a faint glow.

Desperation crept up on her blind side. There had to be something in there she could send. She was almost out of time. The Sanctuary would demand a report, and if she didn't have anything of import, they would take it out on Miri. The torture they would mete out to the werewolf woman didn't bear thinking about. They might even kill her. After all their experiments, the Sanctuary had all but given up creating ways to get her to conceive.

Raisa swallowed. She had to find information. She needed the time it would buy to find Miri's mate. A mystery man whom she didn't know how to find beyond the mental imprint Miri had given her. Someone she couldn't even ask about for fear of alerting the man who'd betrayed Miri to the Sanctuary. Her energy reached for Jared in an instinctive need for comfort. She made a mental grab for it, hauling it back. She couldn't ask Jared's help. Jared couldn't be here now. She couldn't put him in a position to betray his friend.

Standing still, she waited to see if the call had reached him. There was no sound from the bedroom, no disturbance in the energy field around her. After another minute, she relaxed, grabbing the edge of the desk for support. She so was not cut out for this. All she wanted to do was to confess everything to Jared, give her problem to him as she'd been raised to do, but she couldn't. Not only had women evolved past such dependent behavior, but there was no guarantee he'd believe her. No guarantee that he'd put Miri's life over her safety. No guarantee she could trust him with the information. And right now, getting Miri out was her only imperative. Well, that and staying alive long enough to make it happen. She approached the file cabinet.

Getting Miri out was going to take some doing. Her proven fertility gave her the honor of being the number one hope for the Sanctuary's breeding program. They'd taken everything from Miri in their efforts to get her to cooperate, used Raisa against her, but despite all her outward fragility, Miri was one tough wolf. Nothing they had tried had broken her, but this last thing they'd done . . . Raisa clenched her fists, remembering Miri's haggard expression, the flat resolution in her feverishly bright green eyes when they'd discussed the other woman's options. That just might break her.

Raisa clenched her fists. She wasn't going to let that happen. If she had to betray every wolf and vamp between here and perdition, she'd play this out, find this mysterious mate, and make him—*make him*—give a darn about Miri. She just needed to buy enough time to find the no-account.

The cabinet wasn't locked. Not a good sign. Raisa went through it quickly, speed-reading folders and skimming contents. Nothing. Nothing she could use.

She crouched down and tried the next, and the next. Nothing but birth records, health records, deeds, and a lot of other mundane data that she couldn't even fake into making interesting. She needed something to feed the Sanctuary before the deadline.

Then she saw it. A faint glow peeking from under the back edge of the cabinet. A floor safe? She levitated the filing cabinet away from the spot, grateful for the strength Jared's blood gave her. She didn't think she'd have been able to complete any of the mission the Sanctuary had sent her on without it. Which made her wonder if they'd really expected her to survive, because they knew how weak she was. Had used it against her constantly, made fun of her, mocked her, tortured her. She would like to go back just once, as she was now, and make them eat every mocking insult. That would definitely make her feel good.

The floorboards fit seamlessly together. If it hadn't been for her ability to see and manipulate energy, she never would have known from the hair-thin trace of energy that there was a panel in the floor. But she did, and there was.

The boards lifted easily, floating to the side before she lowered them soundlessly to the floor. Beneath was a safe. A strange color of energy surrounded it. She eyed the energy warily. She'd never seen the like, couldn't see a pattern in the shimmering red-gold haze. She squatted there, torn by indecision. She needed something. She glanced at the windows, sensing the descent of night. She remembered the deft touch of Ian's mind to hers. The flash in his eyes as he'd connected. She glanced at the gold edge of the energy surrounding the safe. Same color.

She held her hand over the hole. Nothing. Technically, she should touch her energy to the threads spreading outward from the glow and look for clues, but instinct held her back. She was looking at a trap, one far more sophisticated than she'd ever seen in her limited experience. She could do nothing with this. Tears burned the back of her eyes. She levitated the boards back into place.

"A wise decision."

She spun around so fast she landed on her butt. Jared stood in the doorway, arms folded across his massive chest, naked and furious. He would kill her for this. Vampire and were law demanded it.

*I'm sorry, Miri. I wasn't good enough.*

She was never good enough.

Jared pushed away from the jamb and came toward her one measured step at a time. "Who's Miri?"

She couldn't look away from his chest as he approached. Her energy was all over him, lingering in pale glowing love bites visible to any vampire who cared to look. She'd known what she was risking when she had lain down with him, but she'd also known what she was up against, and once before she died, just once, she'd wanted to know exactly what he'd shown her—the beauty and power of her own body.

She'd used him. No way around it, and now she had to pay the price. Raisa focused on the love bite just above his left nipple, narrowing her eyes so that was all she could see, letting it get bigger and bigger in her field of vision, the closer he got, until it swallowed everything except the remnants of the passion they'd shared.

His hand came around her throat, not hurting her, but all he had to do was close his fingers and he would crush her throat. And she would deserve it. She closed her eyes as he lifted her. She didn't want to see the hatred and disgust in his face. She much preferred the tenderness and possession she'd wallowed in as he'd been loving her.

"You didn't answer my question."

"Someone I promised to help."

"By stealing from Ian? Betraying me?"

What did he want her to say? He saw what she was doing. "Yes."

Keeping her eyes closed, she built his image in her mind, focusing on her favorite, the moments he'd spent inside her, his body deep in hers, his mind entrenched with hers, his face showing the same caring, the same need, the same longing that exploded within her. She built the image and held on to it as her lifeline.

As if he realized she couldn't speak with his hand around her throat, Jared grabbed the front of her shirt with his other hand, slamming her back against the wall. His image shimmied in her mind's eye as she hit the wall with controlled force. Pain reverberated up her back. It was nothing compared to the pain she could feel reverberating under Jared's fury.

He thought she'd betrayed him.

"Why?"

The question grated out at her, lashing her with contempt and anger. And she couldn't fight it. She had betrayed him. It didn't matter why; she had, and she deserved to die for it. That was right, but it wasn't right that Miri would. That wasn't right at all.

"I can't tell you."

"You just expect me to go along with this?"

Grief and guilt threatened her mental shield. She shook her head.

"I know you can't."

Raisa pushed emotion aside and focused on building Jared's image. She didn't have his hair right. It was too short. She lengthened the ends, concentrating on making every strand perfect, knowing she had time. It was going to be a long interrogation. Now that Jared had his passion under control, he'd want to know why. His honor would insist he find out what he needed to do to protect the weres and his own people from the threat he'd allowed into their midst. Her. She just hoped she could be as strong as Miri.

"Who's Miri?" he asked again, obviously latching onto that thought.

She winced at the coldness of his tone and the impossibility of her situation. She was a rather pathetic threat. She hadn't even managed to get one piece of lousy information before she'd gotten caught, but Jared wouldn't believe that. Wouldn't be able to believe that just in case he was wrong. When it came to vampire wars, even she knew assuming that she was telling the truth was a deadly mistake. Despair broke her breath. "I can't tell you."

Jared shook her. Her head bumped against the wall. "Don't you even fucking try it."

She blinked as her energy came surging back at her. She'd been reaching to him for comfort, instinct overriding logic. She was even more pathetic than she'd thought. "I'm sorry."

"Not as sorry as you're going to be." He shook her again. "And get that Goddamn picture out of your head."

She'd been projecting her thoughts, too? Dear God, what else had she lost control of? She checked the energy radiating from the implant the Sanctuary had put in her. It was masked, exactly what she'd programmed it to be. Apparently, her subconscious, while misguided, didn't lose touch of the important things.

She didn't remove the image, just blocked his access to it.

Jared's curse whipped around her along with his energy, which was pouring and sliding against hers. He was going to have to do a lot better than that if he wanted her secrets. Sanctuary torture had refined one of her skills. If there was one thing Raisa knew how to do, it was how to direct and redirect a mind probe until the intruder left with only the image she wanted them to have.

To the Sanctuary, she was a not-so-bright blonde with scattered thought patterns that were easily manipulated. To Jared . . . She sighed. She didn't know what she was to Jared. She'd slipped up quite a few times the last few days. For sure she wouldn't get away with the ditzy blonde routine. She decided to take this in steps. Her shirt was cutting into her underarms. "If you're not going to kill me, could you put me down?"

"I haven't decided what I'm going to do with you yet."

She opened her eyes, holding the mental picture she'd built at the ready, gasping as she met his gaze. Hatred, pure and simple, deadly and cold, blasted out at her. She clutched her mental image like a security blanket and maintained the same calm voice. When faced with a deadly predator, it was best not to show emotion. "Then let me clarify. If you're not going to kill me *now*, could you put me down? The shirt is hurting my arms."

"Good."

She didn't doubt he meant that. It was natural that he'd want to hurt her the way she'd hurt him. Maybe more as she'd struck him in the emotions, and Jared wasn't a man who let anyone close. Tears burned her eyes. If only he'd stayed asleep, she wouldn't have had to hurt him like this. She blinked rapidly. His gaze raked her face. He swore, swung her away from the wall, and set her down a good distance from the safe. "Don't fucking move."

He didn't have to worry. She wasn't going anywhere. Her legs were shaking so badly, she could barely stand. She caught herself on the edge of the desk. She watched as he resettled the boards with careful precision. A couple of seconds later, the taint of her energy was wiped out. This time she blinked for another reason.

"What are you doing?"

Jared levitated the filing cabinet back. Again, all traces of their presence was removed. He turned back to her. His hand lashed out. She closed her eyes, bracing herself for the pain of the blow.

But his hand clamped behind her neck, dragging her against him. "You don't say a fucking word about this to Ian, Creed, or anyone. You don't think about it, you don't do a Goddamn thing that would clue them in to the fact that you're anything other than what you seem."

She licked her lips as her heart raced out of control. He was protecting her. "And what's that?"

It was pointless, but she really did want to know how he'd seen her. "A sweet little vamp with a big heart in need of protecting."

Those damn tears stung again. That was such a nice way to see her. It made her sound so much more than the weak woman at the mercy of circumstance, which she always ended up being.

"Thank you."

He shoved her toward the door. "For what?"

She glanced at the hard implacability of his face. "For seeing me that way."

"I never said I did."

Yes, he had. At least, for a little while. He'd told her that with every touch and every concession to her requests, but she knew better than to rub his face in it. She dropped her gaze. And sucked in a breath. He was aroused. "Oh."

She stumbled on the threshold. Jared grabbed her arm and then steered her down the hall. Instead of heading to the bedroom, he shoved her into the living room. He kept pushing until she fell, face forward over the back of the couch, so wildly relieved that he still wanted her that the knock at the door never registered until she heard a gasp and felt the whip of foreign male lust. Jared's hand at the back of her neck kept her pinned when she would have jerked up straight. His body shielded hers from view. "Get out."

"Sorry."

From the corner of her eye she saw Creed's hard expression and then Ian's amused one before he closed the door. Jared kneed her thighs apart and stepped between them before she could close them. A trill of fear and excitement went though her as his shaft notched to her center. She braced herself for the painful thrust that was coming, his need to dominate and punish crashing over her.

*Oh God, not like this.*

His thoughts thrust into her mind with the brutality she expected from his body. *Exactly like this.*

Except he didn't move, didn't do anything, just loomed over her, his big cock threatening her with the ultimate disrespect while he sucked hard breaths into his lungs.

And then he moved, his free hand coming around to her breast, his lips to the back of her neck.

*Mine.*

It was a sigh of acceptance she didn't understand. She couldn't help her flinch as he slid his hand between the lapels of her shirt and wrapped his fingers around her nipple, expecting the bite of pain, finding instead a gliding invitation to pleasure. She didn't move, didn't breathe, didn't do anything but freeze as he did it again and again. While her mind stayed frozen, her body didn't. It softened and pulsed to the rhythm he set, arching into his touch, the softness he offered, piteously grateful for the reprieve, this chance to pretend one more time, answering his call with the helpless response he'd drawn from her from the instant she'd met him.

*I'm sorry.*

His hand left her breast and went lower, tucking between her stomach and the couch until she was resting on his palm. His fingers pressed into her slick folds, finding her clitoris, and then rubbing gently, persistently.

*That doesn't change anything.*

*I know.*

*You can trust me.*

*No.*

*You will.*

She might have been able to hold out if he had been rough, but surrounded by his pain, her guilt, and the persuasion of his touch, she didn't have a prayer. Passion rose to his command. Her body softened, entreated, and gladly accepted him into her heat. Her energy soothed over his, surrounding him in her apology, her passion.

His curse exploded into the room as his shaft glided into her body—not violently, not reverently, but resolutely. She gasped and then arched back as his finger stroked pleasurably, driving her to seek more. She wasn't picky; anyway she could get him worked for her.

The thought intruded again—a simple statement of fact. *You're mine.*

Yes, she was, but it wasn't the same as before. There were walls between them, a resistance to her energy, but there was passion and gentleness and maybe a slight hope that they could recover from this. Raisa let the passion roll over her, consume her, taking the energy he fed her—pure animalistic lust with no emotion coloring it—and mirrored it back as she rode his desire to the waiting climax.

As it shimmered before her, he leaned over her back, dominating her fully with the sheer size of his body and the force of his personality. A carnal possession that everything feminine within her relished. His wrist brushed her mouth.

*Feed.*

She shook her head and tried to turn, wanting the intimacy of his chest. A dip of his shoulder prevented the instinctive twist. Again his wrist tapped her mouth.

*Feed.*

At the same time that he pressed his wrist against her mouth, his hips pushed against hers in a compulsive drive for completion. His fingers were equally ruthless, driving her passion before them, giving her no choice but to succumb. Her climax exploded through her in a screaming array of brilliant energy—his, hers, together— for an instant in perfect harmony.

The sound never left her throat as his wrist was shoved into her mouth. She bit down, instinct driving everything now. She convulsed around him, her body jerking wildly under the command of his, her mouth working on his flesh. The echoes of her climax faded as Jared's began.

"Oh no, you don't, Raisa," he said when she would have wiggled away. Not "Rai" or "sunbeam," but "Raisa." "You're not fucking up everything now."

She saw the line of her back through his eyes, felt how the image of feminine submission drove his lust, how the tight grasp of her sheath burned him with the same friction it burned her. Felt his balls draw up tight as she took his blood, felt his satisfaction as her clit tingled under his touch. And felt her own vicious hurtle back to climax as he tugged and stretched the eager nub and manipulated her emotions to follow his. As he drove into her one more time, her "God, yes!" echoed around them as she accepted his seed, his dominion, his utter right to do with her what he wanted. Because she'd betrayed him when all he'd done was help her. And because all he wanted from her was her pleasure.

She was his mate, and she'd betrayed him. She owed him this. Owed him everything. As his fangs sank into her shoulder, holding her pinned for the last burst of his seed, he drew from her, completing the ritual. She reached back and cupped his face, giving him the softness he so badly needed, expecting his rejection, accepting it when it came. Offering herself again with her energy, wincing as he ruthlessly shoved it back.

Dropping her head against the back of the couch, she let the tears fall.

When he was done feeding, the act that completed the bond between them, his big chest pressing into her back with each breath, she simply asked, "Why?"

## ❧ 11 ❧

HE pulled from her and straightened her shirt over her hips, the same calm efficiency in his movements as in his voice.

"Weres scent emotion."

She stood, her body still trembling from the possession of his, her emotions still bouncing between hope and despair. "And your point is?"

"I want them to scent something other than your duplicity. Your pleasure works well."

He was using words to hurt her now, to put distance between them, the way he hadn't been able to when he'd made love to her. For a man like Jared, who valued his strength and his honor, his weakness for her would eat at him. And she could expect to pay the price. "Yours didn't hurt, either."

He waved her toward the bedroom. "Get dressed."

She didn't like his tone. "Why?"

"We're leaving."

A spurt of resentment slowed her steps. She wasn't his slave. She didn't have to blindly follow his orders. "For where?"

"Home. And the hell you don't have to blindly follow my orders," he snapped, obviously reading her mind.

She paused in the doorway. He was right behind her. "Let me clarify. I won't blindly follow your orders."

"You don't have a choice."

"I have lots of choices. You don't know how stubborn I can be."

His hand in the middle of her back prodded her toward the bedroom. "Maybe you just don't know me."

The thought that she might not terrified her. She turned her back on him. Rage and another emotion she couldn't identify, and he couldn't control, slammed into her, making her stumble as surely as if she'd been pushed. Jared caught her arm. Her head snapped around as he jerked her up short. Another hot retort teetered on her lips. It died after one glance at his expression. His rage she could handle, but that other something she'd felt—pain, blinding pain. Neither of them was in control of that. Instinctively, she reached for him, wanting to take that wildness into her, soothe it, calm it. With a coldness that encased her hope in ice, he rebuffed her effort. His gaze met hers. "Be advised, Raisa, if you try any of your games in my home, I won't be so lenient."

She didn't flinch. All of this was his choice. He had mated with her, completed the process. As much as she'd been unable to resist the bonding, she *had* warned him against it. "You don't have to take me anywhere. Your home can remain untainted."

"You're my wife. Where I go, you go."

"Then you're just going to have to deal with me, warts and all." She looked pointedly at his hand on her arm. "Do you mind?"

For a moment, the same indecision warring in her flickered in his gaze, then his eyes darkened to stone-cold emerald. His fingers circled her arm with the same cold deliberation with which he studied her. He watched each digit touch the other as he completed the circle, as if fascinated with his ability to do so. Maybe even tempted by it?

The tension ratcheted tight between them as he lifted her arm and tightened his grip. She didn't know him like this. "Either break it or let me go." She was amazed at how calm she sounded when, in reality, she was terrified. Terrified that he'd do it. That she'd pushed him past who he was to the demon on the other side.

A muscle in his jaw leapt. "Don't tempt me."

She moved a fraction of an inch closer. Into his grip. "I'm tempting."

Again that muscle jerked. His gaze lifted to hers. "Why?"

There was nothing subtle in the probe of his mind. There was nothing subtle in the way she opened to him.

"I would rather know the worst from the start than build false illusions." The weight of that truth thickened her accent. "I find it easier to cope."

It was always easier to have no hope. "Since you didn't offer me the same consideration, why should I offer it to you?"

She didn't have to even think about the answer. "Because you're a better person than I am."

"What makes you so sure?"

She looked at him, at his tough-as-nails expression, his hurt-to-his-soul eyes. "Because I know you."

"If I were you, I wouldn't bet on what you think you know of me."

She relaxed into his grip, ignoring his snarl. She did know him and of what he was capable. "But you are not me."

"Lucky for you."

"Yes."

Though she didn't feel lucky. She felt like she'd lost something invaluable. She'd been hurt many times in her life—deeply, irrevocably—but she'd never before delivered the kind of pain to another human being that Jared was experiencing. She'd always been the one betrayed. Being on the other side of the betrayal, even if it hadn't been her intent, was infinitely worse. "For what it's worth, I didn't use you."

"Uh-huh." He pushed her into the bedroom. "You can work on

a believable explanation to go with that lie on the way to the Circle J. Right now, I need to get you out of here."

*I need to get you out of here.*

She paused in the door to the bedroom and looked over her shoulder at him. He was protecting her. He thought she had betrayed him, thought she might be in league with the Sanctuary, yet he was protecting her from pack law. She shook her head. And he said she was too soft. "Thank you."

"There's nothing to thank me for." He stood there, arms folded across his chest, filling the space with the breadth of his shoulders and the cold fury radiating off him in icy waves. "You're not off the hook. I'd just prefer to have the answers I want before tossing you to the wolves."

She squeezed between him and the door frame. He'd rather die than have her think he was soft. She understood that. "Thank you anyway."

"I don't want gratitude."

He wanted an explanation he could accept. "I was just looking for some—"

That fast, his hand covered her mouth. Fear flared as she looked around. She didn't see anything, but everything in his body language said there was a threat. *Don't say another fucking word.*

Or maybe it was just her imagination making excuses for him. She pushed at his hand. *I don't like your language.*

*And I don't like your morals. Guess we'll both have some adjustments to make.*

Adjustments meant future. Did this mean he wasn't dumping her?

*Why not just leave me here?*

*Because you're mine.*

She raised her brows.

*And I take care of what's mine.*

As if that explained everything. He removed his hand.

"Get packed."

"I don't understand you."

It was his turn to lift his brow. "You don't have to, but in five minutes we're leaving, whatever state you're in."

That she understood. She cast a longing glance at the shower. No way did she have time for that. She settled for a hasty cleanup with a washcloth, wincing as she caught a glimpse of the tousled bed. How different the lovemaking between them had been before. Warm, intimate, a sharing and a blending for all that it was passionate and wild. And then there was the time after he'd found her in Ian's office. She shuddered. She hadn't liked it when Jared had made love to her like that—with his emotions held in check, giving her his body but nothing else. They were married. His choice, but she hadn't fought him when he'd moved the commitment forward. She'd wanted the bonding. Wanted to believe forever was possible for them. She still did. Which meant she was a partner in this relationship. Which meant she had a say. Which meant from here on out there would be emotion between them, whatever it was, but never that cold distance.

She grabbed her clothes up off the floor, pulling them on rapidly. She shoved pencil and paper into her bag, along with a spare set of clothing the were women had given her. She wasted precious seconds searching for her gloves and hat. She found the gloves under the bed and finally remembered Jared had gotten rid of her hat.

Raisa glanced out the frosted window. The night looked to be a cold one. Hopefully, Jared's blood would hold long enough this time so she could continue to regulate her temperature until they got to wherever the Circle J was.

She walked back into the bedroom. Jared stood by the bed, completely unconcerned with his nakedness. Unconcerned with her. She might have bought into his act of extreme indifference as he began to dress, except for the way his energy kept reaching for hers. It gave her hope.

Her thoughts must have bled over because he shot her a disgusted glare. "Just keeping tabs on a treacherous little vamp."

She gritted her teeth. Without knowing what was going on,

he was entitled to a few shots. "So good of you to keep an open mind."

His gaze narrowed. "Unless you want me bending you over that couch again, you won't keep picking a fight."

That wasn't going to happen. "You won't touch me again until the anger's gone."

"Then it's a damn good thing we're immortal." Picking up her backpack, he slung it over his shoulder. "Because that's going to take forever."

With a hand on her arm he escorted her roughly through the door. She grabbed the jamb, slowing them down.

"If you're not going to kill me, Jared . . ." Her fingers popped free. She shot into the living room and caught herself on the recliner. "There are things you need to know."

He glanced at the front door and held up his hand. "Not now."

There was a perfunctory knock. When the door didn't open immediately, Jared smiled sardonically. "And they say weres can't learn."

*How had he . . . ?* She didn't finish the thought. She knew. He'd scanned. Just as she could have if she'd thought about it. She was just so used to conserving energy, the sheer luxury of having the strength to do what she wanted when she wanted was taking some getting used to.

A quick check revealed Ian and Creed were outside the door. Great. Just what she needed to round off a horrible night—coming face-to-face with the men who'd seen her with Jared. Heat seared up from her toes, burning her cheeks. Oh Lord, she didn't have the sophistication for this. She pointed over her shoulder. "I forgot something in the bedroom. I'll just go—"

He caught her arm. "Stay put."

She didn't know if it was old-fashioned manners or sheer male possessiveness, but she could have kissed Jared for tucking her behind him before he opened the door. Kissed him for those broad shoulders of his that acted as a shield. Kissed him for whatever it was that was holding his anger in check enough to provide her with this courtesy.

"I'm sorry about the interruption earlier," Ian said.

"No harm done," Jared replied.

Raisa felt the weres' combined mental scan. She took a step forward, placing her fingers on the middle of Jared's back. Again he surprised her. First his hand came around to cover hers, and then his energy draped over hers in an impenetrable cloak. She pressed into his back. Let them all believe it was because she was mortified. She was, but also she didn't think she could deal with any more chaos right now. She was getting a headache. And not the good kind.

"You're leaving?" Creed asked.

"I want to get Raisa back to the Circle J."

"I figured that."

"Good thing I brought this over, then." Creed held out a package to Raisa.

Jared intercepted the bundle. "My woman doesn't accept gifts from other men."

Raisa perked up. "It's a present?"

She'd never gotten a present. When she was a child, there'd been no money. When she'd gotten older, there'd been no one close enough to give her one.

Raisa's excitement cascaded through Jared like a waterfall. How the hell could no one have ever gotten her a present? Jared clenched his teeth. "What is it?"

Creed cut Raisa a glance, a conspiratorial smile on his lips. "The latest Jan Vandor novel."

Raisa gasped. "How did you get it?"

"We have a book exchange here. This was an extra copy."

Raisa's excitement spiked along Jared's anger. She very much wanted that book.

"No one has extra copies of her books."

"We do."

Jared blocked her step around him with his arm. The grip of her fingers on his biceps connected them, steadying the jumble of emotion inside—anger, want, jealousy.

"Are you sure?" she asked the wolf, such longing in her voice that Jared wanted to snarl. Raisa had jeopardized the Johnsons' relationship with the D'Nallys, an alliance they desperately needed. She'd betrayed his trust, but she was still his mate and he still wanted to be the one to give her pleasure. Even while he wanted to wring her neck.

It was Ian who answered. "Very sure."

Raisa pinched Jared's back. "Get out of my way."

Her excitement at the gift of a book rolled over him, making his denial harder. "No."

"It's my present."

"From another man." Who had known she had a favorite author when he hadn't.

"So? This is the twenty-first century."

"And if we were still human and he wasn't wolf, that would make a difference?" He shoved the book back at Creed. "Thanks, but no, thanks."

Raisa's hands punched into his back, her knuckles leaving little imprints of pain. "That's my present."

"Presents from wolves come with strings."

"Not this one," Creed interrupted.

"Uh-huh." Even with the mate bond in place, Jared didn't trust Creed as far as he could throw him. The were was too handsome, too male, and had too damn much experience pleasing women. As evidenced by him selecting the perfect gift for Raisa. Jared nodded to Ian while blocking Raisa's next attempt to come out from behind his back. "I want to thank you for your hospitality."

Ian smiled. "It's been amusing having you here."

He just bet.

"By the way, Caleb says since you're coming in, you might as well get in touch."

Jared raised his brow. "How does Caleb know I'm coming in?"

Ian shrugged. "It was a logical assumption that you'd want your mate safe."

Mate. The primitive were description of the marriage he'd put in motion settled easily into his sense of possessiveness. That sense of familiarity pissed the hell out of him. He didn't want a potential Sanctuary collaborator as a wife. He wanted to respect his woman, trust her, not have her hanging around his neck like a liability.

*Then you picked the wrong woman.*

The resentful intrusion into his thoughts hit on his last steady nerve.

*I'm well aware of that.*

Except he wasn't. Not in his gut. And that was playing hell with his sense of logic.

Silence from behind him, and a flicker of . . . hurt? Dammit! Raisa would not make him feel guilty. He grabbed his rifle and guided her through the door. He heard her making her farewells but ignored them, focusing his attention outward, scanning with his energy as the frigid air hit his face. Her heard the rustle of paper behind him, which could only be Creed offering her that damn book. Without looking he said, "Don't, Raisa."

He heard her sigh. "Thank you anyway."

Immediately thereafter, she pinched his arm. The sting did nothing to disguise her disappointment. She'd really wanted that book. Before he caught himself, he gave her hand a sympathetic squeeze. She didn't squeeze back, and when he tested her energy with his, he met stony silence.

He turned when he got to the bottom of the porch steps, that silence poking at him. He raised his rifle in a small salute to the two weres standing on the porch. "Watch your backs."

Ian nodded. "Watch your mate."

Jared kept his face impassive, though a start went through him. Did Ian suspect something? There was nothing in the man's stance or amber eyes to insinuate anything, but Jared couldn't shake the feeling that Ian knew a hell of a lot more than he was letting on.

"I will."

Ian called to Raisa. "It was nice to meet you."

She waved. "Thank you for offering me shelter."

Ian nodded and the smile on his face could only be described as soft. "Anytime you wish it, it is yours."

Jared tucked her under his shoulder. "She won't be needing it."

As Jared turned her away, she called over her shoulder, "But thank you all the same."

Through the gratitude, he could feel the longing and loss within her. She was still thinking about the book. Random scenes invaded his mind, slipping from her to him with an ease that still shocked. Scenes of passion, love, emotion. Scenes of past books she'd loved. Scenes that moved her to the point of sighs. Slices of life that she enjoyed because they were hopes she harbored for herself. Hopes of being loved. Valued. He got them halfway across the yard before he couldn't stand the hammering of her longing anymore. He stopped at the road. "Don't move."

Jared strode back to the porch, cursing himself as an idiot as he stomped up the steps. He shot Ian a glare. "Don't say a fucking word." He held out his hand toward Creed. "Give me the book."

"Thought you didn't want her to have it."

"Shut the hell up."

Jared grabbed the book and turned around, Ian's and Creed's laughter riding his back. Raisa stood before him, hands folded in front of her. Her excitement hit him first, anticipation reaching out ahead of her hands to wrap around the book.

Anger flared within him, but before it could feed on the resentment that another man was giving her this pleasure, another emotion flowed from her to him, sweeping over his anger in a soft kiss of gratitude. She knew how much pride that had cost him.

"Thank you so much."

"Just don't expect me to act like one of the men in that stupid book."

She blinked and then smiled sweetly. "Do not worry."

Her accent was back. The possible "Why" grated. "I can be romantic with the right woman."

She nodded. "I am just not the right woman."

It grated more that she'd leapt to that conclusion. "You made your choice."

"I'm sorry. I had to—"

"Not now."

He didn't want to discuss it where the weres could overhear. He shifted his rifle up onto his shoulder and held her pack open for the book. As she put it in, her scent flowed over him. Everything in him responded with the need to possess and protect. Whether she deserved it or not. Raisa's fingers touched his wrist, lingered. The violence of his emotions eased. He yanked his arm away. He didn't want to be soothed. He wanted to hold on to his anger. He shut his mind to hers, ignoring the growl of protest from his vampire. With a "Keep up," he headed for the tunnel.

They were halfway through the two-mile stretch before Jared realized something was wrong. He couldn't feel the tap of Raisa's energy and couldn't hear the soft scuff of her footfalls. She was no longer following. He turned. She was a hundred feet back, a black-and-white snapshot of distress, on her knees on the frozen floor, her hands clutching her skull as she bent over.

The two seconds it took to get to her stretched like hours. He dropped to his knees beside her, lifting her into his arms, anger forgotten as her sob broke against his throat. He put his hand to her stomach. There were no spasms, no echoes of agony. "What is it?"

Her talons dug through his shirt. "My head," she gasped.

Her head? He brought his hand over hers, feeling the pounding emanating from one spot at the base of her skull. The pain was wrong, discordant. Not a headache, but then what? He slipped his fingers beneath hers and pressed.

She grabbed his wrist and yanked. "Don't!"

There was something hard under the skin, about the size of a pea, a foreign body attached to the top of her spinal cord.

"What the hell is that?"

She pulled his hand away. He allowed it because, until he knew what he was dealing with, he wasn't going to mess with it.

Her brown eyes about melted his heart as they met his. "You were right not to trust me."

"I'll decide what's right and what's not."

And it definitely wasn't right. There was a device implanted in Rai's skull. His fingers itched to go back to that spot. His mind and body pulsed with the urge to remove the object.

"You can't."

He'd been projecting. Another pain swept over her, centralized, sharp, and directed to do damage. Son of a bitch, this had Sanctuary written all over it. "What in hell did they do to you?"

She didn't ask him who he meant. "It's to control me."

"Yeah, I figured that, but for what?"

"I'm supposed to get information."

"On what?"

Her eyes were wild, lost. "On the Renegades, but I'm not good at it, don't know what to look for to satisfy them."

"Which means?"

"Eventually my head will explode."

She was serious. "Like hell."

He put his hand over the spot again, reading the energy. Nobody was popping her head while she was his mate. "You can't control it?"

"If I break the energy, they'll send the detonation signal."

"And since you don't know what that is . . ."

"I won't be able to block it."

Another pain shot through her. He siphoned off as much as he could, thankful that he was already on his knees as the shock of it hit him.

"Can you stop it?"

"Yes."

He thought a second. "By giving them information?"

She nodded and immediately winced. "It's a transmitter."

He hazarded a guess. "Which you turn on."

He took her whimper as a "Yes."

She grabbed his hand and squeezed through the next pain. He held her, sustained her, while his own mind worked. They could use this. "If you give them something, will the pain stop?"

She shrugged. "If they like it, supposedly."

"You don't know?"

She cut him a glare. "It's my first time as an impressed spy. I'm not familiar with all the ins and outs."

Neither was he, but no one had the right to hurt his wife. "Tell them you heard the weres are planning an attack on a compound west of here."

She stared at him for a long time, her gaze searching his, indecision in the depths. She didn't know whether to trust him. He was tempted to let her stew in the same agony consuming him, but then the Sanctuary kicked up the pain in her head. She fell against him, wavering in and out of consciousness. He lifted her chin, her extreme pallor reflecting a ghastly white in his night vision. Her eyes were almost flat black with agony, giving the uncomfortable impression of a corpse.

"The only person you have to fear killing you is me." And he couldn't hurt her, no matter what the provocation.

She blinked. A tear rolled from the corner of her eye. He smoothed his finger over its path, breaking it. "That being the case, you can send the information. They'll like it."

After a pause, she nodded and took a breath. Using his shoulder as a brace, she struggled to her feet.

He stood with her, steadying her with a hand on her arm, the fineness of her build emphasized by the amount of pain she was enduring. She was too delicate for all this shit. "What in hell are you doing now?"

She pointed down the tunnel.

He grabbed her hand again. "Send the information."

She shook her head, cried out, and took one step and then another. He caught her before she could fall.

"Not here," she gasped.

"Why?"

"Because I think," she stumbled again, dragging him forward with her. "I think they can track me when I transmit."

"Can they track you otherwise?"

She shook her head and immediately her knees buckled. "They think it's defective."

He noted the wording. "They think?"

She nodded, moaning as the movement sent pain knifing through her skull. "It took a couple days, but I figured out how to block it."

"How?"

"It's a constant signal. I learned it."

That made sense. "So they can't track you that way?"

"No."

"But they think it's because their equipment is defective?"

"Yes." The look she cast him was wry. "They don't think I'm very bright."

She said that like she was sharing a secret between friends, reminding him again of what he'd thought they had. The trust he'd almost given her. How she'd betrayed him. And as the next wave of pain rolled over her, he didn't damn well care about any of it. Sinner or saint, she was his, and she was going to stop hurting.

"There's one thing I don't understand."

"What?"

"If they sent you out, why are they hunting you?"

She licked her lip. A hard shudder put a quaver in her voice. Sweat dotted her temple. "The ditzy blonde factor."

"I'm not following."

"They think I'm lost." Her whisper was strained. "They're trying to get me back to the right place."

They thought she was just lost. Jared shook his head and stared at her in amazement. One of the smartest women he'd ever met and she'd convinced them she was the type to get lost.

She grimaced and grabbed his hand. "We need to go now."

"Why?"

Sweat beaded her brow, dripped over her cheekbones. "It hurts too much for me to hold out much longer."

"Damn, you are something."

He scooped her up in his arms, wrestling with his rifle as she looped her arms around his neck.

"Good something or bad something?" she asked.

"I don't know."

"But you like it?"

He shook his head, getting to his feet. "At this point, sunbeam, I don't think it matters."

"Oh." Such a small disappointed noise in the midst of such pain and turmoil. It shouldn't have mattered to him that her feelings were hurt. Hell, he didn't even know if she was the enemy. There were also more important things to focus on, like getting her to a place where she could transmit the information to make her pain stop. But it did matter, and he couldn't get that small disappointed "Oh" out of his mind as he ran through the tunnel, scanning as he went, listening to the sounds around them. He stopped at the entrance, manipulated the illusion covering it and then carried her out into the frosty air. She shivered in his arms, with pain or cold he didn't know. She pressed her mouth into his shoulder burying her whimper against his chest.

Son of a bitch! "Make the call."

She shook her head. "Too close."

"How much longer do you have?"

"I don't know."

He stopped dead. "What in hell do you mean you don't know?"

"I told you this is my first time!"

He'd been operating under the assumption she knew how long she had before things got lethal. "You didn't think to ask?"

She shook her head. "It doesn't matter. We can't risk the D'Nallys."

Another bloody bead of sweat dripped down her temple. He swiped at it with his thumb. It was supposed to be a simple gesture, but the minute he touched her skin, his need was to linger. Caress. The same need rasped in his voice. "I'm not risking you."

Raisa patted the back of her neck. "You forgive me?"

He hadn't forgiven her, he hadn't forgotten, but right now, none of that mattered. "You're dead set on this?"

She trembled. "I can't hurt anyone."

Interesting choice of words. Sweat left a dark smear on her pale white skin. A bloodred tear escaped her control, to run in a bright trail down the side of her cheek. Damn stubborn woman. "Then we'd best get going."

He ran, hugging the shadows, aware he was going too fast, aware it wasn't safe, but helpless to do anything else. Every beat of her heart, every whimper that passed her lips was a countdown to a resolution he couldn't accept. Halfway between the were compound and the safe cave he tucked them into a rock fall. Buried in the shadows, he growled, "Make the damn call."

Her pale, bloodless lips shaped around a word. "Where?"

"Far enough from anything pertinent you don't have to worry. Now make the damn transmission."

She closed her eyes and reached behind her head. Her brows drew down into a frown. He waited one minute. Two. He didn't sense any lessening of her pain. "Well?"

"Give me time." She frowned at him from under her lashes. "This isn't as easy as they made it out to be."

"You'd better not be telling me you don't know how to do this."

"Technically, I do."

"You left it to the last minute, and you don't know how to transmit?"

"We don't know this is the last minute."

Considering she was about to pass out, he was pretty sure they were at the last level of whatever system the son-of-a-bitch Sanctuary had put in place. Suddenly the tension in her sharpened.

"Tell me again exactly what I'm supposed to say."

He didn't waste a second. "Tell them you heard the weres are planning an attack on a secret compound west of here."

She focused, licked her lips, and then grabbed him. "If it's not enough, I just want you to know—"

He scooped up a handful of snow and wiped the blood from her face. The shock of the cold snow cut off her statement. "Not now."

"It has to be—"

The pain stopped. She froze, and he stilled right along with her. He scanned, ready to block any incoming energy, but there was nothing. No pain, no energy, just the calm of the night enfolding them in its embrace.

For three heartbeats, Raisa didn't move. Then she smiled, a bright-as-sunshine smile. "It worked."

He wiped the snow and blood from her face with his sleeve, covering the shaking in his hands with brusque movements. He couldn't live like this, ripping between anger and fear. He drew a shield up around her, strong enough to hide her presence from anyone who might be in the area. Hopefully strong enough to scramble any signal that would be sent after them. Or out from them. He glanced down into her smiling face.

"I told you it would."

Her brow arched as the lines the pain had carved in her face eased. "And I should have believed you because . . . ?"

It was hard to look into that open face and see her as a traitor. He set her on her feet. "Because I'm never wrong."

# ❖ 12 ❖

THE sensation came to her across the snap of wind. Fragmented traces of energy—no source, no consistency, blips on her radar, but spaced out in a rough half circle. They were coming for her.

She caught Jared's hand. "Time to go."

His brows snapped down. His energy flared out. "Trouble coming?"

Flickers of flame appeared at the edges of his eyes. Everything in her responded to the image of pure predatory male with an ecstatic declaration of *Mine*. She was in such trouble. "Definitely."

His frown increased. And right along with it, his suspicion. "How many?"

"Three."

He cut her another glance. She could sense the war going on inside him. Whereas he had believed her implicitly before, now he didn't. She got to her feet. "Just because you can't sense them doesn't mean they don't exist." She brushed the snow off her butt. "But just in case you want to stay and chat, expect them to come at you from . . ." She pointed to the right. "There." Straight ahead. "There." She pointed to the left. "And there."

Raisa grabbed her pack off his shoulder and slung it over her own. "I, however, am out of here." She headed in the only direction open to her. Twenty feet later a hand clamped down over her arm. She sighed and glanced up at Jared. His expression was unreadable. Cold as the night, emotion as untraceable as the energy of the approaching weres. Just flickers of what-might-have-beens combined with what was. Doubt, resentment, frustrated anger. Need. It was the need that gave her hope. "What?"

"You're going the wrong way."

"I'm going the way I have to."

"What makes it a have to?"

The urge to confide in him was strong. Illogical, in the face of his doubt. More of the vampire bonding that went so much deeper than a human one. However, Miri had been explicit in the prejudice against her, what would be lost if the wrong person found out, and as far as Raisa could see, Jared was as anti-were as any vampire. "The fact that there are three killers coming at me from the other directions."

He didn't let go of her arm. "We're going this way."

Naturally, his direction involved up. "No, thanks."

He raised an eyebrow at her. "You're better now."

"That doesn't change the fact I'm still morally opposed to going up."

"Well, since I'm morally opposed to being herded like a sheep to the slaughter, I think we'll go up."

She hadn't considered that. "You think there are more ahead of us?"

"What I think is that if we were horses and I wanted to catch us, I'd set up men in a fan pattern behind and let the horse run into the trap I'd set ahead." He paused and lifted his head, scanning she knew. "It's a hell of a lot less work."

Trap. Oh shit. She hadn't even considered that. "I thought they just wanted to kill us." "Us" sounded so much better than "you." She was pretty sure they wanted to kill him. Everyone did, but they had a plan for her.

"I don't think so." He started up the hill, the direction he'd chosen perpendicular to the course she'd sensed the enemy taking. Since he'd clamped her wrist in his hand, she had no choice but to go with him. It was a lot easier levitating, but she still didn't like it. "That doesn't make sense. They just sent me out."

She forgot to adjust for obstacles. She ran into a log, lost her concentration, and landed on her side in the snow. Jared dragged her two feet before he could correct for what had happened. Snow was in her hair, her ears, her eyes, and worse, down the collar of her shirt.

"Son of a bear."

At least he was back to monitoring his language. "I'm sorry."

"If you're hoping to slow me down, you've got another think coming."

Even, she amended, if he did think she was some sort of conniving two-faced evil bitch. His shadow blocked the view of the stars. Beneath the shadowed brim of his hat, his eyes glittered at her like twin flames. He wasn't happy. He grabbed for her arm. She flinched. He paused and bent over her, the sheer size of him blocking out everything else from her field of vision. His fingers touched her cheek and brushed a gob of snow from the edge of her hairline, before sliding around and grabbing a handful of snow from her collar. "What am I going to do with you, sunbeam?"

"Let me go?"

The softness left his mouth. "No."

"That's the vampire side of you talking."

"When it comes to you, baby, there isn't anything else."

That was not something she wanted to hear. She wanted the tenderness of a human for his wife, the care, the consideration, the bigger scope of emotion than the vampire's need to possess. Jared's fingers curled around the back of her neck and lifted. She went with the pressure.

"You do know how to make a girl's heart go pitter-patter."

"Apparently, with you, it's not hard."

"No, it isn't."

Her honesty gave him pause. He blinked before asking, "Don't you have any sense of self-preservation at all?"

She shook the snow out of her hair. "Yes, but I tend to save it for battles worth fighting."

"You don't think I'm worth it?"

"In your present mood, you're completely hopeless." She turned in the direction they'd been going and resolutely started up the hill.

He was right behind her. "You're the one who was sneaking around Ian's office."

She tugged more wet snow from her hair. "You're the one who decided it was for all the wrong reasons."

"Son of a bitch, now you're going to tell me there was a right reason?"

She stopped and put her hands on her hips as he came up to her. "No, because all you want to do is pick a fight and then twist things."

He caught her arm and carried her forward with him. When she tugged, he didn't let go. "I don't think I even have to give it a twitch to have the mess of your logic revealed."

"As I said, picking a fight."

"Dammit, look at it from my side."

"No."

"What in hell do you mean, no?"

"Precisely what I said. I don't care to see things from your point of view."

His grip tightened on her arm. "You are a nutcase."

A few minutes passed in which they continued relentlessly up before he asked, "What in hell would you have done if I'd been the one messing in Ian's private papers?"

"You mean if we had just spent the night in bed together and I had just decided you were worthy to be my husband and had made you so and, therefore, had declared my loyalty to you above all others?"

He eyed her warily. "Yeah."

"You know exactly what I would have done."

"You would have called me a son of a bitch."

"No. That's what you would have done. What you did."

"I protected you."

"By not revealing my supposed duplicity to the weres? By screwing me on the couch with all the emotional connection you would have for a plastic doll?"

His brows came down over his eyes, and anger whipped around them. "Yes."

She smiled her sweetest smile. "Then, I guess I'd better thank you, hadn't I?"

"Don't fu—" Another glare as if his upbringing were her fault and then he said, "Don't bother."

He took four more steps. Long strides that forced her to skip on the third step to keep up. "And I didn't screw you."

Like heck he hadn't. She held on to her temper with difficulty. Fighting with him now would get her nowhere. "I'm sure there's a more colorful term for it, but it's pretty much semantics."

"I was angry."

"You were hurt."

He looked at her hard. "I was angry."

"Fine, you were angry." The man was seriously out of touch with his emotions. She had to skip again. "Could you slow down. My legs aren't as long as yours."

"That depends."

"On what?"

"How fast are the Sanctuary coming up?"

How could she have forgotten about them? She checked the flickers of energy. "Very fast."

"How's your strength holding up?"

"Good, I think."

"You're not sure?"

She rolled her eyes and took a breath to keep from snapping at him. "I've never done this before; therefore, I don't know."

"In that case"—his hand left her arm and slipped around her waist—"lean on me."

She only had time to grab hold on to the back of his shirt under her pack before he took off. Beneath her grip, his muscles worked with smooth precision as he effortlessly carried her across the distance. Trees and rocks flashed by in a blur of gray, streams flashed in slashes of black. And through it all he carried her, without an ounce of strain. She leaned into his side and let his power flow over her as her mind wandered. She wished things could be different, that she'd met him before the Sanctuary had captured her, that there wasn't everything ugly standing between them. That Miri wasn't depending on her. That she hadn't made her promise to keep the secret.

*You asleep down there?*

*No. Just enjoying the ride.*

*Anything on the bad guys.*

How could he make her forget about the bad guys?

*It's my masculine charm.*

*Right.* She'd lost it to the point that she'd forgotten to protect her thoughts.

*They're still following the same course. We're past the one on this side.*

*Good.*

Her side was beginning to hurt.

*Hold on a little longer.*

*I'm fine.*

A brush of his mind over hers. She took the comfort he offered. He owed it to her, after all.

She ignored the snort her unguarded thought drew from him and clung to the moment of softness. Five more minutes and he put her down. She wrapped her arm around her ribs. "Remind me to build up my strength so I can do my own running."

Another strange look crossed his face, and a twitch of his lips preceded his "I'll see what I can do to oblige."

She closed her eyes and counted to five. "I mean, find my own men to feed off, so I can build up my muscle."

"You're not compatible with anyone else, remember?"

He was entirely too smug. "Yet, but the fact that I'm compatible with you raises all sorts of possibilities. I've just got to keep experimenting until I find a few more."

"Starting with Creed?" The predatory warning growl underlying his tone made the decision for her.

"Not at this point. One overly macho pain in the butt this side of forever is enough."

He grabbed her chin and lifted her face to his. "If I catch these pretty fangs going near any other, I'll be ticked."

She jerked her chin, aggravated beyond belief when she couldn't get clear of his grip. "I don't think you can be any more ticked than you are now."

His thumb brushed her lower lip. "Flash those fangs at another man, and see how fast I can turn pure mean."

She slapped his hand away and bared her fangs in a growl of her own. "Threats aren't going to do a thing to move me one way or another."

His thumb pressed into her mouth. "You don't think so?"

"No. And if you want these *pretty little fangs* anywhere near you, then you're going to have to raise your game."

"To what?"

"To one I want to play."


JARED took her to the same cave where they'd spent their first night. This time she wasn't so exhausted that she couldn't appreciate the skill of the illusion that protected the door.

"Nice work," she murmured as he waved it away.

He cocked an eyebrow at her. "I thought you were giving me the silent treatment?"

"I was. You just got the whole treatment."

"Have a hard time keeping your mouth shut, huh?"

She sighed and rubbed her hands up and down her arms. It was dank in the cave. "No. I just can't hold a grudge."

"Seriously?"

"It's the bane of my existence." Especially with Jared. She moved to the back of the cave, to the little room. It would be so much easier if she could hate him, but everything in her just wanted to be with him, however he would take her. When she looked back, the illusion at the front of the cave was replaced. In her night vision, Jared was a stark silhouette of strength and power outlined by the pale yellow of the illusion's energy. "I'm working on fixing it though."

It only took him three strides to get to her side. "Don't fix it on my account."

She watched as he opened the room, memorizing the pattern of the energy he used. "I plan to do it for myself."

The illusion disappeared. The room hadn't gotten any bigger. If she stood in the middle, she could touch the side walls. And lengthwise, well, the only way Jared would fit was if he bent his knees. She remembered how they'd slept before, with him as her bed, her nestled securely in the cradle of his thighs.

She looked over her shoulder at him. He was standing there, staring at the room also. A muscle ticked in his cheek. Because she was still mad at him and because it was the perfect opportunity, she asked, "Afraid being cooped up next to me might create a compromise in your principles?"

His eyes narrowed. "Being close to you won't make me forget what you did."

No. Probably nothing would. Men of honor could be very rigid. She held out her hand. "Could I have my pack please?"

He gave it to her, a tight set to his mouth. "You lied to me."

"No." She dug in her pack for her brush. "I didn't. If you're feeling betrayed, it's because you prefer making assumptions to asking questions. Part of that delusion you have that you're always right."

The minute she put the wide-toothed brush in her hair it snagged on a snarl. She gave it a yank. Out of the corner of her eye she saw Jared's hand twitch. He was furious. Well, tough. She was also getting annoyed all over again.

"I'm not wrong."

She bit back a curse as the snarl grabbed hold of the brush and wouldn't let it go. She tugged at the imprisoned strands. Her day just needed this. "So you keep telling me."

"You're with the Sanctuary."

"So are a lot of women. Doesn't mean I buy into their grand scheme." She got a strand loose. She sat back against the wall. "Heck, I don't even understand what it is."

"They have your picture."

"They also have my DNA. I didn't give it to them willingly, but they still have it." They'd strapped her down and stole it from her for reasons she didn't understand, but the possibilities haunted her. She raised her brows at him, noting the fires in his eyes. "Does that mean I should be shot at sunrise?"

He took one slow breath and then another. Flames glimmered in his eyes. His fingers twitched again. "Vampires would more likely put you to the squad at sunset."

He had missed her point completely, wielding a literal view as if it were a defense against everything, including her. "You are so completely unemotional. It's a wonder you can function at all."

The brush slipped out of her grip, spun, and wrapped in her hair. From the corner of her eye, she could see it dangling. She left it there, a heavy reminder of how much she'd messed this up.

"Whereas you don't have the common sense God gave a gnat." His fingers opened and closed. His arm jerked just a little before he motioned to the brush. "Aren't you going to get that?"

"I think I'll just wait and see if it catches on as a fashion accent."

She fished around in her pack until she felt the soft wool of a blanket. She drew it out, ignoring Jared's frown as she pulled it around her shoulders.

"You're cold?"

She didn't look at him. "No, I just thought I'd see how well the blanket accessorizes with the brush."

In reality, she *was* getting cold, which meant his blood was starting to wear off, which meant in a little bit she was going to have a whole new set of issues to cope with. She drew up her knees and rested her head against them. The brush swung forward, pulling painfully at the trapped hairs. She ignored it along with the moisture it brought to her eyes. She needed a moment to get her emotions together; otherwise, when the pain started, she was going to fall apart like the basket case she was beginning to feel she was.

Jared's long-suffering sigh was almost the straw that broke the camel's back. He sat down beside her. She refused to look at him.

"You can't leave a brush in your hair."

"I can do anything I want."

She felt the weight of the brush lift. "So you told me before, so why don't you want this out?"

Because it was going take concentration and effort, and she just didn't have it to spare right now. "I told you."

"Sunbeam, even you're not so illogical that you expect me to buy into that bunk."

She rubbed her forehead against her knees. "An endearment and an insult in one sentence. Which would you like me to respond to?"

"How about you just sit there and let me take care of your hair?"

"Why would you want to?"

"How about we just say it bothers my sense of logic to leave that brush hanging there?"

She could believe that. She waved one hand. "If leaving it sitting there is going to make you grumpier, run amok."

"It will definitely foul my mood."

The rustle of his clothing against the wall as he shifted position scraped her nerves raw. She didn't want him near her. All his nearness did was make her want to throw herself into his arms. How could she have given herself to such an infuriatingly unfeeling man? Her vampire had a lot to answer for.

She didn't say a word as Jared slipped his fingers under the hank of hair caught in the brush. She did sigh a little as he lifted, taking the sting off her scalp. She waited for his growl, curse, anything that would indicate his frustration with the stubborn curls that first wrapped and then rewrapped around the bristles. There weren't any. He just addressed the problem with endless patience.

As time passed, she began to realize the longer he worked on the snarls, the more muted the anger coming from him became. Apparently, working with her hair was soothing him. For that reason, she didn't complain when her right butt cheek began to feel bruised, just sat there and endured until he slid the brush from her hair with a grunt of satisfaction.

"All done?"

"Yes."

She shifted her weight. He was still angry, but not as touchy as he used to be. Her buttock immediately sent a stab of pain down her leg. "Thank you."

His hand on her shoulder kept her put. "No sense leaving the job undone."

"My butt begs to differ."

His energy immediately poured over her, searching, seeking for the hurt he'd missed.

The flood of concern softened her voice despite her best intentions. "I'm just uncomfortable from the hard floor."

"I can fix that."

"It's not necess—" She never got a chance to finish. With that easy strength that always thrilled her, he lifted her and settled her down on the cushion of his thighs. "Better?"

That depended on what angle she looked at it from. But if she were strictly talking from the perspective of her bruised butt . . . "Yes."

"Good." The press of his fingers in the middle of her shoulder blades was gentle but insistent. "Lean forward."

She did, knowing what he wanted. A touch on her nape had her dropping her head forward. His hand stroked from the crown of her hair to the base, slipping beneath the curls to lift them, holding them . . .

"What are you doing?"

"Just admiring the view."

His comment made her self-conscious. She reached back, covering the strands he held. "It's just hair."

She felt the shake of his head in the slight vibration that shook his body. "With my night vision it's like moonlight rippling on water, and in the light . . ." Another shake of his head. "It's like all the hues of the sun contained in silk."

Jared Johnson, the poet? Next thing she knew he'd be tossing aside logic and going with the moment. "You're obviously overtired."

His chuckle was a harder vibration. "Or maybe you just need to see your hair through my eyes."

"Thanks, I'll pass."

"Now that's a shame."

She sighed and drew her knees up, wrapped her arms around her shins, and rested her forehead on her knees. "I know how you see me."

"Do you?"

"Yes, and I don't need any more blows to my self-image, thank you very much. It's taken me two hundred seventy years, but I'm just beginning to like myself."

"I find that hard to believe."

"You find everything about me hard to accept."

"That's different than believing."

"I'm sure there's logic in there somewhere."

She felt him gather the breath to explain. She held up her hand, forestalling whatever completely sensible, totally ludicrous reasoning he was harboring in regard to the differences between believing and accepting. "You might as well save it. I'm not in the mood for it right now."

She just wanted a moment of peace. No thinking. No arguing, no impending tears. Just peace. As if he, too, were reluctant to disturb the moment, Jared just kept brushing her hair. It felt right, natural to lean back a bit and let him take her weight as he reached her crown, right to stay in his arms after the last snarl had left her hair. Wonderful to let him draw her back against his chest, surrounding her in his strength and his power. The soft click of the brush being set on the rock floor barely broke the moment. And then his fingers were at her temple, rubbing gently, steadily.

She leaned into his massage. "I'll give you five bucks if you never stop."

"And here I'd do it for free."

She turned to look at him. "Why?"

"You're my woman. It's what a man does for his wife."

She turned farther, relying on him to catch her as her balance shifted. "You're the one who thinks I'm scum."

"I don't think you're scum."

"Then what do you think?"

He touched her chin and, with that logical honesty that was so much a part of him, said, "I think you're beautiful. I think you're sweeter than honey, crazier than a horse on loco weed, more fragile than china, aggravating, courageous, and . . ."

He didn't finish. She waited. "And?"

He sighed. "You just might be Sanctuary."

"And if I say differently?"

"It doesn't change the facts."

God, she hated facts. "I guess that says it all."

The man she'd mated with forever didn't trust her. She could feel the cramp gathering in her stomach. As if a bad situation wasn't bad enough, now there was this.

Jared's fingers stopped massaging and moved to her stomach. "You need to feed."

"I'm fine."

The stab of pain tore a gasp past her throat, making a liar out of her.

He presented his wrist to her mouth. "There's no need for you to suffer."

His wrist, as if she were a stranger. The emotional pain of that stabbed deeper than any unfed hunger could. She'd been so stupid to let her heart get involved in this. She shoved Jared's arm aside and rolled off his lap. Grabbing her pack and pushing it up against the wall, she flopped down upon it, punching it into a plumper shape. "I'll pass."

"What in hell is wrong with you?"

"Beyond the fact that I don't like you swearing?"

"Yeah."

Rage boiled up inside her, so did screams, curses, accusations, but she didn't let any of them out. What would be the point? Histrionics wouldn't change anything. Jared's nature would force him to believe what logic told him, and she'd always be on the wrong side of it. The way she had been when her parents had decided to sell her to relatives. The way she had been when she'd been betrayed to the Sanctuary. The way she had been when she'd finally found a man she thought she could love.

Oh God, she could love Jared. Raisa closed her eyes and drew the pack under her cheek. That was such a dangerous thing. The Sanctuary could use it against her, which would endanger him. He could use it against her, which would endanger her. And considering the position she was in, the mission she had yet to complete, that would be a disaster. She brought Miri's face, as she'd last seen her, to mind in vivid detail—the gaunt cheeks, swollen eyes, bloody lip. The desperation. Heard again Miri's admonishment that nothing out here was what it seemed and the Sanctuary had spies everywhere. Raisa shook her head. She didn't know who to trust, who to confide in. Oh God, there was no way this couldn't all blow up in her face.

She gave the pack a punch. Not to mention the fact that, beyond the physical demand between them, Jared didn't seem to want anything to do with her. Two hundred seventy years, from mortal to immortal, and nothing had changed. When it came to her love life, she sure could pick them.

With a sigh, Jared rolled to his feet, stepped over her, and then came down behind her. "You are a stubborn woman, Raisa Slovenski."

She was learning to be. But one thing was for sure, she was never giving more of herself to a relationship than she was getting back. And if that meant resisting Jared, herself, and that wild vampire part of her that didn't care about common sense, so be it.

He curved himself around her back, his hand spreading over her stomach, massaging gently. "You know you're going to have to give in."

"Not if I don't want to."

His lips nuzzled her ear. "But there's the catch. You want to, don't you?"

"No."

His laugh stiffened her resolve. "Liar."

"It could only be lying if I denied I wanted you. I'm not denying that, just stating that I don't intend to give in."

"You're putting yourself through hell for nothing."

"It's my hell. I'll play in it any way I want."

He pressed his wrist against her mouth. "Feed, Raisa."

"No." *Not like you're a stranger.* The thought whipped through her head.

She must have projected because his answer came swift and sure. *I'm not a stranger.*

She closed her eyes, ignored temptation, and gave him the truth. *Like this, you are.*


**THE** pain came at her from the darkness within, ripping at her like shards of broken glass, making mincemeat of her determination. A demon enemy with talons so long they shredded right through all her principles.

Behind her Jared stirred. If he offered her his wrist again, she knew she'd take it. She wasn't a strong woman. Never had been. But she'd always tried to be happy and make others happy, too. It had gotten her very little as a human. Even less as a vampire. She just didn't know how to be anybody else.

With a sigh that stirred the hair at her temples, Jared tugged her onto her back. Night vision and shadows cast his features into an austere blend of angles and planes. Still handsome, just so much more a part of the night. More vampire. He touched the sweat at her temple. For a second his expression softened. "Ah, hell."

His hand slid behind her head, pulling her against him. The heat of his body was like a drug, lulling her, the scent of his skin a lure. His cheek brushed hers. "Why in hell do you have to be so stubborn?"

She didn't have an answer. His knuckle pressed against her chest and then pressed into his own. The scent of blood, rich, life-giving, pain-stopping blood filled her with her next breath. He drew her down.

She shook her head. He cradled her closer, that same softness she'd seen in his expression extending to his touch. "Shh, sunbeam, let me take care of you tonight. Just . . ." His lips grazed the line of her jaw and the slant of her cheekbones, the smoothness of her brow. "You need me, and I want to give you what you need. Just let it be that uncomplicated, this once."

The tiredness in his voice found an echo within her. She slipped her arms around his neck and nodded. She closed her eyes and wiggled her fingers through his hair and opened her mouth over the gift. As her fangs sank carefully into his skin, his moan reverberated around her. His forehead dropped to the top of her head, and his breath sighed out.

*Right.*

The conviction flowed from him to her, entering her along with his essence flowing through her veins, lodging in her heart.

*Yes.* For however long it lasted, this was right.

# ✤ 13 ✤

*F*OR *however long it lasted.*

Raisa couldn't get the thought out of her head. The only thing that lasted long in her life was her hope that the next good thing would be the one to break the mold. Bottom line, the good times in life were short, and expecting too much was the surest way to deprive herself of what enjoyment she could have. The whole expanse of her life, mortal and immortal, she'd never really felt connected to anyone. Not her family, who were so poor just trying to survive took up all their energy. Not with her cousin, who'd seen her as a means to an end, and not as a vampire, which had only put her in the position of something to be used, either for sexual gratification or bizarre experimentation.

Now that she was literally a ticking time bomb, she'd found a man who, though he considered her untrustworthy, treated her with respect and could make her body sing. And she was putting boundaries on their relationship that assumed they really would have an eternity together when in reality, she'd be lucky to have another twenty-four hours. If there was a more idiotic thought process than that, she had yet to come across it.

She closed the wound on Jared's chest with three slow flicks of her tongue. The expansion of his ribs as he sucked in a fast breath was gratifying. At least the man was not immune to her.

His fingers sifted through her hair. "Whatever made you think I was immune to you?"

She had to learn to keep her mind from drifting open to his. She shrugged. "Your general dislike for what you see as my moral code."

"That, sunbeam, has nothing to do with my attraction to you."

She looked up. "You can't be serious."

"I'm always serious."

No, he wasn't, for all he liked to give that impression. "Well then, that's just disgusting."

"Man or vampire, the male of the species is a pretty simple creature."

Raisa propped herself up on his chest, tangling her pinkie in the sprinkling of hair lightly covering the center. "That is not something I'd be bragging about."

His hand cupped the side of her hip, encouraging her up and over. "That's because you're a woman bent on complicating everything."

She followed his lead, angling her hips over his pelvis, the teasing note underlying the statement found her sense of fun as she settled her weight along his body.

"That's not entirely bad," she pointed out as she adjusted her weight. There were real advantages to taking up with a man so much bigger than she. The differences in their heights allowed her cheek to fit naturally into the hollow of his shoulder, the curve of her breast swelled into the hollow of his abdomen, the softness of her stomach cradled his erection, her thighs fell naturally between his. "If you think about it, my complicated thought processes actually rescue your life as a simple male from terminal boredom."

His right eyebrow went up, and the sexiest of half smiles cocked up the corner of his mouth. "It figures you'd see it that way."

"Are you saying you don't?"

"I'm not saying anything that's going to ruin your mood."

She kissed his chin. "Smart man."

"Just keeping it simple."

She could work with simple. "Does that mean you might be open to extending this moment?"

His hand opened on her buttock, the heat searing through the cotton of her jeans. "That would depend on which moment you are talking about."

She could tell he knew what she was referring to from the way his lids dropped down over his eyes, and from the way his expression grew heavy with sensuality. "The moment where you need, and I want to take care of that need."

His gaze measured her reaction. "Nothing's changed."

She shrugged. "And it might never in the time I have left, so why let it ruin what we have?"

Grim determination shadowed desire. His fingers found the base of her skull, pressing on the chip. "You're going to be fine."

Wishing didn't make it so, but a man like Jared didn't just accept the inevitable. He fought it to the grave, and so would she, but not tonight. Tonight she just wanted to pretend no complications existed.

"I know." She let go of that seductively masculine strand of hair. Why settle for a strand of hair when there was much bigger territory to play in? She popped the top button of his shirt and then the next, spreading the material with a stretch of her fingers, exposing the deep groove between his pectorals, the first ridge of his abdominals, the pure perfection of his body. She couldn't take her eyes away. "But right now that's not what I want to focus on."

The next button slipped free. She flattened her palm over his chest. He was hot and hard, and the rhythm of his heart was definitely perking up. His breath pushed his chest into her touch. She smiled, drawing her nail down his breastbone. He shuddered, and when she wiggled her hips, he released that breath on a sexy rumble.

His thumb rubbed against her throat. "You're not going to die."

Not tonight, she didn't think, but she couldn't be sure. She cocked her head to the side and drew her nail back up his chest, heading in a northeasterly direction, not stopping until she met the distraction of the shallow well surrounding his nipple. She circled the small nub tantalizingly. "But if we pretend I am, then we can just enjoy ourselves without all that heavy thinking about the Sanctuary, betrayal, and lack of trust."

Jared gathered her hair up in a ponytail, exposing her face. If it weren't for the change in his breathing, the faster beat of his heart, and the erection throbbing between her thighs, she'd think her touch was having no effect on him whatsoever. He studied her expression intently, no doubt looking for some sign of a trick or indecision on her part. He wasn't going to find any. She'd gotten very good over the years at living in the moment. "You want to play 'let's pretend'?"

He didn't have to sound so skeptical. She unbuttoned three more buttons before spreading his shirt wide. He had a beautiful chest, well muscled with just enough hair to intrigue. "I want to play with you."

As she tugged his shirt free of his pants, she realized it was true. She'd always been the recipient in lovemaking, passively accepting what was handed to her, hoping it was going to be at least a little good, but with Jared, she wanted to be the aggressor, to learn what pleased him the way he knew what pleased her. She wanted to have fun with him. The kind of fun that left them both panting with satisfaction.

Raisa braced herself up on her arms and looked down on him, her hair falling round them, sliding over his skin, looking amazingly light against his darker complexion. His hiss of breath made her smile. And do it again, rocking against him so her hair brushed his chest in silken whips of pleasure while her hips promised him more. Against her finger, his nipple drew to a small tight peak. She flicked it with her nail, her smile broadening at his indrawn hiss of breath. "So, are you going to let me play?"

The harsh line of Jared's mouth softened. Heat deepened the green in his eyes. A half smile took up residence on his mouth as his energy reached out and stroked slowly, deliberately along hers. "I'd be crazy not to, wouldn't I?"

Oh God. Her abdomen clenched on a surge of desire. When he looked at her like that, everything in her snapped to sexual attention. He was such a beautiful man. Ruggedly compelling, all raw masculine power and grace. He was the epitome of sex appeal and little of that had to do with him being vampire. It was hard to get the answer past the constriction of her throat. "Yes, you would."

She eased the right side of his shirt over and then the left, fully exposing the washboard tightness of his abdominal muscles. She poked. There was no give in the man. He was the perfect killing machine. One by one, she flattened her fingers on his chest, centering the demand of his nipple into the hollow of her palm. The perfect lover. She let her other finger ride the hills and valleys of his stomach, heading south to the intriguing area still hidden by his jeans, meeting his gaze. "I bet women have been chasing you your whole life."

"I'm only interested in one."

She flashed him a quick smile. "Good answer."

He tugged on her hair, calling her gaze back to his serious one. "It wasn't a joke."

She petted his chest. "I know." Her fingers naturally drifted down the curve of his pectoral. The roughness of his hair was exciting against the tips. She licked her lips, remembering how those tight curls had felt against her nipples the night before, rasping, sensitizing. "It's just, I'm not really into being serious tonight."

"Suddenly, neither am I." His hand came up to her breast as she rubbed her fingers over the hair on his chest. Little flames flickered at the edges of his irises. Desire thickened his natural drawl. "You liked that, huh?"

"What."

"My chest rubbing on your breasts."

Why did it sound so much *more* when he said it out loud than when she thought it? Her breast peaked to his touch. Pressing back against the flat of his thumb in a wanton invitation he was quick to accept.

"Yes."

His cock surged, brushing the juncture of her thighs in an illicit little touch. Her gasp broadened his smile. "You like that, too? Me wanting you?"

"Do I look like a fool?" She quickly covered his mouth before he could answer with something logical and mood killing. "You're a wonderful lover, Jared. Any woman would be thrilled to be where I am now."

To prove her point, she wiggled her hips down, receiving another of those erotic surges in return. He kissed her palm. His tongue, hot and moist, tickled the center. Raisa cautiously took her hand away, revealing the hint of a smile and the edge of his fangs just visible through the seam of his lips. Her desire honed to the promise within reach.

"I'm not interested in other women."

She smoothed her palm over his chest. He shook his head, lifting his chest into the press of her nails as she found his flat nipple and flicked it.

"Just you."

"Yes." Satisfaction flowed over her. Tonight he was hers, to do with as she wanted. "And I'm really looking forward to indulging myself."

That right eyebrow of his arched up, spicing the intensity of the moment with a hint of humor. "Don't I get a say in that?"

She canted her head to the side. "No, I don't think you do."

He let her hair go, his eyes following how the strands curled about her face, lingering on the one she could feel tickling the corner of her mouth. "Why not?"

"Because no one ever lets me play, and I'm tired of being the doll lying in the bed accepting what comes her way."

"You don't like the way I make love to you?"

Hurt flicked over her with the memory of their last time. "With the exception of that one time, I love it."

He pushed her hair back, studying her expression. "I thought we weren't going to dwell on the past?"

"We're not. I was just explaining."

"Explaining what?"

"That I intend to take advantage of the fact that I don't think it will bother you if I'm on top for a while."

Now both brows went up, along with the corners of his mouth. Whatever he was thinking, he wasn't turned off by the idea. "Looking to take over?"

From another man, the phrasing of the question might have given her pause, but from Jared, she could take it on face value. "Will you let me?"

He flicked the hair off the corner of her mouth, replacing the silky softness with the delicate abrasion of his thumb. "Tell me why first."

"Last night you got to have the pleasure of discovery. You got to find out what made me gasp and shiver." She placed both hands on his chest, loving the hardness of muscle under the firmness of his skin, the utter heat and strength he radiated. Spreading her fingers wide, she drew them down toward his stomach. His breath sucked in, increasing the incline of the ride. "I just want the chance to know you the same way." Her thumbs settled into the ridge defining his abs before gliding to the well of his navel, where they snagged and stuck. "Do you have any objections?"

He arched into her hands, his hips lifting her knees off the floor, pressing his shaft into the cradle of her thighs, and suddenly he wasn't the only one gasping.

"Not a one." The curve to his lips was almost sweet. "Go crazy."

She would, just as soon as she got over the near-divine sensation of his cock pressing up into her core. Her talons sprang free, piercing his skin, leaving behind eight tiny pinpricks of blood.

"Easy."

She yanked her hands from him as her knees reconnected with the cave floor. "I'm so sorry."

With a deft motion he brought her fingers to his lips. "Not a problem." He kissed first the right hand and then the left before replacing them on his chest. "Just want to get to the good part with all my organs intact."

"I'll be careful." She had to be careful. He never hurt her when he touched her. She'd be darned if she'd hurt him.

Again the touch of his fingers on her cheek. "You can sink those pretty little claws into me all you want, sunbeam. I just want you aware when you do it."

"I'll keep that in mind."

With a swift yank, she had his shirttail free of his pants. The twin valleys defining his abs drew her eye. Deep and inviting, they tempted. Working her hips back, she brought her mouth even with the right valley, hovering just above his skin. She took one breath, two, letting the moist air blow across the firm flesh. His stomach sucked in. A trail of goose bumps dotted the path of her breath. Between his flesh and his denims a more intriguing trail opened. She touched her tongue to his skin.

His hands cupped her head. Not pushing, not pulling, but definitely encouraging. He wanted her mouth on him. Just knowing that, feeling the stroke of his energy over her skin in a tangible caress, gave her the courage to continue. Raisa explored the hollow with teasing flicks. He tasted as good as he smelled. Clean, with a slight male musk tinged with salty spice that was addictive. She fumbled with the buttons of his jeans as she brought her lips and teeth into play, nipping and nibbling the tight flesh as she worked her way down, struggling with his jeans, wanting to bite with frustration when the buttons wouldn't give.

Her chin bumped the waistband. She pushed until she couldn't go any farther. And still she couldn't get the darn button undone.

Jared's hand left her head. She caught a blur of movement from the corner of her eyes, and then there was a harsh rasp and the material parted under the slash of his talons. She leaned back, staring at the denser patch of hair positioned so much lower. "Thank you."

His "Anytime" poured over her in a husky timbre that stroked along her arousal, fanning the embers, creating flames of intensity deep inside.

She pressed her finger to the thick base of his shaft, just visible above the V of his fly. A tickle of her nail and he snarled, his energy sinking into her with a wild thrust. His fingers fisted on either side of the material. The touch of her hand on his stilled his wildness. "It's my present. Let me unwrap it."

For a second she didn't think he was going to, his naturally dominant nature wrestling with his promise, but then his thumbs grazed her thighs, sliding inward, rubbing suggestively, warningly. "If you do, don't expect miracles when it comes to my control."

A furtive thrill shot from her head to her toes, bouncing back up to lodge in her center where it tingled and grew. She'd never made a man lose control before. She kissed the pulse pounding in his strong throat, measured it with her lips, her tongue, before answering. "I'll keep it in mind."

She scooted lower, riding the lure of temptation. Her feet bumped into the wall long before she got to her destination. If she wanted this to work, she was going to have to change her plan. She sat back on her heels. Bracing her hands on Jared's rock-hard thighs, she drummed her fingers. "We've got a slight problem."

The glance he shot her from under his brows was full of lazy sensuality, but not a lot of help. She motioned with her hand. "You're going to have to sit up."

He did, that same sexy, languid ease in every movement that said he knew how to stretch the pleasure out, make it last. For both of them. She crawled over him, noting the narrowing of his eyes as she climbed his body, the flare of energy swirling around him. She slowed her movements, holding his gaze as she ran her tongue over her lips, matching her pace to the depth of his respirations. One breath, one foot. Two breaths, two feet.

His hand dropped to her shoulder, and his finger slipped beneath the collar of her turtleneck, playing with the sensitive skin of her neck. "Take off your shirt."

"I thought this was my show."

"It is, but there's no reason I can't enjoy the view of those gorgeous breasts of yours while you're about it."

Her breasts were so small they were almost nonexistent, yet he though they were gorgeous?

"Absolutely." Jared gestured with his finger. "And if you bring them up here, I'll prove it to you."

She shook her hair back over her shoulder, arching her back as she did, feeling wanton and beautiful under the touch of his heated gaze, smiling when his gaze followed the few strands that insisted on falling over her breasts. "Maybe later."

He drew a line from her neck to where the hard protrusion of her nipple poked through her shirt. It was a short journey from base to tip. He climbed it with the diligence of a man climbing Mount Everest, making sure to cover every contingency to pleasure, lingering in those areas that had her shifting, biting her lip, moaning.

His cock stretched down his thigh, fighting the constriction in his jeans. Feeling daring and nervous, she grabbed hold of the bottom of her shirt. The way Jared immediately froze, his attention coming to point, was more potent than the deepest kiss. She lifted the material that first inch.

"Oh yeah."

All it took to complete her metamorphosis to temptress was a glance at Jared's expression. The man was completely enthralled with the prospect of seeing her breasts.

"You're easy, Johnson."

"And you, sunbeam, are gorgeous."

She smiled, pulling the shirt up another inch. "You need glasses."

His thumbs rode up her thighs, dipping into the well between. "No, I need you."

His certainty flowed over her, through her. She pulled the shirt off with a flourish and gave it a toss. She hadn't worn a bra. As the shirt floated to the floor, he growled and lifted her up and over, leaving her kneeling beside him while he stood. She suddenly felt exposed and incredibly vulnerable, which was silly. A rustle of clothing and he was kneeling in front of her. One hand sliding behind her back, the other engulfing her breast.

"Sweet baby, come here."

He pulled her against him—hard, hot, and in charge. His skin melded to hers in a perfect culmination. A tiny sob of pure joy welled.

"You know what I like, Rai?" Dark and sultry, Jared's voice whispered in her ear, rising and falling on husky notes of enticement as he drawled, "I like the way your hair slides across my skin when you kiss me, the heat of your mouth, the delicacy of your build, the way your nipples rise against my tongue with such delicate eagerness. But mostly, I like the way you hold me when I take you, all hot and eager, as if you're holding your world in your hands." His tongue traced her ear. "Nice and tight." He followed the inner curve in searing flicks she had to concentrate to feel. "Very, very tight."

His lips touched the side of her neck. Her womb clutched on a wild flutter of sensation. "Oh God."

"And that," he murmured, sucking the skin into his mouth, extending the shivers, the moment. "I like that best of all."

She tilted her head away, giving him more room to play. "What?"

"The perfect culmination you experience every time I touch you. I bet I could give you a thousand tiny orgasms before you'd need the real thing, couldn't I?"

She nodded her head. He clasped her nipple between his thumb and forefinger, and pressed.

"Oh." Pleasure gathered, bit by bit, with each teasing second, building before shooting outward as he rolled the engorged nipple between his fingers. Her hips bucked against him.

"That's it. Let me feel what I do to you. Share, baby."

She was finding she didn't have a choice. Even though it was completely embarrassing to know everything she was experiencing was transferring to Jared, she was helpless to stop it. He demanded everything from her. Another pinch of his finger, another buck of her hips. An answering groan from him. He pulled her against him. So close she could feel the beat of his heart, the depth of his breath. He wanted her. So much it was a need, yet beneath the desire, there was the hum of determination. Was he counting on this to change anything?

"Jared?"

"I thought we weren't thinking."

He was right; tonight was just about the pleasure they could give each other. She linked her arms around his neck, pressing her breast deeper into his grip, feeling his heat and strength all along her torso. "We're not."

"Good."

She turned her face to his. His mouth found hers. She was expecting a kiss as fierce as the energy pounding though him. Instead, she found gentleness, patience, a lure.

One she couldn't resist. She shifted position to better accommodate the angle, parting her lips to the brush of his tongue, opening wider when he tapped the side of her mouth with his finger. Giving him her pleasured cry as he rolled her nipple with firm pressure, all but crawling into his lap in an effort to get closer. Oh, she needed to be closer.

With a deep growl, Jared's arms came around her, hauling her up against him as the kiss transformed to a hungry seduction. One meant to destroy her inhibitions and release the lust pulsing within.

Her inhibitions were ridiculously weak. More token than substance. Raisa rose onto her knees, pushing her mouth to his, needing more. Demanding more. He gave it to her. Passion and energy crashed over her in a giant wave so strong she thought it would overwhelm her, but then something in her grew, too, rising to the challenge, pouring into the kaleidoscope of emotion coming at her, meeting it, matching it, encouraging it.

She had to have more. She shook her head, understanding riding hard on the heels of the thought, breaking the kiss. No, not have more, give more. She wanted to give to him this time. Placing her hands against his chest, she pushed. Hard. He cupped her head in his hand. Their lips separated with a sibilant glide of flesh on flesh. "What's wrong?"

"Nothing." She nibbled at his jaw, finding the cord of his neck, scraping down, letting him feel her fangs. This time he was the one who shuddered. His grip drew her in. She resisted.

Scooting her feet back, she kissed her way down his magnificent chest. Out of the corner of her eye, she saw his nipple. While much smaller than hers, it was pulled taut. She homed in on it, lapping delicately at first, taking her cue from his hands and his breathing, centering it on her tongue when Jared directed her closer, lapping it before catching it between her teeth.

Both hands cupped her face. His breath hung up in his lungs. There was no doubt he wanted this. She made him wait until his whole body was strung as taut as a wire. And then she gave it to him, a soft bite that pierced his complacency and dragged a curse from his lips. She sipped at the drop of blood that welled, holding his dark gaze as she licked her lips, the passion spiking through him whirling within her.

She lapped the bite, healing the tiny puncture, before kissing his pectoral and nipping the top edge of his muscled stomach. Scooting farther back, her butt rose as her mouth lowered. A slash of her talons, and his cock was free. Hard, hot, and big, it sprang into her hand. She took it into her mouth, sucking lightly at the heavy head, drawing intangible sustenance from him as his pleasure screamed through her mind.

He held her to him, hips jerking to the rhythm she set, his breath coming in searing hisses. Oh yes, she liked him like this, in control but generous. Letting her please him. Giving her pleasure in return. A small slap on the right cheek of her rear made her jump. There was tension in the fabric covering her flesh, and then the cool rush of air over her buttocks. He'd cut her jeans from her. The next slap added more heat to the fire between her thighs. His hand came back down, not to spank but to caress. She pulled her lips back from her fangs, stretching her jaws to align them.

"Damn!"

Both hands landed on her rear in dual incentives. She bit down ever so slightly. His shout exploded into the small cavern. His shaft jerked and thickened. She braced herself for the explosion.

"No, not like this." He dragged her up, away from what she wanted, ignoring her protests as he lifted her.

"Spread your legs." As soon as she complied, Jared was lowering her, slowly, deliberately, until his cock pressed against her opening. Thick and intimidating.

She grabbed his shoulders, her inner tension communicating to him through the press of her talons. "Nice and easy, sunbeam."

She didn't want nice and easy. Her body took him; the soft flesh clinging, rippling, massaging along his length, she took the first few inches. Her knees hit the floor. He steadied her until she caught her balance, and then his hands were on her waist.

"Gently now."

She shook her head. She knew what she wanted. "No. Hard."

"You're new to this."

"Not that new," she gasped.

"Humor me."

She worked him deeper, pleasure pitching her voice to a throaty hum as she met his challenge. "*You* humor *me*."

He laughed, he actually laughed, and then his thumb was there, between her legs, pressing against her clitoris. Once, twice, gathering up her moisture before coming back to swirl delicately. "My pleasure."

"Oh my God."

His eyebrow rose; his amusement flowed with his own desire, tangling with hers, blurring the line between, just flowing and flowing, filling her thoughts even as he filled her body. "It's just the two of us, baby."

Yes, it was. Just him and her, joined together. Her passion, his passion. His thumb on her clitoris, rubbing and stroking. His cock in her body, pulsing and pushing, spreading the burn of his possession to a consuming ache that seared to her core before shooting outward in all-consuming ripples of flame that called to her to burn along with him. She dropped down, crying out at the perfect culmination.

She held them together for an instant, a perfect blend of male and female, her body softening to the demand of his, her heartbeat finding the rhythm of his, holding them together because it would never get better than this and she wanted to savor the moment. Build a memory.

She couldn't hold it forever, though, and when Jared's fingers bit into her hip and his thumb stroked her clitoris, her passion rose in a wild call to his. One he answered with a pulse of his hips, his energy. She rose and dropped back down, moaning at the sheer perfection weaving through the moment. Over and over they moved together in a perfectly choreographed dance, one that blended both pleasure and emotion, twining around them in a golden shimmer of energy that felt so right, drew her so irresistibly.

Raisa buried her face in Jared's throat as it became too much. His lips brushed her ear. "Come for me, sunbeam." His thumb stroked one last perfect time. "Now."

The order ripped through her a half second before her orgasm did. She bucked on him. He caught her with a hand behind her head, keeping her face pressed to his neck. His fangs scrapped her shoulder as his cock thickened and pulsed inside her, bathing her in his seed, his passion. A hot sting and then he was taking from her everything she wanted to give—her blood, her emotions, her thoughts, her secrets. Oh God, her secrets. With a desperate groan, Raisa slammed the mental door closed. As the last ripples of her climax hugged him to her, she prayed she'd been in time.

# ❧ 14 ❧

SHE was hiding again. Jared observed Raisa as she sewed the rip in her jeans with items from the kit she carried in her pack. Nothing of what she felt inside showed in her face. For all intents and purposes she appeared serene. She wasn't, but she could be surprisingly adept at presenting a false facade. That ability had taken him by surprise at the D'Nallys', made him assume the worst, but nothing was a given with Raisa. She had depth, and in those depths lurked a world of hurt, layered in secrets and covered with a belief that, if she just kept going, something, somewhere would eventually change and it would all be good. No matter what happened, she always believed in good, in doing good. Women who believed in doing good weren't coldhearted traitors. But they could be desperate. He sighed mentally.

She was just a slip of a thing. So small he could toss her with a flick of a finger, overpower her with a surge of his mind, yet nothing ever made him feel as vulnerable as she did. With a toss of her head, she could make him forget what he should do and make him burn with the desire just to touch her, and he'd be damned if he knew how to fight it. Or even if he should.

Jared folded his arms across his chest and leaned against the wall. He wanted to growl with frustration. He'd caught her red-handed, riffling through Ian's office. Why couldn't he believe it was that simple? That she was a Sanctuary plant who had suckered him. He'd blame it on pride if something inside him didn't rebel at that description also.

A thick swathe of hair fell over her shoulder. She pushed it back in a now-familiar gesture. The lighter strands at the crown glowed almost white as they shifted. His own little angel, dressed in one of his extra shirts because she was still too shy to sit in her own clothes that would leave her extremities bare. She was a strange mix of bold-ness and modesty. Charmingly sweet and seductive, and as sexy as the groin-baring view of her in a turtleneck and nothing else would be. He liked seeing her in his dark green shirt, the tails barely pre-serving her modesty. He liked the fact that something of his cov-ered her, comforted her. He liked that as much as he didn't like to see her hurting. He sighed again, accepting what he'd tried to ig-nore while clinging to his anger. She was hurting. Because some-where along her life she'd gotten the idea that forgiveness wasn't for her. And in the whirlwind course of their relationship, he'd never given her reason to believe that he had any to offer her. He'd just assumed she'd know she had his loyalty and what that meant. They'd both probably assumed they knew too much about the other, but the assumptions stopped now.

She looked up, feeling his stare, and tugged the needle through the waistband of her jeans. With a jerk of her chin, she indicated his mended pants, forced pleasantness in her expression, also in her voice. "Aren't you glad I came prepared?"

He shifted his stance, letting his eyes roam over her from the top of her head to the tips of her dainty toes. "Oh, I don't know. I like the way you look in my shirt."

"Ha!" She tied a knot and bit off the excess thread. "You'd have a conniption fit if another man saw me this way."

Yes, he would. He eyed the amount of white flesh visible on her right thigh. Creamy and soft, it drew down his fangs in a surge of desire. He'd like to mark her there. A love bite to emphasize his possession. Leaving his scent and energy on her wasn't enough. A human wouldn't recognize them. And that meant they wouldn't recognize her as taken. He didn't want Raisa vulnerable to anyone. She was his. "But," he pointed out, the darkness lifting from his spirit as he accepted the truth that his instincts screamed at him. Rai would not betray him. "There isn't anyone else around."

The lightest of blushes touched her cheeks. "We can't stay here having sex forever."

"Having sex" instead of "making love." A significant choice of words from his little romantic. She was putting distance between them. Building a wall with words behind which she could hide from the hurt she expected him to inflict. He couldn't blame her. Back at the D'Nallys', he'd reacted rather than asked. Expected her trust, rather than let her learn that she could trust. Been impatient when he should have waited her out. And with every minute that passed, he grew more and more certain he'd had hold of the wrong end of the stick when he'd accused her of spying for the Sanctuary. Spies needed a certain hardness to succeed. Raisa was pure softness from head to toe. "I don't see why not."

She stood and shook out the jeans and tucked her foot into the leg. And she managed it without giving him a glimpse of the honeyed territory he was interested in admiring. Dammit.

"Probably because I can feel your impatience to leave all the way over here."

All the way. As if four feet was miles. Tugging the shirttail down, she stuck her other foot into the jeans. With a sexy little wiggle a man could never imitate, followed by a hop that sent her breasts bouncing, she had the jeans up and over her hips. He sighed as she zipped and buttoned and wobbled.

He steadied her with a hand on her arm. "I want Slade to check you out."

Her hand went to the back of her neck where the implant was

buried. "Fine, but don't get your hopes up that he can undo it. The Sanctuary is loaded with geniuses, and I'm pretty convinced they all have a diabolical slant to their minds."

"Ah, but we have Slade."

She smiled slightly as she reached for her turtleneck. "Well, everything will be all right, then."

She was so cute when she was humoring him. "We think of him as our secret weapon."

"Do I look like I'm arguing?"

He waved his hand. "You reek of skepticism."

She turned her back. His shirt slid off those slight shoulders beneath the fall of her hair. The shirt continued the slow glide down, revealing the hollow of her back above the low-slung waist of her jeans. He took the necessary step forward to catch the shirt before it hit the floor. He dropped it on the pack and caught her hips in his hands as he knelt, pressing a kiss into that sweet, feminine hollow. He slid his right hand along her addictively soft skin, cupping her abdomen, connecting the points of her hip bones with the heel of his palm and the tip of his finger as he pulled her into the caress. Her grip dropped to his forearm.

"Jared."

He stood, letting his arm travel upward, along with his body, until her breast rested on the shelf of his forearm. Such a small, dainty gift. His gift from whomever decided which men got blessed. His heart-bruised gift, who didn't understand her importance to him. Brushing his lips over her hair, breathing her scent into his lungs, he drawled, "I made a mistake with you, Raisa, and you're going to have to forgive me for it."

He felt her heart jump, scented the spice of her uncertainty.

"You can't order someone to forgive you."

He smiled into her hair. "Then consider it a request."

"What mistake did you make?"

"I leapt to conclusions."

The tensing of her muscles was infinitesimal. "You caught me red-handed."

"But I never asked at what."

She waved her hand as she added another layer to the wall she was trying to build between them. "Does it matter?"

Yeah. It mattered. The tip of her ear tucked neatly into the seam of his lips. He gave it a little nip, then a kiss, before he made her a promise. "I'm going to take care of you, Raisa. From here on out you can count on that. You first, with nothing between us. Whatever your secrets are, you can trust me with them."

She went absolutely still against him. Just for a heartbeat, but he felt it. Then she patted his arm and pulled her turtleneck over her head as if nothing was amiss. "Thank you."

This was one instance where he was not willing to be humored. Turning her around, he walked her backward, staying close so she couldn't bring her arms down, couldn't untangle them, just had to face him with those pretty breasts exposed, her vulnerability exposed, her fear exposed. He didn't look any lower than her face. He pinned her hands with one of his, the other he cupped under her chin. "The only thing you're accomplishing by hiding whatever it is you're hiding is to endanger us both."

"There's nothing I can tell you that you don't already know."

Not an out-and-out denial but a hedge. "Do you really think word games are going to put me off?"

"I would never think that."

He raised his brow. "And yet you thought it was worth a try."

She tugged her hands. He just stared at her, waiting her out, not letting her go. She sighed and sagged back against the rough stone wall.

"Does this mean our moment is over?"

"Are you ready to confide in me?"

Her lip slipped between her teeth. She bit down, driving the blood from the plump flesh, leaving it pale. "I can't. I promised."

Someone else. "This Miri?"

She nodded.

He pulled her lip free. "Some promises aren't meant to be kept."

"I can't."

"Then how about we talk about something else?"

The relief in her expression showed how little she knew him. "How did you end up at the Sanctuary?"

Pain flashed through her eyes. The slow blink allowed him a glimpse of humiliation before her gaze ducked his. "I was handed over."

"By whom?"

She shook the hair out of her face. Her gaze fastened on a point over his shoulder. "My boyfriend at the time."

She said it with such calm, as if it hadn't mattered, didn't matter, but that would make three times in her life the people she'd trusted had betrayed her. A person didn't just walk away from something like that without scars. "I'm sorry."

She shrugged. "You get used to it."

"Sunbeam, no one gets used to that."

She frowned. "How would you know?"

"Because I know what it feels like to have a choice like that taken away by someone you love."

Her head canted to the side and the frown deepened to twin furrows between her brows. "Who hurt you like that?"

"My brother turned me."

"Against your will?"

"It wasn't Caleb's fault. He was still crazy from the bitch who turned him while he was dying."

"You blame her for your conversion?" She sounded surprised.

"She knew what she was doing. Caleb didn't."

Jared had seen it a thousand times in his head. Caleb down on the ground, gut shot, delirious with the agony and blood loss. And in the falling twilight, she approached. A shadow separating from

the dark—faceless, cold, ruthlessly taking advantage of Caleb's inability to fight. Changing him and then leaving him clueless as to
how to deal with the conversion. How to deal with the first hunger
that had turned him savage because he hadn't known what he'd
become. Hell yes, he blamed the bitch, and when he found her,
she'd pay.

She licked her lips "Maybe she felt sorry for him."

He didn't think so. "And it snows in hell."

"Were you there?"

"No."

"Then you don't—"

He cut her off. "I know."

"There could be other reasons for what—"

"There aren't, and all your color-it-pretty views can't paint it
any differently than it was, because if she'd cared anything at all
about anything except her own amusement, she would have given
him a choice, respected him when he made his decision. At the very
least she would have told him what he'd become rather than leave
us all to find out the hard way."

Raisa paled. "He didn't know what had happened?"

"No."

"That must have been awful."

"We got through."

"I don't see how." Her big brown eyes searched his face, sympathy shining from her, reaching from her, as if after what had happened over two hundred years ago, he would still need comforting
today. Jared didn't want comfort from her. "In the end, there's no
choice involved. Life goes on."

"And you went on."

"Yes. Which doesn't get you off the hook."

She wiggled in his grip. "My arms are getting sore."

"No, they aren't."

He'd been monitoring her very carefully.

"There's a rock digging into my spine."

"I can fix that." He pulled her forward and then slipped his hand between her spine and the wall, easily finding the protruding rock and protecting her from it. She took the move one step further, snuggling those hard tipped breasts into his chest, casting him a glance from under her lashes so hot it singed his short hairs.

"I'm cold."

She was no more cold than he was. With the small amount of blood he'd given her earlier, she could easily regulate her temperature. He had a hard time containing his smile. "What you're bucking for is a spanking."

She rubbed her hips against him, touching her tongue to her full lower lip, leaving it there for a breath-stealing, tempting second. "Promises, promises."

He kissed her because he couldn't help it, his mouth fitting to hers naturally, his tongue easing between the lush curves of her lips, tracing their sultry shape, tasting her, letting her feel his teeth, anticipate his bite. Drawing out the moment for as long as he could before ending the connection with a soft kiss. She was so full of sass and fire. And so determined to distract him from his questioning, he almost felt guilty for continuing. Almost.

"What happened to you at the Sanctuary?"

Rai blinked at him, clearly not yet back on stable footing. Her energy slid over his in a clear invitation that everything in him rose to accept. His cock throbbed, and his senses opened fully to her presence, taking in her scent, her uniquely feminine essence, the rhythm of her heart. If the flick of her satisfaction hadn't touched the edge of his consciousness, he might not have been able to resist.

He repeated the question.

Raisa frowned up at him. "You were much more fun when you were kissing me."

"Tell me what I want to know, and I'll get back to the kissing."

She sighed. "No, you won't. You'll just order me to pack up. And my arms really are beginning to hurt."

He lifted her up and dropped her hands around his neck. Her legs wrapped around his waist. He braced her against the wall.

"Watch the rock."

He shook his head. He'd already compensated for it. "Now, no more excuses; tell me about the Sanctuary."

"There isn't much to tell. I'm not even sure why they wanted me. They took tests initially, and then they just locked me in a room."

"For how long?"

"Four or five years, I think."

He tried to imagine that, being locked in a room for years on end. He couldn't. He needed wide-open spaces and room to roam. Then he tried to imagine being a small woman constantly sick and in pain, locked in a room with Sanctuary males as her guards. Unfortunately, he could all too easily imagine that. He cupped her face in his palm and forced her to look at him.

"Did they hurt you?"

"Nothing happened that I couldn't handle."

Which didn't tell him a damn thing. She had a tendency to think she could handle a lot more than she could.

"Now is not the time for playing word games."

The thought of a man, any man, forcing her ate at him. He should have been with her. He should have been there to protect her. He should have met her earlier.

"I wasn't aware that I was."

Tightening his grip on her hair, he held her gaze to his. If she wanted blunt, he'd give it to her? "Did they rape you?"

"Do you really think that's the worst thing they do to a woman?"

"No." Jared had seen the bodies of the women the Sanctuary had finished with—broken, perverted shells of the vibrant women they'd once been. He touched the nape of her neck, feeling the obscenity of the implant. "But I figured it was a place to start."

Her fingertips massaged the tops of his shoulders in an unconscious effort to soothe. He didn't think she was even aware of making the effort. He was beginning to understand that about her. It was her nature to make peace, comfort, nurture. An inner prompting that commanded everything she did. The same way it was his nature to war, command, and fight.

"There were a few attempts, but they ended when my reputation got around."

For what he couldn't imagine. "Care to explain?"

To his utter shock, she blushed and averted her gaze. "I'd rather not."

Now she had him intrigued. "Why?"

"Because you might think twice about being intimate with me again."

"Honey, there isn't a force in this world that could make that happen."

"Men always think that."

The weariness with which she said that sent a chill down his spine that ended in his balls. "Just exactly what was this reputation?"

"You know that I can manipulate energy, right?"

He nodded.

"Well, there's all kinds of energy."

"I'm not getting your point."

She held up one finger in front of him and slowly, deliberately curled it downward.

If he hadn't been holding her, he would have crossed his legs. "Son of a bitch."

"Exactly." She shrugged. "After the first few times, they were content to slap me around a bit and then just brag about the rest."

And now he wanted to kill somebody. He probed her mind, not caring about finesse, needing the images of the men who'd touched her. He had a glimpse of faces swirling together, expressions of shock, anger, and horror blending into a collage of images. Enough to know there had been more than a few.

Her talons dug into his shoulder before she shut him out. "No fair, cheating."

"It's a husband's right to protect his woman." His fingers unclenched from her hair, letting the springy curls wrap around his hand, letting them bind her to him. "Even when that woman makes it difficult."

That soothing touch rose to his nape. "I don't need protecting from the past."

Though he didn't want it to, the brush of her energy calmed the violence of his. And suddenly he had a very good idea what her attackers experienced. And he was willing to bet they'd never put two and two together. Rai was about as far from a ditzy blonde as a woman could get. "Tell me, did they even know you were the one making them impotent?"

She raised her eyebrows. "Who me? The scatterbrained, emotional blonde? The weak and sickly vampire who was pretty much the laughingstock of the collection?" She shook her head. "No. I'm completely harmless."

Jared smiled and touched the grin lurking at the corner of her mouth. "Almost makes a man pity the sick bastards."

She leaned her head against his chest. She fit nicely under his chin. "Then maybe you could let it go."

"Not a chance in hell." Her start made him shake his head. She needed to understand something about him. "I'm not a tame little teddy bear that you can wrap around your finger or trick into doing what you want, Rai."

"I don't want you risking yourself for me."

"I'm also not a child you need to protect. I'm a man, and I take great exception to anyone taking advantage of you."

"They hardly took advantage."

He placed his thumb over the spot on her upper lip where the memory of a cut lingered. He met her gaze, letting her see his fury, his determination. "They'll pay for touching you."

Her response was another roll of her eyes. "Life is too short to be so hung up on things that can't be changed."

"We're vampires. We've got forever, and maybe you're right, the past can't be changed, but parts of it sure can be corrected."

Her smile dimmed. "I shouldn't have said anything."

She really couldn't give a damn about the Sanctuary bastards being punished. In her mind, she still saw herself as living on borrowed time and that made the past irrelevant. As if anyone hurting her could ever be irrelevant to him. As if he'd ever let anyone who'd hurt her live. "I can protect you, Rai."

Her smile returned. "I certainly hope so."

"You'll be safe at the Circle J." He rubbed gently at the implant. "Slade will take care of this."

"Not if we sit here playing twenty questions."

She had a point. He lifted her arms over his head and stepped back. She unwrapped her legs. He let her slide down his body, groaning as the pleasure of the contact whipped though him. Her soft hiss of breath spoke of her own desire. He helped her untangle the turtleneck and pull it down over her head.

As she tugged the collar down off her face, she said, "You're a very dangerous man, Jared Johnson."

"I try, sunbeam." He turn her in the direction of her stuff and slapped her butt smartly. "Now, go pack up your stuff and let's get moving. The night's wasting."

She shot him a grin over her shoulder that should have made him feel all warm and fuzzy inside. Instead, it just made him want to hug her for the pain it hid.

"You are so predictable."

"Tell me that again tonight."

She stopped mid-bend, giving him a delectable view of her ass. His cock throbbed. The toss of her head was pure challenge, a blatant cover for the stress that lingered beneath the false gaiety. "What do you have planned for tonight?"

He pretended not to notice. The damage to their union needed repair. If faking play created a bridge, he'd take it. "You'll see when we get to the Circle J."

The arch of her brows was a pure feminine challenge. "Is that supposed to be an incentive?"

He grabbed his shirt off the floor and shrugged into it. "Definitely."

**JARED'S** SUV was hidden in a copse of trees about ten miles down the road. In the faint moonlight, it was very hard to see even though Raisa knew where it was supposed to be from Jared's approach. He walked up to an empty space between two big trees. He grabbed at something and yanked. Camouflage netting separated from the surrounding bush. Glows of energy immediately appeared.

Holy heck. Raisa blinked. "What is that?"

She hurried over to the mysterious netting, awe and excitement surging through her at the chance to examine the strange material. Anything that messed with the properties of energy fascinated her.

"Something Slade came up with to cut down on car theft," Jared said, gathering up the edges of the portion he held.

She reached for the netting where it rested on the hood and then stopped, glancing at Jared. "May I?"

He smiled and waved her on. "Go ahead."

Raisa ran her hand under an edge. The energy glow disappeared from around her fingers and the upper part of her palm. The part that was covered by the heavy netting.

"You might want to move your hand."

Jared gave another tug. The netting began to slide down the windshield. "I'll help."

"Get back."

Faster than she could blink, he yanked her out of the way of the tumbling mesh. She fell, slipping out of his grasp. A portion of the netting fell on her foot. It might as well have been the SUV. She couldn't move. There was a strange sucking quality to the weight. Before she was done studying it, Jared pulled her clear. The pressure on her joints was immense.

"Are you okay?" His hands were all over her, probing, searching.

She didn't take her eyes off the netting. She pushed his hands away. "I'm fine."

She rolled up onto her knees and crawled the two feet to the strange mesh. It looked about as substantial as gossamer. She glanced over at Jared as he squatted beside her. "It shouldn't be so heavy."

"Yeah." Jared grabbed the corner and slid the rest off the vehicle. It hit the ground with a solid thump. "Slade's not real happy with that. If you want to get his goat, just ask him how his mesh issue is going."

She lifted the edge. It took all her strength. "What makes it so heavy?"

"It has something to do with the way it absorbs energy."

He didn't make any effort to roll it up. She hazarded a guess as to why. "You can't lift it, can you?"

He shrugged and pushed his Stetson back. "Not yet. I will be able to in a second though. It releases the energy pretty quickly once contact is broken."

"Doesn't it absorb energy from the ground?"

"No. It's not tuned to natural energy. Just mechanical."

She touched it again. So it was tunable. She experimented with a light probe. It felt strange and discordant until she realized that was because she was used to fielding energy that emitted rather than drew. Once she made the adjustment she could sense the pattern.

Jared stood and took a step forward. "That should do it."

He took the edge next to her and tossed it over to the other side. The fabric floated through the air. She got to her feet and grabbed the other corner. She could lift it with one finger. She gripped the edge and brought it up to Jared who held the opposite side.

"This is amazing!"

"I told you Slade was impressive."

She could hear the pride in his voice. He took the edges and folded them lengthwise before rolling it up. "You love your brothers very much, don't you?"

"They're tolerable." As dry as the tone was she could hear the love. Men! Always having to keep things cool. He glanced over at her, those hazel eyes sharpening as he asked, "How about you? Did you have any siblings you were close to?"

"There was such a gap between my sister and I. She was only two when I came to work for Nicholai. So no, there wasn't a chance to really form a relationship."

"I don't think I could have done this without my brothers."

"You mean live as a vampire?"

He nodded, walking over to the truck. She followed as he continued. "It's pretty much always been the Johnsons against the world."

He unlocked the hatch and tossed the netting into what looked like a terra-cotta box. Picking up the lid from the floor, he settled it on the box and then strapped it down.

"What keeps it from draining the energy from the car?"

"The box."

The innocuous looking container sat on what looked to be a rubber bed, no doubt to keep it from being tossed around on the rough mountain roads. If the energy coming off the mesh was intriguing, the energy coming off the box was positively fascinating. She reached for it. He caught her hand. "You can study it later."

The hurt caught her by surprise. She'd forgotten the distrust between them, the time in the cave having lulled her into a false sense of security.

Jared stepped back, taking her with him. He closed the hatch. "We need to get going."

The comment jerked her head up. Was there danger? She scanned, detecting nothing. "I thought we were safe here."

As far as she could tell, nothing stirred.

"There's no such thing as safe anymore." He opened the passenger door. "Your coach awaits."

Just for the heck of it she asked, "What makes you think that I want to go with you?"

"You don't?"

"Maybe, maybe not."

He pointed to a pass way up the mountain. "The next Renegade compound is that way, through there."

"Over the mountain?"

"Exactly."

She glared at him as if the location of the next compound was completely his fault. "I hate up."

"So you told me the first time we met."

"I didn't say a word."

"You whined the whole way."

"I did not!"

"Not out loud, but you sure did project."

She grabbed the handle. "You can't hold me responsible for what you hear when you snoop." Halfway up to the interior, his hand cupped her butt and gave her a boost, not pulling away immediately, lingering to give the sensitive flesh a little squeeze.

"But I can hold you responsible for insisting I can't block you."

"I didn't do that." She gasped, settling into the leather seat.

He smiled at her, one hand on the door frame, the other on the edge of the open door. "The heck you didn't. You have a real problem keeping out of my head."

She couldn't think of anything to say fast enough. The door closed with a decisive click that implied the final word. She grabbed for her seat belt. No way was he having the final word. The problem was, by the time he got settled in his own seat, she still couldn't come up with a response. Dammit. Mostly because it was true, but that didn't mean she liked it.

His grin as he slipped the key in the ignition was knowing.

"Oh, shut up."

"I didn't say a thing."

"You were thinking it."

He raised his eyebrow. "How do you know that?"

"Not because I was in your mind."

His hand cupped her chin, turning her face toward him. "I don't

mind you in my mind, sunbeam. Unlike you, I don't have any secrets, and there's always the upside."

"Upside?"

His eyes gleamed and his grin turned as wolfish as a vampires
could get. "You've got damn sexy energy."

"Oh, for heaven's sake!" She threw up her hands, bizarrely em-
barrassed. "Energy is not sexy. It's just . . . energy."

He actually laughed. "Tell that to me next time you stroke it,
soft and sweet, along my cock."

"I'm . . . I'm . . ." Good grief, what could she say? That she was
sorry? That would just sound ridiculous because there probably wasn't
a man alive who wouldn't enjoy that. Another thought hit her. A
horrifying one. She wasn't always in control of her energy. "Do I do
that to . . . everyone?"

As soon as the words left her mouth she knew she didn't. She
didn't know how, she just knew.

"No." The glance Jared cut her from the corner of his eye was
razor sharp. "That pleasure you reserve just for me."

"If I ever slipped?"

His hand tightened on the wheel before relaxing. The powerful
SUV surged onto the road with a low growl that barely covered the
laugh that rumbled in his throat. "That's not a worry. I keep a very
close eye on your energy."

# ❈ 15 ❈

RAISA grabbed the hand grip above the door as Jared turned the SUV onto what appeared to be little more than a cow path. On either side of the vehicle, along the edges of the woods, she could see and sense flickers of movement.

"Jared?"

"You see the wolves?"

"Yes."

"Don't worry, they're McClarens."

"And that means . . . ?"

"They're friends."

"You have an alliance with more than one were pack?"

"The McClarens are damn near kin. With Ian's pack we have a reciprocal tolerance. As long as no one brings up my younger brother's name, we get along well enough."

Raisa could see "well enough" between vampires and weres still being a scary thing. "What'd he do?"

Jared shrugged and the corner of his mouth twitched. "No one's talking, including Jace. But figuring it's Jace, and figuring no one's talking, it's bad."

"Jace is a troublemaker?"

Jared cut her a surprised glance. "Nah, just a wild card. Never know what's going to take his fancy or how far he's going to take a point."

"And he made a point with Ian's pack?" she hazarded a guess.

"That's our guess."

"That couldn't have been convenient when the Sanctuary made its move."

"It made things sticky up until Ian's natural contrariness came to the fore."

"Ian is what you'd call another wild card?"

Another glance in her direction. "You've met the man, what do you think?"

She remembered Ian's energy. Incredibly strong and intensely focused. She could see him taking a stand on what was important to him and devil take the hindmost. She could also see him not involving himself in issues that did not concern him. He was definitely an all-or-nothing man. "I think he'd be a very bad enemy to have."

He looked surprised.

"What?"

He shrugged. "It just sounds strange coming from you. You're always looking at the upside of everything."

"That was the upside."

"Yeah?"

"For whatever reason, Ian decided not to be your enemy. I'd think you'd consider that a good thing."

More shadows appeared. No longer hiding, wolves ran alongside the SUV, pacing it easily. Their mouths half open in grins that showed very big, very sharp teeth. Rai cast them a wary glance. "You're sure they're on our side?"

Jared smiled. "Positive." He lifted his hand in a casual wave. The largest wolf, with amber fur and light-colored eyes, tilted its head back and barked before veering off to the right.

"And you're right. We were lucky Ian landed on our side of this conflict. Though he could have made the decision a bit sooner than he did."

"When did he make it?"

"When we were knee-deep in Sanctuary warriors and losing badly."

"That would seem like perfect timing to me."

His "It would" was dry.

The SUV hit a rut, about the hundredth in the short drive up the road, bouncing her around and snapping her teeth together. "Uh-huh."

She dug the fingernails of her left hand into the seat and grabbed the hand bar above the window harder. "Are you testing the suspension of this vehicle on purpose?"

His eyes cut to her white-knuckled grip on the seat. "Sorry." He eased off the accelerator. "Just in a hurry to get home."

Home. The word jerked her attention away from the wolves. It suddenly dawned on her that Jared wasn't just taking her to another compound, he was taking her to his home. Where his family and friends lived. Oh shoot. She licked her lips with her suddenly dry tongue. In her day a man only brought a woman home to his family for one reason. Of course, it was no longer her day. And maybe things had changed, but she eyed Jared from under her lashes. This could get sticky.

"What are you going to tell them about me?"

"The truth."

The truth could be umpteen different things, depending from which angle a person looked at it. "And what would that be?"

His energy stroked over hers with the softness of a touch. "That you're my wife."

"That's not the truth."

"It is, if I say it is."

"You can't just declare me your wife."

His eyebrow went up. "Sweetheart, when it comes to pretty little vamps like you, I can do whatever I want, and you know it. Bonding choice is in the hands of the male."

She did. Vampire society was very much a might-makes-right world. Chauvinistic in the extreme. Which was why she'd stayed away from all the male vampires that she possibly could. "And you want to bond with me? Permanently?" She hadn't expected that. There were levels to vampire mating, from very light to the permanent bonding that came from marking. She and Jared were playing somewhere in the middle.

"That's a done deed."

Or so she'd thought. Her heart hung up in her throat, and she asked, "Since when?"

"Since the first time we made love." His hand came to her neck, his fingers slipping beneath the stretchy collar to touch the spot where her shoulder and neck joined. It pulsed at his touch, heated. "But I made it permanent yesterday."

He'd marked her. She slapped his hand aside. "You didn't." She explored the spot with her fingers, felt the increased heat. "What did you do?" Dear God, what had he done?

She tipped the visor down and flipped open the mirror. Pulling the neck of the shirt away, she looked. Energy—bright and pure—tinted red at the edges, radiated off the spot. Oh damn, he'd marked her. She gasped and wheeled on him, only to find him waiting for her. His hand curved around her head and pulled her toward him as he kept one eye on the road.

"You're mine, baby, from now until hell freezes over and we cock up our toes."

She braced her hands on his side. Her muscles were no match for his. She went where he wanted, sliding across the bench seat until her hip met his and her shoulder notched under his. "You had no right."

His lips brushed hers. "I had every right."

She shook her head, ignoring the warmth of his mouth, his pull on her senses. He'd taken her choice away. Risked everything. "You ruined everything."

He shook his head and let her go. "I put it right."

She sat back in her seat, reeling with the ramifications of what this meant. She put her hand back over the spot. "I don't understand, how could I not know?"

"I expect you were a bit distracted at the time."

She wanted to slap him for the satisfied smile on his lips. Not that it would do any good. He'd gotten what he wanted. A claim on her that all other males would recognize. That the Sanctuary would recognize. He'd marked her, branded her. Imprisoned her. Sitting back in her seat, the anger started, building deep inside, gathering strength as it rose. He had no right. "Well, I'm not distracted now."

"What does that mean?"

"I'm not accepting your claim."

She was the most illogical woman he'd ever met, Jared decided. She sat beside him, chin up, resolutely staring out the windshield, arms folded across her chest in a declaration of war. A war she couldn't hope to win. Immortal law was pretty cut and dried when it came to marked matings. They were permanent without revocation, the bond deeper than law.

"For a woman who claims to have embraced the vampire life, you sure are picking and choosing the laws which you intend to follow."

"Well, getting married is something I always intended to have a say in."

"Is that why you ended up working in a saloon?"

"One has nothing to do with the other."

"Whoring sure would have cut down on your marriage options."

"The same way my suspected connections to the Sanctuary have ruined my marriage options as a vampire?"

The retort stung. "You act like you didn't want it."

"I didn't!"

"Bullshit." He wrestled the vehicle back on the path as it lurched over a rock. "You were with me all the way."

"In the sex, yes, but I don't remember your asking me if I wanted to spend eternity with you."

That was so much bull. "You agreed to be mine."

There was a pause and then, very deliberately, she clarified, "During climax only."

During climax only, his ass. "Right."

Ahead, the rock wall illusion loomed. The SUV barreled toward it. Beside him, Raisa gasped. Her hand tightened on the seat, nails denting the leather. At least she had the sense to be afraid of something. Jared stepped on the accelerator. Her grip transferred to his thigh. The edge of her talons pricked his skin through his jeans. She didn't, however, say a word. She just stared at that mass of rock coming up fast, and breathed through her nose, slowly and steadily, clinging to him in her fear. Suddenly he felt like the ass she'd all but accused him of being. "It's an illusion."

Her grip on his leg didn't ease. "Then, it's a very good one."

"Thank you."

She was still staring straight ahead, but he could feel her energy stretching out, encompassing the illusion, finding the trap.

"Don't."

She stopped probing immediately. "What would have happened if I'd continued?"

"You would have blown us both up."

"Nice touch."

"Thank you." He unlocked the trap, not hiding the secret from her curious mind. She followed his moves easily through the multi-level process, excitement building as he got to the last level, anticipating the correct move before he made it, barely holding herself back from doing it before him.

It was a strange experience, having someone so tuned in to him. Surprisingly, not unwelcome. In many ways, right. The illusion shimmered but held. The SUV shot through. He repaired the protective illusion and pulled his SUV to a halt. "Did those Sanctuary fools really think you were a featherhead?"

Her attention was still on the illusion. "Yes."

"They were idiots."

She shrugged. "They were men."

Apparently his entire gender was in hot water at the moment. Jared rubbed his hand over the back of his neck. She was pretty, even in profile, the slight tilt of her nose over those full lips giving her a tousled pixie look, the point of her jaw emphasizing that she wasn't anyone's idea of easy. "Rai?"

She did look at him then, those chocolate brown eyes flat with anger. "There's nothing to say."

"Not even, I'm sorry?"

"Are you?"

"I'm sorry you didn't realize what was happening."

She turned in the seat, her knee drawing up and to the side in a purely feminine pose that complimented her beauty. Everything about her was lushly, perfectly feminine, from the cream of her skin to the silky beauty of her hair. And it just continued on down to the depth of her soft heart. "Tell me something. If you had to do it over again, knowing you'd find me in Ian's office, would you?"

She wanted him to tell her yes. She was waiting for him to tell her yes. He could feel how much. "That's not what happened."

"But, if it had happened that way?"

Her gaze searched his, no doubt searching for something to hold on to. He didn't have a damn thing to give her. Not before he'd turned vampire and certainly not after. "It didn't, and I'm not going to speculate on otherwise."

"Then tell me, why did you do it?"

"Because I wanted you." Because his vampire had been in control. Because he hadn't been able to stop himself.

"And that made it all right?"

Anger and disappointment edged the question that he was pretty sure was rhetorical. Jared hooked his hand behind her head and dragged her forward, planting a hard kiss on her lips before she could protest.

"No, it doesn't, but it's done and there's no changing it, so we both have to accept it."

Her fingers touched her lips. And then her tongue. "How do you know?"

He couldn't take his eyes off the lazy movement of her pink tongue over her full lower lip. "Know what?"

"Know there's no changing it?"

"No one ever has."

The way her eyes narrowed as she said, "There's a first time for everything," did not give him a warm fuzzy.


**AS** soon as the SUV pulled into the yard, the front door to the house opened. Allie, his brother's wife, came running onto the porch, her long brown hair flaring in the breeze, the smile on her face as broad as her belly, which was about eight months gone with child.

Jared swore and threw open the door. If she hit the stairs at that speed, she'd go headfirst down them. He needn't have worried. Caleb was hot on the heels of his impulsive wife, and if he hadn't been, the two weres on guard duty were at the top step before she reached it.

Jared relaxed against the door. Caleb's expression was grim as he slipped his arm around Allie's waist and caught her hand in his. The weres' faces were just as grim as she took the first step. Allie's "Good grief, you'd think pregnancy had snatched my brain cells bald. I do know how to go up and down stairs" carried to him clearly.

"Jared?"

Jared leaned down and looked into the interior of the SUV. Raisa stared at Allie, her shock evident. "That woman's a vampire."

"Yes." Jared closed his door and came around to Raisa's side, opening the door. She was sitting in the seat staring at Allie as if she were the eighth wonder of the world. Which to the vampires, she was. The few who knew about her condition, that is. Raisa took his hand, letting him help her out of the vehicle, still staring at Allie.

"Vampires can't get pregnant."

"So we're told."

"Jared!" Allie came running—well, waddling—up with her normal enthusiasm.

Her stomach reached him first. Jared steadied her with his hands on her arms. "Careful of my nephew there, Allie."

She waved away his concern. "The baby is fine. And it's going to be a niece."

He leaned down so she could hug him, mentally checking her energy to make sure the small collision hadn't upset anything. Before he'd completed his inventory, Allie was out of his arms and ducking around him.

"And who is this?"

"My wife."

"Your wife?" She spun back and gave him another quick hug before zeroing in on Raisa again. "I'm so happy for you."

He heard a soft gasp and was in time to see Raisa's shock as Allie collided with her in an enthusiastic hug. She wasn't looking at Allie though. Her attention was on Caleb, tracking his progress as if tracking the progress of a stalking cougar.

"At last, a bit more estrogen to balance out the overload of testosterone around here." Allie hugged her again.

Caleb came up beside him. "Think your wife is going to survive the greeting?"

Jared chuckled. "Raisa will survive, but you might want to get in there and save your son from a pancake head."

Caleb grinned. "Allie insists a little jostling isn't going to hurt him."

"The same way she insists it's going to be a girl?"

Even the oldest vampire wouldn't remember a vampire girl being born to a couple.

"Pretty much." Caleb studied him, his green eyes serious. "Are you all right?"

"Yeah. Just a few scuffles, but nothing to write home about." Jared glanced over at the women. Allie was talking up a storm. Raisa was just standing there with that peculiar expression on her face.

"Was Jace able to pick up the slack?"

"Yeah, but he just called in. It was a waste of time."

"The meeting didn't happen?"

"No. It looks like we were spoon-fed a bit of deception."

"Damn." Jut what they needed. Another Sanctuary mystery. "Where's Jace now?"

"He's on his way back. He should be in tomorrow or the next night."

"Good."

Caleb glanced over at Raisa. "About the only thing that came out of this whole trip is the woman you found."

There was a note to Caleb's voice that Jared didn't like. A frown on his face that boded ill.

"You might as well spit out whatever's bothering you."

Instead, Caleb tilted his head to the side and studied Raisa with unnerving intensity. "Introduce me to your woman."

The hairs prickled on the back of Jared's neck. He probed Caleb's mind. It was closed, an event unusual enough to cause concern. "Why?"

"Just do it."

Jared stepped into Caleb's field of vision. "Why?"

"I'm just interested in making the acquaintance of the woman who's managed to evade both Sanctuary and Renegade patrols this last year."

The hell that was it. There was something else going on. The whole time he had been talking, Caleb hadn't taken his eyes off Raisa. And the whole time he'd been staring at Raisa, she'd been staring right back at him, eyes wide, lip between her teeth, anxiety coming off her in waves.

"Come here, Rai," Jared ordered.

She didn't move, just stared at Caleb like he was the Pied Piper from the storybooks. A strange energy arced between the two of them. Jared checked. Caleb didn't have her enthralled.

"What in hell are you doing?"

"I'm not doing a damn thing."

"The hell you're not."

"Uh-huh." Caleb held out his hand. "Allie?"

"What?"

"Come here."

"I'm busy."

Caleb shook his head, stepped around Jared, and took Allie by the arm.

She looked up at him in confusion. "What are you doing?"

Caleb didn't give her any choice, just tugged her three steps away. "I don't think our guest is what you think she is."

"Well, of course not. No one is. That's part of the experience of getting to know someone. Finding out who they are."

Raisa reached out, her hand hovering between them a split second before it dropped to her side.

Caleb shoved Allie behind him. "Derek?"

The big were came up immediately. "Take Allie inside."

Allie dug in her heels. "Get macho on me, Derek, and you're going to be swallowing your balls."

Derek smiled at the warning but didn't haul Allie away, more than likely for fear of hurting the baby than anything else. As leader of the McClarens, he didn't fear much, but he did have a were's respect for a pregnant woman.

"Now is not the time to get stubborn, Allie," Caleb advised, without looking at his wife. All his energy seemed to be projected at Raisa.

Allie folded her arms across her chest above the mound of her belly. "Too late. I passed stubborn three minutes ago."

Jared moved to Raisa's side. This close he could feel her trembling. "What in hell are you doing, Caleb?"

"Do you know who this is, Jared?"

He put his arm around Raisa, absorbing the fine trembling that shook her from head to toe. "My wife?"

Raisa shook her head and stepped to the side. Away from his protection. Was she denying being his wife or denying whatever she was afraid Caleb was going to say?

"Oh, she's more than that. Aren't you, Raisa?"

At that point Jared didn't really damn well care. "Back the hell off, Caleb."

Caleb tipped his hat down, shifting right along with Raisa, keeping himself in front of her, keeping his gaze locked with hers. "No."

A ripple of unease went through the onlookers.

Derek stepped between Allie and Caleb, taking her arm. "You'd better come with me."

"Not until I know what's going on."

"Caleb isn't a man to overreact. If he feels Raisa's a threat, you need to trust him."

"Do you think Raisa's a threat?" Jared asked.

"What should I tell him, Raisa?" Caleb asked.

Around them, other weres stepped in, tightening the circle. Jared sent out a wave of power, driving them back one step. He reached for Raisa. She wasn't there. He looked over his shoulder. She'd taken another step back. Her anguished gaze met his. She shook her head helplessly, those beautiful brown eyes awash in tears. "Caleb, if one of her fucking tears falls, I'm going to rip you a new asshole."

No one had a right to make his sunbeam cry.

"Don't you find it strange, Jared, that on the way to a once-in-a-lifetime opportunity to end this civil war, you come upon an un-claimed woman?"

"No."

He heard Raisa take another step back. "Come here, Raisa."

He didn't know what was going on with Caleb, but he wanted Raisa near enough to protect, if necessary. Raisa didn't obey any better than Allie had.

"And don't you find it interesting," Caleb continued in that same speculative tone, underlain with menace, "that this same woman just happens to be your mate, guaranteeing you'd bring her here at a time when we're keeping the biggest secret we've ever had?"

"Caleb, that's just ridiculous!" Allie exclaimed, from where Derek had placed her. "Raisa's aura is as pure as it gets."

Jared backed toward Raisa. The folded-up picture of Raisa in his pocket crinkled a quiet rasp of suspicion. Inside, a trickle of unease stirred. He met Caleb's gaze. "No."

"I do." Caleb cast a quick glance over his shoulder at Allie. "No disrespect to your assessment of her aura." He motioned to the weres. "That being the case, she needs to be confined."

"No." Jared spun around and threw himself at the closest were, blocking him with his body, shoving Raisa to the side.

*Stay.*

She didn't. With one wide-eyed look of horror at the men bearing down on her, she took off running like her feet had wings, toward the woods on the other side of the square-set lab. Two weres sprinted in pursuit. She looked over her shoulder, screamed, and ran harder.

The scream lingered in Jared's mind. While he knew the weres wouldn't hurt her, Raisa didn't. With a thrust of his elbow, Jared knocked aside the next were that came at him. He threw up his hands and didn't reengage. In wolf culture one man did not come between another and his mate. Bloodlust rose as Rai's terror exploded out toward him in a panicked prayer.

*Oh God! Don't let them get me. Don't let them get me.*

The muscles in his face ached as he morphed. Caleb came into his field of vision. Fangs extended, Jared snarled at him, "Don't."

It was all the warning that he wasn't in control, that he was capable of.

Raisa disappeared behind the lab, the two weres, now in wolf form, loped right behind. They'd catch her soon. The thought of them bringing her down, pinning her, scaring her, hurting her, drove reason from his mind. He reached for her and ran into a wall. She'd closed off her mind.

"Stop it." Allie hollered. Out of the corner of his eye he could see her straining against Derek's hold, one hand on her stomach, the other swinging at the blonde man. Caleb didn't blink. "Think on it, Jared. How convenient has it been? How sudden?"

The men circled, waiting for an order. "Mating can't be faked."

"The Sanctuary has managed to fake a hell of a lot more complex things than need."

"Bullshit." He knew what he felt for Raisa.

*Do you?*

Fuck. How had Caleb managed to get past his guard?

*Because it's weaker* came the immediate response.

Hell!

A scream carried across the yard. It ended abruptly. The energy Jared threw out whiplashed back so fast it made his head spin, blocked way before it reached its destination. The questions was—by whom?

Allie's frustrated scream came hot on the heels of Raisa's. Derek's curse echoed in his ears. Caleb grabbed his arm, yanking him back. Spinning with the move, Jared threw a punch. Blood sprayed from Caleb's nose as the blow landed. Jared snarled. "She thinks they're going to kill her, damn you."

Caleb stumbled back and cursed, but he didn't let go, just hung on, letting his blood soak the bond between them, reminding him of the promises they had made each other.

"She's a threat."

"She's my wife." And she needed him. Instinct taking a tighter hold, obliterating reason, he wrenched his arm free. He had to get to Raisa. Allie took a step forward, nothing more to him in that moment than a potential threat. He bared his fangs and snarled. She gasped as he lunged. Through the red haze of his rage he felt the tendril of energy coming off her. Soft, sweet, gentle. Compassionate. No threat.

Figures moved in his periphery, circling him. He spun around, ready.

"No. Let him go."

Caleb's voice. Caleb's order. Jared snarled at him. Caleb was the reason Raisa thought she was running for her life. The men fell back. And then there was nothing between him and the glowing path of Raisa's energy.

*Hold on, sunbeam.*

The lack of response made him howl inside as he raced after her. He'd kill them. Rip their throats out and feed them alive to the Sanctuary carrion if one hair on her head was disturbed. Jared rounded the edge of the lab. A faint pulse of Raisa's energy reached him. Around her flowed the energy of two weres and a vampire. Only the vampire's energy was strong and vibrating with tension.

Slade. And he was wrapped around Raisa.

With a roar Jared sprang the last few feet, clearing the shed before stopping dead. The two weres who had been chasing Raisa were on the ground, in human form now, rubbing their jaws, looking at Raisa, frowns on their faces. At the edge of the woods beside them, Slade knelt with Raisa in his arms, the skeletal array of winterkill branches a sparse backdrop for the violence strewn about him. Dirt spattered his lab coat and his features were still morphed with vampire rage.

Slade looked up at Jared as he approached, his fingers resting against the side of Raisa's head.

"Yours?" Slade asked.

"Yes." Completely. Forever. Until hell froze over and he gave up his immortal soul to the higher power who had created it. Jared took Raisa's slight weight against him. Her head lolled against his arm.

"She panicked when those two got close, slipped, and hit her head," Slade explained, getting to his feet.

Jared looked at the fallen weres and then at Slade. Sometimes

he forgot how much hard-fisted outlaw still lived in the man beneath that lab coat.

"Thank you."

"Anytime." Slade got to his feet, all six foot one of him radiating
barely contained rage.

Jared melded his energy to Raisa's, calming the lingering panic,
shielding her from the pain in her head. He brushed a kiss across
her cheek, savoring the softness of her skin, her scent.

*Wake up, sunbeam.*

Slade looked past his shoulder to the people approaching. Four
steps and he was between Jared and the group, the curl of his fist,
the flash of his talons reminding Jared that while his brother might
be slow to rile, when he got pissed off, he was the most deadly of
them all, as likely to face off against a tribe of irate Sioux as he was
against a cheating gambler. And when Slade got pissed, it was never
a matter of odds, but of right or wrong. And mistreating a woman
was always wrong in his book. "Since when do Johnsons condone
terrorizing women?" he asked Caleb.

Caleb's energy was as grim as his expression. He stood there
under his brothers' censure, pinching his nostrils to stop the flow of
blood and drawled evenly and carefully, "Since a Sanctuary bitch got
her claws into our brother."

# ❖ 16 ❖

"THE need to call names is a sign of a small mind," Raisa rasped, her hand coming to her head. Jared caught it in his, bringing it down to her chest.

"I'm going to have to agree with that," Allie puffed.

"I told you to stay away," Caleb growled at his wife.

Allie, with her usual disregard for orders she didn't like, waved Caleb's logic away. Instead, she waddled up to him and lifted his hand from his face. She cut a glare at Jared after looking at the wound. "Lucky for you, it'll heal straight." She then cuffed Caleb on the side of his head. "And what do you mean by calling my new sister-in-law names?"

"I have it on good authority that she's Sanctuary."

"I distinctly heard Jared say she was his wife. That makes her your sister-in-law, and it's bad karma to call your new sister names."

"Allie." Caleb's frustration was about to boil over.

"Don't you 'Allie' me." She pressed her hand to her side. "I'm sick of how this war has changed everything, warped everything. No one knows who to trust, everything is suspicious to the point when your brother brings his wife home"—she eyed him meaningfully as she stressed the word "wife""—World War III erupts." She stomped her foot and promptly burst into tears. "I'm not having it anymore, Caleb. Do you hear me?" She wiped at her cheeks. "I'm not."

If Jared hadn't been so torn between keeping Raisa in his arms and killing every male around him, he'd have laughed at his brother's expression. Allie was Caleb's one weakness and her uncharacteristic tendency to burst into tears had had him in a tailspin since about her fourth month of pregnancy.

"This is Renegade business, Allie."

She shook her head, her deep brown hair swinging about her face. She wasn't a classically beautiful woman, but she was always an animated one. "This is family business. My family, so I'm not running along back into the house so you can just get the idea right out of your head."

"In about a minute I'm going to take the choice out of your hands," Caleb growled deep in his throat.

"Is this where I'm supposed to go all weak-kneed and obedient, because if it is, you ought to know I plan on missing my cue."

Raisa's hand touched Jared. He looked down. "I like your sister-in-law."

"You copy her, and I'm paddling your butt."

"Don't believe him, Raisa," Allie called over. "Caleb pulls out the same threat every time he doesn't get his way."

Jared glanced over at Allie, just beginning to appreciate how Allie's free thinking could mesh up unfavorably with the stubborn softness Rai often displayed. "The difference would be that I mean it."

To his surprise, it was Caleb who snorted. "You just go see how far meaning it gets you."

"I can handle my wife."

"Now those are famous last words," Slade put in, his face resuming its normal form. The familiar banter eased over the tension. It was common knowledge that Caleb adored his wife and would cut off his arm before he let anything hurt her. He went to ridiculous lengths to make sure she smiled. Jared brushed his lips over Raisa's hair, breathing in her scent. She placed her fingers over the cut on his knuckle. It immediately felt better.

Caleb rubbed his hand over the back of his neck. "Do you swear she can be trusted, Jared?"

It was just like Caleb to put him on the spot. Jared touched Raisa's hair where it rested against the black of her shirt. If he said no, Caleb would lock her up. If he said yes, he would be swearing she was no threat, and he couldn't say that. Not with the chip in her skull. Raisa's hand fell from his cheek. The cut immediately started stinging.

"It's a pretty straightforward question, Jared."

Yes, it was, but he couldn't bring himself to betray either side.

Raisa blinked and then sat up, moving away from him on the frozen ground. He helped her to her feet. The downed weres sat up, watching her. She shifted away. Jared went with her, curling his lips back from his teeth as the men stood up. Slade fell into step beside him.

Shit, now they were brother against brother.

*No.*

Raisa's denial slipped into his mind. Sad. Resolute.

Raisa pushed her hair off her face and wiped the leaves off her sleeve.

"Raisa."

She ignored his warning. "The person to answer that question should be me."

Caleb's eyebrows went up as he glanced at Jared. "I can see you've got her right under your thumb."

"Shut up, Caleb."

Caleb motioned to Raisa. "Be glad to just as soon as I hear what the little woman has to say."

Allie groaned at the little woman comment and rolled her eyes. "Way to win friends and influence people. That is so not politically correct." She turned to Raisa. "I swear I've been working hard to bring him into this century."

Raisa folded her arms across her chest. Then, when one of the weres collapsed after trying to get up, took a step forward, instinctively reaching out. Her fingers brushed his shirt. There was no missing the motive behind the movement. The man needed help. Raisa tried to provide it. Again, not exactly the behavior of a cold-blooded spy.

"Son of a gun, Slade, for a mild-mannered scientist you sure have a mean fighting style," the were said, getting up. He nodded to Raisa, keeping a safe distance.

"You should have listened when I told you to back off," Slade cut in.

The were wiped the blood from his hand. "Hell, Caleb sent us after her."

"Caleb was wrong."

"That hasn't been determined yet," Caleb interrupted.

Derek took the necessary steps to Raisa's side. He cupped her chin in his hand and tilted her head, studying the bruise forming on her temple. He looked at his men. "You caused this?" .

Ty and Logan, the two weres who had been chasing Raisa, fell in beside him, checking out the injury for themselves, regret putting the frown on their faces. "We didn't realize she thought we were going to hurt her until she panicked at the end."

Derek nodded, accepting the explanation. He touched the bruise with his thumb. "The McClarens apologize for the offense and offer you protection."

An offer of protection from the wolves was all inclusive and to the death, against all comers. It effectively tied Caleb's hands. Ty and Logan took a position slightly in front of Raisa, their position clearly backing the decree. Caleb's curse was as vicious as Allie's pat on his arm was soft. "Sometimes, sweetheart, you have to go with your instincts."

"This isn't a democracy."

Slade grinned. "It doesn't seem to be much of a dictatorship, either."

Jared felt sorry for his brother. Caleb had never wanted to be part of any of this, but when the Sanctuary had gone after his wife, he did what any Johnson would have done. He had taken on the threat. Unfortunately, there was no getting away clean when the conflict was a civil war. And Caleb's natural tendency to bossiness had landed him as one of the leaders. Normally, it would be a source of amusement, but with Raisa's future on the line, Jared didn't appreciate the decision on the table.

"Well, Jared?" Caleb asked, "Can she be trusted?"

Before he could answer, Raisa pushed past the men. "No, I can't."

Caleb took more of Allie's weight as she shifted uncomfortably. "Why not?"

Rai folded her arms across her chest. "You have the reports that tell you why."

"Actually," he watched her, his green eyes alert, his energy probing. "I don't think I do."

Allie rolled her eyes. "At last he sees the light."

Jared reached for Raisa. She slapped at his hands before lifting that chin and squared those shoulders. "You can't protect me from this, Jared."

"The hell I can't."

Caleb's big hand came over Allie's bigger stomach, sheltering their future as he said, "You'd be surprised by what a Johnson can do when he puts his mind to it."

"What's more, you shouldn't protect me." Raisa's gaze dropped to Allie's belly. Her lip came between her teeth. She backed up, cutting him an accusing glare. "You had no right to bring me here. None."

"This is my home."

"It's more than that. It's everything they want."

" 'They' being the Sanctuary?" Caleb asked.

Raisa backed up another step. "Yes."

For all that he looked relaxed, Jared knew Caleb was studying her the same way Slade was, and he was missing nothing. There was an explosion building inside of Raisa. An impatience and frustration that bubbled and welled. "You're not Sanctuary, are you, Raisa?"

"I'm worse." She glanced at Allie. "I'm so sorry."

Jared grabbed her and pulled her close, aware of all the eyes upon them, the speculation. "Enough, baby."

She pressed her face into his chest, her nails digging through his shirt. "But it's a secret. A big secret, and now that I know it, it's only a matter of time before they do."

Jared cupped her head in his hands. His thumb settling on the spot of the implant. "That's not a given."

"It's more likely true than not. You know that. You have to lock me up, drug me, so when they call, I can't answer."

And watch as they blew her up? "Not a chance in hell."

He felt a weight on his shoulder. Caleb's hand. His brother squeezed once. "What's going on, Jared?"

"The Sanctuary put an implant in her head." He kept Rai's face pressed to his chest and met Caleb's gaze. "If she doesn't feed them information they find satisfactory, fast enough, they hurt her. If she doesn't respond or give them what they want, they'll detonate it."

"Son of a bitch."

"That was my reaction."

Raisa stiffened in his arms. He stroked her back. She didn't have to worry. He could, and would, protect her.

Allie came closer, touching Raisa's back. "I think we need to bring back that whole string-them-up thing that was so popular in your day, Caleb."

"It does have its upside." There was a pause during which Caleb looked down on Raisa. His hand moved as if to touch her, then it dropped back. "She's right, Jared, she can't be trusted."

"I said, she can."

Another long silence, and then Derek inserted quietly. "Not at first."

Raisa just stood in Jared's arms, neither condemning nor rejecting him, just accepting his lack of faith as if it was expected. Just one more person owing her loyalty but selling her out.

"You didn't because you know she's right, and we're right."

"And this secret is too big to risk," Derek added.

"No." Jared's fangs surged as Derek moved forward. Being were, Derek would put the life of Allie's child over all else. "Back off."

"You said yourself, I can't be trusted," she reminded him over her shoulder as she strained to get away.

"I didn't say a damn thing."

"You didn't have to."

His silence had said it all. Raisa tried not to focus on that. Tried to stay on the logical reasons. She had a stupid bomb in her head, but it didn't keep her from wishing, deep down inside, that just once in her whole life, someone would put her first. Would she ever grow up?

"If you all are done with the drama, I'd like to make a suggestion."

Everyone turned to face Slade. Mud spattered and wearing a lab coat that should have made him look innocuous, he was in some ways the scariest of the brothers because of the energy that poured off him. Relentless. He was relentless.

"What do you propose?"

Slade shrugged. "I was thinking we'd just take it out. No bomb, no kaboom."

Watching Slade approach was like watching a cougar stalk his prey. He did it with the same intensity, the same unblinking intent.

Allie asked the question on Raisa's tongue. "Can you do that?"

"Not with you within a hundred miles," Caleb retorted.

Slade didn't take his gaze from Raisa's. "Anything can be done."

"Safely," Jared clarified.

Raisa didn't care about safety, she just wanted the bomb gone.

Slade came to a stop in front of her, his head canted to the side. His energy reached out, testing. "It's a bomb. Safely is a relative term."

Jared's response was succinct. "Shit."

"How long do we have before they contact you again?"

"If they do what they did before, a few hours."

He reached for her head. His hands were covered in scars from half-healed wounds. She drew back. "What happened to your hands?"

"One of my experiments didn't work out. Let me see your neck."

Not the kind of information she wanted to hear right before he planned on operating on her. "How did you know the implant's in my neck?"

He shrugged. "The most logical place to put it would be the base of your skull."

Behind her Jared drew a breath and held it. All around them people did the same, an instinctive effort to hold off the inevitable disaster they all feared.

One side of Slade's mouth kicked up in a wry smile. "You can all breathe, I'm just checking where it is and its depth."

Raisa didn't share in the nervous chuckle that rippled through the air. She could feel the probe extending from Slade's hand. Subtle, it was almost the equivalent of a magician's sleight of hand. She caught his wrist. "Not with Jared here."

If Slade blew her up, Jared was not going to be anywhere around. He'd had enough pain in his life. She wasn't leaving him injured, or worse, with the guilt of watching her die and thinking he could have done something about it.

Slade's gaze met hers. "Agreed."

"Agreed, hell."

Jared's forearm locked across her chest, pinning her back against him. "You don't come within ten feet of her unless I'm present."

"That's not your call," Raisa pointed out, not struggling to be free because she could feel the desperation in Jared, the need to protect her at war with the need to protect his family. It was a no-win situation. She understood that even if he couldn't accept it. Slade's response surprised her. "I know what she means to you, Jared. I wouldn't risk her needlessly."

"I don't think you should risk her at all." Allie cut in.

"She's got a bomb in her head, baby. It's all about risk."

"Shut up, Caleb."

Instead of getting angry, the man merely lifted his brow at Allie. "What? That's not the truth?"

"It's not the way I'm coloring it, thank you very much," Raisa interrupted. "And if you keep shattering my rose-colored-glasses view of my situation, I'm liable to freak out."

Immediately, Jared came to attention.

"You tell him, Raisa." Allie piped up. "He so does not get it's all in the perspective."

"In that case, we'd better get you to the lab." Slade slid his arm between Jared's chest and her back, neatly separating her from Jared's embrace. "Because sure as shooting, Caleb's going to put his foot in his mouth within the next few seconds."

"What makes you say that?"

"His need to have the last word."

That was from Jared. He walked beside her, nothing in his expression or his energy implying happiness. She wanted so badly to soothe him, but what could she say? She felt like she was being swept up in a tornado of events. "I'll be fine, Jared."

"You're scared."

"Of course, I'm scared. As everyone keeps pointing out, I have a bomb in my head." Along with a couple more secrets she didn't dare reveal. "But, Jared, I don't want you with me."

He glared at her. "Tough."

She clearly wasn't going to get anywhere this way. She turned to Slade. "I don't want him there."

He glanced at Jared, then Caleb, then back to her. "You don't ask for much."

"Just asking for what I need."

He studied her for a second. If he was questioning her resolve, she only had one answer to give him. She meant it. He sighed and motioned with his hand. Derek and the two other weres grabbed Jared from behind. Relaxed, in the company of his family, he was easily taken off guard, but still it took Caleb's strength added to the weres to subdue Jared.

"Son of a bitch, Raisa."

"This is one of those things I have to do my way." It was an explanation and apology in one.

Jared's *The hell you do* followed her as she walked away.

"**SO** what exactly are we doing?" Slade asked as soon as they stepped into the sterile coolness of his lab.

She looked around the room. It would have done a James Bond movie proud with all its beeping lights and impressive lineup of monitors, computers, and other gizmos she didn't recognize. She took a breath and rubbed her hands up and down her arms. Terror and flight had taken its toll on her strength. She wasn't heavily depleted, but she was definitely diminished.

"Are you feeling all right?"

"Yes, why do you ask?"

"You're rubbing your arms, which would suggest you're cold."

Except vampires didn't get cold. Healthy ones at least. "Nervous habit."

"Hmm." That hazel gaze of his, so much like Jared's, ran over her. "How long have you been a vampire?"

She knew where he was going but didn't see any way to avoid it. "Two hundred seventy years."

"Long time to be holding on to a habit."

Smart men, she decided, once and for all, were annoying. "It hasn't been that long."

He motioned her to an office chair over by a very fancy-looking screen. "Oh?"

She sat in the chair, scooting back and resting her feet on the pedestal bottom. "I'm probably the most sickly vampire in history."

He grabbed another chair and wheeled it over. He spun it around and straddled it, folding his hands across the top. "How so?"

He looked very relaxed. Too relaxed. "Don't you want to check out my implant?"

"Right now, I'm more curious about this sickliness."

The screen beside her flashed in an exploding pattern, the burst of light making her jump.

"It's not relevant."

"How do you know? The implant could be linked to your chemistry."

"It's not."

"You know this because . . . ?"

"Because Jared's blood made me better, but the implant hasn't changed."

He straightened. "Better how? What happened before?"

"Pretty much, taking blood has always been a miserable experience for me. It kept me alive but made me violently sick. Almost like I was allergic."

"You don't look sick now."

"Apparently Jared's blood doesn't have that effect on me."

Slade's eyes narrowed, his thick lashes shadowing the thought processes going on behind his lowered lids. Something that made her very uncomfortable. "What?"

"Nothing. Just thinking."

"Care to think out loud?"

He shook his head. "It ruins my thought processes."

She had her suspicions that wasn't the truth, but she didn't know him well enough to argue it. "And what are your thought processes telling you?"

"That between your difficulties in accepting blood and your ability to manipulate energy, you're going to be interesting to study."

"Why do I suddenly feel like a speck under a microscope?"

His chair creaked as he stood. His smile was as subtle as his energy as it skated the edges of hers. "I have no idea." He made a quick circle with his finger. "Open up and say 'Ah.'"

He wasn't talking about her mouth. "If you fiddle with the implant, it will send an alarm back to the Sanctuary."

"It won't self-detonate?"

"Not that they told me, but—"

"That doesn't mean anything when dealing with the Sanctuary," he finished for her. He motioned with his hand. "I'll be careful."

She forced herself to relax and open her mind. His first touch was light. She braced herself for the mind probe every man indulged in, but Slade was very single-minded in his approach, focusing on the energy humming from the device. Touching on the energy with which she countered the homing signal.

"You're blocking the tracking component." He glanced up, his eyes more blue than green. "Do they know?"

She shook her head. "They think it's defective."

His eyebrows flicked up and then down. "Nice work."

He sounded sincere. "Thank you."

It was strange to be talking with someone as they probed her mind, but the purely analytical way Slade went about it made it less offensive than it normally would be.

"Do me a favor while I'm doing this?"

"What?"

"Breathe in my scent and tell me your gut reaction."

She did. He smelled clean and slightly metallic from the things he worked with. Trace scents of dirt from the spatter on his coat mixed in. Underneath it all was a pleasant masculine scent. Nothing to really bother her. But the voice inside shrieked, *Wrong*.

"You smell fine."

His eyebrows rose. She felt him testing the vibration at the attachment point to her spinal column. "That was your gut reaction?"

She shrugged. "That's all that's important."

He tilted her head to the side, his finger pressing into her nape. "How about you let me be the judge of that?"

He pressed on a sensitive spot. "Ow."

"Sorry. Now give. What was your gut reaction?"

She pulled away and closed off her energy, rubbing the spot on her neck. "You smell wrong."

"Interesting."

What was interesting was he wasn't surprised. "Why aren't you surprised?"

"Allie had the same problem when she got pregnant."

"I'm not pregnant."

He straddled the chair again, exuding that easy Johnson charm she'd noticed so inherent in the brothers' mannerisms. It came from the inner confidence that they carried forward from their previous lives. Unlike her, who carried forward a legacy of uncertainty.

"I know, which just makes it more interesting."

"Why am I feeling like that speck under the microscope again?"

He smiled. "I have no idea."

"So, can you take it out?"

"Yup."

She froze. "Then why is it still in there?"

"Because I want to talk about something before Jared comes barging in here."

"What makes you think he's going to barge in?"

"Because no one can keep Jared from what he wants, and he definitely wants you."

"He doesn't even trust me."

"That's a nit."

"Not to me."

"That's just because you don't understand the man."

"What don't I understand?"

He smiled. "That's for me to know and you to find out."

"You are as much a pain in the rear as your brother."

He pointed with a lazy movement of his hand. "That'd have a whole lot more impact if you put a cuss or two in there."

She sighed. "It never sounds right when I try it."

"Probably doesn't sound any more right than Jared marrying up with a woman he doesn't trust."

She wasn't going there. She wasn't letting him build false hopes in her. She'd had too many in the past, and it'd never worked out. "What did you want to talk about?"

"Why don't you want me to remove the implant?"

"How did you know?"

"There were things I should have been seeing that I wasn't."

Maybe when she was in the libraries, she should have spent more time in the science section. "Have I mentioned how much I hate smart men?"

"Not out loud."

She rolled her eyes. "I thought you weren't paying attention."

"There's always bleed over."

"So Jared says."

"I'm sure it's not the same."

"It better the hell not be."

Raisa spun around. Jared. He stood just inside the door, moonlight casting him in a silhouette of power. He moved, coming forward with long strides. As he stepped into the light, the bruises on his face and the cut over his left eye rendered her first question of how he got here irrelevant. He'd fought his way to her side. Because he was worried about her. Was still worried about her. And she didn't deserve it.

"Deserve it or not, he's your problem," Slade said dryly.

Darn it, she'd been projecting again.

Slade pushed his chair away, letting it roll him over to another computer at the glass-top table adjacent to a weird-looking device.

She glared at Slade and then glanced at Jared. He looked angry enough to spit bullets. "Gee, thanks."

No woman in her right mind met a man as angry as Jared at a disadvantage. She made it halfway to her feet before Jared reached her. She braced herself for his yell, leaving her totally unprepared for his kiss. He hooked his arm around her waist. She caught herself with her hands on his shoulders as he lifted her up. Her head fell back into his shoulder. She braced herself for the descent of his mouth. When it came, she took his anger and fear. He was coming at her too fast, too hard for her to give him anything else but understanding.

She opened her mouth at the stroke of his tongue, clinging to his shoulders as he bent her back, dominating her body, her mouth, her mind, and right at the moment she was about to flip from understanding to anger, it gentled and became something else. Something softer, hungrier, something that called up all the emotions she was trying so hard to keep hidden.

"I should probably point out, before this goes much further, you two are not alone."

Jared's fingers clenched in her hair, holding her still for the last sweep of his tongue before drawing a breath away. His gaze locked with hers, his hazel eyes now almost completely green from the emotions pouring through him. "If you ever try to keep me from you again," he whispered, "you won't like the consequences."

"Stop threatening me."

"That wasn't a threat."

With a sigh, she touched a bruise on his cheekbone. "Are you hurt?"

"Just a scuffle."

His fingertips touched her temple and followed the shape of her face down to her chin. "Are you okay?"

"Not a mark on me."

He frowned. "That doesn't answer my question."

Rats. He was beginning to catch on to her evasive tactics. "I'm not hurt at all."

Slade punched some buttons on a keyboard. "Keep that line of questioning up, Jared, and you're going to hurt my feelings."

"Hurt feelings are not my concern."

"Fine." More taps on the keyboard. "Then maybe you can make this a priority because until I have an answer, I can't remove the implant." He turned the screen toward them. "Who's Miri?"

# ❧ 17 ❧

SLADE had peeked after all.

Rai stared at the screen, frozen in the horror at the gravity of her failure. Miri's face stared back at her, unscarred, with full cheeks that spoke of health. Her dream version of Miri. The way she preferred to think of her. And in her eyes, dear God, in her eyes there was such joy, such a love of life Raisa almost didn't recognize her. In that picture, she was a far cry from the pale, tortured, barely sane woman Raisa knew. But there was something in that picture she did recognize: strength.

Miri was the strongest woman Raisa knew. Weathering blows that would have devastated other women, Miri held on, believing in the mate who'd deserted her, believing if she held on long enough, she could save her child. The child who now, thanks to this slip up, might be without hope. She moved away from Jared and Slade. Isolating herself.

*I'm sorry, Miri.*

The need to run was almost overwhelming. The secret was out. For good or bad, it was out. Partially only, but no matter how much she stalled, eventually they'd either pry or figure out the rest. Should she stall? Confess? Lie? Why couldn't she be a natural at this? What was she supposed to do?

"Who's Miri?" Jared asked, holding her gaze, every ounce of his formidable personality focused on her.

"No one important to you."

It wasn't a lie. She'd promised Miri she would find Miri's mate and only reveal her secret to him. Jared wasn't Miri's mate. "Is she in trouble?" Slade asked.

So much trouble, but confiding in the wrong person would put the nail in her coffin. Miri had been emphatic about that, emphatic about the prejudice and politics that would have most preferring she and her child dead. Raisa glanced helplessly at Slade. Out of the corner of her eye, she saw Jared move. It only took one step for him to reach her, one step for him to draw her into his arms. One step for him to eradicate the emotional distance she'd tried to put between then. His power wrapped around her more seductively than his arms. "Does she need our help, Raisa?"

Yes, she did. Raisa closed her eyes against the urge to tell him everything. To lay the problem at his feet.

"Tell me."

"I can't."

"Tell us," Slade echoed.

They were reading her mind. Oh heavens, she was falling apart. Thoughts spilling over the dam she was putting on them. At least the vital one hadn't poured out. She still had a chance to honor her promise. She opened her hands flat against Jared's chest. "I really can't tell you."

"Because you made a promise?" Slade asked, his voice as smooth as silk, reverberating with an otherworldly undertone.

"Yes." And because she couldn't be responsible for the death of an innocent child and that child had only one hope. Its father. A man who wasn't standing in this room.

"Sometimes breaking a promise is the only way to keep it," Slade stated in a perfectly reasonable tone that resonated with logic. That made such perfect sense. Temptation slid up alongside her resolve. Jared and his brothers were born saviors. Much more suited to this kind of thing than she. If she handed them this burden, they wouldn't bumble along with it as she was doing. They'd know exactly who to trust, and more important, who not to. She opened her mouth. Jared placed his finger over it.

"Cut it out, Slade."

The insidious need to reveal all died an abrupt death, disappearing as quickly as it had come, leaving behind a subtle mental trail of energy that led straight back to Slade. Raisa blinked and stepped out of Jared's arms. They dropped away reluctantly, his fingertips lingering on her skin as she grappled with understanding. "You hypnotized me."

Slade dipped his chin in a slight nod. "Quite effectively, too, if I do say so myself."

She'd have told Slade everything he wanted to know if Jared hadn't stopped his brother. Crossing her arms over her chest, Raisa looked at Jared. Everything they both wanted to know. She took another step back, reinforced her mental barriers. It didn't make sense that Jared had stopped Slade. "Why?"

"The only one with the right to screw with your mind is me."

Lovely. Did that mean she could expect him to start screwing with it forthwith? She licked her lips, her gaze darting to Slade and then back to Jared.

"I wouldn't have realized what you were doing in time."

Jared didn't argue. "No, you wouldn't have."

She could only ask again, "Why?"

"It's your secret, your promise."

Things weren't getting clearer. An inner tightening flicked along her awareness. She clamped down harder on her mental barriers. The tightening continued. In the next heartbeat she recognized it. Hunger. Her hunger was returning. As if things weren't bad enough. She dug her fingers into her arms. "Could you move beyond the short-answer format?"

"I'm your husband. Forcing you to break a promise through a mind rape doesn't sit well with me."

So he'd protected her. Sometimes she thought she'd never understand him. Slade, however ... The other man smiled at her, a shift of muscle that went no further than his lips. "I'm not unnecessarily overburdened with a code of honor."

Except he'd taken on two weres—friends—simply because they had been chasing her, and then he'd stayed with her, protecting her until Jared had come. Yeah, he was devoid of honor. "I'll keep that in mind."

"I'd appreciate it."

The scuff of Jared's boot on the floor jerked her around. "You're not alone anymore, Rai. It's my job to protect your honor as well as my own."

"Even when it's not convenient?"

He nodded, not hiding anything from her. "Even then."

She'd never met anyone like him. The chill of the lab seeped under her skin. "You must be thinking, about now, that it totally sucks being my husband."

"No."

"Even when I can't tell you what you want to know?"

"Even then, but you'd do well to remember you're a Johnson now, and that means you have kin with whom to share your problems."

"Would this be the same kin that sicced a pack of wolves on me when we arrived?"

"The weres were only supposed to bring you back. Your running triggered their actions."

"So you say."

"And to be fair, it was kin who took care of the matter, and the weres have since put you under their protection," Slade added. "Which means you can count on them to help this Miri woman if she needs it."

"So you say."

He shrugged. "So I say."

Jared brought her face back to his with a press of his index finger on the side of her jaw. "It doesn't matter what anyone else says. I give you my word, Rai. I'll do whatever needs to be done to keep solid the promise you made."

"Even if it could cause you trouble with the weres and other Renegades?"

His right eyebrow went up. "It's that kind of promise?"

"Yes."

"Shit."

"Shut up, Slade," Jared snapped out.

"Sorry, just thinking how we're barely on the edge of acceptable now with most of them."

That wasn't good. Raisa knew how strong the Sanctuary was and how small Renegade numbers were, comparatively. "You can't afford to be involved in this, Jared."

He closed the distance between them. "I already am."

She tipped her head back to see his face. "But if you just let me walk out of here, you're none the worse for wear. Things will go on normally. It'll be as if I never existed."

Pain in her arms alerted her to the fact that her nails were cutting into her skin.

Jared smiled, the corner of his lip twitching as he slid his fingers under hers, rubbing the backs of his index fingers over the small stings. "That's the best out you've got to offer me?"

"What more do you need? You haven't exactly been thrilled with being with me."

"There are all sorts of thrills."

His hands slid around her back.

"You don't even like me!"

"You're pretty, sweet, got a sharp wit and a smart mind. What's not to like?"

She folded her arms across her chest, needing the barrier between his heat and her weakness for him. "You don't trust me."

"I can't justify a reason for trusting you, that's true."

For a woman who avoided lying by shading sentence structure, that was a significant phrasing.

*Probably doesn't sound any more right than Jared marrying up with a woman he doesn't trust.*

Could Jared actually trust her on a gut level but be having difficulty accepting that because he couldn't rationalize it?

She wrapped her fingers around his wrist, placing her fingertips on his pulse. It was steady. Constant. Like Jared himself. If she involved him in this, he wouldn't flinch. He'd do what he thought he needed to do.

"You don't want to take this on."

He turned his hand and caught her fingers in his, bringing her palm to his lips. His kiss seared the center. "I already have."

Slade's chair creaked as he leaned back. "In case you haven't figured it out, pretty much we're just waiting on your telling us what kind of crap we're neck deep into."

This wasn't all about them. "What if Caleb objects?"

"Objects to what?"

She spun around toward the door. Caleb stood there. She licked her lips, fortified her mental barriers, and braced herself against Jared's chest. Caleb came out of the shadow into the artificial light. Like Jared's face, what she could see of his under the hat brim was bruised and cut up. Unlike Jared, there was no softness of greeting about him. And the smile on his lips could only be described as cold. In his hand he held a black hat.

Slade asked, "Where's Allie?"

"My wife is resting."

"Resting?" Slade scoffed. "What'd you do, tie her down?"

Caleb shrugged and tossed the hat. Raisa flinched as it came at her. Caleb's eyebrow arched at the instinctive gesture. Jared caught his hat.

"Nothing so drastic," Caleb answered, still watching her. "I mentioned I'd tried some cinnamon buns the next town over that had a unique citrus accent."

"That was a low blow. You know she's not going to be able to rest until she duplicates it."

Caleb leaned his hip on one of the desks. "Which is going to be hard to do without an example."

"Which means she's going to be cooking all night." Jared shook his head, settling his hat on his head. "That's not just cruel, that's evidence of a mean streak."

"It's not my fault the woman has a competitive nature."

"Just your fault that you feed it."

Raisa closed her eyes as the banter continued. The hunger was growing. Her defenses were weakening. It was only a matter of time before Jared noticed.

"Well," Caleb tipped his hat back. "It was either that or tie her down, and I don't have the stomach for the fuss she'd kick up if I tied her."

"Hell," Jared agreed. "No one has the stomach for that."

Caleb waved at the screen. "So who is the pretty lady?"

"A complication," Jared answered, catching Raisa's arm, preventing her from moving away—from Caleb and from him. Not for the first time in her life, she wished she had more strength, the strength to fight physically instead of mentally, because frankly, she was fresh out of ideas, and all it would take for the Johnsons to learn what they wanted to know was for the two of them to combine their psychic powers. With her link to Jared to open up a chink in her armor, they'd succeed.

Providence came in the form of pain. Deep, cramping, blessed, there-is-a-God pain. She wrenched away from Jared, taking two stumbling steps before she was swept up in someone else's arms. Slade was too far away, which only left Caleb. She opened her eyes to see him staring down at her, his expression concerned. "You're hurting." He studied her for a split second before clarifying, his mind brushing hers. "You need to feed."

"It's nothing."

"Why is it you women always say that when you're hungry?"

"We're worried that you'll see us as gluttons?"

His laugh was a surprise. So was the way a smile made him look so approachable.

"Now, you remind me of my wife."

"I'll take that as a compliment."

"You do that."

He carried her over to Slade's worktable. She caught her weight on her palms as he sat her on the edge. With a sweep of his hand he sent papers flying. The expected protest from Slade didn't come. The next pain did. Hard and vicious, doubling her over. She would have fallen off the table if Caleb hadn't caught her. He laid her down easily, catching her head before it could thunk to the cold steel. "The thing you women never seem to realize is that no amount of pain is fine with us. Jared?"

"Right here."

"When's the last time you fed?"

"Two days ago."

"When's the last time she fed?"

"Before we left." He came over to the other side of the table.

"And before that?"

He slipped his hand under her head, supporting her, blessedly familiar, infusing her with the illusion of strength. "Before we rested."

Caleb's head whipped around. "She pregnant?"

Her "No" coincided with Jared's.

"No need to bite my head off. It's a valid question."

"Just an invalid conclusion," Slade murmured.

Raisa glanced to the left. Slade was busy at the computer, frowning at whatever he saw on the screen.

"That, at least, explains why I was able to pierce your shields," Caleb said to Jared. "You're giving her too much."

Was he? Raisa studied Jared's face as Caleb placed his hand on her stomach, absorbing the next contraction of her abdominal muscles. He did look a little pale, but it could be the lighting as much as blood loss.

"Have you been giving me too much?"

"No."

Jared turned to Slade, "This is like what happens with Allie."

Slade tapped some more on the keyboard. "I know."

He didn't look away from the screen. Raisa had a strong urge to throw something at him.

She caught Jared's eye. "Some help he's turning out to be."

He was watching Slade very intently. "Give him time."

"I don't have a lot of that." She balled her hand into a fist and bit back a whimper.

"You're going to have eternity."

Saying it didn't make it so, the same way wishing away the agony of hunger didn't make it stop. The pain clawed inside her, ripping through her control, her reserves, leaving her nerve endings raw and hypersensitive. She couldn't bear the touch of her clothes, the weight of Caleb's hand, or the brush of Jared's fingers over her cheek. She tugged at Caleb's wrist. It didn't do her any good. Like Jared, he was big-boned, heavily muscled, and as stubborn as a mule. And he believed he was helping her.

"Why is it the same?" Caleb growled at Slade.

"If I knew that," Slade answered, "I'd pretty much be in the position to solve all of life's little problems."

"We don't need a solution to all of them, just this one."

"Then you are going to have to wait . . ." He hit three keys in rapid succession. "Until I find it."

"Shit."

Raisa echoed the sentiment. Another wave of pain came at her. She braced herself for its arrival, she blinked when it came to her in a soft echo of its usual force. Above her Caleb flinched. The muscles in his arms jerked. She blinked again. He was diverting the pain. The ease with which he did it spoke of familiarity with the process.

She didn't take her hand from his wrist. "Does Allie hurt like this, too?"

"Not anymore."

"How did you stop it?"

"By giving her what she needed." He pressed his wrist into her thumbnail. Jared's growl filled the room, a real and mental warning. The scent of blood wafted around her. Fresh and powerful. *Wrong.*

She turned her head away.

Caleb's eyes searched her face as his mind skimmed hers. "Just like Allie."

"Allie doesn't like your blood?"

He smiled, showing even white teeth. "She likes my blood just fine."

He stepped back, closing the wound on his wrist.

The hunger burgeoned past the barricade he'd left behind. She might not be able to drink Caleb's blood, but the scent did serve to remind her of what she was missing. With succinct brutality.

"I hate this." It was an empty protest against the inevitable.

Jared rolled her toward him with a hand on her hip. "What's there to love?" She placed her palms on his chest as he lifted her up, panting through the worst of the pain before shaking her head, too aware of the men who watched. "Not here."

He tugged his shirt open. Two of the buttons hit the table in light pings. "Now is not the time to get finicky."

"There's no getting. I'm already there."

"You might as well save your breath, Jared." Caleb observed, looking away from the screen that held Slade mesmerized. "You'd have better luck getting her to undress in public then to get her to feed in public."

"You're my brothers."

"They're not mine." Raisa growled, annoyed at how dense he was being. Feeding was as much sexual as anything else. She was not doing it in front of another man.

"You will if I say so."

She shook her head, wrapping her arms around his neck, stroking her fingers across his nape as the hunger rose to a roar and his scent encompassed her in its perfect embrace.

*Right.*

His big body went rigid against her as the need arced between them.

*This is private between us.*

He didn't argue, just lifted her up and headed for the door. "Then, sunbeam, let's get you to private."

"And you, Slade," Caleb said behind them, "can tell me about the lovely complication on your screen."

**COLD** night air nipped her nose. Raisa shivered. Jared hitched her higher.

"Where are we going?"

"The house."

The house where Allie was baking and presumably weres and others gathered. She pressed her fist into the knot in her stomach. "Isn't there someplace more private we can go?"

If her head exploded later, she did not want to take anyone with her.

Jared stopped dead, his body going hard against hers. Flames licked the edges of his gaze. "Just how noisy are you planning on being?"

It took her a second to realize he wasn't talking about the big bang during which her head exploded. Images spilled from him to her. Images of the two of them entwined, his mouth on her breasts, her head tipped back, an expression of complete carnality on her face as his body blended with hers.

She gasped. "I do not look like that!"

"The hel . . . heck you don't."

Heat burned up from her toes as more pictures poured into her mind, images of all the ways he saw her, all of them of a woman she never saw in the mirror. A lushly sensual woman she never thought she could be. "Oh, for heaven's sake, I'm too old to blush."

She would have smacked him for his immediate grin if it wasn't so engaging to see him smile.

"But you do it so charmingly."

The only way out was to bluff. "You do realize that that's a very old-fashioned expression?"

His path angled to the right. "Lucky for you, I'm an old-fashioned guy."

She tucked her hands inside his shirt, finding the mat of hair, sliding through it until she found his nipple, which was so intriguingly different from hers, yet so similar. She flicked it. His gasp was music to her ears. "Why does that make me lucky?"

His drawl was noticeably thicker as he answered. "Because you're an old-fashioned girl."

"Woman." Some of the changes of the last few centuries she highly approved of.

"My woman," he elaborated.

She didn't have an argument for that. At least that would hold water in light of the way she was stroking him. They stopped in front of a quaint log cabin.

"Where are we?"

"One of the guest cottages. I think you'll find it *private* enough." He leaned over, chuckling as her blush intensified to searing. "Open the door."

She did. He flipped on the lights. She blinked as her regular vision came into play. The bright, cheery southwestern flavor of the decor soothed her. "I never get used to it," she confessed as he set her on her feet.

"What?"

"Night vision. I miss the color."

Like how bright the green of his eyes could be or how the blue flecks added depth to the intelligence and strength she saw when she gazed into them. "I love color," she gasped, grabbing the back of a couch with one hand and her stomach with the other as the next spasm of hunger built.

"Me, too." Jared held her arm for a second. "You okay?"

"Peachy keen."

The quirk of his lips could have been impatience or amusement. "It's almost dawn. I want to secure the place before I take care of you, because afterward, I doubt I'll be thinking at all."

There was no mistaking his meaning. She took her hand off the couch for the split second it took to wave him on. "Safety first."

He glanced at her face. She could feel the sweat gathering there, could only imagine what she looked like. "Maybe you'd better sit down."

Where she was, was fine. Standing with her feet spread, her back bowed, and her fist pressing into her gut seemed to be soothing the beast for a minute. "This is working."

The glance he shot her added the "for now" she'd left off. With one last hesitation, he headed off. She followed him with her senses, relying most heavily on sound. She could hear shutters being drawn in and locked. Doors being opened and then shut. Too many doors for such a small place. He was checking the closets? A spike of alarm shot through her. Immediately, his energy stroked over her with the comfort of a touch.

*I'm the cautious sort.*

Logical and cautious with a tendency to grin. His personality didn't add up unless she factored in the trauma of his conversion. He hadn't wanted that. Being converted against his will by a brother he obviously adored would have left him, as they said these days, conflicted. He'd obviously reconciled with his brother by shifting the blame, and he dealt with the betrayal by being determined not to trust again, but where did that leave her?

"Waiting for me?"

He stood in the doorway, his shoulder leaning against the jamb, one booted foot crossed over the other, his shirt half undone, gaping to showcase the broad expanse of his chest, letting her peek at the washboard perfection of his abs. Beneath his hat his eyes glittered with promise, and below the shadow cast by the brim, his mouth quirked in a sensual grin.

"Yes." She had been waiting for him, this lifetime and the last.

Before she'd been turned she'd envisioned him as her knight in shining armor, the man she'd hoped would come into the fragmented hell of her life and sweep her out of the debris because that's what women did in those days. Hoped, prayed, or finagled for a man to save them. After she'd become vampire, she'd only known the restless aching hunger for more than what she had. A need to fill the emptiness inside her. She'd thought it was because she couldn't find a proper diet, but now, seeing him standing in the hall, his shoulder propped against the doorjamb, his energy stroking around her, she realized the truth. She straightened and held out her hand. "And I think you've kept me waiting long enough."

His eyebrow went up at the softness in her voice. He pushed away from the wall with a languid grace. As intertwined as their energy was, she couldn't miss the start of surprise and desire. She smiled and curled her fingers in invitation. His grin broadened.

He came to her in even strides. One, two, three, and with each step the certainty inside her grew. This was the man she'd spent her life searching for, the man who'd always been meant to be hers, the reason her energy had drawn her to the American West in the first place. Every step she'd taken in her life had been designed to bring her here, to this time.

She tipped her head back as Jared's arms came around her. Her body fitted neatly into his. To this realization. Jared was hers. Why she hadn't been able to resist Caleb's pain when he'd been thinking so hard of his brothers and worrying. She blinked. Oh God, he didn't know she was the one who'd converted Caleb. She licked her lips, remembering how he'd looked that first time she'd seen him, an avenging angel bent on delivering justice, how he'd helped the young couple because she'd asked him to, how he'd kept her warm. She owed him better than a lie. Even one of omission. "There's something I have to tell you."

She didn't want any more interaction between them without him knowing.

His lips grazed her cheek, the corner of her mouth. His need to care for her, his need *for* her poured over her in a blaze of hunger that found an answering yearning in her. She brought her hands up to his back, hugging him to her. She'd come all this way, taken all these years to find him, and in the next second when she confessed everything, it would have all been for nothing.

"Jared."

"What if I tell you I don't want to hear it?"

He caught her earlobe between his teeth.

"Then I'd have to say, you need to."

He bit down gently. "But I don't want to. Not if it's going to take this away."

A shiver shook her from head to toe. She turned her lips into his neck, breathing in the clean, musky scent of his skin. "You always smell so good."

"Not nearly as good as you do. You smell like sweetly spiced honey."

"Honey's all sticky."

He laughed. "I'll work on a better analogy."

She licked her lips and gathered her courage. Another graze of his mouth over her cheek. Another buss to the corner of her mouth. "Remember how the other night you wanted to just forget everything outside the cave existed?" Jared asked.

"Yes."

His fingers played with the bottom of her turtleneck, lifting it and letting it drop, teasing her with the promise of his touch as he tempted her with the option of not disclosing. "I'm asking for that favor for tonight."

"I don't think I can offer that to you."

His palm slid under her shirt to rest against the hollow of her spine, the heat from his touch extending from side to side. "Why not?"

"Because you'll hate me for it later."

"I could never hate you."

"Just because you can't imagine it, doesn't mean it can't happen."

She felt the sharpness of his talons. "Uh, sunbeam?"

"What?"

That razor-sharp talon cut downward, slicing through cloth and conviction. "Yes, it does."

The waistband of her jeans gave without a whisper of protest, sliding down her hips as the hunger dug into her gut, gathering for another strike.

His mouth closed over hers, gently, sweetly, completely, edge to edge, seducing her past her common sense, past what she knew she should do, beyond what was right and wrong.

*This is right.*

The thought pushed through her conflict.

*This isn't real*, she answered back.

*This is all I want.*

She knew he wasn't talking sex. He was talking about the perfect blending that happened when they came together, the way their energy meshed, their thoughts meshed, the way his mere presence drove away the emptiness she'd dreaded over the years more than the pain of hunger. This was the completeness that seeped into her soul when he held her.

She cupped his cheeks in her hands, pulling her mouth away from his, taking his breaths as hers as she whispered, "You have to promise even if you hate me later, you'll remember that you didn't want to hear it now. That it's your fault."

He didn't flinch. "I promise."

That talon snagged the back of her shirt. It didn't tear as easily as her jeans, the stretchiness working against a clean cut, but Jared didn't seem to mind, actually rather seemed to enjoy the struggle. He was such a contrary man.

She worked her hands up around his neck, straining up on her toes to link her fingers behind his neck. The material gave with a staggered rip. Cool air caressed her back. The warmth of his breath caressed her mouth, The heat of his smile warmed her soul as he dropped his hand to her rear, steadying her. "Need a little help?"

"Absolutely."

With an efficiency that might have raised her brow at any other time, he tore through the rest of her shirt. The halves fell away from her back. His hands spanned her waist. He lifted her up. She wrapped her legs around his hips and snuggled into his embrace. Pressing her forehead into his throat, her groin into his erection, she let him support her. Her fingernails sank into his neck. The scent of his blood spiced the air. The musk of his arousal surged to the heart of her own.

His hand cupped the back of her head, wrapping in the strands of her hair. "Sweet little sunbeam, warm me."

She'd give him anything. "Just tell me how."

"You're doing fine just the way you are, but if you could see your way to slipping your arms out of those sleeves, the temperature would go up a degree to two."

She smiled. He wanted to feel her naked skin against his. "I just bet it would." She scraped her fangs over the artery in his neck. Absorbing his shudder against the points of their connection, his anticipation heightening her own. She tugged the right sleeve off and then the left. Not pulling the material away from between them, just letting it pool between their chests, loving his growl at the insubstantial denial. With another growl he reached between them. With an upward yank, her shirt flew through the air and landed on the floor. His followed close behind, and then it was her turn to shudder as her breasts sank into the crisp mat of hair on his chest.

"Yes." Jared dragged his chest back and forth against hers, tormenting her nipples with the exquisite abrasion. "Give that to me."

Locking his hands on the back of her head, he held her still as he walked backward three steps, the reverberation of each step another heated pulse to the hunger throbbing between her thighs. His shoulders hit the wall, jarring her. She blinked as the world came into focus.

"No, baby. Stay with me." With a skim of his callused fingers down her spine, Jared re-centered her focus on the energy arcing between them. "Bite me."

Her fangs tingled and ached, but she didn't immediately obey. He wasn't the only one that enjoyed teasing. She ran her tongue over her lips. "Isn't that supposed to be an insult?"

He canted her head to the side, pressing her mouth to his throat. "Between us, it's an invitation."

"An erotic one at that," she whispered against his pulse, feeling it catch and then race as her meaning sank in.

"Hell yes."

Goose bumps sprang up against her lips. She tested the intriguing roughness with her tongue, smiling when Jared arched his neck, giving her free access to run amok. She licked daintily, preparing him, while pleasuring herself with the salty flavor of his skin, the sensation of his heart beating against her mouth.

"Son of a bitch." Another shudder shook his big frame, and she smiled as pure feminine delight flowed through her at the knowledge that she could make a man this big and this strong weak at the knees.

Some of her joy must have spilled over to him because an aggressive surge of masculine demand came right back at her. Hot and thick with desire, it melded with her own lust, driving it higher. His hand jerked her fangs to his neck. That wonderfully addictive flavor that was so uniquely his poured into her.

It was all over for her then. She couldn't hold back, couldn't tease. Need slammed her gut, backed by another surge of masculine demand. She bit. His shout of *Yes!* ricocheted through her mind. He held her close against him as she fed, surprisingly, more tenderness than lust in the stroke of his energy, his hands. She clung to that softness as hunger and passion swamped her, hoping the bond between them would be enough to carry them through the revelations yet to come. She dug her hands into the back of Jared's neck and pressed herself closer. It had to be. She didn't know if she could survive if she had to return to that awful aloneness.

*Never.*

He drew her almost painfully close.

*You'll never be alone again.*

She closed her eyes and hoped it was true.

# ✳ 18 ✳

RAISA was limp and sated beside him, exhaustion tugging at her safeguards. Her right hand draped across his chest. Her fingers swirled lazy patterns in his chest hair. Jared covered her hand with his, feeling her smile stretch against his chest. He had the illogical impulse to stay like this, to not bring up anything they needed to talk about. To just linger here in the bed, letting the intimacy insulate them from the real world.

"It would be nice, wouldn't it?"

Apparently, Raisa's guards weren't the only ones that were lowered.

"Yup."

"But we have to talk."

"Yeah, we do."

A little sting in his chest as her finger caught on his hair and then a turn of her head as she pressed an apologetic kiss to his pectoral. "You need to know about Miri."

"Among other things."

She kissed him again. "She's a were."

"Not seeing the reason for secrecy."

"She's mated to a vampire."

The shock of that immobilized him. Vampires and weres had a competitive relationship. And in the last six months in which alliances had become a necessity, he'd learned a lot about the history of both and one fact stood out. The two never mated. The reason was simple. Leadership in the were world passed through the female to her mate. A male vampire marrying up with a were female from an Alpha family would put the power of the pack outside the species. Not something anyone was comfortable with.

"Breathe, Jared."

He had been holding his breath.

"What pack is Miri from?"

"I don't know. We thought it was safer that way."

"Sounds excessive."

Her fingers wrapped around his, squeezing. "You won't say that when you hear the rest."

How much worse could the rest be? "Just spit it out."

"Miri had a baby."

"Son of a bitch!" Worse didn't begin to cover it. If the child was female, every pack leader in the world would want the baby and the father dead because of the threat they represented. Potential vampire rule of were society. As a fertile female, another mate would be found for her, whether she wanted it or not, but this mating would not be allowed. "Tell me the child was male."

She stared at him, her big brown eyes wide and pleading.

"I don't know for sure."

"But?"

"I don't think so; otherwise, Miri wouldn't be so adamant about me not telling anyone." Raisa's nails dug into his hand. "They took her baby, Jared. They took the baby away as soon as it was born, and the things they've done to her since . . ."

He kissed the top of her head, stroking his energy over hers in pulses of comfort. "I know what they do."

And it wasn't pretty.

The rest of it wasn't, either. If the Sanctuary had gotten rid of the baby, that would solve the problem and the alliances the Renegades had formed would stay solid. At least maybe long enough to win the war. He wanted to think of that as a solution, but babies were meant to be spoiled, not tortured. And women were meant to be cherished, not abandoned to anyone's fanatical pursuits.

Rai's energy smoothed back over his. In an apology and a release from responsibility.

*I'm sorry.*

"There's nothing to be sorry about."

"This isn't your fight."

"It's everyone's fight."

"This will ruin everything."

"Then it will ruin it. But when it's done, Miri and the baby will be safe."

She went so still, he doubted she was even breathing. "You'll try?"

"We'll all try."

She was shaking her head before he finished speaking. "You can't tell the weres."

"Not all of them." He was in agreement on that. No one outside the Circle J could know. "But I will tell my brothers and the McClarens."

She pushed herself up. "Can they be trusted?"

He cut her some slack on the question, considering her first introduction to them, settling for a succinct "Yes."

"But Caleb—"

"Would never leave a woman or child in danger," he finished, pulling her back down. She twitched and fussed beside him. So much for enjoying the lingering intimacy.

"Rai?"

"What?"

"You're crushing my fingers."

Immediately she let go. "I'm so sorry."

He caught her hand again. He liked having her hold on to him. "Nothing to be sorry for. You've got cause to be nervous. Your friend's in a bad situation that could get worse once we rescue her."

"Nothing's worse than where she is."

He could think of some things that were worse for a were. "What if her family turns their backs on her?"

She shook her head, propping herself back up. "Nothing's worse, Jared."

She probably had a point, but her friend was going to have real issues coming up. It probably would help if she had strong family or a strong mate. "I assume her mate is dead?"

"No."

What in hell kind of mate left his pregnant wife? Jared scooted back in the bed, sitting up, pulling her with him until she knelt beside him. "Then where the hell is he?"

"I don't know, but I've got to find him."

"What's his name?"

"I don't know."

"Then how will you find him?"

"By his energy."

He blinked at the sheer ingenuity of it. If Raisa had a man's name, it could be tricked out of her, stolen from her, but how a person saw energy, that was unique to that person. Stealing it would be a waste of time. Except for a very rare few, like Raisa, who were extraordinarily sensitive, it wouldn't transfer. "You thought of everything."

"I had lots of time to think."

While she'd been a prisoner of the Sanctuary. The urge to explode into her mind and find out the truth of her experience took him again. The only thing that held him back was the trust she was showing him. And the anxiety pouring off her in waves. "And when you find Miri's mate, what are you supposed to do?"

"I'm supposed to convince him to save Miri."

"We're not going to wait on him any longer."

"Good."

"And when we have Miri and her baby safe, we'll find her mate." And then Jared would be having a few words with him about why he'd left her in such a situation in the first place.

Raisa's mind was apparently traveling down the same road as his.

"What if he's a scoundrel?"

"Then I'll kick his butt, and we'll keep her safe here with us."

She tucked her knees deeper under her, her eyes searching his. "Why are you willing to do all this?"

He shook his head at the foolishness of the question, giving her hand a small squeeze. "Because you're my wife, because this matters to you, and because it's the right thing to do."

She nodded. "More of that overabundance of honor Slade mentioned."

Like Slade didn't have the same code and wouldn't be doing the same thing as soon as he heard of Miri's situation. "Apparently."

She stroked her hand down his arm, pride and possessiveness in the gesture. "Good." He found he liked that more than he liked her passion. "How are we going to find him?"

"You sure she wants him found?"

She shrugged, wry humor chasing the sadness from the corner of her mouth, her finger tracing across his collarbone. "Maybe just to kill him, but, yes, she wants him found."

"I can see that. A woman has a right to expect a bit more of her mate than your friend seems to have gotten."

"Absolutely."

A few days ago, he might have seriously thought she was intrigued by the way his shoulder hooked up to his collarbone, but a few days ago, he hadn't known the insecurities that lurked beneath her upbeat front. He curved his index finger around the point of her chin and drew her eyes back to his. The answer was in the glimmer of insecurity shadowing her gaze. She was putting herself in Miri's position and wondering.

"Just for the record, so there's no misunderstanding between us, there's no way in hell you'd ever be in Miri's position."

She licked her lips, leaving them moist and glistening in an unconscious invite he took advantage of, fitting his top lip to hers, aligning the center with precise care. "You can't know that."

"I know this. If you were taken from me, Rai, I'd tear the Sanctuary apart, piece by piece, member by member, until I found you."

Raisa blinked as the full force of Jared's will poured over her. Images of destruction and blood pounded at her awareness, the violent mix wavering around the perimeters of her consciousness in a mental bleed from him to her. She gathered it. Muted it. Absorbed it. And when she was done, she had no doubt. He would come for her. She wondered if he knew how much it meant to her, knowing she had someone to count on to that extent? Probably not. He'd always had that security. The question just slipped from her, a hint of sound, traveling on her breath to him. "Why?"

He didn't blink, didn't hesitate. "Because you're mine."

The descent of his mouth punctuated the declaration, his mouth claiming hers, the depth of his hunger surprising her as it always did, stunning her into a split second of immobility before finding an answering chord within her, one that flowed easily into the jagged edges or his passion, smoothing them into something bigger, stronger. He responded with a growl that prowled through her mind.

*Mine!*

A declaration of possession, not love. She tried to make it enough, but inside her, the starving part of her soul wailed a protest. She didn't want to be owned. She'd been owned many times in the past. She wanted to be loved. Practicality told her not to reach for the moon, to be satisfied with what she had, which was much better than anything she'd had before, but irrational tears pricked her eyes. She fought them back, sliding her arms around Jared's neck, enjoying the welcoming flex of muscle at her touch, relishing his strength as he pulled her up against him. Accepting the dominance that was so much a part of him, reveling in it because it meshed so well with that old-fashioned part of her that had been brought up to expect to be the softness in a man's day, and fed into her natural tendency to give comfort to those she loved. Oh God! She loved. Her gasp at the realization was as involuntary as her flinch back.

With another growl that reverberated down her spine, Jared followed her, knocking her off balance. She tumbled to the side. Jared didn't catch her, rather he tumbled with her, a big, lean predator with hunting on his mind.

His growl turned to a chuckle as his chest came over her, inch by exquisite inch as he followed her down to the mattress. He caught a curl in his fingers, lifting it from her shoulder, rubbing it between his fingers as he asked, "Hungry, sunbeam?"

What would be the point of denying it? "I'm always hungry for you."

He took the long strand of hair and wrapped it around her breast, pulling it taut. The man seemed fascinated by her hair. He cut her a glance, the smile quirking one side of his mouth, both sensual and mocking.

She suppressed the urge to cover her breast with her hand but the "I'm sorry" just came trotting out on its own.

Jared's right eyebrow flicked up as his gaze met hers. "What on earth for?"

She was going to hedge, but then decided against it. Who was he to mock her anyway? "For whatever put the mockery in your expression."

The left eyebrow joined the first for a heartbeat before both came down into a frown. Then, surprisingly, that smile that tugged her heartstrings spread from his eyes to his lips. He kissed her quickly, the puff of air against her lips probably laughter.

As soon as his mouth separated from hers, she warned him, "If you're laughing at me, I'm going to hurt you."

He pulled back, humor lurking in the creases fanning out from the corners of his eyes. "Well, if I wasn't before, I am now, after hearing that threat. A little bit of a thing like you couldn't hurt me."

"Trust me, I have my ways."

Jared might think he knew everything about her, but if he pissed her off, he just might run up against her less pleasant side. She touched the crease in his right cheek. "I like it when you smile."

"And I like it when you tempt me."

"Do you want me to tempt you again?"

"Your very existence is more temptation that I can resist." He again pulled that thick strand of hair taut around the base of her breast, the tension in her scalp, and her breast as it was lifted, sparked little perks of interest deep inside. Her nipple tingled and plumped. His head lowered. "Which might explain that mockery you saw on my face."

He bussed the sensitive tip once, twice. "It's hard for a man to accept that he doesn't have any willpower when it comes to a woman."

She gasped and arched her back, offering herself to him. "And you have no willpower when it comes to me?"

"Zilch."

Raisa riffled her fingers through the cool strands of his chocolate-brown hair. "I like that."

He accepted the invitation, curling his tongue around her nipple, sipping gently, his smile measured in the pressure around the nub. "Why am I not surprised?"

She pulled him to her, desire replacing weariness, hunger replacing worry. Need for the tenderness within his touch the impetus behind her sigh of satisfaction as he opened his mouth, taking what she offered, binding them together for this one moment. Maybe the last they would have before the truth broke them apart.

**JARED** slipped from the bed. Rai stirred. He stroked his mind over hers.

*Sleep.* She turned her cheek into the pillow with a little snuggle. He grabbed the covers, meaning to pull it up over her. Shadow covered her shoulder with the move, providing deeper contrast for his night vision. Her skin glowed satiny white in the darkness. Impossibly smooth, deliciously rounded, the curves tempting him to touch, explore, to follow the sultry lure of that sweep down her arm to that spot just inside of her elbow that made her gasp and shiver. He'd like to linger there a bit, tease that little gasp from her lips again, the one that she made right before she lowered her defenses and gave herself to him. He wanted it like hell on fire, more so now when she was at risk from the Sanctuary, from the bomb in her head, from the promise she had made that would put her in greater danger. The promises he was forced to respect because of his code of honor and hers.

He wanted to wake her and watch her smile that witchy little smile as he slid into her, feel her hands soft on his back as she accepted his possession. Her moan of satisfaction as their energies mingled and she possessed him as well. Hell, he just wanted her, period.

He forced himself to drop the cover over her shoulders and step away from the bed. That first step was always the hardest, the initial separation a poignant pain, but once made, he found it easier to manage the call to return. He reached for his shirt and tugged on his pants while watching her sleep, part of him monitoring everything about her, from her health to her emotions, as if she were an extension of himself. Which he was beginning to believe she was. He had to wonder if all mated pairs felt this way or if his and Raisa's bond was unique. He'd have to ask Caleb about it. Sometime when the man wasn't so on edge with distrust and the need to protect him.

Jared slipped out the back door into the sealed alley that connected the guest house to the main one. He opened the door into the kitchen. The rich scent of cinnamon rolls filled the big room.

He took a deep breath, the fragrance blending old and new for him: the days before conversion where home had only been a hope and today where it meant home and his sister-in-law's smile.

"Morning."

"Morning."

He waved to Derek, who was sitting at the kitchen table sipping a cup of coffee, eying the oven.

"Allie nesting again?"

The closer the time came for the baby to be born the more Allie fussed about all the little things, cooking, cleaning, decorating.

Derek frowned "Yup. Almost got some of that Mexican hot chocolate out of her before Caleb whisked her away to bed and left me to my own devices."

"He's worried she's overdoing."

Derek shook his head. "He's going to drive her nuts trying to pamper her when she's bursting with energy."

"I imagine he finds ways to burn it off."

The were's eyes went dark with hunger, reminding Jared that the wolf had been alone a long time, and being alone was harder for a were than a vamp. Whereas a vamp might know that he could find a mate someday, a were was born knowing that he was incomplete to the point that the knowledge drove some insane. Derek took a sip of coffee. When he brought it down, the hunger was gone and his usual calm mask was in place. "I imagine he does."

Jared poured coffee into a cup and joined Derek at the table. "When are the rolls going to be done?"

"Three minutes." Derek was counting.

That meant Caleb would be here in about two and a half. The man was addicted to Allie's cinnamon rolls. Even if he did have to vomit them up afterward because his digestive track no longer appreciated the food choice. Slade wouldn't be far behind. There were just some things that were too nostalgic to give up. Sitting around the table sipping coffee and eating sweet rolls while discussing the day's events was one of them.

Right on cue, the door to the back stairs opened. Caleb stepped through. No sign of their earlier fight on his person. There was, however, a satisfied look to his expression that had Jared snorting with disgust.

"Good God, man, the woman's eight months gone with child."

Caleb cast him a wry expression. "Hey, I put up a fight."

"If it was anything like the one you put up last night in the living room," Derek grinned, "I'd say it hardly counts."

"It counts." Caleb opened the oven door and breathed deeply of the aroma flooding into the room. "Perfect."

Jared shook his head. "You've got to be shortening your life with that addiction."

Caleb pulled the rolls from the oven. He tipped the door closed with his knee. "I'll chance it."

The back door opened. Slade strolled in. He had the harsher features of their uncle, and with the lab coat gone and his hair falling over his forehead, he looked a lot like the brother Jared had ridden with in the old days.

Jared watched as Caleb spread icing on the rolls, putting twice the amount on that Allie did. He barely suppressed a shudder. There was sweet and then there was *sweet*. "Go easy on the icing on mine."

Caleb cocked a brow at him, "Who the hell said you were getting any?"

Jared arched a brow back at him and took another sip of his coffee. Hot, strong, and bitter, it would go perfectly with the rolls. "Who the hell said I wasn't?"

"Me for one," Slade declared, dropping into a chair to the left of Derek.

"Me, too," Derek tossed in, watching the rolls like a hawk.

Caleb brought the laden baking sheet over to the table. He lifted a roll off. Slade sneaked in behind, reaching for the tray. With image-blurring speed, Caleb snapped around and knocked him back and over. His chair hit the floor with a resounding clatter. As one, the men glanced at the interior door.

"I swear if you have that woman down here again," Caleb ground out, "I will personally kick your butt from here to Sunday."

After thirty seconds in which there was no call and no sign of Allie, the men relaxed.

Slade got up and straightened his chair. "A wife is supposed to mellow a man," he informed Caleb as if it were an ancient truth.

"Who said I wasn't mellow?" He passed the rolls around. Everyone took two, except Caleb. Allie always cooked a baker's dozen and the extra always went to him. A rule Allie had set out early on. One of the small considerations a wife did for a husband. Jared looked at the second roll. He grabbed a napkin off the pile in the center of the table and set his second roll on it. Raisa might like it when she woke up.

Caleb eyed the roll. "For your wife?"

"Yeah."

Derek sat back in his chair. The wood squeaked under the big were's weight. "He's a goner for sure if he's forgoing rolls."

Jared took a bit of his roll, letting the flavor spread through his mouth. "Maybe."

Caleb popped the last bite of his pastry into his mouth. "How much a goner?" The cup he raised to his face hid his expression, but Jared felt the probe of his brother's mind.

"All the way gone." To the point he'd protect Raisa from anyone who threatened her, even his own brothers.

"Well," Slade murmured, "that's going to complicate things."

Jared leveled him a look. "Yes, it is."

"Ease off, Jared. We're just looking out for you."

The order came from Caleb.

Jared turned on him, his fangs cutting through his gums in a feral tingle. "Do you remember what you said when I decided to use Allie to make you want to live?"

Aggression came off Caleb in a wild arc at the memory. "I do."

"Multiply that by two, and you'll have an idea of what's waiting for anyone who threatens Rai."

"No one's going to hurt her, Jared."

"I know." He put his cup on the table. "She's got me to guarantee it."

"She's got us, too," Caleb put in quietly.

"No matter what your suspicions about her?"

"You give me your gut how you feel, and I'll go on that."

Jesus! He would ask that. It was one thing to risk himself on a hunch, but his brothers?

"For what it's worth," Slade put in, "I'd trust your gut more than cold logic anyway."

Caleb cut him a look. "And in the old days, so did you."

"I'd like to have known him back then," Derek injected casually. "Though it's hard to imagine Jared abandoning logic for anything."

"He was someone to know for sure."

"I'm the same person," Jared told Caleb.

"No, you're not. You've walled off all emotion and just become a machine."

"And who the hell's fault is that?"

"Mine." Caleb sighed a bone-weary sigh. "And I wish to hell you'd just blame me like you should and get over it."

"There's nothing to blame you for."

"I'm the one who converted you."

"You didn't have a choice."

Caleb's fist slammed down on the table. "For the last time, I did! I didn't have to convert you. I could have let you die a natural death, but I didn't have it in me to let you go. It's as simple and as selfish as that."

"It was that bitch's fault."

"No, it wasn't, and you need to accept that pretty damn soon."

"Why?"

"Because things can't continue the way they are."

"Why not?"

Caleb opened his mouth and then snapped it shut. "Because they can't. We've both got wives. I've got a child on the way, the whole

damn Renegade coalition is on the verge of shattering, and we just
don't have time for your delusions anymore."

"Well." Jared leaned back in his chair. "I've gotten pretty attached to them."

Caleb shared a glance with Slade. Jared looked at Derek, who
shrugged, indicating he had no idea what was going on.

Caleb shoved him the extra roll. "I repeat, get over it."

Jared took it, tilting it sideways. "What's this, a peace offering?"

"Call it whatever you want. Now, tell me, what's your gut on
Raisa? Can we trust her or not?"

Jared shook his head. Caleb was a stubborn shit. "It's not in Raisa
to deliberately hurt anyone." He remembered the way she'd blown
away the Sanctuary were. "At least without cause."

"Meaning what?"

"Meaning she blew away a were who got the jump on me."

"I'm liking her more already." Derek finished off his roll.

"So am I." Caleb tapped his fingers on the table, the aura of command he wore so easily very much in place.

"Why?"

"Because you need a strong woman, otherwise you'll walk all
over her."

Raisa was strong. She looked delicate, was more than comfortable letting him take over any area she didn't care about, but when
it mattered to her, she had a core of steel. "Then you're going to
love her."

"Good."

"Did you find out what her secret is?"

"Yes." He glanced at Derek. "Do the McClarens stand by their
promise for her protection?"

Derek nodded. "Absolutely."

"Even if what I say is were business?"

Derek sat up straighter. "What kind of were business?"

"Ascension business."

"Shit!"

Jared waited for the information to settle before asking, "Do you still stand by your promise? Does Raisa have the McClarens' full protection?"

Derek inclined his head. "Yes."

"And what I'm going to say won't go any further than this room?"

Derek nodded. "Yes."

"Good, because we've got a mess on our hands."

# ✦ 19 ✦

**T**HE knock at the door woke Raisa from a sound sleep. She reached across the bed for Jared, sensing he wasn't there long before her palm hit the empty mattress. The knock came again. She grunted in annoyance. She rolled out of bed and grabbed her clothes, dragging on her jeans and picking up her turtleneck. The tattered remains weren't going to cover anything. She dropped it back on the floor. She didn't have another top. She tugged the coverlet from the foot of the bed and wrapped it around her. Sun weariness caused her bones to feel like lead, as she headed to the door. She never did well when the sun was up. She put her hand on the wood frame, half to test the energy on the other side and half to prop herself up. The energy was bright, happy, and feminine.

"Who is it?"

"Allie Johnson."

That's what she'd thought. Raisa unbarred the door and opened it, hugging the sheet around her torso. "Hi."

Allie stood there, a pile of clothes in her hands. She took in the sheet and jeans. Her lips fought a smile and lost. "The Johnson men are rough on the wardrobe, aren't they?"

"Just a bit."

She held out the clothes. "Then I picked the right peace offering."

Raisa looked at the clothes. "I wasn't aware we were fighting."

"I believe in covering all the contingencies, just in case you hold my husband's overprotectiveness against me."

Raisa glanced beyond the overhang. The sun was coming up. "I wouldn't do that."

"Then, why don't you invite me in before my husband figures out I'm not tucked up in bed where he left me."

"So, you're not supposed to be here?"

Allie shrugged, her ordinary face becoming beautiful with her irrepressible smile. "I won't tell if you won't."

"I've got a bomb in my head."

"I've got a miracle in my stomach. Both are touchy subjects; which do you want to address first?"

Raisa blinked. "The miracle, definitely."

"Then in that case, you'll have to open the door, because said miracle is killing my back."

Raisa opened the door and stood back. "Caleb isn't going to like you being here."

"Probably not."

"He's going to find out where you are sooner or later."

"Let's hope later." Allie eased her bulk past. "You have no idea what it's like to be cooped up twenty-four-seven with all that raging testosterone."

Raisa followed Allie to the living room. Jared's testosterone had raged a time or two. "I've got an idea."

Allie handed her the clothes. Raisa had no choice but to take them. "Uh-huh." Allie settled her hand on the ledge of her stomach. "You've only had to deal with Jared. Try dealing with all four Johnson brothers at once and then add on the fanatical protectiveness of the McClarens." She shuddered, leaned back and to the side, braced herself on the edge of the couch, and sort of dropped back onto the cushions and raised her brows. "You know they're fanatical about babies, right?"

Allie put the clothes on the arm of the oversize chair and perched on the edge, catching the sheet before it could slide off. "The Johnsons?"

"No, the weres. Though I've got to admit, the brothers aren't too far behind."

Allie wiggled in the cushions until she got comfortable. "I don't suppose there's any chance of you getting pregnant soon to take some of the pressure off me?"

"I don't think so. As far as I know, vampires can't get pregnant."

"So everyone keeps telling me." She patted her belly with a grin. "Apparently, the mound didn't agree."

"The mound?"

"I won't let Slade tell Caleb the sex. He kept trying to trick it out of me, so I came up with a neutral term for the baby."

Raisa couldn't help the twitch of her lips. "Can't he just get the information himself?"

"He could, but he won't. It wouldn't be honorable."

"The brothers are pretty big on honor."

Allie nodded. "If they give you their word on something, it's as good as gold." She looked around. "You wouldn't, by any chance, have any coffee around, would you?"

"I don't know. I haven't had a chance to look around."

"Would you mind checking?"

"Sure." She got to her feet and glanced over her shoulder as she headed to the kitchen. "I thought vampires couldn't eat."

"You actually can a little, but Caleb has cut me off coffee, saying it's not good for the baby."

"Then maybe I shouldn't make any."

"Hey, we females have to stick together. Besides, the mound is craving the stuff." She pulled the saddest face Raisa had ever seen. "You wouldn't deny a growing mound what it craves, would you?"

"Well, considering I've never made coffee, denial might be the best course of action."

Allie struggled on the couch. "Good grief, that won't do. This might be the last cup I get before the baby's born."

Raisa watched her battle with the cushion for a few seconds. Finally she couldn't stand it anymore. "May I help?"

Without an ounce of pride, Allie held out her hand. "Heck, yes!"

Raisa hauled her up. Allie hit her feet with a smile. "Caleb was right, you've got a soft heart."

"More like a soft head," Raisa muttered, grabbing a blue T-shirt and pulling it over her head before following Allie into the kitchen.

"I heard that," Allie called over her shoulder as she started opening cupboard doors. "There has got to be coffee here somewhere."

Raisa opened the fridge. "What makes you so sure?"

"The McClarens drink it like it's water, and they're the ones who normally have guests here."

Raisa didn't see any coffee in the fridge, but as soon as she opened the freezer door, she hit pay dirt. "Got it!"

For a woman who had a distinct waddle, Allie closed the distance between them in the blink of an eye. She grabbed the bag from Raisa's hand and glanced at the brand. "Ah, the good stuff."

Personally, Raisa didn't know how anyone could think of coffee as good, but as long as Allie was happy, she was fine.

Allie made quick work of prepping the coffee, the only interruption in her moves the moment she opened the bag and breathed deeply. "Oh, that's good."

"Will it satisfy the mound?"

"Definitely." Another grin, and Raisa could see why the serious, too-handsome Caleb had fallen in love with Allie. There was a light about Allie, a perpetual willingness to laugh combined with a deep intelligence that was very attractive.

Allie glanced over her shoulder from where she was measuring out beans into the coffeemaker. "You're wondering what Caleb saw in me, aren't you?"

There wasn't a trace of offense in her voice. "Actually, it's the other way around."

"You're kidding, right?" She looked over her shoulder again. "Did you, by any chance, miss the width of those shoulders or not catch a gander at that tight butt?"

There was no good way to answer that. "I was a bit distracted by other things at the time."

Like having a pair of wolves sicced on her.

Allie poured water into the chamber, put the carafe back underneath, and pushed the button with a flourish. The beans ground with a raucous noise. Raisa wanted to cover her ears. Allie patted the black plastic sides of the coffeemaker lovingly, almost hugging it as she made shushing noises. "Shh, baby. We don't want Caleb to hear, do we?"

Raisa glanced over her shoulder toward the kitchen door. "His hearing is that good?"

"Either that or he's got me bugged. But I swear"—she turned away from the machine and braced her hands against the counter— "every time I get near a whiff of caffeine, he pops up and wrecks my day."

She remembered Caleb, his brilliant green eyes so cold and hard as he watched her, his suspicion and anger enveloping her.

"What does he do when he catches you?" If he hurt Allie, she'd have to do . . . something.

Allie rolled her eyes and groaned. "He lectures me. For a man for whom I once had to imprison"—she cupped her palms in front of her chest—"the girls in a Wonderbra just to get him to talk to me, he can really get on a tear."

"Caleb was shy?" That she couldn't picture.

Allie shook her head. "Playing hard to get. He thought I'd have some sort of prejudice against vampires."

The way she had of wording things made Raisa smile.

"And didn't you?"

Most humans would, if given a choice.

Allie raised her eyebrows, her blue eyes alight with humor. She gestured with her hand. "I repeat, did you get a glimpse of those shoulders and that tight butt?"

Raisa couldn't suppress her chuckle. She could really get to liking Allie.

"I'll take that as a no."

Allie shook her head and pushed her bangs out of her eyes. "Truthfully? By the time I realized he was a vampire, he either had to convert me or watch me die." She cut Raisa a glance from under her lashes as she checked on the coffee. "Caleb's not good at watching those he loves die."

Was that a warning? "I don't plan on harming him."

Allie shifted her weight against the counter, bracing herself on her elbows. "Well, hell. I'm just not very good at this subterfuge crap."

Everything inside Raisa went very still as alarm flared through her. "Subterfuge?"

"In case you missed it, that was an attempt to lead into the subject that I know you're the vampire who converted Caleb."

Oh God, this was bad. Raisa licked her lips, keeping the panic in check through sheer force of will. "Fudge."

"Fudge? Good God, woman, let go. That kind of announcement is worth a shit or a damn, at least."

Raisa pulled out a chair as the ramifications swept over her. "I'm not really good at swearing." Feeling like all the hope she'd harbored for someone special for her was shattering in one fell swoop, she asked, "Are you going to tell Jared?"

"Of course not. Caleb and I both agreed that was between the two of you."

Raisa watched her knuckles turn white as she gripped the back of the chair harder and harder in an effort to keep her emotions under control. "What do you want in exchange?"

It always came down to this, someone wanting something from her.

"Well, Caleb doesn't want anything, and he totally understands if you never tell Jared." She waved her hand. "In case you haven't noticed, the man is completely irrational on the subject."

"And you?" Raisa forced the words from her throat. "How do you feel about it?"

Allie poured herself a cup of coffee and came over to the table. With a calm Raisa couldn't imitate in a thousand years, Allie pulled out a chair and sat down. Her gaze, when it met Raisa's, was completely devoid of humor. "I think if I had come across Caleb dying, heard his anguish and worry at leaving his brothers, I would have given him his wish in a heartbeat."

"How did you know?"

"That he was consumed with worry about leaving his brothers?"

"Yes."

"I know my husband, and I know his willingness to sacrifice himself for his brothers. Heck, for anyone he loves. And I imagine his desperation to stay with them was pretty much overwhelming."

As the old pain and guilt rose, Raisa fought to suppress the anguish that swamped her as thoroughly as it had that day. "It was."

Allie took one look at her face and motioned to the chair she was holding. "Sit down before you fall down."

Raisa blinked, realizing her legs were shaking. She sat. She'd never talked about what she'd done that night. She grabbed a napkin off the middle of the table because it gave her something to do with her hands. She started shredding in the corner, feeling like she was tearing off pieces of her soul as she worked inward. "I just wanted his pain to stop, he was hurting so." She smiled wryly, catching Allie's eye. "He thought I was an angel at first."

"He told me that."

"I didn't know how to tell him who I really was, what I was. I just wanted to help him, but I was so sick myself, I didn't even know if I could do anything, but I had to try."

"And you succeeded."

She nodded, remembering every horrible agonizing detail. "His blood made me so sick, I almost couldn't complete the act."

Allie's brows arched up. "His blood made you sick?"

"Every kind of blood except Jared's does, apparently."

"How long have you been a vampire?"

"About two hundred seventy years."

"That's a long time to be starving."

"Yes." An eternity.

"I have the same problem now that I'm pregnant."

Raisa glanced up. "I'm not pregnant."

Allie smiled. "And I bet that little idiosyncrasy is just fascinating Slade to no end."

"It seems to be." Which she actually didn't think was a good thing. Allie seemed to have forgotten about her coffee, twirling the mug in her hands, staring into the black brew as if the secrets of the universe shimmered in the depths. When she looked up, she was completely serious. "I know exactly how it feels to take in incompatible blood, the incomprehensible agony, so I want you to know how eternally grateful I'll always be that you made that sacrifice for my husband. It's a debt neither of us will ever forget."

Raisa didn't want any lies between them. "I wasn't noble, just weak. I couldn't walk away from his pain."

"Did you ever think you weren't supposed to? That maybe you were supposed to be in that spot at that time with that choice to make?"

"No."

"Well." Allie raised her cup to her lips. "Maybe you should."

"My wife is a great believer in fate and destiny."

Allie sighed. "Told you he had radar."

Raisa turned to the kitchen door. Caleb stood there, filling the opening with his broad shoulders and the sheer magnetism of his presence. Behind him stood Jared. She didn't even want to know what that meant. She grabbed the edge of the table, her survival instincts screaming for her to run.

"Don't, Raisa." That growl was Jared's. She obeyed simply because there was no place to go that he wouldn't catch her.

"And don't you take a sip of that coffee, Allie girl. You made me a promise."

She arched her brows at Caleb, not one wit upset at his tone. "And that promise was to not drink coffee when you weren't in the room."

"I'm still not in the room."

Jared gave him a shove, pushing him into the room and out of his way. "Now you are." As he strode past Caleb, Allie took a sip, sighing in exaggerated bliss as she swallowed.

"Dammit, Allie."

Raisa didn't look at Jared as he came closer. The heat of his energy, the torn shreds of his control, were enough to tell her everything. He came up beside her. She crumpled the napkin in her hand, squeezing it hard. "You heard."

"I didn't need to. You projected every thought just like you always do when you're upset."

"I've really got to get a handle on that." Was that her voice sounding so calm and rational when her world had just fallen apart? Across the table, Caleb removed the coffee cup from his wife's hand and pulled her chair back. "C'mon, wife." He bent and slid his hand behind her back and under her knees. "Time to go receive your punishment."

Allie yawned and slid her hands around his neck. "I'm tired."

"If you'd stayed in bed where I put you, you wouldn't be." Caleb nodded to Jared and Raisa. "'Night all."

There didn't seem to be any anger in Caleb's voice or handling of his wife; still she had to ask Jared in a low whisper, "Will he hurt her?"

"No."

That was good. She plucked at the edge of the napkin that peeked from the clenched fold of her fist. "Are you going to hurt me?"

At the door Caleb paused.

Jared's "Good night, Caleb" pushed him through. Raisa didn't look up as the door closed. She couldn't. She didn't want to see the hatred on Jared's face. She'd rather remember him as she'd last seen him, smiling down at her with amusement and arousal.

He sighed and put a napkin-wrapped bundle on the table. "We need to talk."

"Fine." She tore off a piece of napkin and dropped it on the table and then fished for another. His hand covered hers. Emotion poured over her with the contact—anger, frustration, old hatred, new confusion. "Look at me."

She pulled her hand free. "I'd rather not."

He motioned to the napkin wrapped bundle that smelled of cinnamon on the table by her hand. "I brought you a cinnamon roll."

"Thank you."

"Dammit, Raisa."

"There's no need to swear."

"There's every need. Why didn't you tell me?"

She gave him the truth. "I was in no hurry to see you hate me."

"Raisa." His fingertips skimmed her head. She flinched. He swore again. He didn't remove his hand. "I don't hate you."

He didn't love her, either, which just left her in some half-life zone where he needed her and tolerated her while she . . . she just wanted so much more.

"I'll leave as soon as it gets dark."

"What about Miri?"

She closed her eyes and took a breath. "I'll think of something."

"You already have. It's Renegade business now."

Just like fate had made her his. The problem was, even though Jared would honor both responsibilities, he hadn't wanted either and that just made her, at least, a burden.

She blinked rapidly. "I relieve you of the responsibility."

His hand grew heavier. "It's not that easy."

"It's not that hard."

"Sunbeam, look at me."

The napkin was all gone, the last piece too small to shred. She pinched it between her fingers. "Don't call me that."

She'd built such stupid dreams around that nickname, made it into so much more than the casual, meaningless endearment it was. His fingers sank into her hair, the tiny stings from the pressure of his grip found an echo in the pain bursting free inside her. "I'll call you whatever the heck I want."

"You won't call me that."

"You're mine."

The tug at her nape was an order. She ignored it. "Not in any way that matters."

His growl rumbled over her head, a warning of the storm to come if she kept pushing him. She didn't care. "Growl all you want. It doesn't change anything."

"Who the hell said I want anything to change?"

She slapped at his hand as he tugged her head back. "You want me to be everything other than what I am. Stronger, funnier, tougher."

"I want who you are."

"Bull feathers." It irritated her even more that she hadn't used a curse word. Jared's grip didn't relax and neither did the demand. Well, she wasn't looking at him right now. Not when she had stupid tears in her eyes that would just make her appear even more pathetic. She grabbed his wrist, curling her fingers so her talons dug into the inside. The scent of his blood spiced the conflict between them. "And you'd really prefer I be anyone other than the cold . . . bitch who converted your brother."

"You're right, it doesn't come out right when you swear." His fingers curled under her chin. "Look at me."

She shook her head and yanked on his wrist. She should have known the battle was useless. Jared had tons more muscle that she, and he wasn't above using it when he wanted something. In the end

Raisa didn't have any choice but to look at him. Jared pulled her chair back as she raised her face. His eyes were a turbulent green, his mouth a hard line that creased at the corners as he took in her expression. He touched the moisture gathered at the corner of her eye.

"Ah, hell. Come here."

And then he was lifting her out of the chair, into his arms, his gaze locked to hers, no answer in his expression as to how he felt, what he wanted, just the inexorable draw of her body to his. For an instant she stood against him, her toes barely touching the ground, the majority of her weight suspended on his forearm placed in the middle of her back. The softness of her breasts pressed onto his upper abdomen, and then he lifted her higher, drawing her into the flames of his eyes, into those stupid what-might-have-beens that she couldn't get out of her head. He pulled her head farther back as his mouth lowered. She braced herself for the force of his kiss, for the taint of anger to poison all that had come before.

Nothing could have prepared her for the utter gentleness with which his mouth plied hers, the tenderness that infused the next brush of his lips against the corner, lingering on the emotion that quivered there. The understanding edged with impatience that absorbed the emotion pouring from her in a wave she couldn't control.

A sob heralded the break in her resolve. Jared took that, too, along with her weight, lifting her completely into his embrace, taking full responsibility for supporting her, comforting her. Oh God, he was comforting her. Raisa wrapped her arms around his neck, her legs around his waist, and pulled herself harder against him. Surely that meant something. The plea came from the deepest corner of her soul.

*Don't hate me. Don't hate me.* "Please don't hate me."

The last sighed into his mouth. On a groan, he ended the kiss. His cheek slid against hers in a sensual brush of hope as he pressed her face into the side of his neck. "I could never hate you, sunbeam," he murmured, the tendrils of his breath softening the roughness of the declaration.

"Then what do you feel?"

"I don't know, but it's not hate."

Which was a far cry from love. "I turned your brother."

Jared sighed. "Which just goes to show how reality can shatter a really good focus for a man's anger."

When his grip on her back loosened, Raisa clutched his neck and held on for all she was worth. "Just say whatever it is you have to say."

"I'd like to look at you while I do it."

"I wouldn't."

And as long as Jared didn't force her arms from around his neck, he wasn't getting his way. For a heartbeat she worried he planned to do just that. His intent was there in the stillness of his body and the tension creeping into his muscles, but then he took a step back, his shoulders hitting the wall as he braced himself. Just holding her, letting her do this her way. "What are you worried about, Raisa?"

*That you'll look into my face, and the hatred you've nursed for two hundred fifty years will ruin all your good intentions.* "Nothing."

"Right, nothing."

Something disturbed the hair at the top of her head. A kiss?

"Would it help if I told you that I've gotten to know you quite well the last few days? And that I can hardly see a woman who frets about the degree of perceived cruelty I apply in killing a man cold-bloodedly converting a man against his will?"

"It would have been cruel to make them watch."

His puff of laughter parted her hair. "That just makes my point. You've a soft heart, Rai. Soft enough that I can see you converting a man because of it."

"You're not mad?"

"I had been working on not being mad on that point long before you came into my life. I just wasn't ready to give up on it."

She licked her lips, her tongue grazing the warm skin of his neck. His taste infiltrated her mouth. "And now you are?"

"When I have to choose between keeping you or holding on to an irrational anger, it's not hard at all."

"It can't be that easy."

"I won't let it be that hard."

Heavens, she hoped that was true, that he wouldn't hate her tomorrow. Memories she couldn't suppress swept over her. She turned her face into his neck, taking strength from his scent. "He was so cold, Jared. So cold and in so much pain. I wasn't going to stop. I swear I wasn't. I just wanted to get out of the wind before the pain got too bad, but he kept swearing at God and the Devil. Bargaining with both for help. He was lying there in the middle of the prairie, in agony, the last of his blood leaving him, and all he could think about was you and your brothers and how someone had to warn you about the friend who was going to kill you."

"Damn!"

"I was really sick myself, and I didn't even know if I could help him. I just . . ." She shrugged.

He finished for her. "You had to try."

"Yes."

"The same way I would have."

That brought her head up. He didn't flinch from her surprise. "It came to me on the way over here, that if it had been you out on that prairie, in agony, and converting you would save you, I would have done it in a heartbeat."

"No, you would have held my hand, but you wouldn't have—"

He cut her off, his drawl a flat statement of fact. "I would have converted you whether you wanted it or not."

"Why?"

"Because it would have balanced the scales, made things fair." He cupped her head in his hand as she leaned back, supporting her as her legs slid down his thighs. His energy enfolded her along with his arms. "But mostly, because I couldn't have borne your pain."

She let that soak in along with his body heat. Beneath her cheek, his heart beat slowly, steadily. He was always so warm. "I still think you wouldn't have converted me."

His finger slid under her chin, lifting her face. "Then you've got another think coming. I'm not this nice man you keep making me out to be. I'm a selfish bastard, and one look at you and I would have done anything to keep you with me."

"What makes you say that?"

His gaze never left hers. The fingertips of one hand grazed down her back, flirted with the bottom of her shirt, then slipped beneath. They were deliciously rough against her bare skin. Shivers chased up her spine. Jared raised his other hand to place a finger to the hollow of her throat, over the throb of her pulse. "The fact that I already have."

She closed her eyes. "It's not safe for you to be around me."

"I don't care."

"I do." She stroked his forearms. "I couldn't bear to be the cause of your death."

He tapped the underside of her chin. She opened her eyes. Flames flared in his eyes. "You'll never get rid of me that easily."

## ✳ 20 ✳

BY nightfall, there still was no buzzing in her head, no call for information, and Raisa's nerves were shot.

"A watched pot never boils," Jared offered from where he sat on the side of the bed, pulling his boots on.

"What in heck does that mean?"

He leaned over where she lay against the pillows, bracing his arm on the other side of her torso. He kissed her lips lightly, pulling back an inch to murmur, "If you'd give swearing a chance, you'd find these moments much more satisfying."

"What would satisfy me is to have the headache begin."

"That would *not* satisfy me." He pushed the sleep-tousled hair out of her face, tracing the frown pleating her brow. "As soon as you feed, we've got to head over to the lab. Slade's got some experiments he wants to run, but if you want, we can have the bomb taken out."

He felt the temptation to agree tug at her. Instinct demanded he force whatever would keep her safe. For a second, it got past his control. Raisa blinked, sensing his presence. "No, Jared."

It took a considerable amount of effort to rein in the instinct, especially when she was looking up at him, her lips swollen from his kisses, the scent of their lovemaking perfuming the air, his love bite marking her neck. "If they don't buzz you, they'll never know."

"And if they do buzz me, they'll kill Miri."

"Don't take this wrong, but when push comes to shove, I'm more concerned about you."

"It's not just her. There's a baby, too."

She didn't have to remind him. He covered the bite with three fingers. Around his touch, golden energy glowed, the darker flickers around the edge were his, as if his energy was a taint that just couldn't blend with the purity of hers. "I know."

Just as he knew she'd never risk a baby. He pushed away, delivering a light slap to the side of her hip. He stood up.

"Which means you need to get up and get showered, so we can see what Slade has worked up overnight."

Instead of getting up she snuggled deeper into the covers. "What makes you think he's come up with anything?"

"This is Slade. The man's brain never stops."

"Uh-huh."

He buttoned his shirt. She looked so comfortable in the bed, he hated to disturb her. "I'm going to go heat up the shower. When I come back, you're going to have to say good-bye to the bed."

The lazy wave of her hand sent him on his way. He smiled as he headed into the bathroom and turned on the hot water. It was interesting watching how a feeling of safety changed her habits. She was like a sleepy kitten now, coming awake by degrees, playing with him, trusting him. He tested the water. It was hot, but not burningly so. He headed back to the bedroom. In the three minutes he'd been gone she'd managed to make a mess of the covers and was all snuggled down in them, chasing sleep again.

"Come on, Rai, time to rise and shine."

She cracked an eyelid at him. "Just a couple more minutes."

He'd played this game with Jace often enough to know how two minutes stretched to two hours. He tugged the covers off her. For a split second he had an unrestricted view of the perfection of her body—the slender bones, the ultra-feminine curves that complimented her slight build rather than overwhelming it, the satiny white skin that glowed like cream in the overhead light, and the healthy pink of her toenails on her slender toes. And then she was in motion, diving for the covers. While she was grasping for them, he scooped her up in his arms. Another gasp, a bubble of laughter, and then her arms came around his neck and she was nestled into his arms. Where she belonged.

By stretching his thumb up, he could touch the spot where the implant threatened. Rage welled along with an unfamiliar panic. He wouldn't let the Sanctuary take her from him. Immediately, the soothing stroke of her energy found him, hugging him as he held her.

"It'll be okay, Jared."

"I know." It was a lie. He didn't know a damn thing, and after he talked to Slade today this playing Russian roulette with her life was going to end. The Sanctuary wasn't being predictable and that changed everything. He set Raisa down outside the stall. The way her hands lingered on his chest soothed the restlessness prowling inside.

"There's no time for that," he teased, putting the growl in his voice that always brought that little flicker of interest to her lids and the smile to her lips.

Her first reaction was predictable. A flush crept up her torso, but her second was the more intriguing. Those lids came down over those gorgeous eyes of hers in a pure invite, and her finger trailed past the low-slung waistband of his jeans. "There's a nice warm bed in the other room."

He chuckled, desire rising in him at the temptation of the invite. "There's a hot shower right here."

With a gentle push, he sent her into the hot spray. Water poured over her head and down the slope of her breasts in tiny waterfalls, sluicing down from the peaks to moisten the tawny tangle of curls between her legs. He shut the door on the temptation she presented.

Her "Coward" came to him easily over the sound of the water.

"I just know when I'm outgunned," he countered, admiring the blur of her silhouette through the glass. She pushed her hair off her face, her back arching, presenting the curve of her breasts to his starving eyes as she turned into the spray. Damn, he craved her like a drug, and while that should scare him witless, it didn't. Needing her, wanting her, it was all good.

"I'll wait for you in the kitchen."

"Are you making coffee?"

"Why, you want some?"

The subtle scent of gardenia came to him. Exotic, like her. He could imagine how the scent would linger on her skin later when he collected on the promises she was making him now.

"I thought I might try some now that I'm stronger."

"You ever have it before?"

"No."

"In that case you might want to hold off until we get to the main house. Allie has a lighter hand with the beans."

A pause and then, "Can I have my cinnamon roll, too?"

Damn he'd forgotten about that. First he had to watch her shower and not touch, and now he was going to have to watch her eat and get no taste. "I don't see why not."

Her chuckle floated out to him on the mist of gardenia and heat. *If you scrub my back, I'll share with you.*

He turned and unbuttoned the front of his shirt. A man could only resist so much temptation. "Well, if you put it that way."


**FROM** the frown on Slade's face, he wasn't pleased with the delay in their getting there.

"What was the holdup?" he asked impatiently, looking up from the computer screen he was sitting in front of.

"We overslept," Jared answered evenly. The blush that rose up from the collar of Raisa's shirt and flooded her face with a deep rose was a dead giveaway to his lie.

Slade arched a brow at them. "Uh-huh. Was there any contact from the Sanctuary?"

Jared pressed his hand into the middle of Raisa's back, moving her farther into the room. "No."

"Good."

"Good?" Raisa echoed. "I don't think it's good."

Slade rolled his chair away from the computer screen to the other side of the corridor to pick up a bulky rectangular device. "Well, maybe not from a peace-of-mind standpoint, but considering what we're dealing with and all the ramifications to your—" He paused and then obviously rephrased. "Health. I wanted to have this ready before the next signal came in." He motioned them forward as he hit a few buttons on the keyboard.

There was no enthusiasm in Raisa's steps. "He's not going to hurt you, baby."

"Logically, I know that," she whispered back.

"But?"

"I have an aversion to being experimented on, and your brother does have that certain gleam in his eye."

"The one that says he can't wait to test out his new toy?"

"Yes."

Slade looked up and smiled as they stopped in front of him. He held up the device, which had a couple of wicked-looking metal points underneath. "Want me to test it on Jared first?"

Jared felt Raisa's start as she looked at those metal points, and then, incredibly, she stepped in front of him. "No. That's all right."

Jared put her firmly behind him. "Sure, why not."

Slade watched the byplay with open amusement. "You two sure

are well matched in the suspicion department. This"—he pointed to the device—"is a rather crude mock-up of an energy blocker. If it works, I'll create a much sleeker design." He flipped a switch on the side. Jared didn't feel the pulse of power he expected. Slade intercepted his look.

"Pretty slick, huh? I have an energy neutralizer attached to it, which is why I was worried about it working. I created it to record incoming energy while negating outgoing, but the premise is pure speculation." Slade held the device out. "Focus some energy on me."

Jared sent him a beam. Raisa stepped forward and slid her fingers through his. Slade looked at the needle and then checked the computer screen. He frowned.

"Raisa, step back. No, Jared. You keep focusing."

Slade's frown deepened. He hit a few buttons on the keyboard. "Stop focusing, Jared. Come here, Raisa."

After one anxious glance, Raisa went, the set of her shoulders reminding Jared of a woman facing her executioner.

Slade put the device in his lap. "Touch me."

Jared took a step forward, the growl welling from within.

That got him an exasperated look from his brother. "On my hand is fine."

As soon as Raisa's hand touched his, Slade started typing with the other, his fingers flying on the keyboard, his frown deepening with every second. The flurry of activity ended on a "Hot damn."

Slade sat back in his chair and stared at the screen. "Well, this is going to complicate things."

"What?" Raisa turned to Jared, who merely shrugged. Slade would get to explanations when he had all the elements sorted out in his own mind. Raisa took a step back. Jared wrapped his arm around her and dropped a kiss on the top of her head as she leaned back against him. She was definitely getting more comfortable with him. She reached up and grabbed hold of his forearm.

She no sooner said, "I don't like the look on his face," than Slade barked, "Stay just like that."

Neither of them moved. He punched out a command on the keyboard and then approached them with the energy meter in hand. He ran it over them and then, motioning them apart, did it again. He then went back to the computer, not saying a word.

"Are you feeling as much like a rather unattractive bug caught under the microscope, as I am?" Raisa asked.

"Speak for yourself. I'm feeling like a rather handsome bug this morning." He tugged her back into his side. "Thanks to a certain little vamp who had her way with me in the shower."

She blushed and slapped his shoulder, but he noticed she didn't pull away.

"Come over here and look at this," Slade called.

For all her nervous talk, Raisa had him by the hand and was at Slade's side faster than he could say "spit." The woman was as curious as a cat.

Slade waved to the screen where three graphs resided with varying heights of red lines.

Even though he had no idea what he was looking at, Jared nodded.

Raisa looked at the screen and then at him. "There's no way you know what in earth you're looking at."

"There's not?"

She put her hands on her hips and stared harder. She tossed her head and glanced at him over her shoulder. "No."

"Prove it."

That got a snort from her and a laugh from Slade. "She probably can't, but I can."

"I'm your brother. Your loyalty should be to me."

Slade leaned back in his chair. "But she's a heck of a lot prettier."

Raisa flashed Slade her sweetest smile. Slade's gaze lingered on her mouth. Even though he knew it wasn't personal and his brother's attention was just a man's appreciation for a pretty woman, jealousy whipped though Jared.

Slade, damn his hide, just grinned at him before angling the flat screen toward them. He pointed to the graph on the left. "This is Jared's natural energy pattern. Note all the spikes. Usually a vampires pattern is a steady line at some unique frequency, but Jared has a natural ability to throw energy that he doesn't always control, nor does it always stay in his frequency zone."

The look Raisa cut him was knowing. "Rebel."

"Hey, I'm the straitlaced one of the brothers."

"Uh-huh." The amount of skepticism Raisa managed to pack into those two syllables did his ego proud.

"Actually," Slade added, "he is."

"That doesn't say much for you all."

"I think it says a lot," Jared countered. "However, now that you're one of us, you'll have to 'up your freak factor' as Allie says, to keep up."

Slade pointed to the graph with the lines etched in red and blue. "I don't think she needs to up anything."

Jared frowned, trying to make sense of what he was seeing. "That Raisa's chart?"

"Yup."

"How come I have all those blue spikes mixed in with my red?"

"Because, like Jared, you can throw energy, but it's not your real strength."

Raisa stepped back into Jared. He dropped his arms over her torso. She brought her hands up and rubbed her fingers on his forearms. He didn't think she realized she was doing it. "What is?"

Though her voice was even, he could feel her energy tugging at his. He covered her hand with his. "Not all news is bad news, sunbeam."

Slade looked startled at the very thought, which wasn't a surprise. The man lived for discovery. "Who said anything about bad news?"

"Not having to up my freak factor doesn't sound good."

He shook his head. "You, my dear sister-in-law, are a conductor."

Jared waited for Raisa to ask why, for an explanation. She didn't. "You can tell that from that little device?"

"Yup." Slade cocked his head to the side and motioned to Raisa. "But you knew that didn't you?"

"What makes you ask that?"

"Because while I was up last night working on your problem, I couldn't help but wonder how you'd survived all these years."

"I don't see the correlation."

Neither did Jared. "What's your point?"

"My point is, whenever you get pissed, Jared, you tend to lose control of that energy of yours and it tweaks those around you like an electric shock. And you were damn pissed yesterday, yet Raisa, who was closest to you, didn't even twitch."

He hadn't realized he was shocking people. Literally. He instinctively slid his hand from beneath Raisa's. She dug her nails in. He had a choice—get scratched or stay put. He opted for the latter. "Maybe she just understands me."

"If I were a romantic, I'd believe that," Slade continued. Then he pointed to the third graph. "But when you look here, you can see what happens to the spike in your energy when she's near you, let alone touching you."

The graph for both their energies was an even line with the spikes leveled.

"It also explains why Raisa's always hungry. She expends a lot of energy balancing you." He shrugged. "Actually, you balance each other."

"Seems to me that's just one more sign that, as a couple, we were meant to be," Jared offered.

Raisa shot him a startled glance. Her surprise flicked him on the raw. What in hell did she think he'd been telling her for the last twenty-four hours except how he felt about her?

Slade paused, considered the matter, and then shrugged. "That's one way to look at it."

As far as Jared was concerned, it was the only way to look at it, but he could tell from the building tension in Rai and the intentness with which Slade was studying her that there was something he was missing. "What other way would there be?"

"That you've got your arms around the most potentially deadly vampire ever created, seeing as her ability to drain energy is about limitless."

**"FOR** God's sake, up until a week ago, the woman couldn't even levitate."

"Which might have saved quite a few Sanctuary lives, I'm thinking."

"No." Raisa whispered, not wanting to go through this again. "I don't want to hurt anyone."

"No one said you wanted to, just that you could."

That was semantics. Once people knew a body could suck their energy out, and for all intents and purposes, make them implode at will, it colored the way they looked at a person. "I wouldn't."

"Raisa?" Jared's drawl rolled over her in a familiar command.

Oh God, she didn't want to look at him. Jared was an old-fashioned man, the kind who liked to be stronger than a woman. This was going to change everything between them unless he could accept it. His grip shifted to her shoulders. His hands were warm and strong, creating an illusion of protection and gentleness. She closed her eyes and savored the feeling, appreciating it all the more for how fleeting it was going to be. He pushed with one hand, pulled with the other, and she turned. One step at a time, her heart in her throat. His finger under her chin tipped it up in that gesture that was so familiar it was another form of caress.

"Is that true?"

"Of course it's true," Slade grunted. "Look at what happened to my energy when she touched me."

Jared didn't even glance at the screen. "I don't give a shit about your experiment."

"What do you want to know?" Raisa asked him. "Do you want to know if I killed someone with my touch?"

"Did you?"

"Once."

"Who?"

The knot in her throat made it hard to speak. "Your brother."

Slade came to his feet. "You're the bitch who killed Caleb?"

She flinched. Jared moved. With a slam of his hand to the center of Slade's chest, he knocked him back into the chair. It rolled six feet under the impact, before he caught his balance. "Stay out of it, Slade."

"The hell I will." His feet hit the floor with jagged thumps. "Caleb's my brother, too."

"And even if he will, I won't."

The new voice jerked her around. Jared swore, catching her arm. She barely felt his restraint. All her attention was on the man approaching her. He had the Johnson jaw, the Johnson build, and the Johnson confidence. Three steps closer and she also saw he had the Johnson temper. His slate-blue eyes flickered with flames that belied his easy manner.

Wild. The description flashed in her mind. This brother was the wild one. His lips curved in an easy smile that sent a chill down her spine. "Is this the little vamp you've been looking for all these centuries, Jared?"

Raisa braced her spine and lifted her chin in a challenge. "Who's asking?"

Jace touched his finger to the brim of his gray Stetson. "Jace Johnson."

She noticed he left off the "ma'am" that the other men had tacked on to show respect. She didn't think it was accidental. Jared pulled her back to his side. The hairs on her arms stood on end as his energy seethed. "You're talking to my wife, Jace."

"From what I heard, I'm talking to the woman who killed my brother."

He took another step forward. His energy reached out. Behind her, Jared responded to the threat with a gathering of force. If she didn't do something, this was going to get very ugly, and for all that Jared felt he had to protect her, she couldn't be responsible for him hurting his brother.

"I also saved his life," she pointed out.

"Not with his permission."

"He hasn't exactly been complaining, has he?"

"Not lately," Slade interjected, watching the brothers. Watching her.

"What if I said I didn't particularly care?"

With one yank of his arm, Raisa was where she didn't want to be. Behind Jared and out of the way. "Then I'd say you and I have a problem."

Raisa placed her palm in the middle of Jared's back. His muscles were knots of preparation, belying the hip-shot stance he'd adopted. "I don't know why you're bothering to pretend," she muttered for his ears alone. "No one believes you're relaxed."

It carried farther than she wanted. The last thing she expected was Jace's snort of laughter.

"She always this blunt?"

Short and to the point, Jared's answer was simple: "No."

The soft clack of a keyboard was the only sound for the next few heartbeats. The tension in the room was thick enough to cut. Raisa tried to sort through it, but all she could sense was Jared. His energy surrounded her, crowded her, distracting her while Jace stared at them both, doing an assessment of his own.

Finally, Jace broke the standoff. "Seeing how you're set on keeping her, I guess I can't go holding a grudge."

"Especially as Caleb isn't dead," Slade murmured distractedly.

"He does seem rather content right now," Jace acknowledged. He took another step forward and held out his hand. Raisa stepped up to Jared's side. He nodded. She reluctantly accepted the handshake. Jace's energy poured over her, reaching deeply into the shadows of memory, striking a familiar chord. The sensation was familiar, but she couldn't place it.

"Have we met before?"

His smile was pure sensuality. "That, I would have remembered."

She blinked at the sheer charisma in his smile. Jace Johnson was not only wild, he was what, in her day, they would have called a rogue. A ladies' man. Confident in his ability to please a woman. "I think I would have, too."

Another spurt of recognition flowed over her. She grabbed Jace's hand before he could withdraw it, drawing his energy into her, testing it against the implanted memory.

"Rai," Jared asked. "Do you want to give him back his hand?"

"No," She held on tighter as past met with present in her mind.

"Care to tell me why not?"

She shook her head as the men stared at her, frowns forming on their very similar faces. The edges of Jace's energy overlapped the memory perfectly. Edge to edge, curve to curve, indent to indent. It was him. The man to whom Miri had given her heart, her body. The heartless bastard who'd fathered her child and left them unprotected for the Sanctuary to find and torture. It was Jace. Rage blocked her vision. Her fangs cut into her mouth. Her talons stretched for his blood. "You bastard."

He drew back. She followed.

"Rai?"

She ignored Jared and Slade's fussing with the energy device. She only had eyes for Jace. "You horrible, selfish bastard."

She slapped his face with everything she had. Her talons caught on his cheek, laying it open. He grabbed for her arm. Jared yelled, "Don't touch her."

"Then call her off."

"Not until she's had her say."

Jace rubbed his cheek, looked at the blood on his fingers, and narrowed his gaze. "Well, I'm about done listening."

"No, you're not." Raisa's palm stung from the slap. It wasn't enough. She hadn't hurt him enough. Nothing ever could. Miri had suffered so much because of him. She took a step closer, the toes of her shoes touching the toes of his boots. "You left her. She didn't have anywhere to go. She couldn't go back to her pack pregnant, and they got her." She drew her hand back to slap him again, caught herself mid-swing, and placed her hand on his chest. There were better ways to make him pay. "Because of you, they got her," she whispered.

She tuned her energy to his.

"He's Miri's mate?" Jared asked. He couldn't have sounded more shocked if she'd shot him in the butt.

Jace grabbed her arm, hauling her up on her toes. "You know where Miri is?"

"Don't touch her."

"It's all right." She gathered her power into a fine point.

Jared flung Jace's hand off her. "The hell it is."

"Jared," Slade warned. "If you don't stop her, Caleb won't be the only brother she kills."

Jace knocked Jared aside, catching him by surprise, sending him flying backward. In a flash his hand was around Raisa's throat, squeezing as he propelled her backward toward the wall. "She isn't going to do a damn thing but tell me where the hell Miri is."

Raisa hit the wall with bruising force. Air whooshed from her lungs, gathering in a painful knot at the constriction in her throat. She could see Jared coming fast, heard Slade's warning to Jace, but it didn't matter. They wouldn't be in time to save him. Weak, it was a long process. Strong, it would only take one heartbeat, and then his wouldn't work anymore. God, she wished she could kill him.

Jared's hand landed on Jace's shoulder. Jace's fingers relaxed on her throat. She opened her fist over Jace's heart, and let her power do what it did best. In a hard surge she drew his life from him.

Jace jerked as if shot from behind, a horrible noise coming from his mouth. Slade called his name. Jace's grip on her throat tightened with crushing power, cutting off her air for one second before he dropped, taking her down with him. She hit her shoulder and her head. Stars exploded before her eyes. She heard someone call her name, and then Jace's. When the stars cleared, Slade was bent over Jace and Jared knelt beside her. Neither looked happy.

Jared lifted her off the floor, bracing her against his thigh as his hand went to her throat, his expression one of fury and fear. His fingers probed the sides of her neck. Fire burned in his gaze. His touch was gentle. "How badly is Jace hurt?"

"What makes you think I didn't kill him?"

"I know you, Rai."

"I wanted to kill him." She still did.

"But you couldn't."

"I made a promise."

"And because you couldn't."

She glared at Jace where he lay on the floor, unconscious, his hat sitting awkwardly beside his head. "I plan on working on that."

Jared lifted her higher against his chest, sliding his arm under her knees. "You do that, but there's something to remember."

"What?"

He brushed a kiss across her head as he stood. "Jace loves women."

"So?" She slid her hands up around his neck.

"He was ready to kill you to find out where Miri is. A man doesn't go that far off balance unless he's desperate."

Raisa glanced over at Jace again. He was stirring. Slade was hovering over him with his device, glancing at the screen and muttering "Perfect" about every other second. "Or maybe he's just pathetic."

"I take it you're not bowled over by his handsome good looks?"

She shook her head and rested her cheek on his chest. "He's not my type."

"Now that might be a problem."

"Why?"

"Because he's going to insist on being part of the team that's heading out tomorrow to rescue Miri."

# ❦ 21 ❦

MEN with guns were everywhere. Testosterone and energy flooded the air in an overpowering combination as the Renegades prepared for the rescue mission. Jace oversaw it all, cold and deadly, single-minded in his determination to bring Miri home. Raisa could like him for that alone.

Allie came up beside Raisa on the deep wooden porch of the guest cabin, fanning the air in front of her face as if that could remove the oppressive aura. "Makes you nauseated, doesn't it?"

Raisa glanced over at her. "I thought you were told to stay away from me?"

"Caleb tells me to do a lot of things." Allie said, looking totally unconcerned.

"And?"

Allie rested her forearms on the mound of her stomach. "While he may slip and forget which century he's living in, I'm pretty much a twenty-first-century kind of woman twenty-four-seven and make up my own mind what I'm going to do."

"It really isn't safe to be around me."

"Because you might blow up any second?"

Raisa nodded. "And because I can suck the life out of you in a second."

Allie smiled. "Well, I can warp your mind in half that time, but since I see both of us as being too high up the evolutionary scale to so mindlessly indulge, I think we're both safe."

"You can scramble minds?"

"In most instances it's a useless skill, but it did come in handy when the Sanctuary had me."

"I didn't know you were a Sanctuary prisoner."

"They probably don't advertise it." She tipped her head to the side. Her hair swung around her face, catching the moonlight before adding a shadow to her smile. "I wasn't the most congenial of guests."

Raisa rested her hands on the porch rail. "Now, why do I get the feeling that's probably the understatement of the year?"

"Probably because you're an astute woman with well-honed instincts."

Despite her worries, Raisa couldn't help but smile. Allie had a way about her that was at once confident and wry. "You are crazy."

"My family certainly thinks so."

"You have family?"

Allie's smile dropped away. "Six brothers and a father."

Raisa blinked as she absorbed the ramifications of that. "That must be hard."

Allie rubbed her belly. "It is. They think I'm dead."

When Raisa had passed, there had been no one to mourn her. Raisa couldn't imagine what she'd do if there had been someone she'd loved still on the mortal side. "How do you handle it?"

"For now, because I haven't found a way to make anything else work, I'm letting the dead thing ride."

"But you plan on making it work?"

Allie stared across the compound at Caleb. "Absolutely."

Raisa gathered, from the set of Allie's jaw as she stared at her husband, that Caleb was comfortable with the dead scenario. "Then I'm pretty sure you will."

Allie cut her a wry glance. "Thanks for the vote of confidence."

"Oh, I mean it. If anyone can do it, you can."

Allie's eyebrows went up. "Was that an insult or a compliment?"

"Definitely a compliment. Anyone who can handle Caleb can handle anything."

The smile came back to Allie's energy. "You make it sound like such a chore when in reality it's fun."

It was Raisa's turn to look surprised. "Fun?"

"Yup." She rubbed her belly. "My husband is one of the few men who can engage me in a battle of wits and enjoy it."

Raisa couldn't wrap her mind around that. "So I gather he's not part of the family that thinks you're crazy?"

"Caleb? No." Allie's smile softened the same way her gaze did as it searched out her husband who was now reading the riot act to someone about the care he'd demonstrated toward a gun. "He's a pussycat who gets me."

Raisa didn't think the were who was currently at the wrong end of Caleb's temper saw him as a pussycat. "Uh-huh."

Allie leaned against the roof support. Her expression was knowing. "Sort of like Jared when it comes to you."

Raisa grimaced. "It's probably not a good time to go there."

The other woman stared pointedly at the bruises on Raisa's neck. "Why? Because he and Jace are currently at odds?"

"Because about all I've brought the man is disaster, and sooner or later it's going to occur to him that I'm not exactly an asset."

"It won't."

Raisa was just as sure it would. The tension between Jared and Jace was palpable even at this distance. "He loves his brothers."

"Yes, but he needs you."

"Only the part of him that's vampire."

Allie rolled her eyes. "Why am I the only one who doesn't compartmentalize feelings? There is no vampire Jared and human Jared.

They're one and the same person, and that person cares for and needs you."

"You don't understand—"

"Oh puh-leeze," Allie interrupted, brushing her bangs out of her eyes. "I understand a lot. I understand that if your last name is Johnson and you're male, you thrive on conflict and stress. I understand if your last name is Johnson and you're male, your heart is untouchable until you meet one woman, and then you fall like a rock at first sight. I understand if your last name is Johnson and you're in love, there is nothing you hold more dear than your woman, even if you're an autocratic idiot about showing it."

"Caleb doesn't strike me as an idiot."

Caleb turned at that precise moment. He stilled as he noted Allie's presence on the porch beside Raisa. Allie smiled and waved. Caleb frowned and snapped out an order over his shoulder before striding toward them.

"Then pay attention," Allie ordered.

As soon as Jared noticed Caleb's direction, he changed his course. Raisa sighed. "Caleb's protecting you doesn't pit him against his brothers."

"It did."

Raisa really wanted to hear that story. "What did you do about it?"

Allie looked at her like she'd lost her mind. "Let them work it out. I had other things on my plate to cope with."

*Let them work it out.* Allie had said that as if it was the logical thing to do, but logic had nothing to do with this situation. Caleb closed the distance between them rapidly. Jared closed it from the other side of the yard with the same speed. Both men wore hats that threw their expressions into shadow, but nothing could disguise the aggression in the set of their shoulders or the determination in their stride.

"Caleb doesn't look happy."

Allie was remarkably unconcerned with the big vamp's anger. "He's just out of sorts because he has to stay home and miss the fun."

"He's staying home?"

She patted her belly. "I can only take his blood, and I need to feed too often for him to be gone for more than few hours."

"He doesn't mind?"

"Of course he minds, but he'd mind a heck of a lot more if his wife and child suffered. And if there's one thing the Johnsons grudgingly understand, it's the need for compromise."

"Compromise in what?" Caleb asked, his gaze running over his wife before flicking to Raisa.

"Relationships." Allie tipped her face up for a kiss. Caleb gave it, his eyes still watchfully on Raisa.

Just for the heck of it, Raisa gasped and clutched her chest. He whirled and hunched over, shielding Allie.

Raisa could hear Allie's sigh. Her fingers were white against Caleb's dark brown coat as she patted his back, before stepping around him. "You worry too much."

Caleb gave her an irritated glance. "You don't worry enough."

The porch step creaked. The warning had to be intentional. "For Christ's sake, Caleb," Jared growled with exasperation. "Raisa would never risk Allie."

His arm came around her shoulders. Familiar, heavy, and warm. The warmth sank deeper than her skin as she realized he wasn't lying. He truly believed she wouldn't let Allie be hurt. She leaned into his side, feeling his start and then his satisfaction as their energy blended. It was good to know.

"Not intentionally," Caleb agreed.

"Do you really believe, as skilled as she is with energy, that Raisa wouldn't know if a death signal was being sent?"

"She'd only have a split second."

"She's a vampire!" Allie cut in, propping her hands on her husband's chest, the protrusion of her belly forcing her to arch back.

Caleb took her weight easily. "How much more warning would she need?"

"Good point," Caleb dropped a kiss on her cheek before straightening and glaring at Raisa. "But that was still a shitty thing to do."

She shrugged. "Just fulfilling your expectations."

"Serves you right," Jared cut in, "for reacting rather than thinking. The implant is in her head, not her chest."

Allie glanced over at her. "I thought it was funny."

Caleb's "You would" outgunned Raisa's "Thank you."

"Which, naturally, makes it all right," Allie continued as if Caleb's displeasure wasn't wrapping all about her.

"No, it doesn't."

Allie looked pointedly around. "Do you really want to argue with me here? With everyone watching?"

Caleb pretended to consider it. "Yes."

"You'll lose, you know."

His big hand cupped her small face. There was so much love in the gesture. "I'll risk it."

"Well, I for one would prefer you didn't," Jared interrupted.

"Spoilsport," Allie shot back

Jared just grinned. "I know how long you two can draw these discussions out, and we do need to be going."

To rescue Miri. Rai looked out over the yard at the hard-eyed men preparing for battle. The moment of humor died, and the cold reality of the impossibility of what they were going to attempt sank into her bones.

"They know it's not going to be easy, don't they?" Raisa asked.

Jared sobered instantly and nodded. "That's why they're wearing the big guns."

The sarcasm landed on her insecurity. "I know they think they know, but the Sanctuary has a lot riding on Miri. They won't let her go without a fight."

"Neither will we."

"It's just that she's not like the other women they've captured."

Raisa rubbed her hands up and down her arms, chilled from the inside out, not looking at Jared, not looking at Caleb or Allie, just focusing on the men in the yard. Jace in particular. Miri's hope. "They think because they could collect hormone and DNA samples all through her pregnancy that she's their best chance to create the first Sanctuary superbaby, and they won't back off even if the odds turn against them."

"Raisa." The familiar call slid along her nerves.

It wasn't a surprise when Jared's finger slid under her chin and tipped her face up. His expression was dead serious as her eyes met his. "Trust me."

It just popped out. "The way you trust me?"

His right eyebrow lifted, and his finger curled tighter under her chin. "I trusted you enough to bring you to my home. How much more do you need?"

She hadn't ever thought of it that way. To Jared, his family was everything, yet he'd brought her here, to the place where the Renegades hid out, where his brother's pregnant wife waited to give birth, to where Slade hatched all their inventions. She only had one thing to ask, "Why?"

His finger stroked down her cheek. The shake of his head was infinitesimal. Was he shaking his head at her or himself? "Because my gut says to and because you're my family now."

*I understand if your last name is Johnson and you're in love, there is nothing you hold more dear than your woman.*

Was Jared in love with her? Raisa stilled the wild leap of her heart, held the possibility to her, tucking it away like a treasure to be explored in safer times, and asked, "Does that mean I have to thrive on stress?"

Jared blinked. Allie laughed. "There are ways around that."

"Thank goodness." She met Caleb's forest green eyes. Maybe because she felt bad about her earlier joke or maybe because she just needed to do something nice, she told him, "I'd never let the Sanctuary hurt any of you through me."

"Your word?"

She nodded.

Caleb released Allie, steadying her a second while she regained her balance, and then held out his hand. For a second Raisa couldn't move. Caleb waited. Jared stood beside her. Supporting her, she realized, in whichever way she chose to treat the gesture. How was she supposed to resist a man who gave her unconditional acceptance?

*You aren't.*

*Well, pardon me if I don't know what to do with something I haven't had before.*

*You could just accept it.*

That would be risky. She'd trusted people in her past, and they'd ended up betraying her by disposing of her when the need arose. It had taught her to think of relationships as short-term collaborations. That was what she was comfortable with. Now, Jared wanted her to go back to the way of thinking that had left her so devastated so many times.

"Would it help if I pointed out the only ones I bite these days are weres and Allie?" Caleb asked, his mouth quirking with amusement, that stupid hand of his still held out, a powerful enticement to indulge in her old self-defeating ways. Good grief! She'd just gotten done convincing herself this century that she didn't need to trust anyone besides herself to get by.

"Maybe."

Caleb glanced at Jared. They were obviously communicating telepathically. Caleb withdrew his hand, and he studied her in a way that was remarkably like Slade's when he was in the middle of an experiment. "It's the truth."

"And I'm supposed to believe that?"

"At some point you've got to believe in something," another male voice cut in from the foot of the stairs.

Jace. Residual anger sent chills down Raisa's arms. Jared's brother. The man she'd thought had abandoned Miri. The man moving heaven and earth in a crazy plan to get her back.

"The way you believed in me?"

Part of her still held a grudge that he'd tried to choke her. He didn't flinch from her glare. "Miri believed in you. That's good enough for me."

"I could be lying."

"You're not."

"What makes you so sure?"

"You wouldn't betray Jared."

"You have absolutely no proof of that!"

He tipped his hat back, revealing the cold, hard purpose in his eyes and the wry humor edging his mouth. "I've got my gut. What more do I need?"

"Proof positive."

"There's no such thing in this life."

"That being the case, we've decided to put our eggs in your basket," Caleb interjected.

And that faith might be worth something if the Sanctuary believed the message she was going to send. If they didn't decide to blow her head off her shoulders for the fun of it. If they hadn't already killed Miri. If Slade's device worked. If, if, if.

She bit her lip. Jared's hand came around her waist, firm and strong. His chest pressed into her back, solid and thick with powerful muscle. And all around them both in an invisible cloak, his energy threaded with hers, so intertwined there was no telling where hers ended and his began. She blinked. When had that happened? When had she committed to him so completely that anything she said to the contrary now was just word games?

Darn it, these things were always sneaking up on her.

"I guess if you're going to be that way about it, I can't go on holding a grudge."

"I'd appreciate it if you didn't." Jared murmured above her, his shadow stretching over her as he leaned down. "Jace is one of my favorite brothers."

"They're all your favorite," she groused.

"True."

"They're not mine."

"They'll grow on you."

She leaned her head back into his chest to see his face; the angle was off. All she could see was the underside of his hat. Smudges from his fingers abounded under the rim. It could definitely use a cleaning. She reached up and touched the shadow of beard on the underside of his jaw. "You're awfully confident about that."

The back of his fingers skimmed her cheek before his hand captured hers, bringing them both to rest on her shoulder. "You've got an awfully soft heart."

"Not for long. I'm working on toughening it up."

"Then we'll have to work fast at winning you over," Caleb interjected.

It wasn't going to be that hard. "Just get Miri out and you can call it a done deal."

"Miri's freedom is my debt," Jace corrected quietly.

"She's my friend," Raisa countered, just in case he thought his claim was bigger.

"And my responsibility."

"Oh, for heaven's sake," Allie exclaimed, hands on hips. "Split the obligation down the middle and call it quits. We have too much to do to be fighting amongst ourselves over who cares more."

Was that what they had been fighting about? Raisa wasn't sure. And from the flicker of emotion that crossed Jace's face, neither was he.

Allie balanced herself with her hand on the rail and faced Jace. "Now, I assume Slade will be joining us shortly?"

"As soon as he puts the finishing touches on the last of his devices."

"And there haven't been any last-minute changes to the plan?" The arch of Allie's brow was knowing.

"Just one," Caleb acknowledged.

"And what would that be?" Raisa asked, knowing what it was before he even said it from the way he was looking at Jared and not at her.

"You're staying here."

"No, I'm not."

Jared had been angling for that since the get-go, but the reality was that only she knew the back way into the compound, and explaining it wasn't the same as being there. And if the place had been booby-trapped in the interim, only she would recognize it. Plus there was that other pesky detail.

"Have you forgotten I'm the only one who can sense the bad guys when they're masked?"

Jared's jaw went stubborn. "We'll get past them."

"You need more than to just get past them. You need to get past them undetected."

"We'll manage."

She ducked out from under his arm. "You just don't want me in danger."

"None of us do."

That, surprisingly, came from Jace.

She waved away the concern. "I'm not the one who needs protecting. Miri does."

"Miri needs rescuing." Jared didn't come after her like she expected, but his energy did, holding tightly to hers, keeping them connected. "You, sunbeam, like all treasures, need protecting."

"Good God, Jared Johnson spouting poetry, now I've seen it all," a man's voice called. Derek and Slade approached the house. Both were broad-shouldered and lean hipped, with the easy stride of warriors. The weapons draped over their shoulders merely completed the image.

Jared didn't even glance at Derek. "Talk to me when you get a woman of your own." His hand cupped her cheek. "You'll find there's nothing you'll value more."

Unlike the Johnsons, the McClarens never wore hats. Derek's short-cropped hair gleamed a deep bronze above his handsome, square-jawed face. "There's no doubt I'll be valuing her but not to the point that I'll be spouting poetry."

Raisa couldn't turn her eyes away from Jared's as his thumb brushed over her lower lip. His energy reached out. Hers embraced it eagerly. The touch of his mind followed, and for the first time, she consciously opened hers to his. She felt his surprise and then pure male satisfaction as he measured her response.

"Again, Derek, talk to me when you've found her."

There was a brief silence. Caleb broke it.

"I'll get the men ready." His turned to go. His boot hit the top step, then the next. Raisa watched him leave, telling herself it was okay, but knowing it wasn't. She owed Jared this. She caught Jared's thumb in her teeth, kissed it, and said, "Hold that thought."

She hurried after Caleb, catching up to him five feet from the porch. He turned when he heard her behind him. Now that she had his attention, she wasn't sure what to do with it. She rubbed her palm on her jeans and then stuck it out. His right brow rose in that way that reminded her so much of Jared. She licked her dry lips. "If the offer is open, I'd like to start over."

His big hand swallowed hers. "Welcome to the family."


**JACE** and the small group of men raced through the night, sweeping her along in their center, an army of deadly shadows gliding silently through the forest, blending in and out of the faint moonlight.

Having gotten her way, Raisa levitated alongside the array of men who flanked her, feeling their displeasure every step of the way. None of them wanted her here. She'd like to think she'd gotten her way because of her logical argument, but the truth was, Slade wasn't sure the device he'd fashioned to block the killing signal from the Sanctuary would work in time if the signal was weakened by distance. Hence, her presence amidst the weres decked out with enough fancy electronic equipment to make her feel like the warrior queen in a futuristic novel. A tremor of vibration came to her, reminding her she had a job to do.

"Patrol on the left about a quarter mile," she whispered into the earpiece.

There was a flurry of tapping on earpieces from the men around her.

"Repeat that," came as clear as a bell over her head set. The communication devices, which optimized a man's deeper octave, had trouble with her softer, higher voice.

Raisa rolled her eyes and sent the message to Jared telepathically instead. He then repeated the message in a low whisper. Jace direct their course to the right. It boggled the mind that a man like Slade couldn't figure out there were times when a woman might need to use one of these devices.

*Vampire and were women do not go into battle*, Jared informed her with an edge to the thought.

*Be that as it may, there are obviously cases where we have our uses.*

And it felt darn good. Despite the danger, despite the fact that she probably wouldn't come out of this alive, Raisa was finding it exhilarating being part of the team to save Miri. For so long she'd been a helpless victim, but now she was an integral part of something bigger, and it felt good.

*Don't get too addicted to that feeling. As soon as Slade pops that device out of your skull, I'm wrapping you in cotton wool and tucking you away in a bedroom back on the Circle J.*

She would have argued the point, but she didn't have enough energy. Though the men were adjusting their speed to hers, she really wasn't in the best physical condition, and the strain was telling. She settled for sticking her tongue out at him. A gesture Derek caught sight of, which produced the reverberation of a warm, very male, and compelling chuckle in her ear. She blinked. The earpieces just might be too well tuned to male voices. Distracted, she miscalculated the next leap over a low bush. Her foot got caught in the branches. Snow puffed up all around her as her knees hit the ground.

*Rats!*

Before her face planted in the snow, hands grabbed her arms

and she was lifted, Jared and Derek carrying her as if she weighed nothing until she found her feet again.

Were they really that strong?

"Nah. You just don't weigh anything." There was a murmur of agreement across the channel and a lot of disapproving looks.

She blew the snowflakes off her upper lip and rubbed her cheek on her shoulder. "Give it up," she said into the mike. "I'm not going home."

That just earned her more looks.

"Are you hurt?" Jared asked.

He knew she wasn't. She'd felt his energy all over her when she'd fallen so his asking of the question must be to placate the worry eating him alive. He didn't like her being here, didn't like the risk she was taking, didn't like that it was necessary. She cut him a glance, injecting a bit of humor into the tension. "My pride took an awful beating."

The twitch of Jared's lips could have been a smile. A stray chuckle or too meandered over the com. "If you'd stayed home where you belong, your pride would still be intact."

She ignored the grunts of agreement in her ear. "It was my choice."

"That doesn't mean I have to like it."

They'd been having this argument since Slade had announced he wasn't sure the blocking device would work on a signal weakened by distance. Jared had been willing to risk it, opting for less overall risk. Raisa had not. "No, it doesn't."

From her other side, Derek offered, deadpan, "If you're hurt, I could kiss it and make it better for you."

Jared immediately growled a warning to the were. Derek didn't turn his head but the creases fanning from the corner of his eyes indicated his amusement. The were leader's habit of needling Jared usually irritated her; right now it didn't. Anything to divert Jared from his worry worked for her.

"Hell, man, you're getting so predictable there's not much point in teasing you anymore," Derek tacked on.

"And your point would be?"

"Well, with Caleb out of the game, you down, and Jace following the same path, I'm running out of amusement factors."

"Get a dog."

"It wouldn't be the same."

"Get a wife."

"She's playing hard to get."

"She's playing hide and seek," a male voice she recognized as the new were to the group said. "And she doesn't want to be found."

"Like your mate does," Derek shot back.

"Quiet," Jace hissed over the headsets.

The men immediately dropped back to that intense silence.

Raisa forced a smile to her lips at the exchange, despite the pain beginning anew in her head. The Sanctuary's sadistic version of "knock-knock." They'd been trying to get her attention for the last hour. She couldn't send a message now without revealing her location. She couldn't tell Jared because he had no confidence that the Sanctuary would continue to wait for her to give them what they wanted and, therefore, would insist she transmit, which was never going to happen.

Bottom line, she wasn't going to be the one to jeopardize this mission. Miri needed Jace. Jace needed Jared, and they all needed her to guide them through the Sanctuary patrols. Which meant the Sanctuary was just going to have to tolerate being on terminal hold.

A trickle of that almost energy came from ahead. Raisa focused on it, trying to separate it into threads.

*There are Sanctuary ahead.*

"Jace, we've got company," Jared whispered in a thread of sound into the com.

"How many?"

Raisa shook her head. *Two, maybe three.*

"Two or three."

"Are they tracking us?"

Jared stared at her, awaiting her answer. How was she supposed to know that? She shrugged.

"Unknown."

Jace raised his hand. The men came to a stop. Raisa sat down on a rotting log, hoping it would hold her, because her legs sure didn't want to. Jared took a step toward her. She held up a hand, keeping him at a distance as she focused on the energy that flowed to her in subtle bands. The bands didn't move for endless moments, just held at a steady distance. Did the Sanctuary suspect they were coming? The last message she'd sent said the Renegades knew about a compound to the east and they were heading west, but she could have slipped up. She'd been so nervous, that might have gone through, too, and aroused their suspicions. She waited in an agony of doubt for those bands to give her an idea of what they were doing. She had never excelled at waiting.

Without anything to distract her, she couldn't disregard the next warning throb at the base of her skull. Whoever was in charge of the button was going to get serious soon. She sent another pulse of energy to the implant, disrupting the frequency in what she hoped resembled static. As before when she'd tried it, the pain abated before it came back, slightly altered but not as strong. As if they were testing.

Playing with feedback had bought her an hour so far, but sooner or later the Sanctuary was going to get suspicious. And knowing the Sanctuary, when they did, they were going to be vindictive. Raisa took a breath, stilling her panic at the thought. She'd never been able to adjust to pain or raise her level of tolerance. She dreaded the moment they would decide to punish her. The only thing she dreaded more was letting Jared down again.

With the Sanctuary feed under control, she could refocus on the patrol's energy. It was moving away and slightly perpendicular to their current course. They were moving on.

Raisa touched Jared's arm. At the movement several of the party glanced at her expectantly, waiting on her decree. It was both heady and scary knowing they trusted her with their safety. She made a cutting motion across her neck. Jared nodded and spoke into his com. "The path is clear again."

Another trickle of energy came at her. One she had no trouble recognizing. She quickly closed off her mind to Jared's a split second before the pain lanced into her skull. She covered her gasp by pretending to smother a cough. The men fell back into formation, impatience radiating off them as she took an extra few seconds working up the ability to stand. Derek held out his hand. She placed hers in it. There was no way he could miss the trembling in her fingers. His blue eyes studied her face. She forced a smile, knowing he saw the trembling in the corners. "I'm a little out of shape."

"We've only got an hour more." He glanced over at Jared, who was talking to Jace. "Do you need help, or can you make it?"

She quickly got to her feet. "I can make it."

"I'll just tell Jared."

She caught his arm. "Don't."

If Jared touched her, she wouldn't be able to hide anything from him.

"He should know."

"He'll know soon enough."

But hopefully not any sooner than he needed to.

Derek stared at her for the few seconds it took Jared to come up to them.

"Ready to head out?" Jared asked.

Raisa held Derek's gaze, begging him silently. The nod of his head was almost imperceptible.

She gave Jared a bright smile through the building pain consuming her. "Yes."

From the glances the other men threw at her, she might have just overdone the enthusiasm. From the way they all watched her as they resumed that mile-eating pace, she was sure of it.

Thirty minutes later, four more patrols successfully evaded and one more ahead, her lungs burning, her legs aching, every step bringing a tear to her eye, Raisa ran out of time. The Sanctuary allowed her the luxury of knowing it was coming, letting her feel the buildup of power the way one felt the draw of a wave before it came crashing down. She stumbled on the anticipation of the agony a split second before it arrived, grabbing for Jared. She saw his brows snap down in a frown, heard his curse, and then a bolt of agony struck through the base of her skull, wedging down through the hollow of her spinal column, shattering outward in knife-edge arcs of pain, so much worse than before.

Jared's arm came around her. "Raisa!"

She felt his call against her ear, heard it battering the shields she'd put around her mind. She couldn't answer, paralyzed by the unending torment that ripped across her nerve endings. A blur of black closed around her. A band of steel compressed her ribs. The world tilted. She buried her scream against Jared's side, digging her talons into his flesh. Hands fastened around her wrists and pulled them away.

"The scent of blood will draw the Sanctuary patrols," Jace said, his harsh drawl only audible because of the headset. He was right. She had to retract her talons. She couldn't. The pain was too intense, her survival instinct driving the need for defense.

"Hold on, sunbeam." Jared's deep voice slid like a balm over her distress, soothing the rougher edges. "Just five minutes."

She wasn't going to survive five minutes of this. She grabbed his side and held on. Cutting her talons through his coat and shirt rather than his skin as he carried her along. It was the best she could do.

"The patrol," she managed to gasp.

"Fuck the patrol." That was Jace.

"So close." They were so close to rescuing Miri. They couldn't be detected now, not because of her. Jared's muscles gathered. His energy flared outward. Trees passed in a blur as he put on more speed.

She crawled up against his body, driven to move by the agony and the battle not to call out. She could feel the sweat dripping down her face. "Blood."

Her blood. They'd scent her blood.

"Don't worry about it."

She wiped her face on her shirt, trying to keep the drops from hitting the snow and leaving a trail.

"How bad is she?" Derek asked.

"Very bad."

"Shit. I knew it."

Jared's energy honed to a razor point. "Knew what?"

"Knew she wasn't right back at the last stop."

Jared's "And you didn't tell me?" coincided with Jace's "This has been going on for almost an hour?"

"She said she was just tired."

Jared gritted his teeth at that revelation as Raisa's hands crept higher over his shoulder. She wouldn't want to do anything to risk Miri's rescue. She had a thing, as Allie would put it, about not disappointing people. Dammit, he should have seen the signs.

He cupped her head in his hand, supporting her as she weakened.

"Give them something." He backed the order with every bit of compulsion he could manage. He ran into the brisk wall of her will. She shook her head and immediately moaned. Her body went rigid. Shit. She wasn't going to do it, and she was stubborn enough to make sure she didn't.

*Jace.*

*What?*

*She's not going to make it.*

*Shit.* There was a pause in which Jared could feel Jace's mind working and reworking the plan.

*If we split, and if she can hold on ten more minutes, we've still got a chance. Can she hold on?*

*No.*

Weak and fragile, Raisa's *I can make ten more minutes* overrode his denial. Jace's response was immediate as he signaled the men to split, racing off with everyone except Derek and Slade. *Your call, Jared.*

Raisa's *We have to try* ripped at his guilt, his conviction. If it were him, he'd say go for it, but it wasn't him, it was Raisa, and nothing was more important than her. He looked down. She was bleeding from her pores, her eyes, ears, and nose. She wasn't going to make ten more seconds, let alone ten minutes, and yet, her determination reached out, surrounding him. *No, she can't.*

*Won't fail you.* The thought immediately thrust into his mind, a cry from her heart.

Dammit! Was that what this was about? She thought she had to prove herself to him?

Jared enfolded Raisa in his energy, struggling to keep his rage at bay long enough to give back some of the soothing peace she always gave him so freely.

"Give them something." The order quietly slipped into his head, no accusation in Jace's voice, just acceptance.

Raisa's protest was immediate. *No. Pinpoint us.*

There was a hard break in Jace's connection, a moment of despair and loss, and then he was back in control of himself. *Do it, Raisa.*

Inside Jared, the denial welled. Jace deserved his happiness.

Jace didn't allow it to grow to expression. *Your mate is here.*

And his might already be dead.

Jace was farther away now. *Do what you have to, to save Raisa. If I can get Miri out, I will.*

*And if you can't?*

*I'll die trying.*

It had always been the Johnson brothers together against the world. *Fuck that. I'm not going into eternity short a brother.*

*You have your wife.*

He was the selfish type. He wanted it all.

*Sometimes you just have to take what you get,* Jace answered before severing the connection, leaving Jared with nothing to hold on to except the woman in his arms.

To the right, a darker shadow flashed among the rocks. A cave?

"Slade?" Jared murmured into the com so Derek could understand.

"I see it. Let's hope it's big enough."

Derek glanced at Raisa, his mouth set in a grim line. "It'll be big enough even I have to make it so."

Jared nodded. They were out of time and options.

The cave was small, barely big enough to shelter them from the sun. Derek took up guard at the entrance. Raisa moaned, barely conscious.

Jared glanced at Slade. "Can you get the device out of her head?"

"Yes, but she might go into shock."

"It can't be worse than what she's going through now."

Slade sighed, his gaze sympathetic. "Yeah, this would be hard to top." He opened a surgical pack and laid it on the floor. "Hold her tightly." From his backpack, he took out the energy-blocking device he'd created and set it beside her. "If she moves at the wrong time, we could all get blown up."

Slade set up the equipment with quick, efficient motions. It wasn't fast enough. "Hurry up."

Slade glanced at Raisa. His mouth set in a grim line. "Will do."

Jared cupped Raisa's head in his hand, slipping easily past the few guards she could maintain, tracing the pain back to its source, finding the frequency of the transmitter embedded within, blinking in amazement as he realized she was still blocking the homing frequency.

"You're an amazing woman, sunbeam." His amazing, incredibly strong, unique woman. And they'd tortured and humiliated her. Used her, abused her, and convinced her that she was expendable. Damn them all to hell.

She must have felt his presence.

*Jared.* The mental whisper was very weak.

"Right here."

*Love you.*

The mental cry that punctuated that declaration about ripped his heart out. He wouldn't give her permission to leave him by responding in kind. "Tell me again when you're feeling better."

The shake of her head was more a twitch of muscle than movement. *What . . . tell . . . them?*

Jesus, she was still trying to buy Jace time. He brushed his lips across her eyes, the flutter of her lashes a whisper of butterfly wings against his lips, her life force an uneven pulse.

They were losing her. Grief and fury wrapped around his fear, squeezing it out until there was nothing left inside but ice-cold rage.

"Tell them I'm coming for them."

# ✤ 22 ✤

**S**HE was in a cave. The dark, dank odor of the interior felt embedded into her pores, which meant she'd been here awhile. Raisa kept her eyes closed, assessing her physical condition. It wasn't any more pleasant than her environment. She was weak, her mouth dry, and at the base of her skull, there was a steady throb.

Had they gotten the Sanctuary device out? She started to lift her hand and quickly reconsidered when a sharp jolt of pain shot down her shoulder and across her chest. Further inventory revealed every muscle in her body ached to the point that movement was going to be agony. Had removing the device caused damage? Was that why she was so weak and why it was so difficult for her to move?

She lay there, listening to the sound of water dripping in the distance and tried to remember what had happened. She remembered Jared telling her to give the Sanctuary something, then trying and being too weak to do it. She remembered the cold, deadly intent inside him coalescing as she struggled to send the message. Remembered feeling Jared take over when she failed. Remembered hearing his deep drawl resonate within her even as it reverberated outward in a lethal promise.

*I'm coming for you.*

She shivered at the memory. It was one thing to know Jared was capable of killing. It was another to feel the intent within him, to know the depths of which he was capable. Even if it was for the right reasons. There were some illusions she'd prefer to keep.

"You ready to join us again?"

Raisa licked her dry lips with her equally dry tongue. She couldn't place the voice. "Depends."

"On what?"

Slade. It was Slade who was talking to her. The kernel of irrationality that clung to the hope that Jared had stayed with her rather than following his brother withered. She told herself it was fine. Told herself that it made more sense for him to leave Slade with her than to stay himself. He wasn't a doctor. He was a warrior, and Jace needed a warrior in battle. Telling herself all that didn't make the fact that she hadn't come first with him hurt less.

"Did you get the implant out?" Her voice sounded like sandpaper sliding across metal, scratchy and irritated.

"What?" he asked with a stab at humor. "You don't believe what the pain in your neck is telling you."

She appreciated his attempt at humor even though she couldn't play along. "Don't take it personally."

"I'll try not to."

She heard the scrape of his boot sole on dirt as he shifted position. His energy prodded hers in an annoying poke.

"Are you planning on opening your eyes anytime soon?"

"No." If she did, she might burst into tears. She hurt, and she just wanted Jared. And when she opened her eyes, he wasn't going to be there. Lord, she was pathetic.

He sighed. "Well, that's going to complicate my seeing how your pupils react."

That was an attention getter. "Why do you need to see how my pupils react?"

"That implant was attached to your spine. There's a chance I damaged something getting it out."

He said that so calmly, like it was no big thing, but he was talking about her spine, her nerves. She tried to quell the flood of panic.

"How about you try to move your arms?"

"How about I don't." She had no idea if vampire nerves regenerated like their bodies did. The thought of living through eternity paralyzed was terrifying. The thought of trying to move and failing was worse.

A stroke of calm spread over her panic. *Sunbeam?*

Jared. A split second after she felt him in her mind, he was in the cave, displacing air and panic as he settled beside her, filling the space with his scent, his energy, his strength. "Dammit, Slade, I told you not to wake her before I got back from feeding."

She opened her eyes. Jared's face was averted as he glared at his brother, presenting her with the bold outline of his profile.

"I was perfectly obedient." He motioned to her. "She's the one who broke your rules."

"Tattletale."

Even her voice sounded hoarse. Jared turned and Raisa caught her breath. She'd spent the whole of her natural and unnatural life longing for someone to want her. To look at her like the heroes of romance novels looked at the women they loved. Like she was the sun to his moon, the heart in his soul. In the moment Jared's eyes met hers, she knew she hadn't dreamed big enough.

He knelt above her, the skin over his cheekbones white with the emotion he was trying to suppress. Emotion that buffeted the edges of her thoughts. Fear, worry, and something else, something so intense she was afraid to name it. He reached for her cheek. His hand was shaking, the trembling transferring from him to her as he whispered gruffly. "Welcome back."

She couldn't look away from his eyes. They were very green, very warm.

She had to concentrate to bring her hand up, but she managed it. She wrapped her fingers around his wrist and held on tightly. "It's good to be back."

He shifted his grip, cradling her head. "How do you feel?"

"Like I've been run over by a bus."

His thumb brushed her cheek. "I just bet."

"Don't move her," Slade warned. "I need to check how she's healing first."

"Well, hurry up," Jared snapped, glaring at him again.

"Why, are you in a rush?"

"Yes."

She had to ask. "For what?"

Jared made room for Slade to work. "You're overdue for an ass chewing."

Slade snorted.

"Why? I didn't do anything."

"The hell you didn't. You jeopardized your safety."

"I bought Jace time."

"You risked your life!"

Slade's right eyebrow arched as he placed his hands on the sides of her neck. The skin heated and a strange tingling worked outward. "I thought you were going to wait?"

"I am waiting," Jared snapped.

He might be waiting, but his thoughts weren't. They were flooding into her mind, and along with them came images of her face—pale in his night vision, the blood covering her face in a dark smear, tearing from her eyes, dripping from her ears. And along with the image came the imprint of his anguish. Total and complete. Absolutely devastating. He hadn't wanted to live without her. Because he loved her. The knowledge blossomed inside her, spreading and growing, filling her with warmth. He loved her.

She closed her fingers around his, holding on as Slade skimmed his hands over her body, probing with his energy for the right responses.

"I'm going to be fine, Jared."

His snort was eloquent. "You'd say that no matter what was the truth."

Yes, she would. Because she didn't like him to worry. It was sweet that he knew her so well.

His frown got deeper. "There's nothing sweet about me."

He'd been peeking into her mind again. She squeezed his hand. "Then you'll have to start seeing yourself through my eyes."

The expulsion of air could have been a snort of disgust or laughter. "You romanticize everything."

"Since it works to your advantage, why are you complaining?"

Slade chuckled as he slowly bent her leg. "She's got a point, there." His gaze met hers. "That hurt anywhere other than your muscles?" he asked.

She shook her head. His mind probed hers, verifying the answer. A second later she felt Jared intrude, too.

"What?" She looked between them. "You don't trust me?"

Jared's "Hardly" was in perfect synch with Slade's "No."

"Well, that's not very flattering."

"It wasn't meant to be." Jared slipped his hand under her head and glanced over at his brother. "Can I hold her now?"

Slade waved him on before gathering up his equipment. "Go crazy."

Jared lifted her carefully, easing her chest to his. Her sigh blended with his as their bodies flowed together in perfect symmetry. Raisa stroked her energy over Jared's, finding that same symmetry there, relishing his immediate response.

*Mine.*

*Yes.*

His kiss was as consuming as his emotions, not giving her time to breathe or react, just claiming her mouth, her breath, her love. Drawing it into himself as if he couldn't get enough, couldn't quite believe that she was there. She held him through the outpouring of emotion, stroking her hands up and down his back in small, gentle movements.

His lips separated from hers. "Son of a bitch, I love you, Raisa Slovenski, and if you ever do something so unselfish and self-sacrificing again, I'll have your ass for breakfast."

"Kinky."

"I'm serious, Rai."

"I know you are."

He grabbed her shoulder, his fingers biting into the muscle in a way they never would have if he weren't so upset. "I mean it. Nothing, nothing in this world matters more to me than you, and you will not endanger yourself like that again."

The sheer intensity of his emotions blinded her. She grabbed his wrists. "I'll keep it in mind."

"I'm going to have to agree with him on that one," Slade interjected, zipping his pack closed. "That was too close. And Jared, if you don't lighten up, the woman's going to have bruises."

"Shit." Jared loosened his grip, but his emotions still churned.

Raisa looked into his eyes. "Did they get in? Did they get Miri?"

"They got in."

Her stomach sank, hearing what he didn't say louder than what he did. "But what?"

Jared just shook his head, his eyes filling with a sadness she couldn't accept. She slapped his chest. "No! Tell me they got out."

He kept looking at her with that awful sadness. She hit him again. "Stop it." He didn't stop, wouldn't stop. And he didn't do a thing to protect himself, just said, "I'm sorry."

"We don't know what happened after they found her," Slade said from beside her, catching her hand. "There were several shots and then silence."

She yanked her hand free, sitting up straight, ignoring the pain. "Call them on that communication thingie."

"It's too risky."

Raisa froze, her hand falling slowly over Jared's heart. "They're not dead?"

This time Jared answered. "We don't know. We had a plan B and C in case things went wrong, but the only way we'll know if they worked is if Jace and Miri show up at the rendezvous point."

This time she slapped him for a whole other reason. "Why did you let me think they were dead?"

"I didn't. You told me to tell you they got out. I can't."

And he wouldn't give her false hope. She took a calming breath. "What do you believe?"

His jaw set. "That, until I find a body, I'm not believing anything."

Slade's "Amen" was an approving growl.

He wasn't making sense. "Then why did you say you were sorry?"

"I promised you I'd get your friend out."

And he couldn't tell her that he had. She blinked. "Good heavens, do you think I've confused you with Superman?"

Slade's snort wasn't delicate. "Apparently."

The expression on Jared's face confirmed her suspicions. "You might as well know that I'm not having this."

"Having what?"

"I'm not having you go totally macho on me at inconvenient times. I'm not all that matters. You matter, too! And if you think I've forgotten that it's your brother who is missing, too, you have another think coming. You have got to be as upset as I am with a hell of a lot more reason so . . . so . . ."

She came to a stuttering halt.

Jared's right brow lifted in that way that just begged a body to slap him. "Raisa Johnson, did you just swear?"

She had. She wiggled out of his embrace. "See what you've driven me to? And my name is Slovenski, not Johnson."

"Won't be the first time he's driven a woman to cussing," Slade interjected.

Jealousy, mean-spirited and consuming, snuck up past her guard as she got her feet under her. She'd forgotten about her sore muscles. The room spun as her muscles lodged a protest at the sudden move. The mistake cost her precious seconds, stealing some of the thunder from her declaration. "Well, I'd better be the last!"

"That's a given. Sit down before you fall down." Jared caught her left hand in his, easing her back down. He turned his hand palm up and then opened his fingers, leaving her palm suspended on his much larger one. His thumb rested on the third finger, rubbing just below the knuckle, warming her skin, marking her with his heat. His gaze met hers, dead serious. "Will you marry me, Raisa?"

She stared at his thumb, her finger, his face. Was he asking her to marry him because he felt he owed it to her or because he really wanted to?

"There isn't another woman for me."

There wasn't another man for her, either, but if she accepted now, in these circumstances, she'd always wonder. For three heartbeats she didn't know how to answer and then a fragment of a memory provided the answer. "Ask me again when we're out of here."

He hadn't been expecting that. "What the hell difference will that make?"

"Everything to me."

His mouth opened then snapped closed. He let go of her hand. Derek ducked into the cavern. "Hate to be the bearer of bad news, but we've got company."

Slade slung his pack over his shoulder. "Did you scent them?"

"Nope, but I got a hell of a visual." He motioned with his rifle. "Looks to be an easy dozen coming up the slope."

"Time to go." Jared tossed his pack and rifle to Slade.

He caught them easily. "Did you get everything set?"

"Yup." He picked Raisa up.

She grabbed his neck. "I can walk."

He passed her to Derek. "But I need you to run."

She wasn't up for that. Not without feeding. Derek held her like she was a piece of expensive china until Jared came out of the cave and then he passed her back.

"Which way, Rai?"

She opened her mind, sorting through all the energy fields. She pointed down and to the left. "That way's clear."

Jared flashed her a grin. "Not up?"

She hooked her arm around his neck. "Not if I can help it."

His laugh wasn't the full sound she liked to hear, but at least he still had his sense of humor. And as long as the man could laugh, he could heal.

"Then down it is."

Trees blurred as they ran. She could feel the Sanctuary vamps still climbing behind them. They were close. Too close. All they had to do to spot them was to look down. She checked around. There was no cover for a quarter mile. She glanced back over Jared's shoulder. Two Sanctuary men came out of the cave.

"Jared?"

"What."

The men pointed and shouted at their fleeing party. More men came out of the cave.

"They've seen us."

"Good."

His arm shifted beneath her. Muscles flexed. He stopped and turned. In the next instant, a wall of fire detonated in front of the weres. It was followed quickly by an explosion of sound and rocks that spewed into the air like confetti tossed at a party.

When the smoke and dust cleared, the cave opening was gone and there wasn't a Sanctuary man in sight.

She leaned back as far as she dared to see Jared's face. "We were carrying explosives?"

She felt slightly nauseated at the thought.

"Sort of."

"What do you mean, sort of?" She looked between the three men.

"He means Jared had me tweak that bomb that was in your head," Slade explained.

She looked back at the hollowed-out area where three of the Sanctuary men had been standing and then back at Jared.

"All that was in my head?"

"Yes."

If the Sanctuary had detonated it, the device would not only have blown her up but everyone around her—Allie, Jared, Caleb, and God knows who else. "And you left it for them?"

"I thought they deserved a present."

The men headed back down the mountain. She stared at the destruction over Jared's shoulders, all the what-might-have-beens playing in a grotesque video in her mind. That could have been her, would have been her, if fate hadn't thrown her in Caleb's path. And then Jared's. Maybe Allie was right. Maybe things did happen for a reason.

"Jared?"

"What?"

"Ask me now."

He frowned. "Now?"

She couldn't see the top of the hill anymore. She rested her cheek against his chest and listened to the steady beat of his heart. "Yes."

"Why?"

She smiled and pressed her fingertip to the pulse she could see in the hollow of his throat. Carrying her hadn't even elevated it. She did enjoy his strength. "Because it's later."

"What if I'm not ready now?"

"You are."

"What makes you so sure?"

"Because I love you."

The slight break in his stride was gratifying. She replaced her fingertips with her lips.

"See, I told you it was later," she whispered against his throat.

His pulse did take off then, a rapid tattoo of desire and need. "We're not alone."

She made the small shift that brought his face into her line of sight. Everything else faded out of focus. She gave him her witchiest smile as she drew her finger down his chest. "That's why you're still clothed."

His energy embraced her. His laugh jostled her. With an abruptness that had her grabbing tight, he stopped running. Her body grazed his in a tantalizing slide as he let her feet drop until they found purchase on a boulder. Standing on the rock, she was almost his height. Up ahead, she saw the others stop, saw them glance back, saw them turn their backs, granting them privacy.

"So all it takes to make you bold is a marriage proposal?" Jared asked, his fingers tangling in her hair.

"Absolutely not." She settled herself more comfortably in his arms, looping her hands around his neck. "It takes much more than that. It takes a promise of later. A lot of laters." She kissed his neck, his chin, his cheek. "Laters in which you promise to love me and I promise to love you. Forever."

She brought her mouth to his, breathing the last into her kiss as his energy wrapped around her in the same heated embrace as his love. "Laters in which we build dreams, hopes, and a future."

The back of his hand cupped her head, tilting the angle of her head to compliment the slant of his. His mouth melded with hers. "Hell yes."

She parted her lips, welcoming the thrust of his tongue, glorying in the possession, the claiming. Jared didn't do anything by half measures and that included loving her. Thank God.

She rose up on her toes, deepening the kiss that fraction of an inch that signaled her commitment, to him, to them, because she didn't do anything by half measures, either. "I love you."

He groaned and pulled his mouth from hers, just enough so they could both breathe, their breaths intermingling, their hearts racing in synch. "I love you, too."

She stroked his cheek. "Thank you."

His soft laugh warmed the last little corner of her soul. "You don't thank a man for loving you, sunbeam."

"No?" She cuddled his erection between her thighs and tipped her head back. "Then what do I do?"

There was nothing hotter or steadier than the emotion putting those flames in his eyes. "You just love me from here to eternity."

"I can do that." It would be so easy to do that. "What do I get in return?"

"Me loving you with everything I have."

"That's a whole lot."

"Yes." Jared rested his forehead against hers, holding her close, her spirit closer. "Will you marry me, Raisa Slovenski? Will you let me love you and pleasure you all the days of your life?"

She threaded her fingers through his hair, knocking his hat off. It tumbled to the ground with a soft plop. She smiled into his eyes, giving him her heart, her trust, her soul. Knowing in the deepest part of her that every decision she'd ever made, every step she'd ever taken in her life had been designed to bring her to this moment, in this time, with this man. She stroked her energy along his. "Hell yes."

Turn the page for a preview of the first book
in a new series by Sarah McCarty . . .

# REAPER'S JUSTICE

Coming soon from Berkley Sensation!

**T**HEY'D stolen his sanity.

A hint of dawn watered the darkness to a pale gray, illuminating the doorway in a feeble wash of light. Jeb touched the piece of deep blue wool caught on the shattered wood of the door frame, a tiny lingering fragment of the violence that had invaded the peace he'd found, tainted the haven she'd created. Touched *her*.

He pulled the scrap free of the splinter. It came easily into his grip, as if sensing his need. It was cold, devoid of the heat of her body, empty of that subtle scent he associated only with her. They hadn't taken her recently, then.

He tucked the piece of fabric in his pocket and shoved the hanging door out of the way. He didn't go any farther into the kitchen than the first foot. This was her space, her world—not a place where a man like him belonged. Besides, he didn't need to go into the room to know when they'd taken her. The pink-and-white teacup on the table told the story. She was a woman of habit, going through her day in an orderly manner. No matter what chaos stirred around her, she handled everything with efficient competence, maintaining her balance through the rituals she cherished, and sharing that balance with others who came in contact with her. She never looked deeper than a person's need, meeting it as best she could. It was one of her more foolish rituals and one of the reasons he'd taken to guarding her when he was in town. That and the fact he owed her.

One of her nightly rituals—one he approved of—was to sit at the kitchen table every evening at nine o'clock with a book and a cup of tea. She read for a half hour before rinsing out her cup, putting it back on the shelf, and then going to bed. He knew because he came by her house whenever he was in town, drawn against his will to check on her. The ghost of his existence haunted hers. Except for tonight—the one night she'd needed him.

He forced himself into the room, toward the table where her teacup still rested, guilt driving his feet forward. The scent of sweet dough settled around him, drowning out the other scents, pushing against the inner walls that contained the beast.

One step, two steps. He made it one more before the walls closed in around him. Shit. He hated closed-in places. He blinked as reality wavered and the cheery arbor rose wallpaper disappeared into the memory of crevice-laden dirt walls crawling with damp and cockroaches. He breathed steadily as the slip between past and present persisted, gliding silently forward, roses and roaches shimmering, one over the other. He stopped just short of the table, instinct carrying him through the confusion, and reached out, touching the cup. Her cup.

The room snapped back into focus. He traced the rim of the half-full cup, experiencing the delicate fragility of the china against his rough fingertip. Beside the cup sat a smooth gleam of amber. Her worry stone. It was harder to touch the small, flat sphere, so loaded with her scent and the remnants of her energy. His connection to her was already too strong.

He forced his finger to the smooth surface. He pictured her as he saw her so often, head bent over a book, the stone in her slender hand, her fingers rubbing back and forth in an easy rhythm as lamplight shone on her hair, highlighting the blonde streaks that glowed like lingering rays of sunshine. He picked up the amber and carefully put it in his vest pocket. She'd need her worry stone.

He turned to go and made it halfway to the door before he stopped. He glanced beyond the door, the anonymity of the night calling him. Behind him, the cup and saucer sat, a ritual incomplete. The amber burned in his pocket. Rituals mattered, kept a body sane. He, more than anyone, understood that. He returned to the table. Hesitated a moment and then went back. The sense of connection increased as he picked up the delicate china. Tea sloshed in the cup. A growl rumbled in his throat. She hadn't even gotten to finish her tea.

He rinsed out the cup and saucer, and placed them on the drying towel, completing her ritual. He paused an instant, his fingers resting on the fine material of the lace-edged white towel. Even her mundane items were delicate and fancy, little tells of the vulnerable femininity she tried to hide because she saw it as weak. His dark fingers lay in stark contrast against the fragile needlework, the network of scars on the back of his hands the opposite of beauty. The opposite of peace. And tonight, it was good.

The sound of wind roared in his ears, but outside the window the branches of the willow tree didn't sway. The scent of blood blended with the scent of sweet dough. He blinked slowly.

*Not real. It's not real.*

Real or not, it didn't matter. He felt the icy lash of rain against his cheeks as if it were yesterday, felt the pain as the scars split into gaping wounds that never healed, spilling blood until it stained the field of his vision. He blinked again and pulled his hand away. The towel slid off the counter, but it was white, unmarked by blood. Just another trick of his mind, heralding the split building inside as all the rituals he'd built over the last three years to protect the world from himself tore off, layer by layer. He put the towel back to rights, but inside the destruction continued, and the beast howled to be so near its freedom. And this time he didn't fight it back.

He would have stayed invisible forever, blending with the shadows, enduring the cacophony of his life until something brought it to an end—if they hadn't touched her. But they had. They'd slipped into his private sanctuary and threatened the only thing that mattered. The only good he knew. He turned on his heel, melting comfortably into the shadows of the room, heading out the door, no longer human, no longer anything but the deadly specter he'd been taught to be.

The early morning air took him into its cold embrace. The smooth leather of his knife grip settled into his palm with the familiarity of a trusted friend. He hadn't asked for this. The choice had been theirs. Foolishly and arrogantly, they'd ignored the laws of nature that called for balance, the laws that kept evil circling good, and with their actions, released the evil circling her. Him.

He knelt at the foot on the steps, his night vision illuminating the pattern in the dirt. The prints told the story. Three men, all wearing boots. The one with a tendency to roll his right foot to the inside held her. She'd fought—the scuff marks told that story. He followed the tracks back to the narrow alley behind the building. Dark splotches in the dirt drew his touch.

Blood. He brought it to his nose. Hers. The beast snarled and bared its canines. Inside, the hunger surged. Inhuman. Dangerous. The end to her struggles hadn't been painless. For that they would also pay. He scanned both sides of the alley. No bodies. They'd probably made it to their horses without notice. Which probably meant she was still alive. He grunted, pressing the sand between his fingers, holding on to the essence of her as if through sheer force of will he could keep her alive. She just needed to stay alive, and he would find her. No matter where they took her, no matter how they tried to cover their tracks, he would find her. And he would bring her home.

The remaining splotch of blood pulled his gaze, growing, spreading until it swallowed the ground. Rivers really could run red because the ground wasn't always thirsty to drink of men's violence, and when that happened, there was no stopping the carnage. He took a breath and then another, fighting the urge to tumble into the growing vision, to accept the stain that was so much a part of him, to accept that there was no rebuilding a past stolen so long ago. The old anger rose, feeding the emptiness he'd lived with since before he could remember, before they'd taken away what little he'd had. He pushed to his feet, and with a snap of his teeth, won the battle to stay in the here and now. At the end of the alley, between the rough wood sides of the buildings, the horizon flushed with the first hint of morning. A new day. One more night survived without succumbing.

Jeb rested his forearm on his knee and formed a mental picture of the terrain beyond the town. The men who'd stolen Lorie would likely be relying on their lead to get them through, so it'd make sense for them to take the easier southwest route. If he cut through ambush canyon, he could make up a lot of ground, assuming they continued southwest.

He stood. That was a pretty safe assumption. In his experience, men only kidnapped a woman for one of three reasons: money, lust, or revenge. This had the feel of all three, seeing as the woman was beautiful, saleable, and of good family, with strong protectors. The first two explained what a man would want her for—lust and profit— and the last tied in the revenge angle. Only someone mad as hell would risk setting the Camerons on his tail. There wasn't a more relentless or deadly force in the territory, if he discounted himself, than the Cameron men. The fact that the kidnappers had targeted a member of their tight-knit clan made this personal. The loose thread of why, he'd check out after he brought Lorie back. He didn't leave dangling threads of threat any more than he left witnesses.

The kidnappers would likely ride through nightfall before they felt comfortable enough to stop. And when they stopped, the lust and revenge angle would come into play. His mouth set in a grim line. The thought of nightfall and what that would mean for Lori hardened his resolve. They weren't going to touch her.


**IF** he touched her again, Lorie was going kick him between the legs, and to hell with the consequences. She tossed her hair out of her eyes. It fell back into her face immediately, blocking her field of vision. The even cadence of her breathing snagged on a moment of panic. The leader glanced over at her from where he knelt by the fire. His moustache twitched with his grin. Lorie pulled her hands apart, using the pain of the bonds cutting into her skin to bury the emotions battling for dominance. Oh God, she wanted to scream, cry, throw herself on the ground and rage, do anything but stand here and pretend she wasn't terrified, but giving into emotion wouldn't get her what she needed. She needed her wits about her to get out of this mess, a mess that had just gotten worse through the addition of the ten other men who'd joined her three kidnappers as soon as they'd forded the river.

The leader stood and approached, the cruel-looking spurs on his boots clinking with every step.

"You are a proud woman," he said as he drew even with her, reaching out.

She jerked her head out of reach. He studied her defiance for an instant, his hand open, level with her cheek, the fingers drawn back in a threat. She didn't blink or look away, just stared at him as impassively as she could manage, giving herself a focus for calm: memorizing the details of his face. Her cousins would want to know what he looked like so they could hunt him down and kill him. When they asked for a description, she would like to have something to give them beyond that her kidnapper was filthy and stank of horse and old sweat.

"I was raised to be a lady, no matter what the provocation."

The man looked to be in his thirties, with lank, black hair and

swarthy skin. From the dirt ground into his pores, he obviously did
not believe in the saying cleanliness was next to godliness. He was
missing his right eyetooth and one of his lower front teeth. His face
was broad, so much so his eyes looked too small above his flattened
nose. He had a thick, droopy mustache that hid his lips but showcased the remains of whatever he'd eaten the last few days. She
shuddered as everything else faded to unimportant. Disgusting was
the sum total of the description she came up with. Her cousins
would not be happy with her.

"You're damn uppity for a prisoner," the man informed her, a
rolling accent mellowing the threat inherent in the observation.

She waited one breath before answering. One breath in which
she recovered from the shock of his breath. "I prefer to think of
myself as composed."

His eyebrows went up into the shaggy line of his uncombed hair.
"Composed?"

"Yes. Composed. As in not carrying on and giving in to hysterics
at the least little thing."

Like being kidnapped by the king of filth and his entourage of
dirty minions.

The leader cupped her chin in his hand. She couldn't suppress
her shudder. He didn't bother to hide his amusement. "I think you
will find we are not such a little thing."

She refused to think of him as big. If she did, she'd lose all hope.
His filthy thumb touched her cheek. "I'm sure."

His head canted to the side. "But you still intend to keep yourself composed?"

One of the new men, taller, leaner, *cleaner* than the others, looked
up from where he'd been hunkered down rummaging through a
saddlebag. She couldn't see his face, but she knew he was listening.
And he didn't approve. Of her or the situation, she wasn't sure. "Absolutely."

"Why?"

His accent turned the question into two syllables. She motioned to the double row of ammo draped over his shoulders. "Why are you a bandit?"

His mustache twitched, either with a smile or a grimace, she couldn't tell, beneath the overgrowth of hair. "It is what I do."

She shivered and hunched lower into the horse blanket they'd thrown around her shoulders. It stunk, but it was infinitely preferable to freezing. "Well, being composed is what I do."

His fingers slid down her jaw toward her mouth. "One wonders if you would be so composed were I to kiss you." His thumb crept toward her mouth. "I think you would scream."

She shook her head. "No. I wouldn't."

Again, that twitch of a mustache. His head tilted back as he looked down his nose at her. Who knew bandits could be so arrogant? "You are sure?"

"Yes."

He took a step nearer. She looked him straight in the eye, stopping him with two words that were the absolute truth. "I'd vomit."

She was about to vomit from his filthy hand being so close to her mouth.

"Then I would kill you."

She wanted to roll her eyes. He was probably going to do that anyway. Instead, she breathed steadily through her nose, trying to suppress the urge to gag, as the wind swirled his odor around her. "Vomiting just happens. Threats will have no effect on my reaction."

The man in the black hat made a sound. Laughter?

The bandit pulled out a big knife. He held it near her face. It was ten times cleaner than his hand.

"What do you say now?"

"I'm relived to see you keep your weapon clean, at least."

He blinked. She couldn't blame him. She hadn't meant to say that out loud. She was just too nervous to think straight. The knife caught the sunlight, flashing the glare back over her face. "It will not matter if the blade that kills you is dirty."

It would matter to her. "That would make sense."

His eyes narrowed to slits. "I cannot determine whether you are very brave or very stupid."

Well, she wasn't brave. "Does it matter?"

His mustache spread and his eyes crinkled at the corners. The aura of friendliness was disconcerting. And wrong, because it didn't extend any deeper than his expression. His hand dropped away from her face. "No. Your value rests in other places. What is your name?"

"Lorie. What's yours?"

The mustache twitched. "You may call me José."

Not "my name is" but "you may call me." Which meant she didn't have any more to give her cousins when they came for her. They weren't going to be pleased. She'd have to do better or they'd chew her out. José touched the knife, touched the tip of her right breast through her dress, moving next to her stomach before poking lower into the folds of her skirt.

She forgot all about memorizing details and focused on controlling her reaction. She hadn't expected this weakness in herself. She'd spent the whole afternoon going over in her mind all the possibilities of what might happen to her, and certainly, being raped was number one on the list. She'd thought she'd prepared herself for the eventuality. Logically, she knew it wasn't going to be pleasant, but she was sure she'd survive it. Common sense said the act was survivable. Otherwise, the ladies at the White Dove Saloon would be disappearing faster than Miss Niña could replace them.

José pressed with the knife.

The start of fear that went through her wasn't logical at all. She knew all she had to do was survive until help arrived, but still, when faced with the carnal intent of this filthy man, feeling his gaze crawl over her, she shook inside with a fear that went beyond rational to primal. José laughed a mean, nasty laugh before sheathing his knife. He didn't step away, just leaned in, overwhelming her with the reality of the threat. "But we will have tonight."

Which left her no option but to come up with a plan before

tonight. She would not lay down, willingly or unwillingly, with a man who did not understand the concept of hygiene. It was a firm statement—rational, logical, decisive. It was amazing how little it did to make her feel better. José gave her another look.

"You are going to bring me a very good price."

She'd rather bring him a severe case of indigestion.

He turned and gestured to the men. "Mount up. The day is wasting."

The men stood in haphazard order, including the man dressed all in black. She met his flat, blue gaze. His mouth set into a straight line, and then he turned his back on her, grabbing the saddlebag and tossing it over his horse's flanks with more force than necessary. He acted for all the world like he was mad at her. As if she'd asked for three men to break into her house and disrupt her evening reading. She could really work up to hating men.

She waited for someone to tell her what to do. The faint hope that they'd forget about her in all the hustle of getting ready to ride persisted against the logic that said they wouldn't. Still, when the leader turned his horse toward her, she couldn't prevent a shudder. In her dime novels, this would be the time for the hero to show up on a thundering steed, guns blazing and bandits expiring under the hail of bullets.

She glanced around. No hero in sight. Just winter-killed brush and brown flatlands that rolled into distant mountains. She squared her shoulders and lifted her chin. She wasn't going to cringe, no matter how repugnant the thought of riding with the leader was. No matter how terrified she was inside. This time she wouldn't lose her pride. It was very hard to live without pride.

Another horse sidled up along side the leader's when he was about three feet away. "I'll take the woman up with me."

José put his hand on the butt of his revolver. "Your sacrifice is not necessary."

The man in black glanced at her as he pulled his makings out of his pocket. "I wouldn't call having my arms around a pretty lady a sacrifice."

"Then why should I give this pleasure up?"

He opened up the paper. "Because if her people come after her, we're going to have to split up, and they'll follow whichever horse she's riding." He shook some tobacco into the paper. "Doesn't make sense to lose a leader over a piece of tail."

A piece of tail? Never in her life had Lorie been referred to in that way; never had she heard of any woman referred to that way. It was as shocking as it was disgusting. The man didn't even look at her as she gasped and flushed. With efficient movements, he rolled the cigarette and struck a sulphur, lighting the tip. The acrid scent of cheap tobacco stung her nostrils as he snuffed the flame between his spit-moistened fingers. "It's up to you."

José looked at her then back at the man in black. He didn't take his hand off his gun. Tension thickened the air. The big man in black drew on his smoke. The end glowed a bright red. Lorie reached into her pocket, automatically reaching for her worry stone. It wasn't there. The glow of the cigarette faded. The tension remained. She rubbed the thick wool of her skirt between her fingers. It wasn't the same. It did nothing to stabilize her emotions.

The chill of the wind replaced the heat in her cheeks as José nodded and pulled his horse up. "The woman will ride with you."

The man in black kneed his sorrel forward. He held out his hand. She took a step back, every muscle protesting the movement, instinctively shaking her head.

"You can ride sitting in the saddle or across it, your choice."

It was a simple truth. She forced herself to accept it. And at least she had control of this, even if it was a tiny thing like how she would ride against her will. Control was good. It could be won and maintained in small measures. It should be held on to. She placed her bound hand in his. Her feet left the ground so fast she almost didn't have time to throw her leg over the horse's back. Her skirts wrapped in an uncomfortable knot around her legs as she struggled to find her balance. She tugged at the heavy material, yanking it out from under her thighs, trying to cover the scandalous amount of petticoat and calf showing. In the process, she kicked the horse's side. It did a little hop to the left. She grabbed the man's waist. Nothing but hard muscle met her touch. He swore and glanced over his shoulder.

"What in hell are you doing?"

She dug in her nails as the horse hopped again. She wiggled her right leg. The maneuver ended in another kick that generated another protest from the stupid horse. "My skirts are tangled."

"Well, cut it out. You're scaring Jehosephat."

She tried a tug-and-hop maneuver. This time the horse bucked. "Jehosephat needs some manners."

Controlling the horse with a shift of his weight and tension on the reins, he growled, "He's got plenty of manners, now settle down."

The last rumbled out of his chest more sound than enunciation. Too scary to ignore.

"I can't." She pulled at the hopelessly trapped material. "It's not decent."

He glanced down at her leg and then back at her over his shoulder, his mouth lifting in a sardonic twist. "Lady, showing a bit of leg is the least of your worries."